ALSO BY MEGHAN QUINN

CANE BROTHERS
A Not So Meet Cute
So Not Meant to Be
A Long Time Coming

A not so MEET CUTE

MEGHAN QUINN

Bloom *books*

Published by Bloom Books, an imprint of Sourcebooks
P.O. Box 4410, Naperville, Illinois 60567-4410
(630) 961-3900
sourcebooks.com

Originally published in 2021 by Hot-Lanta Publishing, LLC.

Cataloging-in-publication data is on file with the Library of Congress.

Printed and bound in the United States of America.
LSC 10 9 8 7 6 5 4 3 2 1

PROLOGUE
LOTTIE

"HEY, GIRL."

Hmm, I don't like the cheeriness in her voice.

The smirk on her lips.

The overuse of her toxic, throat-choking perfume.

"Hey, Angela," I answer with wary trepidation as I take a seat at the table in her office.

With a flip of her bright blond hair over her shoulder, she clasps her hands together, her body language conveying interest as she leans forward and asks, "How are you?"

I smooth my hands over my bright red pencil skirt and answer, "Doing fine. Thank you."

"That's so wonderful to hear." She leans back and smiles at me but doesn't say another word.

Ohh-kay, what the hell is going on?

I glance behind me to the row of suited men, sitting upright in chairs, folders on their laps, staring at our interaction. I've known Angela since middle school. We've had one of those on-again, off-again friendships, me being the victim of the intermittent camaraderie. I was her main squeeze one day—the next it was Blair, who works in finance, or Lauren, who works over in sales, and then the friendship would come back to me. We're interchangeable. Who's the bestie this week? I'd always wonder, and in some sick, demented way, I'd have a hiccup of excitement when the bestie card landed on me.

Why stick around in such a toxic friendship, you ask?

The answer is threefold.

One: when I first met Angela, I was young. I had no idea what the hell to do during such a vibrant roller coaster ride. I just gripped the handles and held on for dear life, because frankly, hanging with Angela was exciting. Different. Bold, at times.

Two: when she was nice to me, when we were deep into our friendship, I had some of the best times of my life. Growing up in Beverly Hills as the poor girl didn't lend its hand to many adventures, but with the rich friend who looked past your empty wallet and welcomed you into her world—yeah, it was fun. Call me shallow, but I had fun in high school, despite the ups and downs.

Three: I'm weak. I'm confrontation's bitch and avoid it at all costs. Therefore (raises hand) here I am, doormat, at your service.

"Angela?" I whisper.

"Hmm?" She smiles at me.

"Can I ask why you called me in here and why the FBI seems to be lined up behind me?"

Angela tilts her head back and lets out a hearty laugh as her hand lands on mine. "Oh, Lottie. God, I'm going to miss your humor."

"Miss?" I ask, my spine stiffening. "What do you mean, *miss*? Are you going on vacation?"

Please let that be the case. Please let that be the case. I can't afford to lose this job.

"I am."

Oh, thank God.

"Ken and I are headed to Bora-Bora. I have a spray tan scheduled in about ten minutes, so we need to get on with this."

Wait, what?

"Get on with what?" I ask.

Her jovial face morphs into something serious, the type of serious I don't see very often from Angela. Because, yes, she might be the head of her lifestyle blog, but she's not the one who does the work—everyone else does. So, she never has to be serious.

She sits taller, her jaw grows tight, and through her thick fake eyelashes, she says, "Lottie, you're a true pioneer for Angeloop. Your mastery behind the keyboard has been positively unmatched by anyone in this company, and the humor you bring to this thriving, money-dripping lifestyle blog has made this trip to Bora-Bora a reality."

Did I hear that right? Because of me, she's able to go on her vacation?

"But unfortunately, we're going to have to let you go."

Hold up…what?

Let me go?

As in, no more job for me?

Like a bolt of lightning, three of the men come up behind me, two on either side, flanking me like security. With their heavyset shoulders blocking me in, one of them drops a folder on the table in front of me and flips it open, revealing a piece of paper. My eyes are too unfocused to even consider reading what it says, but taking a simple guess, I'm thinking it's a termination paper.

"Sign here." The man holds a pen out to me.

"Wait, what?" I move the man's hand away, only for it to bounce back right where it was. "You're firing me?"

Angela winces. "Lottie, please don't make this a thing. You must know how difficult this has been for me." She snaps her fingers, and an assistant magically pops up. Angela rubs her throat and says, "This conversation has truly taken it out of me. Water, please. Room temperature. Lemon and lime, but take them out before you give it to me." And like that, the assistant is gone. When Angela turns back around, she sees me and clutches her chest. "Oh, you're still here."

Uhhh…

Yeah.

Blinking a few times, I ask, "Angela, what is going on? You just said I make you a ton of money—"

"Did I? I don't recall making such a statement. Boys, did I say anything like that?"

They all shake their head.

"See? I didn't say that."

I think… Yup, mm-hmm, do you smell that? That's my brain smoking, working overtime, trying to not LOSE IT!

Calmly, and I mean…calmly, I ask, "Angela, can you please explain to me why you're letting me go?"

"Oh." She laughs. "You've always been such a nosy little thing." The assistant brings Angela her water and then rushes away. Sucking from an unnecessary straw, Angela takes a long sip and then says, "Your one-year anniversary is on Friday."

"Yes. That's correct."

"Well, per your contract, it says that after a year, you're no longer under restricted pay, but instead receive your actual salary." She shrugs. "Why pay you more when I can find someone to do your job for less? Simple bottom-line thinking. You understand."

"No, I don't." My voice rises, and two large hands land on my shoulder in warning.

Oh, for fuck's sake.

"Angela, this is my life. This isn't some game you get to play. You told me when you begged me to work for you that this job was going to be life-changing."

"And hasn't it been?" She holds her arms out. "Angeloop is life-changing for everyone." She glances at her watch. "Oh, I have to get naked in five. Spray tans don't wait." She twirls her finger at the guys beside me. "Wrap it up, boys."

Two sets of hands grip me and help me up from my chair.

"You can't be serious," I say, still not quite grasping what's going on. "You're having security drag me out of your office?"

"Not by my choice," Angela says, the picture of innocence. "Your hostile attitude is making me use security."

"Hostile?" I ask. "I'm hostile because you're firing me for no reason."

"Oh, honey, I can't believe you see it that way," she says in that condescending voice of hers. "This is nothing personal. You know I love you and still plan on your monthly invitation to brunch. This is just business." She blows me a kiss. "Still my bestie."

She's lost her goddamned mind.

I'm pulled toward the door, but I dig in my two-seasons-ago Jimmy Choo heels. "Angela, seriously. You can't be firing me."

She looks up at me, tilts her head to the side, and then presses her hand to her heart. "Ahh, look at you, fighting for your job. God, you've always been scrappy." She blows me another kiss, waves, and calls out, "I'll call you. You can tell me about your horrible boss later. Oh…and don't forget to RSVP to our high school reunion. Two months away. We need a head count."

And just like that, defeat whips through me, my heels let up in total shock, my body goes limp, and I'm dragged by my underarms through the offices of Angeloop, the most idiotic and absurd lifestyle blog on the internet, a place where I didn't want to work in the first place.

Peers watch me.

Security doesn't skip a beat as they drag me all the way through the tall glass front door.

And before I can take my next breath, I'm staring at the obscenely large Angeloop sign outside of the office, a box of my office things in hand.

How the hell did this all happen?

CHAPTER 1
HUXLEY

"I'M GOING TO FUCKING MURDER someone," I shout as I throw my suit jacket across my office and slam my door.

"Seems as though the meeting went well," JP says from where he's leaning against the expansive wall of windows in my office.

"Seems as though it went incredibly well," Breaker offers from where he's lying across my leather couch.

Ignoring my brothers' sarcasm, I grip my hair and turn toward the view of Los Angeles. It's a clear day today, fresh rain from the night before eliminating some of the smog in the air. Palm trees reach high to the sky, lining the roads, but look small compared to where my office sits above the rest.

"Care to gab about it?" JP asks while taking a seat in a chair.

I turn toward them, my brothers, the two idiots who have been by my side through thick and thin. Who have ridden the ups and downs of our lives. Who have dropped everything to join me in this crazy idea of taking over the real estate market in Los Angeles with the money Dad left us when he passed. We've built this empire together.

But the smarmy looks on their faces make me want to punt their goddamn dicks out of my office.

"Does it look like I want to *gab* about it?"

"No." Breaker smirks. "But fuck do we want to hear all about it."

Of course they do.

Because they were the ones who said I shouldn't meet with Dave Toney.

They were the ones who said it was going to be a waste of my time.

They were the ones who laughed when I said I had a meeting with him today.

And they were the ones who sarcastically said good luck as I walked out the door.

But I wanted to prove them wrong.

I wanted to show them that I could convince Dave Toney that he needed to work with Cane Enterprises.

Spoiler alert—I did not convince him.

Capitulating to my brothers' stares, I take a seat as well and let out a long sigh. "Fuck," I mutter.

"Let me guess, he didn't fall for your charm?" Breaker asks. "But you're so personable."

"That shit shouldn't matter." I slam my finger into the armrest of my plush leather chair. "This is business, not some goddamn parade of nurturing friendships and coddling one another."

"I think he missed something in business school," JP says to Breaker. "Because wasn't fostering business relationships an entire course?" His sarcasm is grating on my nerves.

"I believe it was," Breaker says.

"I went in there and kissed his ass—what more does he want?"

"Did you wear lipstick? Not sure his girlfriend would appreciate finding another pair of lips on her man's ass cheeks." Breaker smirks.

"I hate you. I really fucking hate you."

Breaker lets out a bark of a laugh while JP says, "Hate to say it, but...we told you so, bro. Dave Toney doesn't work with just anyone. He's a different breed in this city. Many have tried to break into the vast amount of real estate he owns; many have failed. Why did you think you'd be any different?"

"Because we're Cane Enterprises," I shout. "Everyone wants to fucking work with us. Because we have the largest real estate portfolio in Los Angeles. Because we can turn a broken-down building into a million-dollar business in a year. We know what the fuck we're doing, and Dave Toney, although successful, has some dead pieces of land on his hands that are hurting his business. He knows it, I fucking know it, and I want to take those pieces of land off his hands."

JP grips his chin and asks, "What precisely did you say to him? I hope not that? Because although your little speech made my nipples hard, I doubt he'd appreciate the tone."

I roll my eyes. "I said something along those lines."

"You realize Dave Toney is a prideful man, right?" Breaker asks. "If you insult him, he's not going to want to work with you."

"I didn't insult him," I shout. "I was trying to get on an even playing field. You know, let him see that I'm a pretty normal guy."

Both of my brothers scoff.

"I am a normal guy."

JP and Breaker exchange glances, and then both lean forward, and I know what's coming: a classic come-to-Jesus moment. They like to perform them on me from time to time.

"You know we love you, right?" Breaker asks. And so it begins.

"We're here for you, whenever you need us," JP adds.

I drag my hand over my face. "Just get the fuck on with it."

"You're not normal. You're anything but normal. None of us are. We live in Beverly Hills, are constantly invited to premieres and celebrity gatherings, and have been in the headlines on Page Six many times. There's nothing normal about us. Dave Toney, now…he's normal."

"How the fuck so?" I ask. "Because he doesn't get invited to celebrity after-parties?"

Breaker shakes his head. "No, because he's down-to-earth. Approachable. You could easily grab a beer with him in a bar and not feel the least bit intimidated. You're the exact opposite. You're flashy."

"I'm not flashy."

JP nods at my watch. "Nice Movado—is it new?"

I glance down at it. "Got it last week—" I raise my eyes to meet my brothers' knowing looks. "Am I not allowed to spend my hard-earned money?"

"You are," JP says. "The way you live your life is completely acceptable. The house, the car…the watch, all earned and rightfully so, but if you want to connect with Dave Toney, then you're going to have to get on a different level. And that doesn't mean dressing down, because he'll see right through that. He already knows you're a flashy guy. But he needs to see you in a different light."

"Oooh, I like that," Breaker says. "A different light. That's what he needs." He taps his chin. "But what would that light be?"

Irritated, I get up from my chair and grab my suit jacket from where I tossed it. "While you two morons think about it, I'm going to grab lunch."

"If only Toney could see this moment, where Huxley Cane doesn't ask his assistant to grab him lunch but, like a mere peasant, walks the streets of Los Angeles to fetch his own food," JP says.

I slip on my jacket, despite the heat outside. Ignoring them, I cross toward my door.

"Could you grab us something?" Breaker calls out.

Sighing, I call back, "Text me what you want from the deli."

"Pickles. All the goddamn pickles," JP yells as I make my way down the office hallway to the elevator. Luckily, the doors slide open for me, so I step in, press the *lobby* button, and lean against the wall, hands stuffed in my pants pockets.

Get on a different level. I don't even know what that means. And I know I'm a businessman who's made deals with people I've gotten along with, but I've also made deals with people I absolutely despise. The difference between me and Dave Toney is I don't give a fuck who takes my money or who I sell to. Business is business, and if it's a good deal, I'm going to take it.

I offered Dave a fucking good-as-shit deal today, better than what he deserves, if I'm honest. And instead of shaking my hand and accepting it, he sat back in his office chair, scratched the side of his cheek, and said, "I don't know. I'm going to have to sit on this."

Sit on it.

Sit on my goddamn deal.

No one sits on my deals; they take them and thank Jesus Christ Himself for doing business with Cane Enterprises.

I push through the elevator doors when they part, weave my way through the busy lobby, and then head out of the office building toward the hole-in-the-wall deli that's just down the road. Two blocks. I don't usually send my assistant, Karla, to grab me food, because it makes me feel like an asshole—despite what people might think of me—and I also enjoy the second to get out and breathe some fresh air. *Well, it's LA, so fresh air is an overstatement.* But it gives me a second to reset before I get back behind my desk, where I control our billion-dollar operation with my keyboard.

My phone beeps in my pocket, and I don't bother looking at it because I know it's JP and Breaker's orders. I don't even know why I told them to text me, because they get the same thing every time. Same as me. Philly cheesesteak with extra mushrooms. And, of course, pickles. It's our go-to sandwich. Something that we don't eat often, but when we do head to the deli, it's our usual.

The sidewalk is more crowded than normal. Summer has hit Los Angeles, meaning tourists are sweeping in, celebrity bus tours will be at their max, and driving on the 101 is going to be a hellish nightmare. Lucky for me, I only live thirty minutes from the office.

As I approach the deli, a familiar black SUV pulls up in front of it. When the door opens, I catch sight of Dave Toney—speak of the devil—stepping out of the vehicle. What are the odds?

Whatever they are, they look like they're in my favor. Nothing like a good follow-up to try to secure the deal. Maybe JP was right, Dave

Toney might change his mind when he sees me picking up lunch. That's definitely *on a different level*.

I button my suit jacket and pick up my pace. Never miss an opportunity in business. Never. As I grow closer, I'm dangerously caught off guard when I see a feminine hand pop out of the vehicle behind Dave. I slow down and zero in on the hand…the small hand with a VERY big engagement ring on it.

Holy shit. Dave is engaged?

I'm assuming he is, since he's holding the woman's hand.

But engaged…hell, how did I miss that?

Usually I'm aware of such—

My thoughts pause, and I blink a few times as the fiancée turns, giving me a profile view.

Holy…fuck.

Looks like the engagement isn't the biggest surprise of the day.

Thanks to her tight-fitting dress and slender frame, there's no doubt in my mind that Dave Toney's fiancée is pregnant.

Dave Toney, engaged with a baby on the way. How…? When?

He waves to the driver, shuts the door, and then glances behind him, just enough for us to make eye contact. His eyebrows lift in surprise, and then he turns all the way around and waves to me. "Cane, didn't expect to see you on the streets."

Yeah, neither of us expected to see each other, but I'm not going to let the shock of this new development rattle me.

Showtime.

I plaster on a smile.

"Just enjoying the sultry California sun while on my way to get lunch for me and my brothers." I walk up to him and extend my hand. He gives it a brief shake. "This deli is our favorite."

"Is that right?" Dave asks in surprise. "It's Ellie's, too. I've never been, but she was telling me they have the best pickles."

"My brothers are a sucker for the pickles as well." I hold my hand out to his fiancée. "You must be Ellie."

"Shit, that's rude of me," Dave says with an awkward laugh. "Yes, this is Ellie. Ellie, this is Huxley Cane."

"It's a pleasure to meet you," Ellie says in a very sweet southern voice. One that I've heard before.

I shake her hand and then let go, only to say, "Let me guess, you're from Georgia?"

Her smile brightens. "I am. You could tell?"

Yup, this bodes well for me.

"My grandma is a self-proclaimed Georgia Peach. I spent many brutal, humidity-filled summers out on her screened-in porch, rocking on chairs with her as she filled me in on the latest town gossip."

"Really? Whereabout?"

"Peachtree City."

Her eyes widen in delight. She presses her hand to her chest. "I grew up in Fayetteville, just east of Peachtree. Wow, what a small world."

Yes. Yes, indeed. Especially since my grandma actually resides in San Diego, and I've never been to Georgia, actually, but they don't need to know that. They also don't need to know I recognize her accent because I dated a girl in college from Peachtree City. All semantics.

Delighted with the small connection I'm making to Dave's world, I turn toward him, only to be met by a very territorial-looking man. Uh-oh. Jaw clenched, brows narrowed, his eyes find no humor in our small... very small world.

Dude is practically marking his territory with that angry snarl. I wouldn't be surprised if he started circling Ellie and peeing all around her.

Given what he knows about me—flashy, a flirt, Mr. Page Six—not recently, thank God—he must think I'm a threat. Which, I'm not. I mean, yeah, Ellie is a petite bundle of blond. Pretty with blue eyes, but she's also pregnant—total nightmare—and she's engaged, therefore, completely off the market.

But given what my brothers said, Dave probably doesn't see it that way when it comes to me.

Which means, I need to salvage this and fast.

But how…

How can I possibly make it—

Light bulb

Did you see that brilliant flash of light? Yeah, an idea has emerged. It might not be smart. It's definitely not the most intelligent thing I've ever thought of, but Dave seems to be growing more and more tense by the second, so…

Here goes nothing.

Please don't come back to bite me in the ass—famous last words.

"Fayetteville, huh?" I wet my lips. Here goes. "Wow, crazy. I think my fiancée's parents are from Palmetto. Isn't that just north?"

Yeah, fiancée. Told you it wasn't intelligent, but it's the best I've got.

"Yes, Palmetto is just north of it," Ellie says with such joy, while Dave moves his hand around her waist in a protective embrace.

"Fiancée?" he asks after clearing his throat. "You're engaged, Cane?" There's genuine interest in his eyes, and the tension that was collecting in his shoulders is slowly easing.

"Yup."

"Huh, I'm surprised."

I can't read him. *Does he believe me? Is he testing me? Am I making this exponentially worse? I hope to fuck not. I don't want to lose this deal.*

I refuse to let it slip through my fingers, not when I'm so close. To have those properties would be exponentially beneficial to our portfolio, especially with what we have planned for them. And to snag a deal with the elusive Dave Toney would make me that much more victorious. My business mind takes over, leaving my common sense to the wind.

So, before I can change my mind on what's about to come out of my mouth, I swallow hard and say, "Yup, engaged and…expecting."

The minute the lie leaves my lips, a gross feeling takes over, because fuck, I know how hard some women try to get pregnant, and to lie about something like that…hell. And I don't know her circumstances either… if it was hard to get pregnant. All of it doesn't feel right. But like I said, common sense is nowhere to be found at this moment; it's pure idiotic instinct.

"Really?" Ellie cheers. "Oh my gosh." She rubs her belly. "So are we. Dave, isn't that exciting?"

"That really is." Dave's face morphs from unsure, protective boyfriend to…to a look I haven't seen on him before. Compassion.

Understanding.

Dare I say—*camaraderie*?

I stick my hands in my suit pants pockets to keep them from fidgeting as I tell the biggest goddamn lie of my life.

"Yeah, my grandma introduced me to her back in Peachtree. It was one of those love-at-first-sight meet-cutes."

Ellie clasps her hands together. "Oh, I love meet-cutes."

I shrug. "Yeah, and we hit it off quickly." I attempt to gaze off toward the sky as I think about my imaginary pregnant fiancée and how much I *gulp* love her. "We did things a little backwards, with getting pregnant first, but I guess we've never done anything right, according to society's timelines."

"Same," Dave says, and I see it, right there in his eyes. A new appreciation for me. This is what the boys were talking about. This was what Dave needed, to see me as a "human."

This is me, meeting Dave on a new level. Connecting on a new level. In this moment, he doesn't see me as the flashy, take-no-prisoners businessman, but rather, someone he can ask out for a beer and talk through his worries about becoming a father.

This might very well be exactly the kind of in I needed. A little chit-chat, an acute white lie that isn't going to hurt anyone. He doesn't have to actually meet this imaginary girl. He doesn't even need to know much about her. Just the idea of her makes me that much more appealing.

Huh, maybe this wasn't such a bad idea after all.

Maybe this was actually pure brilliancy at its finest.

Mark my words—by this time tomorrow, he'll be calling me up, no longer willing to sit on my offer, but more likely willing to take it.

Huxley Cane, you're an absolute genius.

"Dave, wouldn't it be absolutely divine to have Huxley and his fiancée over for dinner?"

Ehhh, what now?

Dinner?

Ellie clasps her hands together and continues, "It would be so lovely to talk with people in our same situation." Leaning forward, Ellie says, "Family has been less than thrilled about us waiting to get married until after the baby is born. My parents are quite traditional."

Sweat breaks out on my upper lip as I try to keep my face neutral.

A dinner date.

With my "fiancée."

Oh...fuck.

Abort, Cane. ABORT!

"That would be wonderful," Dave says with a jovial smile.

FUCK!

"How does Saturday night work?" he continues.

Saturday night?

Double fuck!

That's four days from now.

Four fucking days to not only find a fiancée, but a pregnant fiancée.

Huxley Cane, you're no genius; you're an absolute moron.

"Oh, give him a second to talk about it with his girl," Ellie says. I'd say thank God for Ellie, but the anxiety-ridden dinner date was her idea. "Why don't you get back to Dave and then let me know if it's a go. I love cooking. I could make us a real southern meal if you'd like."

My mind is already formulating excuses as to why my fiancée and I won't be able to make Saturday work.

"And maybe we can talk about the deal some more," Dave says with a genuine smile.

Fuck.

Fuck. Fuck. Fuck.

Can't say no now. Not at the risk of losing the deal.

Christ.

Despite the desert that is my mouth, I swallow hard and nod. "Yup." My voice cracks. "Saturday sounds great."

"Wonderful." Ellie claps her hands. "Oh, I can't wait. I'm going to make my best peach cobbler and collard greens. Dave will exchange information with you."

"Perfect," I say with a shaky smile. What the hell am I getting myself into?

"Oh, babe, we're going to be late. Let's stop by the deli after our class— that okay?" Dave asks.

"As long as I can get double the pickles," Ellie says while pressing a kiss to Dave's lips.

The PDA makes my stomach roll. It's not that I find them repulsive, but it's a stark reminder of the hole I just dug for myself.

"Okay, we're off to Lamaze class. Talk soon," Dave says with a wave.

I give them a wave in return, hoping my hand doesn't look shaky, and without going into the deli, I turn around and head back to the office, my mind swirling with how to get out of this fuckup.

Huxley Cane, you're a complete and utter moron.

CHAPTER 2
LOTTIE

HANDS ON THE STEERING WHEEL, I stare out at my childhood home and also current place of residence, a small bungalow that has been in the family for years. I mean…years. Grandma Pru bought it back in the fifties and passed it on to my mom, who raised me and my sister, Kelsey, all by herself.

The white stucco has faded over the years and looks more cream than anything, and the red clay tile roof needs more repairs than what Mom can afford despite her live-in boyfriend of thirteen years, Jeff, wanting to replace it for her.

Speaking of Jeff, he's out in the front yard in his oversized jean shorts and classic white undershirt, pushing his mower. Jeff always has an unlit cigarette dangling from his mouth, because even though he doesn't smoke it, ever, he finds comfort in knowing that he could if he wanted. Don't ask me about the psychology behind it; he's great to my mom and he's been a wonderful sounding board over the past ten years for me and my sister as well. So if a cigarette dangles from his mouth, so be it. Could be worse.

But Jeff being in the front yard creates a flaw in my ability to bring my box of office things into my room without questions. And I don't want any questions from Jeff or my mom. They can't find out about Angela firing me. That would be a debilitating disaster.

No, they can NEVER find out.

Why?

Well, because they were the ones who begged and pleaded for me to find another job that wouldn't include me working for someone with whom I've shared a toxic relationship for years.

But you know how it goes. Parents know nothing, we know everything, and then we have to eat our freaking words later on when we realize...we should've listened to our parents.

Ughhh.

Not wanting Jeff to become suspicious, I get out of my dilapidated VW Bug, leaving the box in the back, strap my purse over my shoulder, and plaster on a beautiful smile that I know will bring joy to Jeff's day.

"Hey, Lottie Bug," he says, using the nickname Mom gave me years ago.

"Hey, Jeff." I wave as he turns off the mower and adjusts his sunglasses on the bridge of his nose. "Yard is looking great."

"Thank you. I think the beautification committee will have to notice us this year."

Oh, Jeff, always so hopeful.

You see, we live on the border, and I mean, one street over from The Flats in Beverly Hills. And every summer, there's a committee that walks from house to house, picking out the best yards in the neighborhood and awarding them prizes. We've always walked through The Flats, taking in the fabulously manicured lawns curated by professional landscapers, not the actual owners. It's a bloodbath the week before the judges take their walk, including here at our house, because the last house on the route is across the street, and in order to see the house, you see ours, just past the bushes, and Jeff is bound and determined to be noticed.

"You'll have to get Mom to fix the roof if you want any shot at it."

There's a fat chance in hell that our yard would ever be noticed. The beautification committee is made up of a bunch of rich snobs who would never look across the street. But it's nice to give Jeff hope, especially since he works so hard.

His shoulders slump in defeat. "I told her that. I need the roof to be pristine. Those broken shingles will never get the win. I think I'm going to call the boys over one of these days and fix it while she's at work. Act first, ask for forgiveness later."

"Very smart approach."

"How was work?"

I pause in my pursuit of the front door. Keeping my smile in full force, I say, "Great. Just a typical day." Yup, a typical day of meandering around the streets of Los Angeles, killing time before I could return home, knowing full well my mom and Jeff are aware of my schedule, and if I arrived home any earlier than normal, they'd be suspicious. And luckily for me, during my meandering, I was told to go buy some pantyhose by an endearing homeless man who scowled at my bare legs. I bought some consolation mint ice cream, which fell victim to the summer California sun and ended up dripping down the front of my white blouse, and to top it off, I tripped over a street grate and tore a heel off my Jimmy Choo shoes, which is why I'm walking barefoot into the house.

It's been one of those days.

"Promotion is in a week, right?" Jeff asks. "Are you excited? You can finally find a place of your own."

Insert the deep sigh here.

I give him a thumbs-up. "Super pumped."

Without another word, I open the door to the house and immediately smell Mom's homemade fish sticks. *Lord Jesus, not again.*

This girl can't catch a break.

"Jeff, dinner is almost ready."

"It's me, Mom," I say, heading to my room, but before I can get too far down the hallway, Mom peeks her head around the doorway to the kitchen.

"Lottie Bug, just in time for dinner."

I wave my hand at her. "Not really hungry." I grip my stomach. "Late lunch. I might have an apple later."

"Don't be ridiculous. Go wash your hands"—yes, she still makes me wash my hands before a meal—"and freshen up. I'll have a place setting waiting for you."

Sighing, I say, "Thanks, Mom." I reach my room, shut the door, and then slide down against it until my butt hits the floor. "God, I need booze." I pull my phone out of my purse and text my sister.

> **Lottie:** Booze needed. Day drinking when Mom and Jeff leave tomorrow. You in?

Kelsey, my Irish twin as Mom likes to call her, is only twelve months younger than me, and is an up-and-coming organizer—yeah, I was confused when she told me that little nugget of information as well. Basically, she's started her own organizing business where she goes to different people's houses to show them how to organize their pantries and closets to be more functional—so how to not be pack rats. I asked her how she differs from everyone else jumping on *The Home Edit* trend, and her answer blew me away—because it was actually well thought-out. She focuses on organizing sustainably. Instead of encouraging all of her clients to use clear acrylic bins, she works with a company that offers sustainably sourced organizational products, as well as products made from fully recycled materials. Better for the environment and better for your home. *See? Blown away.* Apparently, she's one celebrity away from being discovered. I believe her. She makes just enough right now to grow her business and to afford a small studio apartment in West Hollywood.

My phone beeps with a text.

> **Kelsey:** Shouldn't you be at work tomorrow?

I stand from my spot on the floor and untuck my shirt before texting her back.

Lottie: I should…

I set my phone down and undress, tossing my clothes in my hamper, not even bothering with the stain. The damage has been done. I put on a pair of shorts and a tank top and tie my long brown hair up in a knot.

Kelsey: Don't tell me that ho fired you.

Lottie: Consider me unemployed.

Kelsey: I FREAKING told you this was going to happen. She's such a…God, Lottie, if you ever talk to her again, I'm going to disown you. Do you hear me?

Lottie: Trust me, Angela is dead to me now, despite what SHE might think.

Kelsey: Let me guess, the narcissist still thinks you're going to be friends.

Lottie: Yup. Anyway, I'm not telling Mom and Jeff, not until I can figure something out. They still think I'm moving out next week when I get my "promotion"—aka downgraded to unemployed.

Kelsey: Your secret is safe with me. I'll be over around nine with tequila and margarita fixings.

Lottie: Can you come with the idea notebook?

Kelsey: Already packing it. I got you, sis.

Lottie: I love you.

Kelsey: Love you. And don't worry. We'll figure this out.

Feeling relieved, I set my phone down on the dresser, because if Mom sees a phone anywhere near the dinner table, she snatches it away and tosses it in the toilet. I've fallen victim to such thievery once and only once. After drying your toilet-water phone in rice overnight, you quickly learn to never do that again.

I head down the hallway and to the dining room, where I catch Jeff press a chaste kiss to my mom's cheek. He whispers, "Thank you," to her before taking a seat. He's changed his clothes as well, hands free from any landscaping dirt. I know he'll be right back outside after this, but I appreciate his understanding for my mom's rules at the table.

"Smells good, Mom," I lie as I take a seat. Jeff loves her homemade fish sticks. I loathe them. But I eat them because I was taught at a very early age, you eat what's on your plate and you don't complain about it. Be happy you have food at all.

"Thank you. I made some of your favorite cobbler for dessert."

Now that's something I can choke down fish sticks for.

"You're amazing. Thank you."

Mom takes a seat, and then as a cute family of three, we link hands, Mom leads us in a prayer, and then we dig in. Thankfully, Mom gave me smaller portions. I can easily take this down for the promise of some fresh cobbler.

"How was work, sweetie?" Mom asks while putting a dollop of tartar sauce on her plate. She passes the sauce to Jeff, who takes a scoop as well, and then to me. I load up my plate with the pickle-ridden dipping sauce because it's the only way I can chew through the sticks of fish.

"It was great," I answer, the lie feeling raw on my tongue.

Three things I learned while growing up with a strong, independent woman—you don't lie, you don't cheat, and you always work for what you want. Well, I just lied, but I can't possibly stomach telling the truth. Not when Mom and Jeff told me—just like Kelsey—what a bad idea it was to take a job from Angela. Hot and cold Angela. Narcissistic and erratic Angela. They told me to wait out the job market, that something would come along for a graduate from UC Irvine with a master's in business.

Something would come.

Anything would come.

Nothing came.

Absolutely zero opportunities.

I became desperate.

Student loans were knocking at my door, responsibility was flooding around my feet.

I needed a job.

Angela was my only option. She offered me temporary placement within the company, a lowball salary that forced me to live with my mom so I could maintain living in Southern California, and a promise that if I performed my job well, that after a year, my salary would triple—yes, triple, that's how much of a pay cut I took—and she'd give me a permanent position. Mom and Jeff said I'd be a fool to take it. That she'd screw me over somehow.

But I had no other options. Absolutely none. So I had no choice, in my mind. I took it.

And I slayed.

Over the next few months, I saw extreme growth of the lifestyle blog. Celebrities started backing it, and before I knew it, Angeloop had become a household name. I was a part of that. I threw a "told you so" right at Mom and Jeff after our first featured spot on the *TODAY Show*. I said I had to put the time in, and good things would happen.

Can you hear the sarcastic laughter now?

Not only do I have no money, but now I have no job, and in a week— unless I want to tell Mom and Jeff the truth—nowhere to live.

As Rachel Green would say, isn't that just kick-you-in-the-crotch, spit-on-your-neck fantastic?

"Did you sign a lease yet? I know you found a place over in West Hollywood near your sister you liked."

That I did, but thank God for my fear of commitment, because I didn't sign the lease. That would've just added to this nightmare.

"I didn't quite like that place; the vibe wasn't there."

Jeff laughs. "Maura, do you remember being twenty-five, searching for a place to live based off a vibe?" He playfully clutches his chest. "The memories."

My mom chuckles and smooths her hand over his back. "I remember I found a one-room square over in Koreatown where the toilet was next to my bed, and I'd use it as a nightstand. It was in those nightstand-toilet-seat moments that I thought, *Wow, the vibe here is real...*" Mom looks at me. "Real poor, that is."

Chuckling, Jeff nods. "Toilet nightstand got me beat there. I just had a neighbor with a broom that wrecked my vibe all the time."

I look between the two of them. "You know I'm borderline a Gen Zer; the sarcasm can cut deep at times."

They both laugh, and then Mom says, "You're a soft millennial. That's okay, honey. You can stay with Mommy and Stepdaddy for as long as you want. We love having no privacy." She smirks and I know she's teasing. She'd never kick me out of the house, but I also know they've been looking forward to my departure for a while.

"If you like having no privacy, then we might as well have a slumber party tonight. We can all cuddle up in your queen-size bed."

Jeff holds up his hand. "Please, spare me."

Poor Jeff, such a good guy, and I can see that he does want to have some privacy with my mom. He's been with us since I was fifteen. I think he's ready to have some serious alone time with my mom. And just like that, the guilt builds. Does it suck that Angela fucked me over? Of course, but what sucks even more is if I don't figure this out, I'm going to be fucking Jeff and my mom out of the freedom they've been looking forward to.

"We really want to walk around naked," Mom says out of the blue. When I give her a horrified look, she says, "Whenever you're hanging out with your sister, that's what we do. We turn on some Harry Connick Jr., strip down, and then dance naked in the living room."

"Oh my God, why are you telling me this?" I set my fork down, the possibility of eating dwindling. Yes, Jeff and my mom are attractive people; Jeff lifts weights in the garage, and Mom keeps up with her physique, but good Christ! Not something you want to envision.

"Just so you know what we're looking forward to." She winks and then dips a fish stick in tartar sauce casually.

"I could've done without knowing." I lean back in my chair and cross my arms over my chest.

Mom waves her fork at my plate. "Eat up, sweetie. Cobbler is waiting for you."

How could I forget?

―――――――

From behind a bush, I peek through the branches and watch as Jeff pulls my mom in for a kiss, gives her ass a squeeze—ugh, old people—and then they both get in their cars and head to work. I don't pop out of the bushes right away. Instead, I wait another two minutes just to make sure they didn't forget anything. With my luck, they'd return home just as I was busting open a bag of chips.

When I feel the coast is clear, I move around the bush, attempting to not snag my black pencil skirt on a branch—can't afford to lose any good interview clothes—and I trudge across the street in my generic black heels. Thank God for seven-foot shrubs, because I don't think they noticed a thing. I tiptoe up the sidewalk to the house, unlock the door, slip inside, and then let out a deep breath.

Mission accomplished. *Although now I'm wondering why I didn't just drive to Kelsey's place rather than worry about all this subterfuge.*

The hum of the fridge fills the rather quiet house. Everything is in order, not a throw pillow out of place, not a single dish in the sink. Mom probably wants this. Peace. The ability to enjoy the home she's worked so hard to keep.

Not that I'm loud or obnoxious or a bad "roommate," but there's something to having a house to yourself, being able to do what you want without the repercussions of someone walking in on you. That's what Mom and Jeff want desperately.

I know this because they mention it almost every day.

I need to find a job, and quick.

Not only because I want to be able to give my mom peace with Jeff, but because this girl doesn't have much in the bank account, and student loans won't pay themselves. Not to mention my high school reunion is coming up, and wouldn't it just be a freaking cactus to the armpit if I show up unemployed, up to my eyeballs in student loans, wearing a dress from five years ago, and still living with my mom?

And it's not as if I can't show up, because if I don't show up, Angela will know why, and I can't give her the satisfaction of knowing I relied on her.

No, I need to figure this out.

I head back to my bedroom and change out of my work outfit and into a pair of shorts and a ratty Taylor Swift shirt that I've had for over a decade.

As I make it back into the living room, my phone beeps with a text.

Kelsey: All clear?

Lottie: Clear.

A few minutes later, Kelsey comes busting through the door with tequila and margarita fixings in hand. "The items to forget all your troubles are here."

I walk up to her, take the tequila, and then give her a hug. "Thank you for coming over."

"What are sisters for? Plus, I have a light day today. Just fielding some emails. I brought my computer with me so I can get some work done as well."

"While drinking?" I ask, brow raised. "Doesn't seem like a smart idea."

"We're going to take it slow." She gives me a pointed look. "Alcohol can ease the pain, but it's not going to fix anything. Unless…have you decided to tell Mom and Jeff? Because if that's the case, I'll get shit-faced with you right now. You say the word, and our heads will be battling for prime-time toilet space in two hours."

I shake my head. "No, I'm not telling Mom and Jeff." Margarita fixings in hand, we both walk to the kitchen, where we set everything on the counter. "I don't think I have it in me to tell them. You should've seen their faces last night when they were talking about having the house to themselves and having the opportunity to finally dance around naked."

"Ew." Kelsey's face scrunches up.

"Tell me about it. It was a visual I didn't need while trying to choke down Mom's fish sticks." I grab two glasses and a shaker from the cabinet. Kelsey goes to the freezer for a tray of ice cubes—Mom doesn't believe her fridge needs to be updated, just like the roof. "But they were excited about me leaving, and to tell them that there's no end in sight at this moment, it makes me want to drink this entire bottle of tequila." I press my hand to my face. "I'm such a failure, Kelsey."

She slips in behind me and gives me a hug. I wrap my arms around hers and hold her tight, letting myself take advantage of the sisterly hug.

"You're not a failure," Kelsey says. "You've just hit a bump in the road."

"You all told me she was going to screw me over at some point, and maybe I thought that in the beginning, but after finding a groove with work and proving my worth at the company, I thought I could trust her. I truly thought I'd found my place." I shake my head. "I'm an idiot."

"You're not an idiot." She pats my hands before releasing me. "But maybe you make some bad decisions at times."

"I make so many bad decisions. Remember that time you told me not to ask out Tyler Dretch because you said he liked you, but I tried to prove you wrong and asked him out anyway? He told me he wanted to date the younger version of me. That was in high school. HIGH SCHOOL, Kelsey."

She chuckles. "I know. I told you not to."

"And then when I bought those peach-colored seersuckers? I convinced you they were the newest fashion that just hadn't hit the market yet, and I wore them to the beach only for them to tear in the crotch seam when I bent over. My ass crack never cinched up so tight and so fast in my life."

"I can still see the horrified look on your face as you felt the first ocean breeze cross your lady bits. Not wearing underwear, another bad decision."

"You see? I don't even know what a good decision is."

"That's not true. Those are just small things. You've made some good decisions."

"Oh yeah?" I ask, pouring the margarita ingredients into the shaker. "Please, regale me with my amazing decisions."

Kelsey leans against the counter and taps her chin. "Uh...you...well, there was the time...hmm, oh, what about...eh, maybe not that..."

"Please, keep them coming," I say dryly. "You're showering me with all my good decisions. I can barely breathe from all the flattery."

"Just give me a second, sheesh—oh, you got your master's in business. That was a great idea."

"Was it?" I ask her. "Because I've spent the last year using my measly paycheck to pay off my hefty student loans. And that master's in business did absolutely nothing for me other than land me a job with Angela, which...we know how that ended."

"Oh, I forgot about the student loans. Are they bad?" Kelsey's face scrunches up.

I shake the mixer and say, "I honestly can't even look; I'm too scared. I have them on autopay right now."

"How much do you have in the bank?"

I wince.

It's bad.

And I knew she was going to ask the question, but it doesn't make it any easier.

I pour the margaritas into their respective glasses. "I don't know. Once again, too scared to look."

Kelsey takes a deep breath, picks up her drink, and says, "Well, if we're going to figure out what you're going to do, then we're going to have to rip the bandage off and take a look at what we're working with. We need to know your level of desperation."

She pulls her computer from her bag and nods toward the dining room table.

"It's time," she says.

Crap…I'm afraid she's right. It is time.

I stand there, lift the glass to my lips, and take a very large sip. I'm going to need it.

We both stare blankly at the wall in front of us.

Not a word.

Not a movement.

Just…staring.

The air conditioner kicks on every few minutes, blowing cool air over my heated body. But that's it. That's the only movement in the house, a slight wisp of my hair floating across my grief-stricken and incredibly shocked face.

I've heard of rock bottom before. I've read about it. I've even seen it on some people.

I thought I was at rock bottom yesterday.

But I was wrong.

This…this right here is rock bottom.

Finally, after at least five minutes of silence, Kelsey says, "So, I'd say our level of desperation is DEFCON 1."

I tip back my drink and finish the contents. "Yup," I say simply.

Over thirty thousand dollars in debt, less than three thousand dollars to my name.

Not enough for a deposit and first month's rent for my own place.

Not enough to keep paying off my loans.

Not enough to consider some money to fall back on.

Nope.

DEFCON 1 is precisely what we're dealing with—nuclear war.

"You really weren't making much, were you?" Kelsey asks.

"No, I wasn't." I press my hand against my forehead, the severity of my situation really starting to sink in. "I hate to admit it, but I think I have to start stripping."

"What?" Kelsey asks.

"Yup, stripping. I've seen how much those girls make. They're raking in the dough." I lift the collar of my shirt and peer down at my body. "I have nice boobs, maybe smaller than what some might enjoy, but guys like that, right? They're perky enough. And I can…sway to the music."

"Strip clubs aren't looking for people to sway to Taylor Swift music, they want you gyrating. Do you know how to gyrate?"

"You're never too old to learn something new. Gyrating is just thrusting your pelvis, right? I say we look up some strip clubs and just, you know, scope out the competition. See what's getting the penises up around Hollywood these days."

"I'm going to tell you right now, it's not the kind of two-step, side-to-side dancing you do. Also, Mom would murder you. And you realize, you'd have to dance in a thong, and your boobs would be out for everyone to see."

I roll my eyes. "I know what strippers do. I'm not an idiot." I tap my chin. "Do you think if I get my nipple pierced, that would help my chances?"

Kelsey actually gives it some thought. "Maybe—wait, no." She shakes her head. "You're not going to be a stripper. There has to be a better idea than exposing men to your bare-breasted two-step." She stands and holds her hand out to me. She helps me stand as well and then says, "Let's go for a walk. Fresh air will clear our heads. Booze is always a good idea to forget, but we can't forget, because we're in DEFCON 1 mode right now. We need ideas, not sorrows."

"Are you saying I'm not allowed to wallow?"

She shakes her head again. "No. We have no time for wallowing. Not unless you're ready to tell Mom—"

"No way in hell."

"Then get your shoes, because we need to get thinking."

Not bothering with sneakers, I slip on my sandals. We lock up, and then we head out of the house. Kelsey walks across the street and turns right.

"You want to walk through The Flats?" I ask her. "Do you want to depress me?"

"Being surrounded by rich, elaborate houses might be exactly what you need. Inspiration."

Dragging my feet, I follow her, and we start our walk through the neighborhood of the most elaborate and ornate houses in Los Angeles. The sidewalks are immaculate, with not a crack in the cement, and the grass is so pristinely cut that, from a quick glance, one would assume it is AstroTurf, that's how perfect it is. A mixture of palm trees and old oak trees line the roads, while cascading bushes and wrought-iron gates protect the dwellings of the wealthy.

"This is depressing," I say as I go to turn around.

"No, this is inspiring. You have to have a mindset change. Who knows? Maybe by walking these streets, we'll run into someone rich who wants to work on a charity case—you."

"Aren't you cute."

She chuckles. "Seriously, though, you never know who we might run into. Haven't you heard those stories about people who meet an investor on an airplane, and next thing you know, their product is in every Target in the country?"

"No," I answer. "I haven't heard those stories."

"Well, they happen. You never know who you might run into." She laughs. "You could possibly meet a rich husband, walking these streets." She glances at me, and then looks me up and down. "Well, not dressed like that, but—"

"You know, that might not be a bad idea," I say.

"What? Meeting a rich husband?" Kelsey asks. "Sis, I was joking."

But it's not a joke in my head. And, yes, it might be the tequila—what little we had—talking, but there have to be men around here looking for someone to marry, right? Some singletons looking for a romp on their luxury mattress that could very well turn into a lifelong coupling? I'm not opposed to impressing with my sexual exploits to snag a man. Remember, DEFCON 1.

"No, this could be something."

"Oh, Jesus," Kelsey says in an exasperated tone. "Lottie, I know you're desperate, but we need to be smart-desperate. Finding a rich husband isn't the solution to your problems. What are you going to do, get married next week?"

"Love can happen that fast."

"I'm going to stop you right there—this isn't a solution. We need something concrete, something we can control."

"No." I gesture to the houses around us. "Look at these places. You can't tell me all these people are living the perfect life. I bet there are some bachelors here looking for someone to keep them warm at night." I point to my chest. "That person can be me. I'm warm. I have snuggly arms, and I'll put out. I have no problem with such behavior."

"Jesus, help me," Kelsey says, pressing her hands together while looking up to the sky.

I lift my phone and open my browser.

"What are you doing?" Kelsey asks.

"Looking up how to snag a rich husband."

"Lottie, you've lost it. Truly, this is an all-time low for you."

"Precisely, which means I can only go up from here. Oh, look." I point at my phone. "An article on how to impress the rich." I click on it and start scrolling. "It says they like braids." I look up at Kelsey. "Rich people like braids? Do your clients have braids in their hair?"

Kelsey thinks about it. "I mean…I guess I've worked with a few who have the cute mini braids in their hair."

"Okay, braids—check."

"Lottie, you can't be serious."

Desperation consumes me, and once I'm fixated on something that I think will save me from my current situation, I go all in. So…yes, I am serious.

"Classy clothes, nothing scandalous." I glance down at my shirt. "Think they would like this Taylor Swift shirt?"

"No," Kelsey says. "No one likes that shirt. It has holes in the armpits."

"Unless you've experienced the kind of breeze received from these holes in the armpits, you have no opinion on the matter. But noted, the rich might not enjoy it." I scan the article. "Makeup, sophisticated conversations. Knowledge on a vast array of topics." I think about it. "Do I know a lot of things?"

"What kinds of things?"

I scan the article again. "Doesn't say, just 'a vast array of topics.'"

"Uh, I mean, you know a lot of random facts about reality TV."

"I do." I perk up. "That can be entertaining."

"Probably not for someone who brings in enough money to afford a twenty-four-million-dollar home."

"Hmm, yeah, maybe you're right. Not to worry, I'll peruse Wikipedia, brush up on some knowledge."

"Yeah, because Wikipedia is the place to do that," Kelsey says sarcastically and then stops to face me. "I think we really need to focus here, Lottie. Come up with a valid idea. I know this isn't what you want to do, but maybe you can ask Ken if you can—"

"No," I say, turning away from her and continuing to walk down the manicured streets. "I'm not contacting Ken."

"But he'd have a job for you. You know he would."

"Ken is out of the question. I'd rather rub my boob on some drunk man's face than call Ken."

"Is it because he's dating Angela now?"

My jaw grows tight as my lips twist to the side. "No, I just don't feel like crawling back to my ex who left me for my boss after I introduced him to her. Begging him for a job at his lame freight-shipping company is something I'll never do. Seriously, my boob on a drunk man's face is so much more appealing than that."

"You know he'd help you," Kelsey pushes.

I shake my head and then turn around to head back home. "This is useless. We should be thinking of useful ideas, not walking around, coming up with ideas like calling up my ex for a job. Honestly, Kelsey, you're not bringing your A game today."

"I didn't get a lot of sleep last night, and I think that margarita mix was old." She holds her stomach.

I take her hand and turn her around with me. "This fresh air idea was a flop."

"Better than sitting on the couch with a pitcher of margaritas."

"I beg to differ," I say as a black car drives toward us, windows tinted black. "You know, that person in that car could be my escape out of this mess. I'm still thinking finding a rich husband is the way to go."

"You're delusional. You realize that? Especially dressed like an unemployed vagabond. No one is going to want anything to do with you in that getup."

"I'll have you know—these are my nice shorts. They're only three years old."

Kelsey slow claps for me. "Bravo, sis."

We cross the street and head toward the house, and my phone beeps in my hand. We make our way up the sidewalk to the house as I bring my phone into view.

And then I stop dead.

Kelsey notices and asks, "What? What is it? Do Mom and Jeff know we're home?"

I shake my head and show her my phone. "Angela texted me."

"Noooooo." Kelsey takes the phone from my hands and punches in my passcode. Yup, we're that close. "What the hell do you think she wants?"

"I don't know, you took my phone."

Together, we lean in, and Kelsey holds the phone out in front of us so we can both read it.

Angela: Hey, girl, now that you have time on your hands, think you want to help me with the reunion planning? I could really use your magic touch. You're so good at everything.

"What the actual fuck?" Kelsey shouts. "She has the audacity to text you and ask you for help? Has she lost her damn mind? And *time on your hands*? Uh, you have no time on your hands because of her; you have to spend all that time looking for a new job."

I just stare down at the text, unable to move. Stunned that she'd say such a thing to me. That she'd think it's okay, after firing me.

It's nothing personal...

Yeah, well, it's personal to me.

I shake my head. "She's the worst human being I think I've ever met."

"Glad you're finally noticing that." Kelsey pats me on the back and encourages me to enter the house, but I stay still.

"There's no way I'm going to that reunion. Do you know why? Because she's just going to spend it humiliating me."

Kelsey turns me toward her and forces me to look her in the eyes.

"Oh…you're going to that reunion. Do you hear me? You're going, and you're going to show up with some hot-as-shit guy on your arm who's going to make Ken look like a freaking troll, and Angela is going to drool all over him."

"It's in two months. Currently, I have no job, I live with my mom, and I have zero prospects for arm candy." I point at her and say, "And if you even joke about hiring an escort, our sistership is done. Got it?"

She nods. "I understand. Escort is not an option." She taps her chin. "Let's go inside, figure this out. Form a plan. We'll get you out of this mess, even if it means you sleep on the floor of my studio apartment for a few weeks."

"And here I thought I'd hit rock bottom, but you just offered up a whole new low."

———

Kelsey: You know, I just measured out my studio. Another twin bed won't fit in here with my furniture. What if we stack some pillows under my bistro table? Might feel like a bunk bed or something.

Lottie: I'm not staying at your place.

Kelsey: We spent all day yesterday trying to come up with something. That's the best I've got. You know if I could afford to, I'd love to hire you so you could take care of all the business things, and I could focus more on client outreach.

Lottie: Working with you would be the dream, but if I want to get out of Mom's house, I need money now. But don't worry, I have it covered.

Kelsey: What do you mean you have it covered? I told you, no stripping, no matter how nice your boobs are.

Lottie: I'm not stripping. I don't think my nips are ready for that kind of exposure.

Kelsey: Then, I'm afraid to ask what your plan is.

Lottie: I'm not saying this is the end goal, but at least it's something until I can figure out more.

Kelsey: Lottie, what the hell are you doing?

Lottie: Just...taking a stroll.

Kelsey: Oh my GOD! Are you in The Flats right now?

Lottie: Nothing wrong with a little exercise. Got to get my muscles moving, you know?

Kelsey: What are you wearing? If you say heels and a dress, I'm going to drive over there and pick you up. This is not a *Pretty Woman* moment. You hear me? Julia Roberts lucked out with Edward. That's once in a lifetime.

Lottie: That was fictional.

Kelsey: Either way, what are you wearing?

Lottie: [picture] Simple workout clothes.

Kelsey: You're wearing a sports bra, no shirt. That's flashy.

Lottie: Yeah, and these people are flashy. High ponytail so I look approachable and fun, with of course a braid on the side. Bright white sneakers because they scream I like tennis. And I found a Fuji water bottle on the ground yesterday when I was pretending to come home from work, and I brought it home, cleaned it, and I'm carrying it now so it looks like I buy expensive water.

Kelsey: Eeeww. Are you drinking from it?

Lottie: God, no. I'm not ready to contract syphilis. It's just a prop.

Kelsey: A prop? I'm sorry, are you in a movie I don't know about?

Lottie: Not yet, but I did apply to some service that gathers extras for TV and film. You can make $40 a day. Score.

Kelsey: You know, I never thought I'd see you like this, but...wow.

Lottie: What's that supposed to mean?

Kelsey: You're excited about the possibility of making $40 a day, while perusing the streets for possible single, rich men, in a neighborhood you don't belong in. CALL KEN!

Lottie: OVER MY DEAD BODY. I can feel it, Kels. This is it for me. Today, my life is going to change, even if it means I have to stay out here all day, walking up and down these damn streets. This is my out.

Kelsey: When you come home, don't be surprised when there's an intervention set up. Because this is a new low for you.

Lottie: I'm going to make you eat your words. Just watch!

CHAPTER 3
HUXLEY

JP PRESSES HIS FINGERS TO his temples. "Hold the fuck on. Let me get this straight." He looks up at me. "You ran into Dave Toney on the street and told him you were engaged to a girl from Georgia and that she's pregnant?"

I wet my lips. "That would be correct."

We're sitting on my front porch, beers in hand, as I break the news to my brothers that I not only fucked up, but I ROYALLY fucked up. I didn't tell them yesterday after I saw Dave on the street, because honestly, I needed a second to process what the hell I'd gotten myself into. Now that I've had more than twenty-four hours to think about it, I realize that, yes, I'm going to need some assistance from my brothers to get me out of this one.

Breaker rests his beer on the armrest of his chair and asks, "What the hell were you thinking?"

I shrug. "I saw an opportunity, and without thinking, I took it."

"Claiming your nonexistent fiancée is pregnant with your child isn't an opportunity—that's a big fucking mistake. Dude, you have to have dinner with them in three days."

I grip my hair and pull on it. "I know. Fuck, what am I going to do?"

"Uh, tell him the truth, that you're a liar," JP says.

"Because that's going to secure the deal." I roll my eyes. "I can't do that. If I tell him I lied, our reputation is going to be tarnished. No one will want to work with us."

"You couldn't have thought about that before you went and made up a fake baby and fiancée?" Breaker asks. "Shit, man."

Yeah, I fucking know.

I couldn't sleep last night, because all I kept thinking about was how the hell I was going to get myself out of this situation. Honestly, I have no idea what came over me.

The property, yes, could be a huge profit for us, especially with what I've lined up idea-wise, but it's not as if this deal will make or break the company. I think there's just a part of me that needs to get what I can't have. And that, right now, is those properties. I have my eyes set on them, and apparently, I'll do just about anything to secure them.

Even if it means putting our business on the line.

And that made me feel sick to my stomach at three o'clock this morning. My brothers and I have built Cane Enterprises into the conglomerate it is today with a lot of hard work, a lot of right moves, and a lot of reinvesting.

That one little mistake yesterday—it could cost us all that hard work, especially if word gets around.

"Do you have any friends that are single women?" Breaker asks.

"I barely have time to hang out with you two; do you really think I have time to nurture a friendship with a woman?"

"Hey." Breaker holds up his hands. "Don't get snarky with me. You're the one who came up with this great fucking idea."

Sighing, I stand from my chair and set down my beer.

"What are you doing?" JP asks.

"Going for a walk. I need to clear my head."

"Fine," Breaker says, standing as well. "I'm going to order food while you do that. And you know what? I'm getting fucking ice cream, too, because this is one of those ice cream moments."

"Cookies and cream, dude. I've been craving it," JP says as they both go into the house.

I jog down the few steps from my porch to my sidewalk and head out toward the street. I use the door in the guard gate, rather than having to open the entire gate, and then turn right.

It's just past six. I came home early, because I couldn't stand sitting at the office any longer than I had to today. And because on my computer screen, in big bold letters, was an e-vite to Dave Toney's house for dinner with the missus. Yup…the "missus."

It was a bleeding reminder of how I lost my damn mind yesterday. At the age of thirty-five, you'd think I'd have the ability to stay more…calm, but that wasn't the case. The pressure got to me.

Maybe it's because I feel the need to be the best. Turning thirty-five has made me realize that I'm still young and have so much potential, and if I continue to make the deals I'm making, we could easily become the youngest billionaires in the business.

Money shouldn't be a motivator, but hell, the prestige of it is.

I grip the back of my neck in frustration. Dad is probably looking down at me, laughing his ass off, thinking I got myself into one hell of a situation this time. Growing up, even though I was the oldest, I was also the troublemaker, the one who pushed the limits. Not the typical firstborn personality, but I'd push and push and push until I was stuck between a rock and a hard place, and Dad would just sit back and laugh while I attempted to become unstuck. I always succeeded, but this time around, I'm not so sure I'll be able to.

I've performed my fair share of miracles, but finding a woman to fall in love with me, accept my proposal, and get pregnant in three days seems like a bit of a stretch.

If only a girl could just fall right in my lap, willing and ready to go through this ruse with me. Someone, anyone…

I turn the corner and almost run straight into a confused ball of brunette.

"Oh, sorry," I apologize as I grip both of her arms to keep her from toppling over into the grass.

"Hey, watch where you're going," she snaps at me while pulling away.

"Jesus," I say, holding my hands up. "It was an accident."

She steadies herself and then adjusts her long brown ponytail. I quickly take her in. She's a small thing, petite, head barely reaches my chin. Her skin has that California glow to it that tells me she has time to hit up the beach or pool, and the definition in her arms makes me believe she has time to go to the gym as well. Probably some housewife out for a walk, trying to get her steps in before the husband comes home from a late night at the office.

When she turns to face me, though, hell…I'm struck in the goddamn chest as her light green eyes meet mine. A seafoam color so light that it's almost startling against her natural, thick black lashes.

Damn.

Her eyes quickly roam my body and then meet mine again, but this time, she's not hostile, more…frustrated.

"Sorry, I'm just…ugh, I'm lost. And I shouldn't be telling a complete stranger I'm lost, because that's an invitation to take advantage of me. But my phone died, and I can't remember which way to go."

"Oh, so you don't live around here?"

She scoffs. "I'm wearing four-year-old leggings from Target. Trust me, I don't live around here." And then, as if she remembers something, she says, "Uh, I mean, I'm from here. I, uh…I'm posh and all those things." With a deep exhale, her shoulders slump, and she rests her hands on her hips. "Who am I kidding? This was a stupid-ass idea, and now I'm lost and hungry, and my mom is going to call the cops if I don't come home soon."

Oh shit, how old is this girl? I assumed old enough to look at, but if her mom is worried…

"Being that it's a school night, I can see why she'd be worried," I say. "You can use my phone if you want."

She stands taller. "School night? How old do you think I am?"

I grip the back of my neck. "I don't know. You said your mom would be worried."

"Because she's an overprotective mother, and I'm a twenty-eight-year-old loser who gets lost in a rich neighborhood while trying to find a rich husband."

"What?" I laugh.

"Uh-huh." She folds her arms over her chest, which props up her breasts in that already spectacular sports bra. "Tried to look for a rich husband today. Not a gold digger, though, if that's what you're thinking. Just seeking revenge for a high school reunion. You know the deal."

"I'm unfamiliar with needing to find a rich husband."

"So, you're not gay?"

My eyebrows shoot to my hairline. This girl holds nothing back. "Do I seem gay?"

"I mean, if you want to lay down stereotypes, then, no, you look more like an alpha asshole you might find in the boardroom. It's the haircut and watch."

I glance down at my watch and then back at her. The watch is really expensive. "I get the alpha in the boardroom, but why the asshole?"

She scans me, her nose scrunches, and she says, "Your cologne. Smells too good. Nice guys never smell that good."

"From this brief conversation, I'm going to assume you found no takers in your rich husband search."

"Nope." She pops the P. "You're actually the first guy I've run into today. Imagine that. Received plenty of judgmental stares from the ladies around here, though."

"It's probably because of your four-seasons-ago Target leggings," I joke.

"Yeah, they can totally tell that kind of stuff." She tilts her head to the side. "Can I ask you a question?"

"Sure," I answer, sort of enjoying this odd encounter.

"You're rich, right?" When I don't answer, she rolls her eyes and adds, "I'm not going to pull out a nail file and try to stab you, if that's what you're worried about. I read this article on how to snag a rich guy, and I feel as though one of the suggestions was wrong."

I stick my hands in my pockets and casually say, "I have money."

She snorts. "Yeah, I'm sure you just *have* it." Shaking her head, she says, "Okay, you're loaded, let's go with that—because it's obvious. I want to know, do rich guys like braids?"

"Braids?" I ask, confused.

"You know." She points to the side of her head, where there's a small braid stretched across her head and then tied into her ponytail. "Braids. Do you like these?"

"Uh, I mean…sure? It's not like I'm super excited about it, but I don't hate it, either."

"I knew it," she whispers while snapping her fingers. "That article was total clickbait. I could tell by the millions of ads on the page that kept popping up every time I scrolled down. Duped again."

"Do I even want to know?"

"Probably not."

I rock on my heels. "So, looking for a rich boyfriend, huh?"

She eyes me skeptically. "Yes."

"You know, I'm single."

I know, I know. What the hell are you thinking, Huxley? This is a random girl on the street looking for a rich boyfriend, not a friend up for a con job to save your ass—and business. For all you know, she could very well be a gold digger. She could be bad news. She could be a decoy for someone driving by in a van to rob you. It's happened before in this neighborhood.

And from the way her leggings fit tightly against her flat stomach, it's a solid guess that she's not pregnant, making this plan of mine exponentially worse. But I don't see any other options at the moment.

She's single, and she's a woman, the only two requirements I'm truly looking for at this point.

Still looking skeptical, she folds her arms over her chest. "You're single."

"Yeah. Single as they come."

"And you're telling me this because…"

Yeah, why are you telling her this, Huxley? Why are you telling a complete stranger that you're single with the intention that you can use her to your advantage?

Because she seems to need help like I need help, and if I've learned anything about business, it's that business deals can go a long way if they can benefit both parties.

And I very well might have a business deal in the making.

"You know, I think we should go grab something to eat."

She doesn't move, doesn't even blink. "Okay, what kind of creep are you?"

"Excuse me?" I ask.

She motions at me with her finger. "I told you I'm looking for a rich boyfriend. You should be running away. You should probably be calling the cops to escort me out of here and back to my mom's modest bungalow. There's no way in hell you should be asking me to grab something to eat. So what's your game, man?"

She's spunky, outspoken, unlike any girl I've met, that's for sure. And she's right. I should be scared. She seems to have the kind of tenacity that would bring a man to his knees, but she also is a qualified candidate for what I'm looking for, and I'm three days away from a dinner date. I'm willing to roll the dice.

"I have no game—"

"Don't bullshit me."

Wow, she really calls it like it is.

"Just tell me what your endgame is."

"Fine," I say, seeing where this is going. "I might be in the need for a fake fiancée." I'll keep the pregnant thing to myself for now.

"A fake fiancée?" she asks. "Why?"

I glance around at our surroundings. "I don't tend to talk business in the middle of the neighborhood. If you're interested in talking about this, then why don't you meet me at the Chipotle on Santa Monica and Beverly in an hour?"

"Chipotle?" she asks, dumbfounded. "You're rich—supposedly— and that's where you want to meet for dinner?"

"I like burritos," I say with a shrug. "Plus, anywhere else isn't going to accept someone wearing four-seasons-ago leggings and a sports bra into their establishment." Even if the sports bra makes her tits look amazing.

She doesn't answer right away, instead taking her time, but when she does answer, she says, "That's fair. Care to direct me back to my house so I can put on something more suitable for Chipotle?"

"Sure." I pull out my phone and open the Google Maps app. I hand her my phone and let her figure it out on her own. "My name is Huxley, by the way."

Her eyes flutter up to mine. "Huxley, huh, that's an interesting name. Any inspiration from *Huckleberry Finn*?"

"Not that I'm aware of." When she goes back to the phone, I ask, "And you would be…"

"Lottie," she says, zooming in on the phone and finding her bearings as she glances around the streets.

"Lottie. Any inspiration from a lollipop?"

Her brow raises when she looks up at me. "No. It's actually short for Leiselotte. But no one, and I mean no one, calls me that. Not even my parents." She points at me. "And don't even think about calling me that. Got it?"

I hold up my hands in defense. "Got it."

"Good." She hands me back my phone and says, "I know where I'm going now. I'm about a mile away."

"Will an hour be long enough for you to get back?"

"Do you think I'll be crawling?"

So fiery.

So fierce.

"No, just not sure how long it would take you to, you know…shower."

Her brows shoot up to her hairline. "Are you implying I stink?"

Jesus.

I drag my hand over my face. "No, I just…I don't know what you need to do to get ready."

She holds up one hand. "Trust me, it won't take long. I'm not here to impress anyone." She takes a step back. "Chipotle, in an hour." She points at me. "You're buying."

And then she takes off at a jog, and for some reason, I keep my eyes trained on her heart-shaped backside.

Business. Opportunity. Cane. That's what I need to focus on, because Little Miss No-One-Calls-Me-Leiselotte might be just the woman I need. Smart. Quick on her feet.

Desperate.

"What do you mean, you're leaving?" JP asks from my dining room table. "And why are you dressed like that?"

"Like what?" I ask as I adjust the cuffs on my button-up shirt.

"As if you're about to go on a date," Breaker answers before taking a sip of his beer.

"Because I am."

Both of my brothers sit up in their chairs and set their beers down on the sandalwood dining room table to which I have no attachment. My designer purchased it because it goes with my "design aesthetic."

"What do you mean, you're going on a date?" JP asks. "You were just outside, trying to dig yourself out of the mess you've made with Dave Toney. You went on a walk, and now you're going on a date?"

"Yeah," I say as I slip on my shoes.

"How?" Breaker asks.

"Ran into her on the sidewalk. She was looking for a rich boyfriend. I happen to be rich. Therefore, it works out perfectly."

"What?" JP asks, his voice disbelieving. "Hold on. You met a girl on the sidewalk, she openly told you she's looking for a rich boyfriend, and now you're taking her out?"

I finish tying my shoe, stand, and adjust my slate gray shorts. "Yup." They're about to open their mouths when I pin them with a steely glare. "Do you have any better ideas? Do you have any other women lining up for the job?"

"Is she lining up for the job?" JP asks.

"She's aware that I need a fake fiancée."

"I don't know," Breaker says. "This seems like a really bad idea. Going out with someone you don't know."

I give him a confused look. "Dude, that's what dating is all about, going out with someone you don't know."

"But this is different. She wants a rich boyfriend, you need a fake fiancée, who's to say she's not going to take advantage of you? How do you know she won't agree to whatever you have going on in your head but then do something like go to the media and fuck up our reputation?"

I stuff my phone in my pocket and say, "That's why we pay our lawyers an extreme amount of money, so they can create contracts to prevent that from happening." When Breaker still looks uneasy, I say, "Listen, I didn't give her my last name, and she didn't seem to recognize me either, so I'm going to feel her out and see if she's interested. If so, I'll get Harvey to draw up an NDA, as well as an agreement for both of us to sign."

"I don't know," Breaker says, leaning back in his chair now. "This seems really fucking risky."

"Then tell me what I should do. Do you have another plan of action?" I ask, arms spread.

"Tell Dave that your *fiancée* isn't available this weekend. That she's away for the next two weeks. So, the dinner date needs to be postponed. Although, I wouldn't have lied in the first place," Breaker says.

"Too fucking late for that," I say in a huff while grabbing my keys. Not to mention, I want this deal done and dusted. Not waiting another fucking two weeks, when I'd probably be no closer to finding a fake fiancée. On my way to the garage, I say, "Be back. Lock up if you leave."

I hate to admit that they're right—this is crazy, slightly stupid, and incredibly risky, but I also dug my hole. I might as well lie in it.

CHAPTER 4
LOTTIE

Lottie: OMG, KELSEY!!!

Kelsey: What? Did Mom and Jeff find out? I swear I haven't said anything.

Lottie: No, I found a rich man.

Kelsey: Uh...what?

Lottie: I don't have a lot of time. My phone is charging and I'm meeting him in about twenty-five minutes at the Chipotle down the street. But, yeah, I found a rich man.

Kelsey: Hold on. What do you mean you found a rich man? What were you doing?

Lottie: **Puffs chest** While on my walk. I got lost, and then BAM, rich man to save the day. Told you I could find one walking through The Flats.

Kelsey: You're fucking with me.

Lottie: I'm not, I swear. I'm putting on some mascara right now, and I'm trying to decide if I go in casual or if I put on a sundress. Honestly, I have no need to impress him. He's the one who wants to discuss things.

Kelsey: Discuss things? What does that even mean? Why aren't you answering your phone when I call you? I need to know what the hell is going on.

Lottie: I can't talk. I don't want Mom and Jeff hearing me. And this guy is looking for a fake fiancée. It works out great.

Kelsey: WHAT? Lottie, are you hearing yourself right now? Do you really think this is safe? You found a random man on a sidewalk, and he just so happens to be looking for a fake fiancée? Do you not see how…coincidental that is?

Lottie: Lucky, right?

Kelsey: Oh my God…you're going to be murdered.

Lottie: No way. The dude is meeting me at Chipotle. He's not going to murder me at a place where you have to pay extra for guac.

Kelsey: What does guac have to do with any of this?

Lottie: Nothing, but I want it to be known that I believe charging extra for guac is outrageous. Anyway, I have to get going. I'm walking there and I don't want to show up as a sweaty mess. I want to take my time. I'll text you when I'm done.

Kelsey: Lottie! I know you're desperate, but this is not better than telling Mom and Jeff. Suck up your pride and just tell them. Meeting a random stranger for food isn't the way to go.

Lottie: People meet up with strangers all the time to share food. That's what dating is all about.

Kelsey: You're not dating him!

Lottie: Not yet. Text you later, sis. Love you.

Yeah, this is stupid.

I'll admit it.

Kelsey has every reason to fret, because this situation screams bad decisions, but I like to think I'm a good judge of character, and this guy wasn't giving me murder vibes. Instead, his eyes reflected the same desperation as mine. He needs me, just like I need him. And that right there is exactly what one needs in order to follow through with such a farce—mutual neediness.

Now, my mother didn't raise a fool, and of course I'll play hard to get, because, yes, getting out of Jeff and Mom's house is the end goal here, as well as finding a new job and bringing a hot piece of ass to the reunion, but I'm also going to see what this guy has to say. I'm going to feel him out, and if the offer or story isn't good enough, see ya, buddy.

I'm all about saving face, but not in exchange for my soul.

I round the corner and find the Chipotle across the street. My stomach growls just from the sight of the crisp white building and burnt red pepper logo. If anything, this will be a free meal. *Burrito bowl, here I come.*

Once I got home, I quickly showered, tossed my hair into a tight bun, and then put on a pair of jean shorts and a simple Aerosmith T-shirt. I paired that with some bracelets and my favorite pair of comfortable Birkenstocks—found them at the Thrifty Shopper, which around here has rich people's used clothing for super cheap—and I headed out.

I charged my phone just long enough to be able to make a phone call if I need a quick out or if I am abducted. Now that I'm crossing the street, almost here, a small bout of nerves is in the pit of my stomach.

For the most part, I have strong bravado, but there are times when that bravado falters and my vulnerability comes out. I'm experiencing flashes of that right now.

When I make it to the other side of the road, I take a deep breath and head into the restaurant, and I spot Huxley immediately. It's hard not to.

I'll admit, the man is extremely attractive. A tall man, he must be at least six foot two, his skin has a golden tan to it, his hair is a beautiful chestnut brown—yes, I said *beautiful*—and he has those dark, penetrating eyes that seem like they could cut any human in half, in the boardroom or on the streets. Currently, he's staring down at his phone, one leg pressed up against the wall he's leaning onto, and he's wearing dark gray chino shorts and a light blue button-down shirt that hugs him in all the right places. His sleeves are rolled up to his elbows and—*hello, man chest*—the top two buttons of his shirt are undone, showing off a little man cleavage. Not too much to be douchey, but just enough to pique my interest. *Not* that I'm here to actually see him as a potential date, but the hot factor needs to be considered for this… transaction. *And…*

He's incredibly good-looking.

He would make Angela drool, for sure.

His eyes lift from his phone briefly, and when they spot me, I feel them dangerously rake over my frame, taking me in, every last inch of me. When they finally meet my eyes, he pushes away from the wall and walks up to me while stuffing his phone in his pocket.

"You're here," he says.

"Worried I was going to stand you up?"

"A little," he admits, but that confidence he exudes doesn't falter, as if he had a bout of worry, but knew I was going to come all along. He nods toward the counter. "Want to order and then get down to business?"

"That would be ideal for my stomach."

We get in line, and he lets me go first—point for him being gentlemanly—and I order my typical burrito bowl with chicken, black beans, and fajita veggies. And since lover boy is paying, I have them pile the guac on. Huxley sweeps in behind me with a steak burrito, pinto beans, no rice, and tons of lettuce and salsa. No guac. Does he not like guac, or is he not willing to pay the extra money? A question for the ages.

When we get to the register, he grabs beers for both of us, as well as chips and salsa, and then pays. When I see him pull out his Amex Black Card to swipe it, my anxiety over him claiming he's rich no longer exists. Uh, yeah…the man wasn't lying about being rich. Good to know.

With food and drinks in hand, Huxley finds a high-top table near the window that offers us enough privacy from the rest of the restaurant that I feel comfortable enough to have the type of conversation we're about to have.

Once we're seated, I say, "From the lack of guac on your burrito, I'm going to assume you don't like it very much."

He shakes his head. "Too slimy. Can't handle the texture of it."

"Are you a California native?"

He nods. "Yup, born in Santa Monica."

"Fascinating," I say, giving him a smooth once-over. "I don't think I've ever found a native Californian who doesn't like guacamole."

"I'm an anomaly. My brothers think I'm weird, so you're not alone in the opinion you probably have about me."

"I don't think you're weird, just…interesting. You also didn't get rice."

"Not a big rice fan." He glances at me while he unwraps his burrito. "Care to analyze anything else about my order?"

"You got beer instead of a soda. You're either extremely nervous or you're the type of person who has no shame in ordering an alcoholic beverage at a quick-serve restaurant."

"I don't know what it feels like to be nervous," he says in such a straight, monotone voice that I actually believe him. I'm not sure he knows that emotion based on his quick and abrupt answer. "I also don't carry around shame. It's a waste of my mental energy."

I pick up my fork and move it around my burrito bowl as he takes his first bite. "Ahh, I see how you are."

He finishes chewing and swallows, following up with a swipe of his napkin across his mouth before he asks, "Oh, you do? Please, educate me on myself."

"You're one of those power men."

"Power men?" he asks, brow raised.

"You know, the ones you read about, the successful ones that have a crazy regimen. They read a self-help book a week, work out every day, are brutal in the boardroom, and drink so much water that their bladder doesn't know what yellow pee is."

His burrito is halfway to his mouth as he says, "Takes me a week and a half to get through a self-help book when a new season of *The Challenge* comes out."

Then he takes a bite of his burrito, and honestly, from the lack of facial expressions, I can't tell if he's being serious or not. Might as well test his knowledge.

"You watch *The Challenge*?"

He nods slowly. "CT for life."

Okay, okay, don't freak out.

Gah...but CT!

"He's my dream man," I say before I can stop myself. "Heavy Boston accent, troubled past, buff—even in his dad-bod era—and just a fine piece of ass. Love him so much. Is that why you like him?"

He wipes his mouth, and in a dry tone, he says, "Yes. Can't get enough of that tight ass of his."

Look at that, we have a funny man. I like that. Makes me feel comfortable. "I knew you were an ass man."

"How do you figure?"

"You just have that type of intense glare in your eyes. Screams ass man."

"Wasn't aware you could tell by someone's glare that they're an ass man," he says while lifting his beer to his lips.

"Easily."

"Funny." He swallows some more beer, sets it down, and says, "Because asses are sexy and all, but I'm all about the neck."

"The neck?" I ask, my loaded fork halfway to my mouth. "You, uh, you like to choke people?"

"No, but there's something so sexy, so possessive about being able to hold your girl at the nape of her neck."

"Possessive, are we?" I ask, trying to feel this man out.

"I prefer to claim what's mine."

"Interesting. If that's the case, why are you looking for a fake fiancée? Claiming what's yours seems like an intense reaction, something you wouldn't take lightly."

"I don't take it lightly. It's why I haven't been able to find the right person, because I take my dating life, or lack thereof, seriously. I'm not going to waste my time on someone if I don't feel an innate demand in my body to claim them."

"I guess that makes sense." I study him. "So, then, why the fake fiancée? I told you I need someone to pretend to be my boyfriend for a reunion. What's your reasoning?"

"We'll get to that," he says. "I want to know more about you first. I need to be comfortable with you before I tell you what I need."

"Okay, as long as I can ask you questions, too."

"A question for a question. That work for you?"

Easy to compromise—I'm surprised. He doesn't necessarily give off that vibe, especially with all the possessive talk. I'm just going to make it known that detail about him is a total turn-on. Not that I'm looking to actually date this guy or anything.

"That works for me. You ask first."

"What do you do?" He takes a large bite of his burrito, and for being a man of "class," he's really munching down on that burrito.

"Currently in between jobs—"

"So, unemployed," he cuts in, and I grow defensive.

"Not by my choice."

"So, you were fired?" He lifts his brow in question.

I puff up my chest. "As a matter of fact, I was fired, and not because I wasn't doing my job, but because my idiot boss believes she can get someone else to do my job for less pay." With a sinister smile, I say, "I hope her business burns up in flames."

He lets out a low chuckle. "Seems like poor management to me."

"You could say that. My boss was one of my best friends growing up. A volatile friendship, very toxic. I could love her and hate her all in the span of one minute. She told me my firing wasn't personal, and then the next day, she asked if I'd help her with our high school reunion she's planning. You know, now that I have time on my hands."

He winces. "Brutal."

"Yes. So she's Satan's daughter."

"Seems like she did you a favor."

I shake my head. "She screwed me over." I smile. "But we can talk about that later. My turn to ask a question. What do you do?"

"Real estate," he answers simply.

"That's it? That's all you're going to say?"

He sips from his beer and then says, "Sorry, don't have a tragic story to tell you about losing my job."

"Are you mocking me?"

He levels with me, his eyes connecting directly with mine. "I'm trying to get you to agree to be my fake fiancée. Do you really think I'd mock you?"

"I guess not."

"Next question. Are you attached to anyone romantically in any way?" he asks.

"If I were, I wouldn't be trying to find someone to take to the reunion now, would I?" I take another bite of my burrito bowl and wish I wasn't trying to be all dainty around this guy, because the chicken is on fire today. I want to shovel it in my mouth.

"So that's a no. I need to hear you say it."

What a formal fuck. "That's a no. I'm not romantically involved with anyone." I motion to my body and say in the voice of the old lady from *Titanic*, "It's been eighty-four years since these breasts have been touched."

He smirks and nods. "Good."

"What about you?" I ask. "Seems like a stupid question since you're looking for a fake fiancée, but who knows? Maybe you got yourself involved in some sort of drug deal gone sideways, and you need a fake fiancée to get you out of the situation instead of throwing your wife to the wolves. So you find an innocent walker in the neighborhood to use as a decoy. Lure her in with promises of extra guac and good-smelling cologne."

Seeming amused, he wipes his mouth and leans back in his chair before tossing his napkin on the table. "I fear what else is going on in that head of yours."

"Trust me, it's a place you don't want to get lost in." I grin and then shove some more chicken in my mouth. *Sweet Chipotle gods, you outdid yourself today. Chef's kiss.*

"Apparently. And to answer your question, no, I'm not romantically involved with anyone. Don't have time."

"Ooo, workaholic, huh? A man who's married to his work, always a catch for a single lady."

"Haven't found anyone to take me away from my work." He finishes up his burrito, and if this guy were my bro right now, I'd offer up a high five for the annihilation of his meal. *Color me impressed.*

"So, you're saying if you found the right woman…or man—"

"Woman," he says, sipping his beer.

"Just double-checking. Can never be too sure. If you found the right woman, you would come home early?"

"If I found the right woman, I'd be far more interested in fucking her against every surface of my house rather than answering monotonous emails or buying a business partner a drink."

Well…okay.

That's…well, that's information.

"So you like fucking. That's good to know," I say awkwardly while nodding.

"Do you not enjoy fucking?" he asks, and I don't think I've ever met someone like him. Bold, brash, domineering, but also equipped with a playful side if you can pull it out of him.

"Well, you know…since it's been eighty-four years, I can't quite draw up any experiences that would remind me what a pleasurable event fucking is."

He slowly nods but doesn't say anything after that. Instead, he studies me, and under that strong gaze, I feel naked, as if he's stripping me down to nothing with every breath I take.

Good God.

"So, is it my turn for a question? I kind of lost track," I say.

"Sure. Ask away."

I nod, but my mind goes blank, because all I can think about is the way he's staring at me with those take-no-prisoners eyes. They're controlling, almost a mindfuck. Steadfast, unwavering, he speaks truth with his gaze; he destroys with his glare. The faint dusting of dark scruff on his jaw makes him exponentially more intimidating, and the way he has one hand casually draped on the table, almost as if he's claiming this space, throws me off, and I can't think of a damn thing to ask him.

"Why don't you ask a question?" I ask, right before I shove a huge forkful of food into my mouth.

"Are you comfortable around me?"

Wasn't expecting that question, even though I should have, since he seems to say what's on his mind. There's no skirting the truth with him.

I finish chewing, swallow, and then say, "I know I shouldn't feel comfortable around you. You're everything my mother has warned me about. Alpha workaholic who seems to get everything he wants. Dominant, holds nothing back, intimidating. You don't scream family man, nor do you have *attentive boyfriend* written across your forehead, but there's also this air about you that makes you seem trustworthy, and I'm not sure if that's comforting or terrifying."

"I'll take that as a yes." He leans forward across the table and eats a chip for the first time. Neither of us have touched them, too engrossed in our conversation. "I'm going to need you to feel comfortable with me, Lottie. I'm going to need your trust."

"You realize trust is earned, right?" I ask.

He nods. "Yeah, but I'm going to need you to be open to it. My intentions are pure, although askew, but they're pure. Going into this meeting, I knew I was going to be asking a lot, but I need to make sure you're open to it first, before I lay it all out on the table."

Huh.

Now I'm really intrigued. I mean, I was intrigued before—and of course a free meal—but he almost seems to be showing a slight hint of vulnerability, something I'm not sure a man like Huxley shows very often.

"Are you open to it, Lottie?"

I set my fork down and pat my mouth with my napkin. "I'm unemployed, I live with my mom, and I have nothing going for me at the moment. Pretty sure I'm open to whatever comes my way."

He nods and then leans even farther forward. "I fucked up big time, and now I'm trying to cover my ass."

"Ooo, a man who knows when he's wrong. Be still my heart."

He doesn't smirk, but he grows more serious. "This fuckup could cost me my reputation, and not only my reputation, but my brothers' as well, and everything we've built together."

"What did you do?" I ask, leaning forward, too. Going into this dinner, I didn't think I was going to gobble up some gossip, but I'm here for it.

"Short story is I was trying to land a deal. The guy who I was trying to work with wasn't biting, and my brothers said it's because he couldn't connect with me on a personal level. I ran into him on the street after the meeting. I met his fiancée, and before I knew it, I was telling him I was engaged as well."

I wince. "Your mouth spoke before your brain could think."

"Yeah, you could say that. Anyway, he invited me and my fiancée to dinner, and it's the first in I've had with this guy. The problem is, the dinner is Saturday."

"Well, that really puts you in a spot, doesn't it?"

"You could say that." His eyes bore into mine. "That's where you come in."

"You want me to go to this dinner with you and pretend to be your fiancée?"

"Yes, but I also need you to play out the farce until the deal is done."

"How long will it take for the deal to go through?"

He shrugs. "Could take a week, could take longer."

I slowly nod, thinking this over. "What would the farce entail? Am I going to be required to play Julia Roberts for you?"

"Julia Roberts?" he asks, confused.

"You know. *Pretty Woman*. Richard Gere hires Julia Roberts to be at his beck and call for all of his important business meetings. Have you never seen the movie?"

He shakes his head. "No."

"Well, basically she moves into his hotel with him and shows up wherever he needs her."

"You wouldn't need to move in with me," he says.

Damn, there goes getting out of Mom and Jeff's house. Not that I'd actually move in with a complete stranger. I'm not that insane.

"But I'd need you to be available when I need you."

"I see." I cross my arms over my chest. "And you think I could just do that given how I've no job?"

"I have connections. I could get you a job."

I hold up my hand to stop him right there. "I don't need your charity job. I'd prefer to earn my own career."

"I can respect that." His jaw tightens. "If I can't hook you up with a job, what can I give you in return? This would be a business transaction, after all."

Shelter would be preferred.

Money to pay off my student loans would be amazing, but I'd never ask that.

The reunion is the only thing he can really offer me, but is that enough? That doesn't really solve much. Just gives me a superficial upper hand. It doesn't solve my money problem or the need to move out of Mom's house.

Honestly, what was I thinking, looking for a rich husband? What was the end goal?

The more I think about it, the more I realize there was no end goal. This was...hell, this was a distraction.

"I'm not sure," I say.

"I can go to your reunion, act as though we're in love, whatever you need." Desperation slips into his voice.

"I'm not even sure I'm going to that," I say. "You know, I'm not sure this is really for me. I have student loans I have to pay off, so I don't think I can be at someone's beck and call when I should be finding a job." I lean back in my chair and stare down at the table. "Jesus, what was I even thinking, coming to this meeting? A job, that's what I need to be doing, finding a job, not worrying about what I look like at a stupid high school reunion." I look at Huxley, whose brow is pinched together in consternation. "This was a mistake. I'm sorry."

I stand from the table, and Huxley says, "Wait. We can come up with something that benefits both of us."

I shake my head. Ultimately, this is another situation where a rich person gets what *they* want by using a poor person. Even though I'm currently lying to my mom and Jeff, I hate lying. *You have the intellect to be more, to find a job that utilizes your skills.* "I know this is going to sound prideful, but I'm not sure I should be taking handouts right now. I need to figure out what I'm doing with my life." I look at the bag of chips and snag them from the table. "But I'm not too proud to take free food." I pat the bag. "Thanks for these and thanks for your time. Good day, sir."

And then I turn on my heel and take off. I last only until I reach the crosswalk before I dip my hand inside the bag and pop a chip into my mouth. Lime salt is my only comfort right now.

Lottie: I'm alive.

Kelsey: Well, thank Jesus. Do I dare ask, are you engaged?

Lottie: No. It was tempting, but I really need to focus on my career. That's what's going to move me along from this nightmare, not some stupid fake fiancée bullshit.

Kelsey: You know…maybe it wouldn't be so bad.

Lottie: You've GOT to be kidding me. Have you lost your mind?

Kelsey: I was thinking while you were eating dinner—maybe you could do this fake fiancée thing and work for me at the same time. I'm so close to expanding, I could really use your help on the business side. I'd be able to pay you soon, and you could live with me for a few weeks. We could make it work. And he could help you.

Lottie: You've lost it. It's okay, sweetie. Get a good night's rest and then call me in the morning. I love you.

Kelsey: I'm serious.

Lottie: Night night.

"Hey, honey, how was work?" Mom asks from the kitchen, where she's preparing dinner.

Pretending to be whupped from a tough day of dealing with Angela, I say, "Same old, same old."

"Still no news on the promotion?"

I swallow hard. "No news." I take a seat at the island in the kitchen and watch my mom stir the pot of spaghetti sauce she claims is homemade, though I know isn't. She says she adds her own spices, which makes it homemade, but the empty Prego jars next to the sink suggest otherwise.

"Well, I'm sure it's coming soon. What about the apartment hunting? How's that going?"

Yup, I get it, Mom. You want me out.

"Found a cute place near Kelsey. Thinking about it." The lie slips past my lips flawlessly.

"Oh, that would be wonderful, you two living close to each other."

"Yeah," I mutter as Jeff comes through the front door from where he'd once again been tending to the landscaping in the front yard.

"Lottie, care to explain these?" he asks, holding a large bouquet of red roses.

What the actual hell?

"Are those for me?" I ask.

He nods. "Yes, they have your name on them."

"Oh, maybe it's Angela promoting you."

Jesus. One-track mind, anyone?

I hop off my stool, take the bouquet from Jeff, and set it on the table. I remove the tiny white envelope from the holder and take out the card. Written in very manly handwriting—slanted, almost illegible—it says *Please reconsider. H,* and then there's a phone number beneath it.

How on earth did he know where I live?

I know rich people have access to things us peasants don't, but the man doesn't even know my last name, nor enough information about me to put together who I am.

"Who are they from?" Mom asks, coming up behind me.

I clutch the envelope to my chest. "No one," I say quickly, and then I grab the flowers and run to my room. I shut the door and, once again, slide to the ground, flowers in hand.

What the actual hell?

CHAPTER 5
HUXLEY

"DAVE TONEY IS ON THE phone," Karla says as she knocks on the doorframe of my office door.

"Send him through," I say before turning to JP. "Can I get some privacy, man?"

He shakes his head. "I'd rather be here for this conversation." When he doesn't attempt to move, I realize he's not kidding.

Rolling my eyes, I pick up my phone. "Dave, good to hear from you," I answer in a casual voice. "How are you?"

"Doing great. I was speaking with Ellie last night, and she was adamant I find out if your fiancée has any allergies or aversions to food. Ever since Ellie got pregnant, she can't even be in the same room as French fries. They absolutely repulse her. But potato chips are fine. I don't get it, but I go with it."

Great question.

Really great fucking question.

Well, if this were an alternate reality and I really was engaged to a pregnant woman, I'd assume she'd have some sort of pregnancy craving, as well as something she couldn't possibly be around, but because I don't have a pregnant fiancée, I don't have an answer for him.

But I'm still counting on Lottie, even though I've yet to hear from her. I know the flowers were delivered—I asked for a delivery receipt—so I should've heard something from her. At least, that's the narcissistic side of me talking. And I'm going to keep holding out, because I could see she was interested. She needs the help. I just need to find the right way to pursue her. I'm also not opposed to playing dirty to get what I want. That's obvious from this entire predicament I'm in.

So, instead of answering about allergies, I'm going to answer about cravings, because if I can nudge them toward something I know she'll eat, then that will guarantee I don't make her eat something she might have an allergic reaction to.

"No allergies that I'm aware of—thank God for no allergic reactions during the time we've been together, am I right?"

Dave laughs. "Talk about ruining a date."

It's sickening how jovial the man sounds. How relaxed. It's as if he's been walking around, doing business with a stick up his ass, and then I come around with a pregnant fiancée, and he's Mr. Dad now, happy-go-lucky, wearing his New Balance 409s and living his best life.

"Yeah, we haven't had that happen. Thankfully. But I do know that she's craving burrito bowls right now. I just had to get her one from Chipotle yesterday." Not a lie, the truth. And she shoveled that thing into her mouth.

"That's crazy. Ellie has been craving Chipotle lately. We had it last night. I'm wondering if we should just get that for dinner. I know Ellie spoke of making a southern meal, but she's been exhausted lately, and this might be an easy out for her. Do you know what your girl likes from Chipotle?"

That I do.

I smile, and for the first time since I picked up the phone, I remember JP is sitting across from me. His arms are crossed, one leg is crossed over the other, and he has a huge smile on his face, enjoying me squirm way too much.

"Yes, I do know what she likes," I say while turning my back toward him. "She likes the burrito bowl." JP snickers behind me. He can fuck off. "Chicken, black beans, lettuce, and she likes to pile on the guac. She's always worried because it costs extra, but you know"—I swallow hard—"what my baby wants, my baby gets."

JP snorts.

Red-hot embarrassment creeps up the back of my neck. *I'm going to get so much shit for this.*

"Perfect," Dave says. He drags it out, as if he's writing it down. "And what about you?"

This is what my life has become, me giving another man my Chipotle order, but not just any man, the man I want to do business with. We've succumbed to no longer talking business or being sharks in the office. Nope, we're handing out Chipotle orders.

I give him my order, and then he asks, "Do you guys like the chips?"

"Love them," I say. I was actually banking on taking those chips home last night and eating them alone in my room while staring out at my pool, contemplating life. But Lottie snagged them as a parting gift before I could stop her. I should've been annoyed, but it actually amused me. Can't say a woman has done that sort of chip dash to me before.

"Great, I'll be sure to have a bunch, then. Ellie is craving salt right now, so I know those will be right up her alley. And are you sure you're okay with this dinner? Ellie will probably be horrified that we're ordering fast food to serve to our guests, but I also know how pregnant women are."

"Trust me, Lottie will be thrilled."

"Lottie, I like that name," Dave says. "That's the first time you've said it. Is it short for Charlotte?"

"Leiselotte, actually." I can feel JP's burning gaze on me, his brain filling up with a million questions.

"Beautiful," Dave says. "I can't wait to meet her. Does six on Saturday work?"

No.

It doesn't work at all. It actually would be helpful if I had time to find someone slightly more stable than the girl I'm trying to chase after right now, but I can't afford that kind of time. I need to make an impression sooner rather than later so I can score that godforsaken deal.

"That works great. We'll see you then."

"Perfect."

I spin around in my chair and casually hang up my phone, ignoring JP altogether. I move my mouse on my desk, wake up my computer, and go straight to my inbox, where I feel the most comfortable.

JP doesn't say anything. He just stares at me. A few minutes pass, and my nerves creep and crawl higher and higher until I break. "What?" I ask him.

"Nothing. I didn't say anything."

I turn toward his annoyingly large grin. "You didn't have to say anything. It's all in your eyes, in your stare."

"Just fascinated, is all. Because not only have you lied about this whole pregnant fiancée thing, but now you've dug yourself an even bigger hole by handing Dave a name, but not just a name, her whole name. And you offered him a Chipotle order. Ballsy man, really fucking ballsy, especially since the girl didn't say yes."

"She will," I say.

"Yeah, you sure about that?"

"Positive. I know her weakness, and if I have to use it, I will."

"Perfect way to get someone to do something for you. Threats." JP claps. "You really are something else, Hux." He stands from his chair. "I think the smart thing would've been to tell him you lied." He buttons his suit jacket. "I just pray you don't fuck this entire thing up. We worked damn hard putting this enterprise together."

"You think I don't know that?" I ask. "It's why I'm going to do everything it takes to save our asses, to make this right."

"You better," JP says. "And Lottie, she better be at that dinner with you, because I doubt pretending she was sick will be accepted. You're just going to have to do the night all over again."

He's right. That was an option, but I know Dave enough to understand his need to make an impression. He wants to meet my fiancée, and he's going to keep asking until he does.

"Good luck, bro, you're going to need it." JP walks out of my office, and I lean back in my chair, letting out some pent-up frustration.

"Fuck," I mutter.

I stare down at my desk and contemplate my next move. Clearly the flowers didn't work, which only means I'm going to have to play dirty.

She'll hate me, but that's fine. As long as I can get her to come to dinner and not make a fool out of me, that's all I care about.

———

This is really fucking dumb, and any person watching me do what I'm about to do would agree. But desperation is at my door, and I'm fucking answering.

Chocolates in hand—because honestly, I don't know what women like, and I've never done this before—I walk up the small path that leads to Lottie's front door. She lives in a small bungalow with an impeccable yard, right around the corner from The Flats. The house must be worth a fortune now, especially on such a nice parcel, right next to a wealthy neighborhood.

I knock on the door and hold my breath.

"I got it, Mom," I hear Lottie call out right before she opens the door.

She's wearing a pair of cotton shorts and a Rolling Stones T-shirt. Her hair is up, pulled away from her face, and her eyes are wide with surprise.

"Hey, babe," I say with a devilish smile. "I've missed you."

Through clenched teeth, she asks, "What the hell are you doing here?"

"Don't you want to invite me in?"

"No...I don't," she says in a snippy tone. Looks as if I have my work cut out for me.

"Lottie, who is it?" a female voice asks from inside the house.

"No one," Lottie calls out. I can sense she's about to slam the door in my face, so I take a step forward and stand in the doorway, cutting her off from an abrupt departure on my end.

"No one? Is that how you treat your fiancé?" I ask. "I thought I meant more to you than that?"

"You're insane," she whispers. "How do you even know where I live? Did you stalk me? Do you have someone following me around, watching my every move? Rich people can do things like that. I know the kind of power you have."

Trying to hold back my smile, I say, "You typed your address into my Google Maps. It was in the previous addresses section."

"Oh." She slowly nods. "Yeah, that checks out."

Jesus.

"Lottie, dessert is…ready. Well, hello." From the vast resemblance between Lottie and the woman next to her, I'm going to assume this is Lottie's mom. "And who might this be?"

Before Lottie can say anything, I hold out my hand and say, "Huxley, ma'am. Lottie's boyfriend."

"Boyfriend?" her mom shouts in surprise and turns to her daughter. "Since when have you had a boyfriend?"

"Three months," I answer once again. "We've kept it really quiet. We wanted to get to know each other before we announced anything publicly. Especially since my job is high profile."

"Wow, I'm shocked. I didn't even know Lottie was dating anyone, but what wonderful news." She holds out her hand and says, "I'm Maura."

I take her hand and give it a soft shake. "Huxley. It's very nice to meet you."

"Huxley, oh, what a wonderful name. Please come in. Dessert is ready, and I'd love for you to join us."

I hand her the chocolates. "Maybe I can add to the dessert table with these," I say, but before Maura can take them, Lottie snags them from my hand.

With a ravenous look in her eyes, she says, "These are mine."

Her mom chuckles. "Don't get between Lottie and her sweets. I'll grab another plate for our guest. Come in, come in, Huxley."

I do just that. I step into their quaint but homey bungalow and remove my black Tom Ford shoes and then my black suit jacket as well. I undo the buttons on the cuff of my button-up and roll the sleeves up to my elbows while staring down at Lottie, who's staring up at me, hatred beaming from her pupils.

"Hey, babe," I say again, this time with a smile.

"You've completely lost your mind," she says quietly. "What do you think you're doing?"

"Playing dirty. I tried to play nice, but you didn't want to, so here I am now. Playing dirty."

"What makes you think I'm going to play along?" She lifts her chin.

"Because I know you don't have a job...and you don't want your mom to know."

Her face goes white, and in this moment, I do feel slightly bad. It's obvious Lottie is going through a hard time, and I watched her struggle with her conscience in Chipotle as she tried to figure out what to do. Respected that. But I don't have time for her to figure it out, and honestly, I don't feel bad enough to end the farce. Especially since I'm in deeper shit than she is.

"You're going to blackmail me?"

"No, just using tools to help me get what I want, and don't act as if you don't need me too."

"I don't. It's why I haven't called, you psycho," she snaps.

Laughing, I say a little louder, "Missed you, too, babe."

"Why don't you two come in here?" Maura calls from the kitchen.

Smiling, I reach down and take Lottie's hand. She attempts to snatch it away, but I have a firm enough hold on her that she doesn't go anywhere. Leaning down toward her ear, I whisper, "I swear, I'll make this worth it for you."

When I pull away, her surprised eyes meet mine for a brief second before I pull her toward the kitchen, hand in hand.

Her mom turns and places a plate on the small four-person table. The table is situated under a large window, offering an expansive view of their well-manicured backyard. A canopy of trees and an old stucco wall offer them privacy from the close-knit quarters of their neighbors. "Jeff is working late tonight, so Lottie and I were taking advantage of some ice cream sundaes, since Jeff is lactose intolerant."

I'm assuming Jeff is her husband.

"I believe Lottie mentioned that," I say, playing along. "Not sure what I'd do if I were lactose intolerant. I enjoy ice cream way too much."

"Me too," Maura says. "I'm grateful my digestive system can handle it. Please, take a seat."

I pull out a chair for Lottie first. I might not have vast experience in dating a woman, but I do know fucking manners, and pulling out a seat for your girl is a sweet gesture. From the look on Maura's face, I'm going to assume she agrees. When Lottie is settled, I take a seat as well and pick up my spoon.

"Wow, I feel spoiled," I say. "This looks amazing."

"I gave you the works, just like me and Lottie. I hope you're not allergic to nuts. I should've asked."

"I'm all good." I spin the bowl around. "What's in this?"

"Vanilla ice cream, hot fudge, chopped peanuts, a dash of cherry juice, whipped cream, chocolate sprinkles, and cherries."

"Looks amazing. Thank you." I dig my spoon into the bowl, take a large helping, and shove it in my mouth. *Damn, it's really good.* I'm not sure the last time I had a sundae, but I've been missing out. "Really good."

Lottie just stares at me, as if she can't believe I'm here, eating ice cream in her mom's kitchen, acting as though nothing is wrong.

Actually, that's exactly what's happening.

If only I could hear her thoughts.

My guess is, she'd just be saying, "I'm going to kill him," over and over.

"Lottie, are you not hungry?" her mom asks.

I press my hand to her thigh and say, "She's probably in shock. I'm not sure she was ready to tell you about me. I assumed no one was home when she was texting me, so I figured I'd stop by." I squeeze her thigh. "Sorry, baby. Cat's out of the bag."

"Oh, honey, what do you have to worry about?" her mom asks.

We both look at Lottie, who looks like a deer in headlights.

"My reputation," I say, covering for her. "It's, uh, not the best, but not by my doing. I'm not sure if you've heard of Cane Enterprises."

Maura's face morphs into shock. "Huxley Cane? You're Huxley Cane?"

I quickly glance at Lottie, who looks clueless. Interesting.

"Yes. And even though Page Six likes to report on what girl I have on my arm one night to the other, it's not true. Don't believe anything you read in those things." Thankfully I haven't been mentioned in a while, because that wouldn't work out well for my story with Lottie.

"Oh, I never believe any celebrity gossip unless it comes from Hoda Kotb herself." Maura waves her hand in dismissal.

Lottie finally comes to life and says, "Mom, you always believe what they say in those gossip magazines. You told me the other day that Jennifer Aniston had triplets and sold them to Will Arnett."

Maura laughs nervously. "It was a joke." She clears her throat. "Anyway, is this why you've been so evasive about moving?" Maura asks Lottie. "Because you're thinking about moving in with Huxley?"

Oh shit...

"What would make you think that?" Lottie asks in annoyance.

"Because when I looked around for apartments near Kelsey, there was nothing available. It seems as if you've been avoiding the whole conversation, and I don't know, finding out you have a boyfriend just makes me think that you might be thinking about moving in with him." Maura turns toward me. "Don't get me wrong, we love having Lottie here, but we've also been excited about her promotion so she could find her own place, finally."

Interesting. So she does need a place to stay; that's not what she said the other night. And since she didn't get a promotion, but was fired, not telling her mom makes sense. I think I have Lottie right where I want her.

Maura offers me a sly grin. "Jeff and I really want to walk around the house naked."

"Mom!" Lottie says, her face turning red.

I lean in and wink. "I totally get what you mean." Clearing my throat, I say, "I asked her to move in, but I'm waiting on an answer."

"Really?" Maura asks, excitement beaming from her eyes. "Oh, wow, that's so exciting. Honey, are you going to say yes?"

We both look at Lottie, whose mouth is full of ice cream. She glances between us, and I know she wants to murder me, because if looks could kill…

I'd be six feet under.

She swallows cautiously and then says, "I'm not sure. He's more attached to me than I am to him." She shoves more ice cream in her mouth.

"Lottie. How could you say something like that?" Maura asks, horrified. Whispering, she adds, "And right in front of him, too."

"Ah, she's only kidding," I say, taking the heat off Lottie. "She was the first one to say, 'I love you,' actually."

Maura's eyes widen. "Wow, I didn't…I didn't know." Maura turns to Lottie. "I'm sad you didn't think you could trust me with this information." Oh shit. I don't need the mom feeling sad.

"It's my fault," I say quickly. "I begged her not to tell anyone. I really wanted to keep it on the down-low. She wanted to tell you and Jeff, but I asked her not to. Please don't be mad at her. If you're mad at anyone, it should be me."

That earns me a soft gaze from Lottie, but it doesn't last very long, not when she turns back to her ice cream and scoops some more into her mouth.

"I appreciate you being honest with me, Huxley." Jesus, if only she knew. "Well." Maura rests her hands on the table. "How did you meet?"

"On a walk," I say, even though that's not what I told Dave. Jesus, this is already twisted and fucked. At least *on a walk* is true. "She was lost, and I helped her find her way back home. But I knew before she left, I needed her number. Couldn't stop staring at her. Those green eyes of hers mesmerize me."

Lottie glances in my direction, a surprised look on her face. *Yeah, I pay attention to the small things.* I'd remember those eyes even if they just briefly glanced at me.

"How sweet. Lottie, you haven't said much."

Because I keep stepping in before she can say anything. Because even though I know she needs me to cover for her, I'm not fully confident she won't fly off the deep end and blow our cover.

"Just observing Huxley," she says. "Seeing how he fits in my environment." She stirs her spoon in her bowl. "Not sure he fits in or not."

"Please excuse my daughter. She apparently has no decorum. Lottie, this is your boyfriend."

Maura is a good woman.

"It's okay, Maura. She tends to bust my balls often—excuse my language."

"Oh, don't bother excusing yourself around here, we aren't proper in any way. And I guess she gets that attitude from me; I tend to throw some shade toward Jeff as well."

"Makes it that much more fun, especially when, at night, she curls into me for a hug and presses those sweet lips on mine. Makes it all worth it, because I know my girl loves me. Truly loves me."

And the Oscar goes to...

Lottie stands from the table, bowl in hand. "I'm done. Huxley, let me show you my room."

"That's presumptuous," I tease while taking a mouthful of ice cream. When she glares at me, I stand from my seat and say, "Maura, excuse me while my girl gains some private time with me. Shall I put my bowl in the sink?"

She waves at me. "No, I got this; you two go ahead."

"Thank you." I take Lottie's hand in mine and allow her to guide me down the hallway to the last room on the left. She opens the door, drags me in, and then shuts the door behind me.

I take in the small but fully decorated room. Posters of rock bands span across every wall. From the Beatles, to ELO, to Boston, everyone is represented, even on the ceiling. Her bed is unmade, there are clothes on the ground, and her dresser is covered in makeup and face products. I feel as though I've been transported back two decades to one of my girlfriend's rooms. Clutter, everything you like plastered on the walls, and even though there isn't a black light in her room, there is rope lighting outlining her door. This girl is not that much younger than me, but man does it feel like it.

"How old are you again?" I ask, turning to face her. I'm greeted by a very angry-looking woman: arms crossed, jaw clenched, foot tapping.

Damn, the girl truly can commit murder with her eyes.

"What the actual hell are you doing here?"

"We'll get to that in a second. I just need to know how old you are first."

She rolls her eyes. "Don't worry, *babe*. I'm twenty-eight. No need to call your lawyers." She passes me, her shoulder bumping against mine as she makes her way to her unmade bed and takes a seat. Her sheets are covered in tiny hearts, whereas her comforter is pitch black and velvety. I'm trying to gain an understanding of this girl, but I can't seem to put my finger on her. She's all over the place.

Rock posters. Heart sheets.

Surly attitude. Cares about her parents.

Snarls from across the table. Will gobble down whatever is placed in front of her.

"Now tell me what the hell you think you're doing," she says.

"Doing you a favor." I stick my hands in my pants pockets.

"How is lying to my mom doing me a favor? She legit thinks we're a couple."

"Which was accomplished by my impeccable acting. You could use some adjustments."

Her brows narrow. *Cool it with the teasing, man, she's not open to it right now.*

"I thought I told you at Chipotle I wasn't interested."

"You were interested," I say. "But you were spooked. Not sure what spooked you, but I saw a shift in you. I knew you weren't through with this; you just needed some encouragement. That's what the flowers were, encouragement."

"Uh-huh. And what would you say today is?"

"Today is a kick in the ass."

"I don't need a kick in the ass. You're the one who needs this more than I do."

"Oh, really?" I ask, feeling cocky now with knowledge. "Because from what it seems like, your mom is counting down the seconds until you leave this house. She also seems to believe you will be receiving a promotion soon, when, in fact, you're out of a job. Care to tell me why she thinks that?"

Lottie moves her jaw back and forth but doesn't answer me.

I thumb toward the door. "Or should I go ask her myself?" I move to leave, and she quickly springs from the bed and grabs my hand, pulling me back.

"Don't say a GD thing to my mom." She sits on the bed and then flops backwards. "God, why is this such a nightmare?"

"It doesn't have to be," I say. "It could be really simple. We can help each other out, but for some reason, you're not allowing that to happen."

"Because you're a complete stranger," she hisses at me. "You want me to be your fiancée, live with you apparently, and be at your beck and call? I have a life I have to live; I don't have time to play your rich-dick game."

"This isn't a game for me," I say. "This is a huge fuckup on my part, and I'm trying to make it better, for everyone. And you won't have to be at my beck and call, just a few dinners here and there, maybe a weekend thing, just until I can secure this deal, and then you can tell me to fuck off."

"And what do I get in return?" she asks, lifting up so she's leaning on her elbows.

"Whatever you want," I say, because I'm at that point. I want her to know the sky is the limit, because I've yet to mention the pregnancy thing. "Need a place to stay? I have a seven-bedroom home. Need a date for your reunion? I'm your man. Need me to make a phone call to this ex-boss of yours, let her know she made a huge mistake by letting you go? I'm there for you. Want a job? I can find you one."

"I don't want a job from you," she says. "I really want…" Her voice trails off as she shakes her head and looks toward her window.

Oh, she does want something. I can see it in her far-off gaze. It's wishful, hopeful, something behind those sultry eyes that she truly, truly wants.

I take that opportunity to sit next to her on the bed. This might be a breakthrough moment for me, where I can move past that tough exterior of hers. "What do you want, Lottie? Trust me, I can make pretty much anything happen."

Her lips twist to the side as she avoids eye contact with me. Just from the way her brow draws together, I know she's thinking about it, considering telling me. Instead of pushing, I wait.

And wait.

Until…

"I want to be able to help my sister," she says quietly. "I want to feel fulfilled with my career, appreciated, and I know I can do that with Kelsey. She's my person, my best friend, and working with her would be a dream." She glances at me. "But she can't afford to hire me, and I need to make money."

"What does she do?" I appreciate the vulnerability in her voice. When she's not hiding behind the snark and sarcasm, she's the most unselfish person I've ever known. Here I am with the proverbial Aladdin's lamp, and she wants to help her sister. True altruism. *Wow.*

"She has her own organizing company. Think *The Home Edit* but doing it sustainably."

"What's *The Home Edit*?" I ask, confused. *Is that something I should know?*

"Ugh, men," she mutters before saying, "*The Home Edit* is all about organizing your house, paring things down, and making sure you live an organized life rather than a chaotic one. They turn pantries into havens, fridges into masterpieces. It's spectacular. Kelsey is on the cusp of being able to push forward and be more than a one-person show, but she's having a hard time keeping up with the business side. That's where I would come in."

"I see." I stare down at her. "You know, I have a lot of connections. My brothers alone could use someone to come into their house and organize. Our offices could use an overhaul. I can make sure your sister's business is not only seen by the type of people who would spend a lot of money for her services, but I can make it thrive as well."

"We don't want your charity."

"It's not charity. I'm not telling people to use her, but if you want to go anywhere in business, Lottie, you have to know connections mean every-thing. Sometimes, just one person is all you need. One person to ignite the flame, because that one person might know five people, and those five people might know five more people, and that's how a business grows at first, word of mouth. I'm that first person, and I know way more than five people."

"What are you saying?"

"I'm saying I want to help you." *How do I make her believe me?* "How about this—you pretend to be my fiancée and go to these business events with me, and in return, you can stay at my house—"

"I'm not living with you. I can move in with Kelsey. There's no way I'm living with a stranger I don't know."

"Fine. You take the job with Kelsey and move in with her, and I help you two with some connections."

She mulls it over, her lips twisted to the side.

"And you know," I add, clearing my throat, "if you could be pregnant as well, that would be ideal."

"What?" she says, sitting up completely. "Have you lost your mind? I'm not letting you get me pregnant."

"Fuck, no, I didn't mean it like that. Pretend to be pregnant. Pretend. I'm not going to be fucking you or anything like that."

Her brow knits together. "Why on earth would I pretend to be pregnant?"

"Because I told the guy I'm trying to do business with that you're pregnant."

"Why? Why would you say that?"

I sigh and grip the back of my neck. "His fiancée is pregnant. I was trying to form a connection with the guy."

"By making up the fact that you have a pregnant fiancée? Wow, Huxley, you really are in some deep shit, aren't you?"

"I am. That's why I need you. So, name it, Lottie." I hold my arms out. "Name what you want and it's yours."

"I don't know what I want."

"Okay." I stand from the bed and pace her room. "In a perfect world, what would you have right now?" I face her and hold my finger up. "Working with your sister, right?"

She nods.

"Not living with your mom and Jeff."

She nods again.

"Showing up this boss of yours, the one that let you go."

"A lifelong friend who has been toxic from the start. Would love to just shove it up her ass."

I chuckle. "Okay, that can be arranged. What else?"

"Perfect world?" she asks with hesitation.

"Perfect world."

Her teeth roll over the corner of her mouth as she says, "Well, I'd be working with my sister, out of my mom's house, could stick it to Angela, my student loans are paid off, and every time it rains, I have a place where I can lie in the rain without judgment."

"Done," I answer.

"What?" she asks skeptically.

"All of it, done. I've got you covered. I'll help with your sister's business so you can work for her. You're going to live with your sister, so that covers housing, we'll make the perfect plan to stick it to Angela, I'll easily pay off your student loans, and I know the perfect place to privately lie in the rain."

She shakes her head. "You're not paying off my student loans."

"Why not?" I ask her.

"Because I'm not a hooker."

I scratch the back of my head. "I don't recall the time where I said I would pay you to fuck me."

"You didn't, but it just feels...weird. You paying me to be your escort."

"First of all, you're not an escort. Let's throw that term right out the window, got it? Second of all, this isn't about me, this is about us. This is a deal. An accord. A transaction between two people. We'll both agree upon a fair bargain and trade services, that's it. Nothing more. Trust me, I'd pay a hefty amount of money to convince you to get on board. I'm sure the student loans can't be that bad. How much do you owe?"

She winces and says, "Thirty thousand dollars."

The corner of my mouth tilts up. "Chump change, Lottie."

Her eyes widen. "I have a thirty-thousand-dollar debt, and you're calling that chump change?"

"Trust me when I say I have billions to work with."

Confused, she asks, "Why are you telling me this? I could extort those billions from you."

"Possibly, but I don't think you will. You don't seem to be that kind of person."

"I'm not," she says, deflated. "I wish I were; it would make this that much easier."

I chuckle. "I'm glad you're not someone who relies on extortion. Bodes well for me." I stand there, hands in my pockets. Head down, I just lift my eyes to glance at her. "Say yes."

She presses her lips together. "How do I know you'll follow through on your end?"

"I'll have my lawyers draw up a contract. Simple."

Still seeming unsure, she stares down at her hands. "I don't know."

"Tell me why you don't want to do it," I say. In order for her to go through with this, she has to admit to whatever is holding her back.

"Just feels…wrong. I know I was the one who crazily sought out a rich husband to solve all my problems, but now that it's halfway true, it just feels wrong. I've worked hard for everything I've earned; this feels like a freebie, and it doesn't settle well with me."

I can understand that feeling. If it weren't for my dad, we wouldn't have the business we have today.

"I understand the pride you have in working for everything you've earned in life. I understand that all too well. But do you know how we started our business?"

She shakes her head. "I honestly know nothing about you."

"Well, it was with an idea and insurance money from my dad's passing. Without that insurance money, there's no way we would be where we are today. Yes, hard work, hustle, and well-thought-out decisions made that money grow, but we needed that boost, that assistance. That starting point. Everyone needs both a strong start and a boost from time to time. Don't look at this as a freebie, Lottie; look at it as a boost."

"I guess that makes sense." Her eyes flash to mine. "You might be offering me the deal of a lifetime, but I need you to know something." She stands from her bed, and even though she's a foot shorter than me, she still walks up to me and attempts to be intimidating. "I owe you nothing other than what I signed up for, and this little stunt you pulled today—it's deceiving and it won't happen again. Blackmailing, holding my truth against me, that's bullshit, and I don't like you very much for it."

"Fair," I say. "But I refuse to apologize for what I did." Her gaze focuses on me. "I don't apologize unless I regret something I did. I don't regret this. As a businessman, I make the best decisions to help close in on my goal."

"So that's what this is—a business transaction?"

"Nothing more than that."

"Good," she says and then points to the door. "You can leave now."

I shake my head. "Nice try, Lottie, but I'm going to need some information from you before I leave, and those things include your phone number, sister's address, dress size, and shoe size."

"Why do you need those things?"

I take a step closer and tug on her old rock band T-shirt. "Not that this isn't sexy on you, but you're going to need something a little more... expensive...if you're going to be attached to me." I lift her chin up with my index finger. "I'm also going to need your ring size. My fiancée will be properly adorned with a ring."

She swallows hard. "Fine, but I'm going to need to know your dick size before you leave."

"Why do you need to know that?" I ask.

"Because," she says with a smile, "I need to know if I have to act like a happy fiancée or a truly satisfied fiancée."

Fuck, the ovaries on this girl. *When was the last time I had such an honest, forthright conversation with a woman?*

The back of my neck heats up as I say, "Trust me, you're fucking satisfied."

She shrugs. "I guess I'll have to take your word for it."

She walks over to her nightstand and pulls out a pen and a piece of paper and starts writing things down. I move around her messy room and say, "If your sister specializes in organization, how come your room is a disaster?"

"She's tried to help me, but I'm a lost cause. Be happy you're not living with me."

You might be a lost cause to your sister, but you could be my victory.

CHAPTER 6
LOTTIE

Mom: [picture] Here's a picture of Jeff and me, naked, in the living room. Spared you with a pic from the neck up. But we're living a free, breezy life.

"WHY, MOM? WHY?" I ASK as I cringe and set down my phone.

"What?" Kelsey asks, fumbling with one of my boxes.

"Two hours after I moved out, and they're already naked in the living room."

Kelsey makes a gagging sound. "I'm all for expressing your true self, but there are things she doesn't need to share with her two daughters."

"Agreed," I say, while leaning against the wall of Kelsey's small studio apartment. "And we still have to sit on that furniture when we go to visit her."

"I'll be standing from now on," Kelsey says, grunting as she shoves one box on top of another.

The space here is, let's just say...lacking. "Kels, I'm starting to get anxious."

"Because of the dinner you have to go to tonight, the contract you just signed, or the fact that we're going to have to make a box castle in order for you to live here, too?"

Yup, that's right, I signed a contract, binding myself to Huxley Cane until all contractual obligations are fulfilled.

And, yes, I'll be acting like the doting fiancée tonight.

Not to mention, there's absolutely zero walking space in Kelsey's apartment. Why did I think it was bigger? Why did I think this was big enough for two people?

"All three," I answer. "Do you think I made a huge mistake?"

"Honestly? I don't know." Kelsey lets out a heavy breath. "I think there are risks and rewards with everything. It's a huge risk being contractually obligated to hang out with this Huxley guy until he secures the deal. But think about the rewards from it all—and I'm not just talking about where the business could go. Think about being debt free from your student loans."

"Yeah, I still don't feel right about that."

Kelsey stacks one of my boxes of clothes on top of a box of shoes. "Think about it this way. Huxley is probably making a lot of money off this deal, or else he wouldn't have gone to the lengths that he has to secure it, right?"

"Right."

"Well, just treat the student loan payoff as your commission for helping him."

"Huh, I guess I could think about it that way."

"See?" She hoists up another box. "These will have to go here until I can figure out the perfect storage system for us." She points to my bed on the floor. "Are you sure you don't mind sleeping on pillows? I can trade with you every other night."

I wave my hand at her. "It'll be fine. And look at how cute you made the bed, too. It'll work." I sigh. "Thanks for taking me in."

"What do Mom and Jeff think you're doing?"

"They think I moved in with Huxley."

"Uh, what are you going to do when they ask to visit your new place?"

"We'll set up a time, I'll take over some personal effects, and then I'll pretend I'm living there. It's not as if they're going to check the bathrooms to make sure my tampons are locked and loaded."

"True." Kelsey laughs. "Didn't imagine that. Well, it seems as if you have everything planned. What about tonight? Are you ready? Do you have your story straight?"

"What story?"

"You know, how you met, how he proposed...how far along you are?"

Oh God, we don't have a story.

Nothing was in the contract.

And I've only heard from Huxley once since he left my house the other day, which just makes things that much more comforting.

Can you sense the sarcasm?

Because it's heavy.

My anxiety peaks as I realize we haven't talked about any of our backstory. The only thing we've spoken about to each other is the contract and if I signed it or not. I had a lengthy conversation with his lawyer, who basically threatened my life with an NDA. I asked him if Kelsey counted in that NDA, and once discussed separately with Huxley—I was left out of the conversation—I was told no, she didn't count, but then they made her sign an NDA as well. It's been an ordeal.

"We haven't talked about any sort of backstory." I nibble on my finger, attempting to tamp down the bile starting to rise in my throat.

Kelsey cringes. "Ooo, I'd text him, see what time dinner is, when he plans on picking you up, and what your story is, because I doubt he'll be thrilled about any slipup on your end. Didn't he say something in the contract about committing to character?"

"Did he? Oh God, I should've read it better."

"Did you not read the contract?" Kelsey asks, horrified.

"It was twenty pages, Kels. That's far too much legal jargon for one sitting."

"Jesus, Lottie. You signed your life away without reading it?"

"I got the gist of it."

"Clearly not."

I can taste the bile on my tongue now. "You're not making my anxiety any better. You realize that, right?" I reach for my phone and shoot Huxley a panicked text.

> **Lottie:** What's our story? How did we meet? How did you propose? How far along am I? Should I be showing? Are we having a boy or a girl? What are the names of the people we're having dinner with? Why on earth did I sign that GD contract?

I toss my phone down and sit at the two-seat oak bistro table. "This was a bad idea," I say. "I promised to stay in character, and I don't even know what the character is. I signed a contract, Kelsey."

"Yeah, not going to lie, I have secondary anxiety for you."

"That's not helpful." I pin her with a stare.

Knock. Knock.

"That's the food," Kelsey says, bouncing toward the door. "Put a pin in that anxiety. Spring rolls don't go well with it."

Does anxiety go well with any main dish?

As the door opens, I rest my head against the wall, but only for a nanosecond, because Kelsey's startled gasp draws my attention. Frightened by what might be on the other side of the door, I hesitantly lean forward just in time to see a man carrying a few dress boxes and bags full of shoeboxes into the apartment. He sets them on Kelsey's twin-size bed and then leaves as Huxley steps forward, looking rather expensive and quite serious. When his eyes meet mine, I'm met with a frown. Why the hell is he frowning at me?

"Can I, uh, help you?" Kelsey asks.

He turns to Kelsey, and his frown lightens as he says, "You must be Kelsey." He holds out his hand. "I'm Huxley. It's a pleasure to meet you."

"Oh dear God," Kelsey says, shaking his hand. She looks over her shoulder and whispers, "You did NOT say how handsome he is."

I whisper back, "You might be whispering, but he can still hear you."

Huxley chuckles and shuts the door behind him. His eyes roam the quaint four-by-four space. His neutral expression slowly changes into a displeased scowl with every second that goes by. He doesn't seem too happy.

"This is where you plan on living?"

"Is there a problem with that?" I answer.

He steps in farther, and his critical inspection falls to the pillow bed on the ground. He toes it with his shoe. "And this is where you're sleeping?"

"Isn't it nice?"

Not answering me, he shuffles past the box tower, which precariously sways. "And where do you plan on putting these boxes?"

"Not that it's any of your business, but Kelsey is going to organize everything. She's a pro, remember?"

That judgmental cast of his eyes extends over our space one more time before he says, "No insult to her profession and skills, but I'd like to see how all of this is going to fit into this tiny apartment and the space still be livable. I see that Kelsey has already used some of the height these taller ceilings have to offer, but I've seen your room and the disaster you're capable of."

Well, he came in fired up, didn't he?

"Kelsey, care to put him in his place?" I ask casually. If anyone can figure out this debacle, it's Kelsey. She's a modern-day marvel when it comes to organization. She sees storage in ways other people don't. If anyone can make it work, it's her.

"Well, I didn't think you were going to bring over this many boxes," Kelsey says, looking less confident than me. "And then who knows what's in those boxes and bags that Huxley just dropped off?"

"Kelsey." I sit tall. "This is what you specialize in."

"I know." She twists her hands together and says to Huxley, "I don't want you to think I'm not good at what I do, because I'm really good, but sometimes you also have to admit that a purge is necessary in order to make things work. I'm a minimalist, and I think we might have to purge some of your things first, Lottie, in order to make this work."

"Purge?" I ask, flabbergasted at the mere notion of doing such a thing. "Do you realize I only brought the bare minimum with me? I didn't even bring all of my clothes. This is what I need to survive."

"I'll take care of this." Huxley pulls out his phone and starts typing away. "I'll have Andre come retrieve your boxes."

"What do you mean, retrieve them? What's he going to do with them?"

Huxley glances up from his phone, one brow lifted, those sultry eyes burning through me. "Take them to my house."

I shake my head. "No way, nope. Not a chance. I told you I wasn't moving in with you."

"Don't be absurd. I have a seven-bedroom house. You could have a room for each of your boxes."

"I'm not rooming with a man I don't know." I fold my arms over my chest.

We stare each other down, a line being drawn between us.

Would living with Huxley be easier? Sure, probably, but I don't know the guy. What insane person would just move in with a complete stranger?

Not me.

And my sister would never allow it.

"You know, it might not be a bad idea," Kelsey says.

Excuse me while I pick my jaw up off the ground.

Excuse me? Not a bad idea?

"Kelsey," I whisper in shock. "What on earth? You're supposed to be on my side."

"I am." She gestures to the boxes. "But one weekend of this, and we're going to hate each other. And look at him, he seems nice enough."

"Nice *enough*?" I ask, completely floored. "Is that all the qualifications you need? Nice *enough*?"

"And he smells heavenly, and we know who he is, so if he tries to do anything, we can report him, and that would ruin his reputation. It's obvious he's going to great lengths to avoid that."

There's some truth to that, but still...

"What am I supposed to do—just live at this guy's mansion?"

Kelsey smirks. "Uh, yeah. Seems like a dream to me."

Leaning toward Kelsey, I whisper, "I don't even like him."

Whispering back, she says, "He can hear you."

"You don't have to like me to do business with me. Remember, this is nothing but a business transaction. The sooner you start thinking of it that way, the easier it will be to take the emotion out of it."

I scowl at Huxley, who looks far too casual, rocking on his heels, hands in his pockets.

"He's right," Kelsey says. When I don't respond, she continues, "What about this? Try it for a week, and then if you want to come back, my studio apartment is open to you, pillow bed and all."

"You're serious? You don't want me to stay?"

"He's not going to hurt you," Kelsey says.

"That's what you say now, but tomorrow in the news, missing-sister reports circulate the interweb."

"You're being ridiculous. We know everything about him. He tries one thing, and his reputation is ruined. Trust me, I'm good at reading people. He's not stupid."

I can't believe I'm even considering this, but when I look between the two of them, I feel myself leaning further and further toward a yes. Not because of the mansion aspect, but because I don't want Kelsey to hate me, and I know after a few days in this tiny apartment, she very well might disown me. Living here is one thing, but working and living here in this apartment is a whole other ball game.

Sighing, I say, "Fine, but I request the farthest room away from yours, no funny business." I point my finger at him.

"Don't flatter yourself," he says casually before going to the bed, where he shuffles the dress boxes. Kelsey snorts and covers her mouth while I steam.

"Well, don't you…flatter yourself, either," I say.

"Ooo, burn," Kelsey says mockingly. "You really got him with that one."

I rub my temples. "Kelsey, I would appreciate it if you were on my side."

"I am, that's why I'm encouraging you to try harder with your comebacks. Think before you react, hit him back where it hurts. You know, something like…your, uh, hair…well, no, that's nice. Maybe that suit… hmm, it's impeccably tailored. Wait, that's a compliment. Oh, I know, your jaw is so tight…it's actually quite symmetrical. His whole face, very symmetrical. Just an absolute specimen."

"Wow." I slow clap. "Thanks, Kelsey, super helpful insults."

Huxley looks between the two of us. "Are we done with the pitiful attempts at comebacks?"

"You're pitiful," I shoot back and then look to Kelsey for approval. She gives me a solid thumbs-up and a head nod. *Ha, got him good.*

His jaw ticks. "I need you to try on outfits."

"You could ask in a nicer tone."

"This is business. I'm not trying to win you over or woo you. I'm your boss in this moment. Therefore, you respond to my commands."

Anger bubbles up inside me while Kelsey fans her face.

"Wow, should she call you Daddy after that domineering speech?"

"Kelsey, for the love of God." I pinch the bridge of my nose. "Could you please keep it in your pants?"

There's another knock at the door, and she says, "Now, that must be the food, unless you have someone waiting for me behind that door." She wiggles her eyebrows and then straightens. "Man, I really do need to keep it in my pants." She goes to the door, accepts the food, and then brings it to her galley kitchen.

Huxley flips open the boxes and holds up a beautiful green maxi dress with an empire waist and flowy dolman sleeves. The plunging neckline is lower than what I'd normally wear, but the fabric looks luscious, so you know...I'll try it on.

"Put this on. I want to see you in it."

I stand from my chair, snag the dress from him, and say, "You know, a *please* wouldn't hurt you."

When I'm in the bathroom, I quickly slip out of my clothes—which I just kick to the side, Kelsey will be horrified—and then put on the dress, letting the smooth fabric fall over my curves.

"Wow," I whisper, while taking in the dress in the mirror. It fits like a glove, it accentuates my waist, and my boobs look spectacular. I guess money really can buy everything, because I've never been able to buy this kind of silhouette before.

Time to show the "boss."

I open the door and walk out of the bathroom, feeling awkward. I don't know what to do with my hands, so I hold them demurely in front of me. "Is this what you were looking for, master?" I ask him.

His facial expression doesn't change, nor does he show a flicker of appreciation. In a stern voice, he says, "It'll do for tonight."

Might as well be the farmer from *Babe*. Pat me on the head and say, "That'll do, pig. That'll do."

Sheesh.

At least he's setting expectations right now. This is business. This isn't some sort of fairy tale where he plucks me from rags and turns me into a princess. Not that I want something like that. I truly want to earn my way through this life, but you know, a little decency or acknowledgement of my usually lacking cleavage would be nice.

"These other dresses are for different occasions. There are notes in the boxes on when to wear them and how, as well as which shoes to pair with them, but now that you're going to be living with me, I'll be able to give final approval before you walk out of the house."

"Final approval?" I ask. "You realize this is my body, right?"

"Very much aware that's your body. But you also signed a contract that stated I get final approval of all outfits before we attend a business event."

"I thought that was just, you know, semantics." I wave my hand about.

"Nothing about a contract is just semantics," he shoots at me. "That's something you should learn right away, especially if you're going to be working within the admin side of your sister's business. It would behoove you to become quite familiar with legal jargon."

"I am familiar," I shoot back. "Don't assume I know nothing."

"When you pass off our contract as semantics, I'm going to assume you need to be educated, especially when taking on your sibling's business that she's built from the ground up. You don't fuck around with that."

"I'm not fucking around with it."

"You need to take it seriously," he says in that commanding voice.

"I am taking it seriously."

"This isn't just a game, Lottie. This is an opportunity to seize, to jump to the next chapter in your life, to level up, and if you're just going to fuck around—"

"What the hell makes you think I'm fucking around?" I spread my arms wide. "I'm standing here in a dress you want me to wear, and some man is going to come here and move my boxes to your house, at your request. I'm going to attend a dinner tonight that, frankly, I'm terrified of attending, just for the mere fact that if I slip up, if I say something wrong, then I fuck everything up for you. And for some odd reason, I don't want to do that." I close the distance between us and poke him in the chest. "So don't accuse me of fucking around. Do you understand me?"

A munching sound fills the silence, and at the same time, Huxley and I both turn toward Kelsey, who has a container of lo mein in hand, chopsticks in the other. She's midbite when she smiles at us and says, "Oh, sorry...just enjoying the show. Lo mein?" She offers the canister.

Annoyed, I spin on my heel and return to the bathroom, where I disrobe once again, but this time, I sit, half naked, on the covered toilet.

The nerve of that man. *It really is time to read that contract.*

The air conditioner in the car is doing nothing for the burning inferno that's ripping through my body.

I know this is business. I'm not looking for anything other than a business transaction, but would it have killed the man to at least acknowledge the lengths I went to, to curl my long hair? Granted, he asked me to curl it and demanded I go with a natural look with my makeup, but a nod of approval would be nice.

Do you think I got one?

When I stepped out of the bathroom—looking damn fine, mind you—he said nothing, other than "Let's get moving."

Kelsey gave me a hug of encouragement before I left and told me to call her if I needed to come back to her apartment. From the anxious look on her face as we were trying to figure out what to do with all the boxes, I'm going to assume the invitation is an empty one.

Huxley drives the car into a quiet street and pulls up next to a large white house that resembles the house from *The Fresh Prince of Bel-Air*, with the grandiose pillars and large dangling light fixture.

I reach for the car door handle, but he asks, "Where do you think you're going?"

I look over my shoulder at him. "I don't know, arriving obnoxiously early to a dinner date?" I point to the clock. "Honestly, who shows up an hour early? Is that a rich thing us peasants are unaware of?"

"Cutting the snark out of your tone would be helpful."

"Cutting the asshole out of yours would cut the snark out of mine, so…the ball is in your court, Huxley."

The animosity between us seems to be strong, and I can't quite pinpoint when it happened. Somewhere around the time he came to Kelsey's apartment and demanded I try on a dress. Whenever it was, it's now filtered into the vibe between us.

The tension is fierce, that's for sure.

His jaw clenches and he carefully turns toward me, his large frame adjusting to the compact space of the car. "This isn't their house. Dave lives down the road more. I figured, for your benefit, we could talk through some of the questions you texted me, but if you want to show up early, looking like a dysfunctional couple, then, sure, let's do that."

I point my finger at him. "That's not cutting out the asshole tone."

"I'll cut it out with the asshole tone when you take this seriously."

"I am taking this seriously," I yell at him. I flip my hair in his direction. "Do you realize the kind of effort it takes to curl this hair? I rarely do it, but while you were enjoying lo mein with my sister, I was sweating like a beast in the bathroom, trying to make myself presentable enough to be on your arm. I'm sorry I'm not Page Six material, but you chose me to help, so deal with what you got."

His eyes remain stern, his facial expression stoic, and for a second, I've an urge to poke his face, to see if he's frozen without me knowing it. But he drops his eyes to his phone and grabs it from the console. He flips through it and says, "You want to know how we met."

So, we're not going to address how long it took me to do my hair? Okay, just making sure that's the case. Insert eye roll here.

"It might be helpful, because I'm sure it's going to be asked. Are we just going with the whole 'ran into him on the sidewalk' story? Because, although lacking in luster, it's an easy one to tell. But in my version, you're a dick. Let me guess; I'm a shrew in yours?"

"Close," he mutters and then says, "We met in Georgia."

"Georgia?" I ask in a shrill voice. "Why the hell did we meet in Georgia? I've never even been there."

"You haven't?" he asks, as if he can't comprehend such a preposterous idea.

"It's not as though I'm a Californian who's never been to Disneyland. I just haven't happened to fly across the United States to randomly visit Georgia, when Nevada is the furthest east I've been."

"How is that possible?"

"Not all of us can drop everything and fly somewhere on a whim, Huxley. Also...you're old. You've had more time to explore."

His lips twist to the side. "Research me?"

I glance down at my nails, examining the wonderful job I did while painting them earlier. Matte white, in case you were wondering. Totally hopping on the trend, and I'm loving it. "Thought it would be helpful. Didn't expect to see you were a cradle robber. Seven years difference really is quite up there."

"I have associates who are married to women twenty-five years their junior. Seven years is nothing."

"Twenty-five years? Jesus, they could be their father."

"Why do you assume it's a man?" he asks.

"Well...I don't know," I say, thinking that he's right. "Men, I just assume, like perky things."

"And older women like stamina in the bedroom."

Yeah, I mean, I wouldn't turn down stamina, either. "So, they're women? A bunch of cougars."

"They're actually men."

I toss my hands in the air. "Jesus Christ. What was the point of all of that?"

"To educate you to never make assumptions, especially in business. It could bite you in the ass."

I exhale sharply. "Dear Jesus, please help me through this nightmare predicament I put myself in." After a few moments of collecting myself, I sit back up and smile at him. "So, sweetie, please tell me how we met in Georgia."

"Don't call me *sweetie*. I don't like that. If you must have an endearing name for me, you may call me Hux."

"Inventive." I give him a thumbs-up.

"I told Dave my grandma lives in Georgia. Peachtree City, to be exact. You grew up just north of there."

"Grew up?" I ask in shock. "How in the hell am I supposed to talk about growing up in a state I've never been to before? Can't we just go with the sidewalk story? Why involve a different state? I don't even have a southern accent."

"Because I already told them my grandma introduced us while we were visiting in Georgia."

I fold my arms. "Well, that was idiotic."

"The interaction was unhinged from the beginning. We can make up for it, though, and say that you were visiting Georgia, family and whatnot. You moved to California when you were ten. It'll help with the no-accent thing, and then you can also be more familiar with California. But we were both visiting family when my grandma introduced us. She's best friends with your grandma Charlotte, and they thought it would be ideal since we both live in Los Angeles and were both visiting them at the same time."

I nod. "Okay, that could work. What happened when we met? Were you taken aback by my beauty?"

"Yes," he says, his eyes not straying from mine. "I couldn't stop thinking about how captivating your eyes were."

Hmm…that's the second time he's mentioned my eyes. I'm beginning to think the demanding asshole might actually think they're pretty.

Not that I care.

But, you know, never hurts to know you have a pretty set of peepers.

"Just my eyes, nothing else?" I ask, batting my eyelashes.

"If you're reaching for compliments, you're not going to find them here."

"Jeez," I say. "What happened to the pleasant guy I had Chipotle with? Or the fella who came over to my house and wooed my mother?"

"He's an act, just like I put on for my business partners."

"Wow." I clap for him. "Well done. You really fooled me into thinking you were a genuinely nice guy."

"I am nice. I just don't need the pleasantries when I'm working. I like to get straight to the point."

"I see." I smile at him and say, "If you want this to work for you, I'm going to need some pleasantries. I understand this is business, but you don't need to be a dick. Technically, we're partners in this endeavor, despite this all being your idea. So instead of tossing out commands, let's try something a little different, eh? Maybe a little *please* and *thank you*?"

He glances at his watch and then back at me. "We don't have time for your nonsensical way of conducting a meeting. And we've wasted time just talking about it. Be quiet, and just listen to the backstory. Retain it. Add, if need be, but we don't need this…fluff."

Aw, look at this little ray of sunshine I've contractually attached myself to. Lucky me.

"Now, our backstory. Focus and listen up, because Ellie, Dave's fiancée, is from Georgia."

Groaning, I lean my head back against the headrest. "You're such a freaking moron…you know that?"

When he doesn't say anything in reply, I like to believe that he's silently agreeing with me.

———

"Before I forget…" Huxley reaches over me to the glove compartment and pulls out a small box. He hands it to me. "Here, wear it."

Isn't he romantic?

I open the velvet box, revealing the biggest diamond I've ever seen.

It's in a nest of more diamonds, and the diamond-encrusted band is in a beautiful rose gold.

Mouth agape, I pick it up and examine it more closely. "What on earth is this?"

"An engagement ring," he says casually.

"Uh, this isn't an engagement ring; this is an ice rink for a family of five." I look up at him. "What the hell, Huxley? You expect me to wear this?"

"Yes."

"Just like that—yes. No reasoning behind it?" I ask.

"Do you need reasoning?"

"Huxley, have you looked at this thing?" I hold it up, and I swear, it weighs at least a pound.

"Yes, I picked it out. Of course I've looked at it. I've studied it very closely to make sure there were no imperfections."

"And you think this is an appropriate ring?"

He shifts his body and looks at me. "You're fake engaged to a billionaire, Lottie. That ring is very much appropriate for what settles in my bank account; anything less would be a joke and unbelievable. Now put it on your goddamn finger and don't take it off."

Stunned by the edge in his voice, I set the box down and slip the ring on my finger. "Wow. Wouldn't have guessed this would be the immaculate proposal I'd get one day. Just 'put it on your goddamn finger and don't take it off.' So romantic."

He goes to open his car door, and I follow suit, but he says, "Don't get out."

"Don't get out?" I ask, confused.

"Yes, don't get out."

"So…you want me to stay in the car the whole night? That defeats the purpose of the last hour."

He drags his hand over his face. "Stay in the car so I can get the goddamn door for you."

Oh.

Inwardly, I chuckle as he leaves, tension set in his shoulders. I want to call out a "sir, yes, sir" to him, but his door is already shut and he's rounding the car. Something rabid crawled up his ass today.

When he whips open my car door, he offers his hand to me and demands, "Hold my hand."

"You could say *please.*" His eyes murderously narrow in on me. *Eep.* "Or not." I take his hand, and he helps me out of the car. I adjust my green dress, loving the fit of it, and he shuts the door behind me.

Together, we walk up to a grandiose stone house where vines climb the entire façade. When we drove through the gate, I almost felt as though we were transported into the English countryside, with the wispy, overhanging trees and stone wall that lines the gravel driveway. Very *Secret Garden*–esque.

"What do you think is the upkeep on those vines?"

"Please don't ask questions like that," Huxley says. "Makes you sound uncultured."

"Have you forgotten how you found me? I was panning the streets for a rich husband. Scraping the bottom of the barrel, Hux."

He glances down at me. "I'd hardly say you're the bottom of the barrel."

I clutch my chest. "Oh, a compliment. I shall cherish it throughout the night as I attempt to play your heart-eyed, pregnant fiancée."

He leads me to the front of the house and rings the doorbell. He clutches my hand tightly, as if he's afraid I'm going to run away. Trust me, I've thought about it. Many times, on the drive over here, I considered pulling the old "tuck and roll right out of the moving car," but two things prevented me from performing such an action-hero move: one, I was worried about road rash, and two, the ironclad contract I signed that holds me accountable. Basically, if I don't follow through, I'll lose everything, and so will my mom, Kelsey, and my unborn children, still chilling in my lady bits.

But I do wonder—is he nervous?

He doesn't look as though he is. Then again, I don't think he knows how to show emotion. He's so stoic, completely different than the man I met on the sidewalk, and the man I had dinner with. Who is the real Huxley Cane? A part of me wants to believe this emotionless man holding my hand is all an act to protect what rests underneath that puffed and proud chest of his.

The doors unlock, and a wave of nerves hits me like a tidal wave as the door opens, revealing two people who are the prime picture of wealthy suburban life. Dave stands there with his arm wrapped around Ellie's shoulders, and she has her hand pressed against his chest.

Smiling. *In love.*

All dewy-like, with their perfect skin and teeth.

Ready to be published in *Home and Country* magazine.

Who opens the door like that, like there's a photo opportunity on the other side? They look positively perfect.

Dave is incredibly handsome. He has that whole "blond hair, blue eyes, nerdy finance guy" vibe going for him, while Ellie is basically the most gorgeous creature I've ever seen. Highlighted blond hair that's curled in perfect waves framing her face. Her makeup makes her glow, and her sweet little red capris with the white flowy top just give her this angelic vibe that I'm totally digging.

"Welcome to our home," Dave says with a huge smile. "We're so glad you could make it."

This is going to be an incredibly long night. I can feel it already.

Dinner in Pleasantville—pretty sure this isn't the place to lie back, pat your belly, and say, "Boy, I couldn't stuff another taco in my face." And then quickly grab the last taco before it's taken back into the kitchen.

I'm so used to eating dinner with Jeff with his napkin tucked into the collar of his shirt and Mom, who likes to give us the rundown on the latest celebrity gossip—which she claims she doesn't pay attention to—that

I'm not sure I'm going to remember my manners, like elbows off the table, small talk that doesn't revolve around a surprise mole that was found on one's back, or what kind of chicken bone was tossed over the fence by our grotesque neighbors.

"Thank you so much for having us," Huxley says in a pleasant voice that nearly startles me out of my designer sandals. "This is Lottie. Lottie, this is Dave and Ellie."

Dave steps up and offers me his hand. I take it as he says, "Lottie, it's such a pleasure to meet you."

"The pleasure is all mine," I say, because that's what people say in movies, when really, I have zero pleasure in meeting this man. It's actually the opposite of pleasure. It's…it's…displeasure. Yup. It's a displeasure to meet him. "And, Ellie, it's so great to meet someone else who's pregnant. All my friends are in a completely different stage of their lives."

"I totally get it," Ellie says, shaking my hand. "I'm in a bit of the same position. Come in, come in. We can talk some more."

I turn back around to take Huxley's hand and catch the smallest glint of appreciation in his eyes as we walk into the house.

Hmm…maybe he'll be nicer to me now.

CHAPTER 7
HUXLEY

"I HATE YOU," LOTTIE WHISPERS into my ear as she stands from the table, her hand lovingly caressing my shoulder as she walks by.

"Thank you, babe," I say. I keep my eyes on her as she takes my glass and heads into the kitchen for a refill. Not a fan of "serving her man," as Ellie said. *Got it.*

Lottie doesn't seem to be a fan of much.

If it weren't for her brilliant ability to slap on a smile and act interested in Ellie and Dave's love story, I know I'd find an unwavering scowl, a gauntlet of sarcastic comments, and maybe a toss of her angry hands here and there.

She's a spitfire. For a little package, she packs a powerful punch.

It was hard to keep a straight face in the car when she kept getting irritated with me. But I assumed finding humor in her annoyance wasn't going to win me any points.

"She's great," Dave says. "I can see why your grandma introduced you. And Ellie seems to like her a lot."

"Yeah, I'm pretty lucky," I say, meaning that. I am a lucky motherfucker that, in such a short amount of time—four days, to be exact—I was able to find someone who had no problem stepping into the role of pregnant fiancée and helping me out.

Such a lucky motherfucker.

Lottie walks back into the room with a glass of water in her hand and a smile on her face as she sashays toward me. That dress, yeah, it's fucking perfect on her. I knew she had great tits from the first time I met her, but seeing them in this dress? They're really fucking nice. Not big at all, but the perfect size, less than a handful. And with her hair floating around her shoulders in loose waves, a beautiful chestnut color, she really is gorgeous. Like I said, a lucky motherfucker.

She hands me the glass and then takes a seat. I lean into her ear and ask, "Did you spit in this?"

She leans in close and whispers back, "If Ellie wasn't helping me, I would've licked the rim, spit in the water, and then added vinegar as a delicious touch."

I pull away and say a little louder so Dave can hear me, "You're perfect."

Her hand reaches up to my cheek, and she rubs my thick scruff. "I know."

Dave laughs loudly, while Ellie giggles. "Perfect response for such a powerful man," Dave says. "I've known Huxley for a few years now, and he thinks highly of himself, as he should because of the empire he's put together. But to not reply with *he's perfect*...that makes my day."

I'm sure it does, Dave.

Lottie smiles at me, and I can see a wicked gleam in her eye as she turns toward Dave and Ellie. "I know he'd kill me if I said this..."

So don't fucking say it.

"But he's far from perfect." Leaning forward, she says, "The man doesn't know how to pick up his socks and put them in the hamper."

Ellie gasps and then points at Dave. "Dave, too."

Dave raises his hand with a coy look. "Guilty. But I've gotten better. The nagging has worked."

"Hmm, maybe I should nag more," Lottie says. Her hand falls to my thigh, her fingernails applying more pressure than I care for, especially as she drags her hand farther north. *Hey there, watch it.* "What do you think, Hux? Care to deal with a nagging fiancée?"

"I thought I already was," I answer with a wink, letting Dave and Ellie know I'm only teasing her.

"Isn't he charming?" Lottie asks. "It's what won me over, his inherent charm that just keeps coming. That, and my grandma said he was a sad and lonely man who needed some fun in his life."

Don't care for that. I can see we're letting loose. Getting comfortable.

That slightly terrifies me, because Lottie is no doubt a loose cannon.

"Aren't we all sad and lonely?" Dave asks, shaking his head. "This business can be incredibly cutthroat. Brutal, at times. Having someone to come home to at night, someone loving, someone who doesn't want to talk business but wants to talk about us, about our relationship..." He lifts Ellie's hand and kisses the back of it. "That's what I want. It's what I needed. I'm sure you're the same way," Dave says to me.

Uh-huh, yup, totally.

I nod. "Long nights at the office have broken me down. I didn't know how much I needed Lottie until she magically appeared in my life."

Ellie sighs. "Aren't they the best?" she asks Lottie.

"Totally," Lottie answers with a nauseating smile.

"So, when are you two tying the knot?" Ellie asks. "Finding a venue recently has been tough. Have you had a hard time?"

I set down my glass of untouched water and place my hand on Lottie's leg. "We were thinking about having something small, maybe in my backyard."

"Ugh, that would be the dream," Ellie says. "But Dave, over here, has a mother who demands the fanfare of a ceremony and reception. She wants the bells and whistles for her son. From the live band, to the sparklers at the end of the night, to the dessert bar that offers more cookies than anyone has ever seen." She leans in and says, "Granted, I'm thrilled about the cookies, but the other stuff, all the people, it makes me nervous."

"Yes, but I'll be there with you, sweetheart," Dave says calmly. "I promise, it'll be just you and me."

Seeing this side of Dave is…enlightening. No wonder we weren't connecting on a business level. He's sensitive. Not something I was expecting going into meetings with him. Not an approach I took. Instead, I
spoke business, I talked numbers, but just from spending this time with
him tonight, I'm seeing he's more than just numbers. He has a heart, and
clearly my straight-talk approach doesn't work for him. He wants to see
the heart of the deal.

Rolls eyes.

Fucking hate that shit.

This is business. Take the emotion out of it. It's either a good financial
deal or a bad deal. It either benefits you financially or it doesn't. If it's not
a viable business decision, move on.

Believe me, what we're offering Dave benefits him greatly.

"What would your dream wedding be?" Lottie asks as she crosses her
leg and leans in toward me. It's the little touches of hers that I appreciate.
The body language, the glances in my direction, the constant hand somewhere on my person. She's good at what she's doing, and I don't know if
I should be pleased or terrified.

Ellie meets Dave's gaze and smiles charmingly at him. "I would love
to get married out on a boat. Dave proposed to me in Malibu, at sunset,
on the water, and that moment has been engrained in my mind as utter
perfection. I'd love to rent a yacht and just have our parents attend the
ceremony. Kiss as husband and wife just as the sun sets."

"Then why not do that?" Lottie asks. I shift in my seat and grip her
leg tighter, not wanting her to start any sort of fight between the couple.
Ellie already stated Dave's family was the one pressuring them to have a
big wedding. Dragging up what seems to be an uncomfortable topic can't
be good for anyone. But Lottie doesn't seem to get the hint, or rather, she
doesn't seem to care, because she removes my hand from her leg and slips
her hand inside mine while keeping a smile on her face.

"What do you mean?" Ellie asks.

"Is the food almost here?" I ask, cutting in to try to change the subject. "Can't be letting my girl get hangry." I point toward Lottie. "Happens with this one."

Dave chuckles and points at Ellie. "This one, too."

Ellie playfully knocks away Dave's hand and then turns to Lottie again. "Are you saying we should have two weddings?"

Back to this? Hell.

"Why not?" Lottie asks. "I mean, it seems as though this is a very special moment for Dave's parents, and I completely respect that." Lottie places her hand on her stomach and says, "When this little one gets married, trust me, I'll be ordering a skywriter and a billboard to let everyone know that my baby is tying the knot. But I wonder if you guys could do a small intimate ceremony, just you, and then maybe even the next day, you have the ceremony that's being planned." Lottie shrugs. "I guess something to just think about. That way everyone is happy."

Dave turns to Ellie and asks, "Would that make you happy, sweetheart?"

Ellie smiles and nods. "It would, actually. I'd really, really love that."

When Lottie turns to me, she has the biggest *fuck-you* look on her face. And here I thought I was the cocky one.

"Then I'll speak with my mom and tell her our plans. She'll have to be okay with that."

Ellie excitedly kisses Dave just as the doorbell rings. "Food is here. Will you get that, Dave? Lottie and I can head into the dining room."

"Of course."

"I'll help you," I say to Dave as I rise from my chair and then offer assistance to Lottie, who thankfully takes it.

Ellie links her arm with Lottie's and says, "I'm so glad I met you."

Together they head toward the dining room, while Dave grips me by the shoulder and guides me toward the front door. "I have to tell you, I don't think I've ever seen Ellie this excited. Lottie, man, she's something else. Your grandma was smart, setting you up with her. She smooths out your rough edges, and she brings light into the room. She's quite the catch."

If only he knew.

But, hell, I have to give credit where credit is due—Lottie is absolutely killing it tonight.

She's more than a catch; she's absolute perfection.

"So, how far along are you?" Ellie asks. "I'm assuming not very far, since you don't seem to be showing at all."

"Eight weeks," Lottie says and then nudges me with her shoulder. "This guy shouldn't be telling anyone, but he seems to let it slip more than he should."

We devoured our Chipotle, the girls actually finishing their meals first. If I didn't know any better, I'd think Lottie *was* pregnant from the way she unapologetically matched Ellie's ravenous appetite. Now we're sitting out back, a fire pit burning between us, Lottie and me in one love seat, Dave and Ellie in another. Lottie is curled against my side with her hair tickling my cheek and her hand resting on my chest. She really is such a little thing; she fits perfectly plastered against me. Not that I'd ever admit this to her—because talk about the world of fucking pain it would be to hear her boast—but she feels good curled against me.

Apparently, I've forgotten what it's like to have a female companion, not that I've really ever had one. But I've dated here and there, and having that feminine touch, the attention, yeah…it's nice.

"I had a hard time keeping the news quiet, too," Dave says. "When you find out your girl is pregnant, it's hard not to shout it from the rooftops."

"Same," I say. "I just can't seem to keep my mouth shut."

"Have you bought anything for the baby?" Ellie asks.

"Not yet. But I've looked at a few cribs from Pottery Barn that caught my attention. My sister is all about sustainability, and Pottery Barn makes a lot of their furniture from repurposed wood."

"Oh, wow, I love that. Dave, we should look at Pottery Barn."

"Anything you want, sweetheart."

Dave is such a yes-man when it comes to Ellie. Wish he were a yes-man with business, too. *Maybe I should butter him up with some of Ellie's tactics.*

What my brothers would fucking do if they saw me curled up against Dave's armpit, slowly stroking his thigh while nuzzling my head into him.

Also…was Lottie really looking at cribs? I doubt she'd say anything that isn't true out of fear of being called out. So, how the hell does she know about repurposed-wood cribs?

"Did you hear that?" Lottie asks me. "Dave is going to give Ellie anything she wants. Is it the same with us?" Lottie pats my chest with her hand and looks up at me. She's inches away, and I know if I were an outsider looking in, we would one hundred percent look like a couple. All because of Lottie.

"You know you can have whatever you want," I respond. "When do I ever say no?"

Her finger plays with the buttons on my shirt. "Just last night, when I asked for—"

"Not around company," I say, not sure what she was going to say but wanting to cut it off before it becomes something it shouldn't. Lottie is a wild card, and she's been on her best behavior all night; I could see the potential of her slipping soon.

Dave chuckles. "Best we go grab dessert while Lottie convinces Huxley to perform…whatever it is she wants."

"Might be best," Lottie says with a wink.

Dave and Ellie retreat inside the house. When the door clicks shut, Lottie stays in place, but the sweetness in her tone dissipates as she says, "I don't appreciate you squeezing my leg when you think I'm about to say something wrong. I'm going to have bruises."

"Don't be dramatic."

Her finger plays with the side of my cheek, her nail scraping against my scruff. "I'm really carrying the team over here. No wonder Dave doesn't want to do business with you. You're like a dead fish in a button-up shirt."

My brows narrow. "I'm not a dead fish."

"Uh, it's like pulling teeth to get you to show some personality. Seriously, where's Chipotle guy? He was way more fun than the one I've been petting all night."

"You haven't been petting me."

"Feels like it." Her finger tugs on my lower lip. "Are we going to have to kiss at some point? Because I'm really not interested in that. Kissing a dead fish is really not an activity I'd care to partake in."

"I'm not a goddamn dead fish," I seethe.

"Could've fooled me," she says. "You barely even laugh. That helps, you know—laughing, interacting. Making a joke on occasion. I know he's a business associate, but lighten up, man. Sheesh."

"How about we leave the business interactions to me, and you just keep doing whatever it is you're doing?"

"Oh, making you look more likable because you had enough sense in that pea-sized brain of yours to ask me to fake marry you?"

"You're foul to be around," I say.

Her eyebrows shoot up, and then her eyes grow round with anger. "I'm foul to be around? Uh, hello, pot, it's kettle…you're black. Also, I'm not sure how I could be foul to be around when clearly I'm the life of this borderline Hallmark movie we've been living in the past two hours." Still whispering, she says, "I'm twenty-eight years old, and I'm having to talk about marriage, babies, and what kind of linens I like to use on my bed. Shoot. Me. Now."

"Then talk about something you like," I say.

"Oh, you want me to do that? Shall I discuss the latest dildo I purchased from an exotic website? Because it has a suction cup, and I love using it in the shower."

Jesus.

Christ.

I shift in my seat and turn more toward her. "Do not bring that up."

She smirks. "But I thought you wanted me to talk about what I wanted to talk about."

"This is why you're foul to be around."

"Coming from the one with the stick up their ass." Her eyes travel to my lips and then back up. "You're unpleasant."

"You're unhinged."

"You open your mouth and put people to sleep," she snaps back.

"You're obnoxious."

"You're an ass."

"You're bawdy."

"You're imperious."

"Aww, look at them," Ellie says, coming back outside. "They're so cute, aren't they, Dave?"

"They do look quite perfect for each other."

If only they knew.

I smile at Lottie and stroke the side of her face lovingly before turning toward Ellie and Dave and the tray of mini trifle cups they're carrying.

"I meant to make peach cobbler, but just yesterday peaches started to make me sick to my stomach, so I hope everyone likes strawberry short-cake." Ellie turns to Lottie. "Lottie, I'll have to share the recipe with you. It's to die for."

Lottie lifts off me, but still keeps her hand touching my leg. "I'd absolutely love that, Ellie." Lottie squeezes my leg tightly as she sits up, and I know exactly what that squeeze means.

She'd rather be caught dead than trade recipes with Ellie.

Do you know what's been the worst part of this evening?

Not having to dodge couples' questions from Ellie left and right.

Not having to pretend to touch Lottie's flat stomach on occasion, like Dave does to Ellie's slightly rounded one.

And not having to see a man I respected in the boardroom shrink to a shell of a man who falls in line with everything Ellie has to say.

Nor is it the idea that Lottie has a goddamn suction cup dildo that she uses in the shower floating around in my head.

I can handle all of that.

What I can't handle is not being able to cash in on one minute of alone time with Dave. I haven't been able to talk about the deal once. I haven't even been able to mention it, because it's not something I'd do around Ellie and Lottie. Business should be kept separate from "family time," but I thought I would be able to sneak away with Dave at some point. But everywhere I look, Ellie has her claws dug into Dave, and he's the happiest motherfucker about it.

Ellie yawns. "Oh, what a night. I've had such a wonderful time."

"Me, too." Lottie yawns as well and then pats my chest. "But we should probably get going. We don't want to keep you from getting that important beauty rest…right, Dave?"

Dave laughs and nods. "Oh yes, Lottie, you know I need that beauty rest, or I'll be a nightmare to look at in the morning."

"I'd say intimidation is never a bad thing for a man in your position," Lottie says, "but after spending the evening with you, I'm going to assume that's not your MO."

"You'd be correct. Very perceptive, Lottie."

She pretends to bow. "Thank you." And then she turns to me. "Are you ready, sweet cheeks?"

Don't care for that nickname, either.

"I'm ready." I stand from my chair and hold out my hand, and she takes it so I can help her up as well. I then turn to Dave and offer my hand for a shake, realizing this is the end of the night and we haven't discussed a goddamn thing. "Dave, thank you for having us over tonight. It was a pleasure getting to know Ellie."

"So glad you two could make it."

They lead us through the house, and when we reach the door, Ellie gives Lottie a hug, and Dave offers me another handshake. It's all so domestic, so…suburban. And it makes me feel claustrophobic. My throat closes up on me, and while Lottie gives them another goodbye, I just nod and walk to my car to open the door for her. My hand falls to her back as she gets in, and then I shut the door once she's settled.

I round the hood and then get in. Dave and Ellie stand at the door, connected at the hip as they smile at us. If *that* is what having a fiancée involves—that domesticity, *docility*—I'm so glad there will never be anything like that between me and Lottie. *Never be anything like that, period.*

I start the car and offer one more wave before I round the circular driveway and head down the gravel path, finally able to let out a deep breath.

So does Lottie, but she slouches in her seat and says, "I feel as if I can finally unclench." A smirk pulls at my lips. "That was…unreal, that entire experience. I felt as though I transported into another body and that body controlled my every word and action. Because if I would've been in my own body, I would've snatched Ellie's shortcake right out of her hand after giving her a knee to the head to make sure she doesn't take it back. That shit was good. Really good. I felt feral eating it. And the fact that Ellie said she'd share the recipe with me? No, I don't want the recipe, I want someone to make it for me."

"I'm glad you didn't knee her in the face for more."

"She was eating it so slow. I swear they were doing some sort of sexual game in front of us."

"They were not performing a sexual game in front of us," I say, debunking that thought quickly.

"Are you sure about that? Were you paying attention? Because you really felt like a robot back there. She was totally licking the spoon sexually and then glancing at him. I saw him shift in his seat a few times. Bet you anything they've already stripped out of their clothes and are fucking against the entryway door right now. Although Dave doesn't seem like the type that fucks against the door." She considers this and then adds, "But it's actually usually the silent ones who are total freaks in bed." She turns toward me. "You're silent—are you a freak in bed?"

"Not something you need to worry about," I answer.

"God," she groans in frustration. "Thanks for the evasive answer. I'll draw my own conclusions, then, and I'm guessing you have a teeny weenie and don't know how to use it."

I grip the steering wheel more tightly. "How about we don't talk?"

I need to sulk, stew silently on the drive. Because here I was, going to a business meeting, thinking I'm about to score a deal, and not once did we speak about business; instead, we spoke about the different variations of the color cream, the impact a simple rug in a dining room can have, and the different ways to serve avocado toast. Christ.

"Oh, I struck a chord. You do have a teeny weenie. That's probably why you're single and spend so much time in the office, why you didn't have a catalog of girls to ask to help you out but had to find a random girl on the streets. This is all making so much sense."

"Lottie, enough."

But she doesn't stop.

"You realize you can catch more flies with honey, right? You can adjust your attitude. We're partners in this endeavor, after all. How would you like it if I took you along to a function of mine and spoke to you the way you speak to me?"

I don't answer. Instead, I think back to the way Dave seemed so comfortable. So…in his place. Not that he's awkward at meetings, but he doesn't seem comfortable, ever. Almost uneasy, untrusting. But sitting in his backyard, with Ellie right next to him, he let down his guard.

"I'm sure you wouldn't take kindly to such an attitude. You should really speak to others the way you want to be spoken to. I don't think that's too much to ask for. And while you're at it, treat others the way you want to be—"

"Can you just shut up for a goddamn second?" I ask, my mind racing, trying to put together the pieces.

"Excuse me?" she asks, folding her arms. "Would you care to rephrase that? Because unless you want me to march back to their house and flash them a negative pregnancy test, I'd change your attitude."

"You're in contract."

"And guess what? I think my family would rather us lose everything, than for me to be verbally attacked by an asshole. I'm a human, Huxley, treat me like one," she snaps at me and then turns in her seat so she's not looking at me at all, but rather out the window.

Fuck.

Guilt swarms me, because she's right.

She is a human, and she did a fucking great job today. I'm not generally an asshole. I know how to be civil, so why have I thrown out all decorum when it comes to Lottie?

I glance over at her. She's closed off; there's nothing I can say right now that will penetrate the wall she's erected, so instead of trying to deliver some half-hearted apology, I stay silent for the rest of the car ride, stewing in my own thoughts and reliving the night.

Dave seems to be his most receptive when at home, when with Ellie, but he also clearly won't talk business then, either. So how can I combine the two?

Normally I wouldn't chase a deal like this. I never have, really. In fact, I've never had to lie nor be a complete asshole to anyone to achieve my goals. But with my eyes set on the ten-million-dollar profit this deal will procure, there's no stopping, as far as I'm concerned. Cane Enterprises needs those properties. *That* is the priority.

They will be mine by the end of this, I guarantee it.

CHAPTER 8
LOTTIE

I HATE HIM.

I hate him so much.

Here I am, performing my ass off, caring about the difference between frozen spinach and fresh spinach as Ellie tells me all about her spinach balls that Dave likes so much. I listen with a smile, respond with thoughtful questions, and even delight in exchanging emails so she can send me, as she said, "all of the recipes."

And what do I get at the end of the night from Huxley?

Are you thinking a *thank you*?

Possibly a *good job*?

I'm not looking for a celebration of my accomplishments, but I'd appreciate a little bit of kindness.

But it seems as though kindness isn't part of Huxley Cane's repertoire.

That's fine. Totally cool. Because guess what? I know what to expect now.

Which would be nothing.

I should expect nothing from him.

Silence fills the car as we make our way through Beverly Hills. Huxley flies through the streets, one hand on the steering wheel, the other on the gearshift, disregarding every speed limit stated on the side of the road. And when I glance over at him, I notice the tight grip of his hand on the finely conditioned leather, the steel of his jaw, and the pinch between his brows. What the hell is he so disconcerted about? I'm the one who has been thrown through the wringer today.

He just sat there and dictated.

Annoyed with him, I keep my eyes forward as we begin to slow down. We pull up in front of a large wooden gate. He presses a button on the visor of his car, and the gate slowly opens to the right, into a white stone wall covered by vines. *Of course.*

Ahh, this must be home sweet home. In my head, he has some ostentatious house with pillars, obnoxiously large fountains, gold fixtures, and marble everywhere, even on the walls, because he can afford it, but as we turn into the driveway, I'm completely surprised by the house that comes into view. A coastal-looking white house with black-framed windows, large southern-looking lamps flanking each side of the main door, and a simple black tin roof.

This was not what I was expecting at all.

It's chic.

Modern.

In style.

Nothing ostentatious about it other than the size.

Huxley parks the car just as someone steps up to his car door and opens it for him. "Mr. Cane, welcome home."

"Thank you, Andre." Huxley hands him the keys. "Everything all set?"

"Yes, sir."

"Thank you for staying late. You can head home."

"I'll park your car in the garage and plug it in first. Have a good night."

"You, too," Huxley says, and excuse me while I pick up my jaw because... how come Andre gets spoken to like a normal person and I don't?

Huxley opens my door for me and then holds out his hand, but since we're no longer under the eyes of Dave and Ellie, I ignore his help and attempt to shut the car door, his grip on the top of the door preventing me from doing so.

"What the hell are you doing?" he asks.

"I can open and shut the door myself."

Leaning in close, he says, "And I have staff around the house that will be watching us interact, so you need to act like you're my fiancée."

"Uh, excuse me?" I ask. "That wasn't part of the deal."

"Did you read the entire contract?"

That godforsaken contract. How many times is it going to come back and bite me in the ass?

"Of course I did."

I didn't.

Who really reads contracts these days? Lawyers, that's who. I read the important parts—at least, I thought I did. There was a section about staff, but I breezed over it. I thought it was just about how he has staff that works for him, so, I don't know...be kind. Something like that.

"Then you'd have noticed that section. Andre is my trusted right-hand man. He knows of our arrangement, but he's the only one."

"Doesn't your staff have NDAs?" I ask.

"Yes, but things always seem to slip. We've fired a few staff members for tipping off the media, so I still don't fully trust everyone in my house."

"Seems stupid to me." I reluctantly take his hand. "Allowing these strangers to come into your house and take care of you, but you don't trust them. Yeah, really intelligent."

"There are very few people I trust."

"Do you trust me?" I ask as we walk toward his grand entrance. The black door feels incredibly intimidating despite the potted flowers welcoming me.

"No," he answers without thought.

"Wow, that's...that's fucked up."

"I barely know you. Why would I trust you?" He opens the front door, and I'm greeted by an expansive entryway, light blond floors, white walls, and a straight shot all the way to the back of the house, where the largest sliding glass doors I've ever seen open to a beautifully lit-up pool and dreamy backyard with enough foliage to block out the neighboring properties. He places his hand on my back and says, "You need to earn my trust."

I glance up at him and say, "You're not the only one who needs trust to be earned."

"You'd be a terrible businesswoman if you offered up your trust right away. I respect you more for making me earn it."

"Oh, yay, I earned your respect," I say sarcastically as I walk into the house. I take in the impersonal décor and the calculated placement of each item. Large vases, sleek-looking bowls, and foliage offer the lack of personalization I'm talking about. He probably doesn't even know half of these decorations exist.

Past the entryway, the house opens up into a great room with vaulted ceilings covered in white shiplap and lightly stained wooden beams. The house is devoid of any color, only decorated in variations of white, with pops of black and green here and there from a plant I'm sure he doesn't bother watering himself. The kitchen is massive. The island traverses the entire length of the kitchen, with marble countertops and black cabinets, but the uppers and lowers around the kitchen walls are white with modern, black hardware. It's an absolute dream kitchen, and I'm pretty sure if Kelsey saw this house, she'd be drooling.

"You're welcome to anything in the kitchen. My chef prepares premade meals and puts them in the fridge. If you've any requests, just let me know, and I'll make sure they're prepared."

"I can get my own food."

"Do I need to remind you, you're my fiancée?"

I turn toward him and catch him with his hands in his pockets, looking somewhat vulnerable as I take in his house. I lean in and whisper, "Fake fiancée."

Ignoring my comment, he says, "Nothing is off-limits in the house. What's mine is yours."

"Oh, so no threat to stay out of the west wing?"

His brow knits in confusion.

"You know, like from *Beauty and the Beast*."

"Are you comparing me to the Beast?"

"Not quite. He seemed to have more manners when dealing with his captive."

"I don't find that amusing."

"Shocking," I say and walk over to the fridge. I pull open one of the enormous subzero doors. Just like he said, there are meals fully prepared and stuck in the fridge with dates marked on the top. Man, the kind of things money can get someone. "Like brussels sprouts, do you?" I ask, seeing a lot of them in the containers.

"They're good for you."

"So I've heard." I shut the fridge and then ask, "Where's my room?" And then it hits me. "Uh, wait…are we going to have to share a room?" I hold up my hand. "Because that's where I put my foot down. There's no way I'm sharing a bed with you. I need my own space."

"This way," he says, walking toward the staircase just off the grand living room.

"That wasn't an answer. Are we sleeping in the same bed? I'm going to tell you right now you won't want to. I like to sleep naked."

"Not a hardship for me," he mutters as he walks up the stairs.

"Was that a compliment?" I ask, trailing behind him. "Are you saying I have a nice body? Wait…it doesn't matter if you did. Don't be a pervert."

"I'm not being a pervert. You're the one who brought up the naked thing."

"I'm trying to tell you why I'm not a good partner in bed." I pause and then say, "Wait, I didn't mean that. I'm a really good partner in bed. I know how to make a man sing to the high heavens with these hands. Miracle workers, they've been called before. I'm a good partner in the sexual aspect, the real deal. Amazing at giving head, in case you were wondering."

"I wasn't."

"Well, I am. And I'm very comfortable with my sexuality. Very adventurous. But when it comes to actually sleeping—not sex but sleeping—that's when things go haywire. I'm erratic. I'll sleep sideways in bed. I have no problem kicking someone to get them out of the way, and I don't cuddle. So, you know...sharing a bed and a room with you isn't a great idea."

When we reach the top of the stairs, he turns right and heads down a long hallway.

"Did you hear me?"

"I heard you."

I catch up to him. "Then how come you're not answering me?"

"Because your incessant chatter is annoying me."

"Wow, you really are such an asshole," I say as he opens a door on the left.

I step into the room, and I'm immediately transfixed by the modern, light-stained four-poster bed, which claims the attention of the room with its soft white linens and fluffy pillows. At the foot of the bed is a bench with pillows, and across from the bed is a fireplace with two mid-century modern black chairs angled toward the flames. Off to the right is an en suite bathroom, which I'm sure is decked out in marble like the kitchen. But what's really catching my eye is the dresser under the large window that overlooks the front yard. Because on top of it are my three dildos. One pink, one purple, and the suction cup dick I recently purchased.

Dear Christ, what are those doing out? And who the hell touched them?

I glance over at Huxley, and to my lack of fortune, he's staring at my pleasure collection as well.

"Did your staff unpack my things?"

"They did," he says.

"Seems as though they came across my lady toys."

"Is that what you call them?" he asks.

"I could say *dildos* if that makes you feel more comfortable. Although, it probably doesn't bode well for you that I have those, huh?" I nudge him with my elbow. "You know, since you're supposed to be keeping me satisfied."

"It's nothing new to them. They know I have toys."

Errr...what?

Did I hear that correctly? Huxley Cane has toys? Talk about a plot twist.

"Uh, what? Where?" I look around the room. "Do you hide them in your nightstands?" I walk over to one and open it, finding absolutely nothing.

"This isn't my room."

I stand tall. "Wait, so we're not sharing a room?"

"No. My room is directly across the hall."

"I see." I fold my arms. "And what will your staff think about that?"

"They've been informed that we're attempting to remain celibate before our wedding."

A loud snort pops out of me, and I cover my nose. "I'm sure that was laughable for them."

"Why would that be laughable?" he asks.

"You know..." I wave my hand at him. "Aren't you always bringing women home?"

"No."

"Oh." I think about that. "Well, I guess that's good for me. Don't have to pretend your wandering eye doesn't bother me."

He closes the distance between us with purposeful, commanding steps. His hand falls to just above my collarbone, and he grips me tightly, his fingers pressing into the back of my shoulder. The position not only commands my attention but steals the breath right out of my lungs.

"Let's get one thing straight," he says, his voice menacing. "I don't have a wandering eye, never have, never will. And I signed a contract with you.

That means I belong to you, and you belong to me until our obligations are fulfilled within our agreement. Do you understand?"

His words pierce me, their meaning strong, poignant.

There's no one else he'll be looking at, no one he'll be fucking until our agreement is up, that's what he's telling me, and it shouldn't have any effect on me. But for some reason, it sends a chill down my spine, an ice-cold chill.

Growing irritated with my silence, he steps in closer, his body an inch from me. His hand slides up my neck and his thumb locks under my chin. He tilts my head up, forcing me to lock eyes with him. "Do you understand, Lottie?"

God, being this close to him, forced to look him in those sinister, dominant eyes…in this moment, I realize just how much I've put on the line. Because even though his personality speaks of nothing but arrogance—and I could never imagine myself falling for a man with such an incessant need for authority—I can't help but feel something when he speaks to me with such conviction, when he claims me with his hands.

Swallowing hard, I say, "No philandering. Got it."

"I'll be loyal to you; I demand the same respect."

"You act as if I have men lining up at the door to take out my hot mess of an ass. Trust me, no need to worry." I pat his chest, trying to lighten the tension in the room and take a step away so I can catch my breath.

That was…consuming. Something to remember—when he commands a room, commands my attention, commands my every move, I can see myself drowning in his presence. There's no doubt about that.

I walk over to my dildos and pick them up one at a time to inspect them. Even though Huxley is an atrocious man with a mercurial attitude, he's incredibly hot, and the way he spoke to me just then, with that alpha tone? That was hot. Go ahead, chastise me. I know I shouldn't think anything about him is hot, especially after our recent interactions, but, ugh, his deep sultry eyes, the way he towers over me, the baritone of his voice…yeah, it's doing all sorts of things to me that will require assistance from one of my vibrating friends.

Maybe I'll use my purple dildo tonight. I love the twisting motion it does. Although, my suction cup penis is calling my name, but that's best used in the shower. It's why I got it, so I could get off from behind, one of my favorite positions.

"What are you doing?" Huxley asks as he watches me run my hand up and down my purple dildo.

Because I think it's fun to test him, I say, "Deciding what I want to fuck myself with tonight. You know, since my fiancé is celibate and all, I need to get off somehow. Your staff most likely understands the circumstances." I pick up my suction cup dick and run my hand over the tip. "God, I love it from behind, but I'm too tired for a shower right now." I hold up the purple one. "Looks like me and Thor will be having some fun tonight."

I glance up at Huxley, and I'm rewarded with a tight jaw and an irritated glare.

Perfect.

Revenge is mine.

I'm not saying I'm a beauty queen over here, turning this guy on with every step I take, but I do know something about men. No matter who you are, if you're stroking a dildo in front of them, they're going to think about sex. And when they think about sex, they get turned on. And a turned-on asshole who has to go to bed alone is satisfactory to me. *I hope he suffers…just to even the scales for the aggravation I've experienced tonight.*

"Breakfast will be at seven thirty tomorrow morning. Make sure you're there."

"Seven thirty?" I shout. "It's a Sunday."

"We have things to discuss." And with that, he shuts my door. I hear him go into his room across the hall and shut the door behind him.

Someone needs help with their anger problems.

Maybe I was wrong, maybe he is treating me very much like the Beast treated Belle.

"An invitation would've been nice, not a demand," I mumble as I set Thor down on the bed. I walk over to the closet to discover that not a single piece of my clothing is hanging up. Instead, it's all designer clothes, ranging from flowy dresses to tight-fitting evening wear, to blouses, to jeans. And then lots of shoes. Okay, that's kind of nice, because—

"Oh my God," I whisper, picking up one and clutching it to my chest. "Louboutin. Sweet heavenly Lord." I set it back down carefully and give it a small pet. "You're beautiful. Always remember that, especially when my careless feet scuff you up, because sometimes I walk like a newborn fawn."

I open the drawers in the closet and…oh, wow. Picking up a white lace thong, I hold it up to the light.

"That's a whole lot of nothing." I glance down and open another drawer to find matching bras. "Do undergarments really matter?" Well, if his staff is doing the laundry, he probably doesn't want my mismatched stuff just floating about.

It's annoying how thorough he's been in such a short amount of time.

I toss the garments back in the drawers and then search for my pajamas, which…seem to be nowhere. The more I look through drawers, the more I notice one thing in particular—there's a lot of lingerie, but there isn't one trace of my oversized T-shirts, my band shirts, or my personality.

I lift up a two-piece silk set—petite shorts that I'm sure will barely cover my ass and a matching slinky top. *This is what he expects me to wear?*

Garments in hand, I storm through my room, out the door, and right across the hallway to pound on his door.

"I need to speak to you," I shout.

It takes him a few seconds, but when he whips the door open, he pulls me in by the hand and spins me against the wall as he shuts the door.

Standing tall in nothing but his shorts from tonight, his immaculately muscular chest rises and falls as he stares at me, his body overbearing, large, fuming. Someone spends time in the gym, and his name is Huxley Cane, because...wow. Just...wow.

Who knew pecs could be so thick? I bet they bounce when he runs.

"What the hell are you screaming for?"

Uhh...

What's the question?

I'm sorry, but I'm sort of distracted by the absolute god who's standing in front of me. Yes, it's easy to see that he's an attractive man. I'd be lying if I said he wasn't. But I never noticed he was hiding so much more under his dress shirts. And I mean...so much more.

Thick flat pecs, carved shoulders, biceps that look like chiseled marble. He has the fit build of a surfer, all muscle, from the neck down, all the way to his perfectly defined abs and the indented V in his hips. And because life isn't fair, his boxer briefs cling to his waist just above where his shorts hang.

It's official—my fake fiancé is a total dreamboat.

Too bad he's the biggest asshole I've ever met.

Still fuming, he asks, "What the hell do you want?"

Oh, right. I'm supposed to be mad at him.

One hand on my hip, I hold up the negligee and ask, "Do you expect me to wear this?"

His eyes fall to the black silk in my hand, and then he looks back to me. "Is there a problem with that?"

"Uh, these are not pajamas."

"I thought you sleep naked, so what's the big deal?"

"Uh, I'm not going to sleep naked in a random stranger's house."

"Then what's in your hand should be suitable."

My eyes narrow. "Where are all of my clothes?"

"In storage."

"Why?"

He drags his hand over his face. "Because they weren't suitable for the role you need to play. This was discussed. Why are you bringing this up when I'm trying to get ready for bed?"

"Because I thought I'd have some of my own clothes to put on at least."

"Not necessary, I made sure you have everything you need. Now if that's all, I'd like to get some sleep."

Could he be any more of a dick?

Probably.

I bet this is just the tip of the iceberg for him. I bet he could be way more of an asshole, which of course makes me wonder how far I could possibly push him. Seems as though I have some time to find out.

Clutching my new pajamas, I say, "You're dreadful, you know that?"

"You're no ray of sunshine yourself."

Even though he's at least a foot taller than me, I step up to him, crank my head back, and say, "I hope you have a sleepless night."

"Sweet nightmares," he replies back with such a level of snark that I think I might have met my match.

Little does he know, he's not the only one who can play dirty.

I may have a contractual agreement with the man, but I sure as hell can make his life a horror film. And that's exactly what I plan on doing.

CHAPTER 9
HUXLEY

JP: How was last night? We didn't hear anything from you, and I'm worried she blew it. Did she? Did she fucking blow it?

I STARE DOWN AT THE text from my brother and pick up my mug of steaming black coffee. I blow on the hot liquid and then bring the rim of my mug to my lips to take a small sip, letting the bitter yet smooth drink slip down my throat.

Did Lottie blow it last night?

She did not.

She didn't blow one fucking thing…

If you catch my drift.

In all honesty, I didn't expect her to look that damn good in the dress I picked out. Nor did I expect her to walk out of her sister's bathroom looking like a goddess with her hair in waves and subtle makeup highlighting her mesmerizing eyes.

And I sure as hell didn't expect to think about her last night, all last night, with that goddamn vibrator. After I got into bed, I swear I barely breathed, just hoping to hear her pleasure herself. After thirty minutes of staying quiet, my dick as hard as a rock, I relieved myself and then went to bed.

Three dildos. What woman needs three?

Lottie, of course. Because not only am I borderline fucking up my entire enterprise with my careless mistakes, but I had to pick the one girl who so easily gets under my skin. She's annoying, frustrating, beautiful, and snarky. A total wild card. She makes me hold my breath with every word that comes out of her mouth, and then she surprises me with her brilliancy.

It's exhausting.

I set down my coffee, taking note of the time. She's two minutes late to breakfast. While I wait, I text back to JP.

Huxley: She didn't blow it. Annoyingly, she exceeded expectations, made Dave and Ellie fall in love with her, and made me look good.

I take another sip of my coffee as my brothers text back.

Breaker: How is that annoying? Shouldn't you be happy?

JP: Uh-oh…is there a problem in paradise?

Huxley: She's a goddamn pill.

Breaker: LOL. Well, that makes me fucking happy.

JP: Difficult to work with?

Huxley: You could say that. She challenges everything, and she's late for breakfast.

Breaker: You set a time for breakfast this morning? Dude, it's Sunday.

JP: Let me guess, you're being a complete ass to her. Classic Huxley.

Huxley: I'm not being an ass. I'm treating our interactions as business transactions. Because that's what this is—business.

Breaker: He's so romantic.

Huxley: There's nothing romantic about this arrangement.

Breaker: So, you're saying you don't find her the least bit attractive?

JP: What does she look like, anyway?

Huxley: Does it matter?

Breaker: Yes.

JP: One thousand percent it does.

Huxley: Why?

Breaker: Because we need to know if this arrangement is going to end in you two fucking.

JP: We need to gear up the lawyers, make sure they're on standby.

Huxley: This WILL NOT end in fucking. Trust me.

Just then, I hear the flop of slippers sliding across the hardwood floors, drawing my attention toward the stairs. Lottie comes dragging into the dining area looking as though she just rose from the dead, but fuck… she's wearing those "pajamas."

The shorts are barely shorts. They just slip past the juncture of her hip and thigh, smoothing over her curves, and the shirt…well, it shows off her midriff, just above her belly button, and then stops, minimally covering her breasts. The fabric is so thin that if it were white, I know I'd see those tight little nipples that are poking against the material.

Her hair is still in waves, but her face is clean and clear of the makeup she wore last night.

She looks, rumpled…cozy…and like absolute trouble.

There's a place setting next to me at the table, and without saying a word, she drops down into the chair, picks up my coffee, and takes a sip out of it before slouching in her chair and resting her head against the back.

"You're late," I say. "And that's my coffee."

I reach for it, but like a rabid beast, she hisses at me, causing me to pull back in absolute fear. "Touch it and die," she says in a deep, possessed voice.

Not a morning person. Noted.

After a few seconds and some large gulps of coffee, she sets down my mug and slowly turns toward me. "Your seven thirty breakfast is absolute horse shit."

Really not a morning person.

From the kitchen, my chef, Reign, brings two plates of breakfast. Each plate has a slice of avocado toast, a serving of scrambled eggs, and a fruit salad, perfectly presented.

"Thank you, Reign," I say. As he's about to leave, I gesture to the devil incarnate next to me and say, "This is my fiancée, Lottie. Lottie, this is Reign. We're very lucky to have him on staff. His food is impeccable."

Shaking off some of the crust she accumulated overnight, she sits a little taller, brushes her hair behind her ear, and says, "Hello, Reign. I love food so I think we'll be best friends."

"Miss Lottie, the pleasure is all mine. Please don't hesitate to ask me for anything. I shall make sure you receive the palate survey, so I'll know which foods you enjoy."

"Thank you," Lottie says with a smile. When he leaves, Lottie turns toward me, a frown on her face, and says, "You could've warned me other people were going to be here. I'm practically naked."

"I told you I have staff in the house."

"On the weekends?" she hisses. "You monster."

"They're compensated extremely well."

"Great, they have money, but how are they supposed to have fun with it if they're always working for you?" She whips open her cloth napkin and places it on her lap.

I study her, the pompous tilt to her chin, the proud puff to her chest, the stubborn set to her shoulders. "If you're so worried about how people perceive you in what you're wearing, then why did you come to breakfast wearing that? I'm not someone you're very familiar with."

Her eyes snake over to me as she plunges her fork into her eggs. "If you've laid eyes on my dildos, then you've seen pretty much everything."

"Not everything," I say, picking up my mug and glancing down at her chest while I take a sip. She catches my once-over.

"Is that supposed to make me melt? Swoon at your feet? That one glance, the deep set in your voice? You're going to have to try harder than that."

"Who says I'm trying?" I ask, setting down my mug.

"Your breathless voice last night, when I came into your room."

"I think you're mistaking me for yourself. You were the one breathless, chest heaving, as you stared at my naked torso."

"*Pffft*, okay, Huxley." She stuffs a forkful of eggs into her mouth.

Great defense. She can be in denial all she wants, but I know what I saw last night. She might hate me, as she so accurately portrays, but she doesn't shy away from ogling me.

"On that spectacular comeback, let's get down to business."

She shoots me a glare but doesn't say anything. I open the folder on the table to the left of me, remove the first piece of paper, and hand it to her. She takes it, looking confused.

"What's this?" she asks.

Casually, I pick up a piece of avocado toast and say, "That's the letter stating your student loans have been paid off. Keep it for your records."

Her mouth falls open as she examines the paper. I can tell when her eyes focus in on the owed amount, which says zero, because her face falls flat. "It's all paid off?"

"That's what was stated in the contract, was it not?"

"It was…but…it's actually paid off?"

"Do you think I'm not a man of my word?"

"You're deceiving a potential business partner into thinking you have a pregnant fiancée. Excuse me if I'm slightly skeptical." She sets the paper down.

I say, "I signed a contract with you. I don't take those lightly. You went to dinner with me; I paid off your debt. Now we move forward."

"Just like that, we move forward? How? We seem to hate each other."

"You can hate someone and still work with them. You need to learn to take the emotion out of business."

"Are you attempting to make me your protégé?" she asks.

"That would be a death sentence on my part. I don't have time to deal with your nonsense."

"Nonsense?" she asks just as Reign reenters the dining room.

"How is everything?" he asks.

Lottie's angry face morphs into a smile as she looks up at Reign and says, "Absolutely wonderful. Thank you."

"Good. Mr. Cane, is everything to your liking?"

I nod. "As always. Would we be able to get another cup of coffee? Although I enjoy having Lottie's lips all over my mug, she's drinking far too much of it."

Reign chuckles. "Of course. My mistake. Miss Lottie, how do you take your coffee?"

"Just like Huxley's is fine."

Reign nods and then returns to the kitchen.

"It's frightening how quickly you can change from angry to pleasant," I say.

"Speak for yourself. You're a modern-day Dr. Jekyll and Mr. Hyde."

Once Reign drops off Lottie's coffee and gives us some space, I bring the conversation back to business. "I'm unsure what the timeline of our contract will be. It seems as though Dave is in no rush to push this nego-tiation along, and I don't want to push my luck and pressure him."

"Figured as much," she says, mouth full of food as she leans back in her chair.

It's odd how different her attitude is around me. She lets loose and has no shame in the way she slouches in her chair or talks with food popping out of her mouth. And even more odd, I don't find it repulsive. Rather intriguing. Does she really have no care for her actions? For her decorum?

And yet, when we were with Dave and Ellie last night, she carried herself with class. The contrast is incredibly confusing.

"Dave was all about Ellie last night. You have your work cut out for you."

"Which means you do, as well. I'm sure I'll receive correspondence from Dave tomorrow, a follow-up on the evening. From what I could tell, Ellie liked you. She'll probably want to invite you out, just you and her."

Lottie pauses, her fork halfway to her mouth. "Excuse me? That wasn't in the contract."

"It falls under additional outings," I say. My lawyers thought of everything.

"So, you're telling me I'm going to have coffee with her? Spend extracurricular time with her? In actual life, we have nothing in common. She's very much...affluent suburbia, and I'm...well, I have a jar full of spare bills that I use as savings, so when Foreigner comes to town, I can buy the nosebleed tickets and finally see them in concert. I'm pretty sure Ellie has no idea who Foreigner is. Do you?"

I lean back in my chair and say, "I'm partial to 'Cold As Ice.'"

Her brows raise. "You are familiar. At least, you know one of their main hits."

"*Agent Provocateur* is my favorite album of theirs."

She sits taller. "Is it now?" I can see the twitch of a smile, the hint of intrigue. "I wouldn't have pegged you as a Foreigner fan."

"What would you have pegged me as?"

"I don't know, constantly playing 'The Imperial March' over and over in your head."

I glance down at my plate, a smile testing my lips, as the thought of walking around to Darth Vader's theme song is humorous. "Consider it my second choice." I clear my throat and try to continue with this meeting. "Concerning your job—"

"That has nothing to do with you."

"I said I'd help your sister's business. I have the connections she needs. Is your ego, your pride too big for you to sit down with me and talk about her business?"

I can tell from the set of her jaw that she doesn't like my approach, but too bad. A deal is a deal.

"No, but I'm not sure we need you butting in, either."

"How much is she paying you, again?" I ask while bringing my mug to my lips, fully aware Lottie is getting paid nothing for the time being.

"God, you're such an ass. Here I thought you were normal for a second because you like Foreigner, but then you go and say something like that." She shakes her head. "Every business has to start from somewhere, so before you start judging—"

"I'm not judging. I'm attempting to help you, but you aren't allowing that to happen."

"I don't want your help."

"Then why are you here?" I shoot back, keeping my voice low.

She goes to answer, but then closes her mouth and leans back against her chair. She stares at her plate for a few seconds, then picks up her napkin, tosses it on her plate, and lifts up from her chair. She walks out of the dining room and back up the stairs.

Great. Just fucking great.

CHAPTER 10
LOTTIE

BEFORE I COULD LAY EYES on Huxley this morning, I slipped out of the house, fully dressed in some silky dress that's far too flattering. The material feels like a cloud gently wrapped around me. Damn these expensive clothes.

I wanted nothing to do with him, nor did I want him asking me questions.

Yesterday was dreadful. After breakfast, I slipped up to my room, where I wrote down all of my ideas for Kelsey's business and how to improve it. Lunch and dinner were spent sitting in silence next to Huxley until I was able to slip away again. I haven't seen him since dinner last night, and I prefer it that way.

When I went to get into my car to drive over to Kelsey's this morning, I realized—guess who doesn't have a car here? So I walked down the block and ordered an Uber to get me to West Hollywood.

Now, with our favorite coffee in hand, I walk up to Kelsey's apartment, excited to see her and give her all the gory details. I knock on the door and wait. It's early, but hopefully she's up and ready for the day.

The door opens and—

"What the actual fuck are you doing here?" I ask Huxley, who stands on the other side of the door.

In a sarcastic tone, he says, "You didn't give me a kiss goodbye."

Pushing past him, I say, "Crawl up your own scrotum and drown." I find Kelsey in the kitchen, eating a bagel with a huge smile on her face. "Why did you let him into your apartment?"

"I thought there was something wrong, like something happened to you. Then he told me you didn't say bye to him, and I felt bad."

I spin around to glare at Huxley. He's dressed for the day in a deep blue suit, white button-up shirt, and a slate-colored tie. Not one hair is out of place on his head, and he has just enough scruff to make him look positively intimidating.

"How on earth are you ready and dressed?"

"If you shared a room with me, you'd know I wake up at four to start my day."

"God, you're mental." I hand Kelsey her coffee and say, "I shouldn't even give this to you, since you seem to enjoy my slow torture."

"He's actually a pretty nice guy," Kelsey says.

"To whom? To you? Of course he is, because he doesn't see you as his puppet. Believe me, if you were in the trenches like me, you'd think differently."

Kelsey fingers the sleeve of my dress. "You consider designer clothes being in the trenches?"

Pompously, Huxley sticks his hands in his pockets and rocks back on his heels, a grin on his stupidly handsome face.

"I'd rather be naked than have to deal with him."

"We can arrange that," Huxley says, causing my sister to chuckle.

"Hey," I snap at her, "whose side are you on?"

"Yours, of course. Always on your side, sis. But this is far too entertaining."

Groaning, I turn back to Huxley and say, "I have no idea why you're here, but I need you to leave so I can talk about you behind your back with my sister."

From his pants pocket, he pulls out a black card and holds it in front of me.

"What's that?"

"The key to your car."

"That's not a key, that's a credit card."

He shakes his head. "It unlocks your car and you need it to drive the car, so yeah, it's a key. It's the white Model 3 in the front parking spot of this building. I expect you to drive it. The PIN number you'll also need to drive it is written down inside the envelope on the table." When I don't take the card from him, he steps up to me and slips it right into my cleavage. "Have a great day...*sweetheart*."

And then he leaves.

I stare at the closed door, card still stuck in my cleavage.

When I turn around, mouth agape, Kelsey chuckles and says, "Oh, this is so much fun for me."

"Why are you a bad sister?"

She laughs and sets her mug down on the counter. "I'm not a bad sister, I'm just taking joy in something new that's happening in your life."

I point to the door through which Huxley just retreated. "There's nothing joyous about that man."

"I don't know." She smirks. "He does seem to have some good qualities."

I fold my arms. "Really? Good looks buy your loyalty?" I point to my chest. "I'm your sister. Your loyalty belongs to me."

"Oh, settle down," she says as she plucks the key card from my cleavage and guides me to one of the chairs at her bistro table. "You know I'm on your side, but I will say, you should probably give him a chance. Not be so...irritable around him. He's helping you out."

"I'm helping him out."

"You are both in this together. But look at what he's doing for you. Gave you a new car to drive rather than that hunk-of-junk Bug that barely gets around; you have all new clothes, which helps us, because, not to be mean, but now you look put together, which bodes well for business meetings; and he gave you a place to stay so you don't have to live here with me—or worse, with Mom and Jeff. He also paid off your student loans, so you don't have to worry about getting a job to pay those back and can work with me instead. He's done a lot, Lottie. And you went to dinner with him, to help him with some deal he's trying to score. I'm not taking sides, but he seems to be doing a lot for you."

"Well…when you put it like that, sure, he looks like a saint, but he's anything but that. Trust me. He's a pompous asshole. He's rude and degrading at times. He doesn't treat me with respect."

"Do you offer him respect, or are you always fighting him? Knowing you, it's probably the latter."

My sister knows me far too well.

"He started it," I say. "He came in ripe with the attitude. What was I supposed to do? Just sit back and take it? Hell no. He makes my life difficult? I'll do the same."

"So glad you didn't lose your maturity in the move," Kelsey says with sarcasm. "And even though this topic of Huxley Cane is entertaining, we have some work to do." She brings her computer over to the table and hands it to me.

"What do you want me to do with this?"

"We need to start getting organized with the business, and oddly enough, that's the part of this job I suck at. We have a meeting later today with a potentially huge client, and I want to make sure we have everything under control. So if they ask questions, we can give them exact numbers."

"Exact numbers of…"

"You know, like inventory and financials. Things like that."

I eye her suspiciously. "Why would they care about that?"

She rolls her eyes. "Rich people want to know how successful you are. I need you to make me look successful on paper."

"Okay…what are you going to do?"

She pulls out her iPad and smiles. "Design, of course."

"Of course." Sighing, I open her computer. All the files we need on her computer are at the bottom, ready to be opened. "Am I going to hate you after this?"

"Possibly. But this is what you enjoy."

"Oddly, it is." I crack my fingers. "Let's get to work, sis."

———

"How do you turn off the car?" I ask, looking for an *off* button of some sort.

"I don't think you turn it off," Kelsey says, slinging her bag over her shoulder.

"What do you mean, you don't turn it off? There has to be an *off* button somewhere."

She shakes her head. "I went out with a guy with the exact same car, and he just put it in park, got out, locked up, and walked away. The car knows when you're not in it anymore." She gets out, and I grumble to myself as I put the car in park and get out myself.

Out of all the cars Huxley could have given me, he gave me one with a mind of its own. I press the key card to the side of the window and watch as the side mirrors curl in toward the car.

"Is it locked?" I ask.

"I believe so." Kelsey checks her watch. "Come on, we're going to be late if we fiddle around with this thing anymore."

Shoving the key card in my purse—key card for a car, strange, by the way—I catch up to Kelsey, who's already halfway to the building.

"Who are we meeting with, by the way? You never gave me any information. All I know is that your bookkeeping is in dire need of help, and I've been able to pull together some rough numbers."

She doesn't answer. Instead, pushes through the large glass doors and into a modern, sleek lobby. There isn't a person in sight other than a receptionist at the front desk.

No signs.

No personalization.

Nothing to indicate where the hell we are.

"Miss Kelsey, Miss Lottie, glad you could make it," the receptionist says. "Please, take the third elevator to the tenth floor. They're waiting for you."

"Thank you," Kelsey says, power walking to the elevator.

I rush to catch up with her and barely make it into the elevator as the doors close behind me. "Jesus, hurry much?"

"We can't be late. It looks bad."

I lift her wrist to look at her watch. "We have two minutes to spare. Calm down."

She looks me in the eyes. "This is important, Lottie. This could be a big break for us, okay? Please understand the magnitude of this."

Seeing the desperation in my little sister's eyes, I say, "Hey, I know this is important. I'd never do anything to mess with that. I'm just trying to calm you down. Going in there looking frenzied isn't going to help the cause either."

She takes a deep breath. "You're right. This is like any other pitch I've made."

"Exactly. We have everything we need, and I'm here by your side to help."

"Thank you." She squeezes my hand, the elevator dings, the doors part, and there, standing in front of a conference room, are three tall, broad, and intimidating men.

But one of them is unmistakable.

"What the actual hell," I mutter as my eyes land on Huxley.

"Decorum," Kelsey whispers as she pulls me off the elevator with her.

"Kelsey, Lottie, so glad you could make it," Huxley says with a grin. He gestures to the conference room behind him. "We'll be in here."

Kelsey starts for the conference room, but I grab her hand and hold my finger up to Huxley. With a smile that pains me, I say, "Please give us one moment. We'll be right in."

He nods, and the three men walk into the conference room, allowing the door to shut behind them.

I turn my back to them and, with eyes that scream death, say, "What the fuck, Kelsey? Why is Huxley here?"

With a grin spread across her face, making sure the guys see that nothing is wrong, she says, "That's why he came by this morning—well, one of the reasons—to set up a meeting with us and give you the car, obviously."

"A meeting for what?"

"For the office." Her smile grows even more. "He wants to possibly hire me to organize and make the office more sustainable. This could be a huge account, Lottie. If done right and efficiently, this could put us on the map."

The excitement in her eyes, the hope blooming inside her, sets me into a tailspin. Because this doesn't feel right, it almost feels too good to be true, and as the older sister, I want to protect her from harm. But how can I express my concerns without looking as though I'm trying to pee on her parade?

I don't trust Huxley.

I don't trust his intentions.

I've seen the extent he'll go to in order to deceive someone into making a deal. Who's to say he wouldn't do that to my sister?

But her begging, pleading eyes are cutting through my strong will. She wants this, this chance to grow, and hell, I can't take that away from her, no matter my level of unease.

Pushing my hesitation to the side, I say, "Okay, but let's proceed with caution. We don't know what this could lead to, and we also need to remember that Huxley is a shrewd businessman."

She smirks. "Trust isn't built in a day; I get it." She takes my hand in hers. "Let's go in there and blow their dicks off."

I chuckle. "Not literally…right?"

Her eyes widen. "Right, no blowing actual dicks."

Together, we walk into the conference room and stand at the end of the table, opposite the three extremely handsome men. Even though they all are extremely attractive—which isn't intimidating at all—my eyes land on Huxley, sitting in the middle with his folded hands resting on the table.

"Mr. Cane, we're so honored you had time to meet with us today," Kelsey says, and I hold back a sneer at her use of *Mr. Cane.*

Ugh, gross. Am I going to have to call him that?

And these two guys, do they know who I am? Am I supposed to walk up to Huxley and give him a kiss?

Oh shit, wait…am I?

Is this part of a test?

When I glance at Huxley, he's staring me down, his eyes fixated on the ring on my finger, which I keep twirling with my thumb out of pure nerves.

Is he trying to tell me something? Is that a hint? I did brush him off right when we got here, asked for space. What if he'd intended to give me a hug? Should I assume these men know we're engaged? Or is this a business setting? His house staff is aware of our engagement.

Jesus Christ, a heads-up would've been wonderful.

On both ends. From my sister and from Huxley.

Sweat forms at the base of my neck, heating up my ears as I take a step forward. I watch Huxley intently as I take another step forward, looking more like an unoiled robot than a confident fiancée. I just don't know the protocol.

WHAT IS THE DAMN PROTOCOL?

"Lottie, are you okay?" Kelsey asks.

Another step, closing the distance, slowly, awkwardly, but closing it.

"Oh yeah, just wonderful. Want to, uh, make sure I say hello. You know…" I gulp, "to my, uh, to my counterpart." I point at Huxley and take

another step forward. "The man I can't stop thinking about." Another step, until I'm right at his chair, the other two men looking up at me awkwardly. I pat Huxley on the shoulder, my gestures erratic. Not a smooth bone in my body. "Hello, dear honey…bottoms." I smile. "You're looking ravishing." With every eye in the room watching me, I lean down, growing closer and closer until my lips meet the top of his head. Instantly I'm met by the smell of his delicious cologne and the masculine scent of his hair products. "Oh, that smells nice." I pat his head. "Not musky at all. Just… you know, like a man should smell. All mountainy and rich. You smell very rich." Awkwardly I finish kissing the top of his head, and then I move away and give him a thumbs-up. "Love getting to sneak in some affection during the day…fiancé." I wink and take another step back as a droplet of sweat rolls down my back.

That was not smooth at all.

"For the love of God, tell me that's not how she acted in front of Dave," the guy to the right says.

Huxley leans back in his chair and props up his chin on his hand as he slouches. "I have no idea what the fuck that was, but it wasn't what she did Saturday."

"Excuse me?" I ask, looking between the men.

"Uh, Lottie, maybe you come on back over here." Kelsey waves her arm. "So, you know, we can be professionals and start the presentation."

"Hold on," I say, holding up my hand to my sister as I turn to face Huxley.

His navy-blue suit makes him look even more sinister when he's sitting in that pitch-black conference-table chair. And his pose—casual yet firm, his eyes fixated on me—unwavering. He's a force to be reckoned with, and I have no problem standing up to the man.

I motion to the two other men. "Do they know?"

"What exactly are you referencing?" Huxley asks with such smugness in his voice that I'm tempted to reach out and kick him in the shin.

"Our engagement of course, sweet cheeks," I answer in a nauseating tone. "Are they aware you've made me the happiest woman on earth?" I clasp my hands together and hold them in front of me.

Kelsey clears her throat. "Lottie. Come over here."

"You didn't seem particularly happy, especially when you came off the elevator." Huxley's index finger travels up the side of his face to his temple, while his thumb positions itself just under his jaw. It feels like a power pose, as if he's attempting to command the room in a casual manner... yet command me. And I'll be damned if he thinks he can command me.

Hands on my hips, I ask, "Now why would you say that? I was shocked to see you, is all. I wasn't expecting to run into such a hunk of meat in the middle of the afternoon."

"Lottie," Kelsey whispers, giving me the *come-here* motion, but I ignore her.

The two men next to Huxley are far too amused as they sit deep in their seats and take in the show.

"I see." Huxley's eyes stay trained on me. "And were you particularly happy to see your fiancé?"

What is he doing?

What game is he playing?

This doesn't seem very professional of him.

It's almost as if he's taunting me, testing me.

Guess what, buddy? Two can play at this game.

I wet my lips. "Very...excited." I lace my answer with innuendo and slowly move my eyes down his chest to his crotch and then back up.

There.

See what he does with that.

"Will you excuse my sister, she's—"

"Kelsey, it's okay, the cat is out of the bag," I say to shush her. "We're engaged. I know it may come as a shock to some, but"—I walk over to him and take his hand in mine—"we're in love."

I glance over at one of the men, and he's snickering behind his hand. *That's fucking rude.*

I look over at the other guy, and his smile stretches from ear to ear, but it's not a joyous smile, it's more of an amused smile. What the hell is going on here?

"Sorry," I say after a pause. "I was sort of expecting a round of applause or something, you know, for our love." All eyes on me still—Huxley isn't helping in the slightest—I lower myself until I'm sitting on Huxley's lap. His hand falls to my side and I wrap my arm around his neck. "So much love," I say, getting a good whiff of his lavish cologne. I hate that it smells so good.

Hand on my hip, Huxley keeps his eyes on me as he asks the others, "Will you give us the room, please?"

Uhh…say what now?

I glance over at Kelsey, who looks more than irritated, but she gathers her things and leaves the room, followed by the two men.

Once the door is shut, Huxley asks, "What the hell was that?" I go to move off him, but he keeps me close, his hand now gripping my ass and keeping me tight against his body.

"That was me trying to figure out what the hell this is." I motion to the conference room. "You couldn't have told me you were meeting with me and my sister today?"

"Why would I tell you when your sister clearly could have?"

"Uh, I don't know, you could've given me a heads-up about who might be in the meeting. Am I supposed to play doting fiancée or irritated shrew?"

"As much as I enjoy irritated shrew…you call the spectacle you just laid out doting fiancée? That was awkward woman unsure of what to do."

"Because you put me in that position. I had no idea how to act. I don't know who knows about us and who doesn't. When I should turn it on and when I shouldn't."

"You should always be *turned on* around me."

My eyes level with him. "Not that kind of turned on. God, you pervert."

"I wasn't talking about *that* kind of turned on..."

"Yeah, okay, surrrre," I answer maturely. "Either way, I had no idea how to react, awkwardness got the best of me, and that's the version of me you received. If I'm prepared, I know how to act, but walking off an elevator only to see you standing there when I'm not expecting it, threw me off my game."

He slowly nods. "Did I intimidate you?"

"No," I answer quickly as his hand reaches up and pushes my hair behind my ear. "What are you doing?" I ask in a panic as a wave of chills stumble down my arm from the graze of his finger over my cheek.

"Everyone can see us," he says, tilting his head to the side. "And since we're in my office, wouldn't you think everyone would need to see us together, see us interact, because the main point of this entire farce is so that I can score a deal?"

"Huh," I say, thinking about it. "Yeah, I guess that makes sense."

"One thing you need to get straight, Lottie—I always make sense."

My eyes connect with his. "You're so narcissistic."

"Confident," he replies.

"A cockhole."

His brows raise. "What the hell is a cockhole?"

"Cocky asshole. Therefore, you're a cockhole."

His hand smooths down my ass and back up. I need to hate how that feels, but for some abhorrent reason, I don't. I don't mind the feel of his large palm skimming over my backside.

Jesus Lord help me. There's something wrong with me.

"So, because I know what I want, how I want it, and when I want it, that makes me a cockhole?" His eyes shift to my mouth and then back up.

Tension builds in the hollow of my chest, a tingling, heavy, throbbing sensation. One I've never experienced before.

"No." I swallow, and for some reason, I look at his mouth for a second.

He has great lips. Not too full for a man, but just enough that I know if he ever had to place his mouth on mine, it wouldn't be a bad kiss. Just from the way he speaks, with such command, there's no doubt in my mind that he'd be a good kisser. "Not that it matters, because it doesn't. You're a cockhole because you don't treat people with kindness."

"I see." His stare is unwavering. "So let me get this straight: I don't treat people with kindness. So what would you say making sure you have a solid mode of transportation is? Or what about the flowers I sent to your mom and Jeff, congratulating them on an empty house?"

He sent them flowers? Mom didn't say anything.

"Or how about the lengths I went to in my house to ensure you'd be comfortable?"

What lengths?

"Or the meeting I took with your sister today, completely rearranging my schedule so she could pitch to us? What would you call that?"

Uhhh...

I'm about to answer when the conference room door opens. Huxley looks over my shoulder as a female voice says, "I'm so sorry to disturb you, Mr. Cane, but Bower is on line one."

He nods and says, "Thank you, Karla. I'll be right there."

The door swishes shut, and Huxley lets go of me, helping me settle on the ground before he stands from his chair and buttons his suit jacket.

Eyes boring into me, he says, "I'll see you at home."

He starts to walk away, and I ask, "Wait, what about the meeting?"

"Looks as though you've used up my time."

"What?" I chase after him and move in front of his large body. I can feel eyes on us, eyes from around the company, so I make sure to keep my frustration at bay as I slide my hand up the lapel of his suit jacket. "Huxley, my sister has been preparing for this meeting all day. She's going to be devastated if she can't pitch to you."

"Something you should've thought of."

He goes to move again, but I stop him. "Please, Huxley."

His eyes meet mine, and for a brief moment, I see a hint of human inside them. This man really does have a soul. It's right there, behind the dark chocolate of his hollow eyes.

"I'll see you at home," he repeats and moves to the side. "And by the way, if you're going to help your sister succeed, you should always do your research on every client you go to meet."

"What do you mean by that?" I ask.

"The men sitting with me. They're my brothers, not associates. And they know everything going on in my life."

My eyes narrow, and I try to keep it together as I ask, "So I didn't have to put on an act at all?"

"No, you didn't. They know exactly who you are and what you're doing for me, but you'd have known that if you were truly prepared. Perhaps I'll take another meeting with your sister when you show that you can actually conduct yourself professionally in a business setting."

Anger shoots to the top of my head as I feel my cheeks darken with embarrassment. "I hate you," I say with such venom that I can taste my hatred for him on the tip of my tongue.

"I'm well aware of your feelings for me. No need to constantly repeat them." And with that, he heads out of the conference room, past Kelsey without a second glance, and into the depths of his office. I glance at Kelsey, who stands there alone, her laptop and portfolio in hand, looking absolutely defeated.

And that's when it hits me hard. I fucked this up for her.

I fucked up really badly.

Kelsey reaches to leave the car, but I grab her arm and stop her. "Please, Kelsey. Please just talk to me."

She lowers her head and shakes it from side to side. "I don't even know what to say to you at this moment. I'm so upset, I don't want to say the wrong thing."

"I'm sorry, Kelsey. I really am."

She looks over her shoulder, and I can see the disappointment in her eyes. It cuts through me like razor-sharp glass.

"I understand you're in a weird position right now. You were fired by someone you thought you trusted, thrust into this odd deal with a very domineering man, a man you don't particularly get along with, and you're trying to find your way through this mess. But that doesn't give you the right to be a martyr."

"A martyr?" I ask in surprise. "I'm not a martyr."

"No?" she asks as she turns in her seat to face me. "Because from where I sit, you're looking pretty cushy at the moment. Not many people are granted the opportunity you've been given. Not only are you living in some mansion with an extremely hot man, but you had your college loans paid for, you don't need to worry about any expenses, and you were granted a chance to live with a businessman who's a wealth of knowledge. You realize he's worth billions, Lottie? BILLIONS. He's built his business from the ground up with his brothers, and instead of capitalizing on that, on his experience, on his expertise in what you spent four years studying in college, you're inciting him to anger. And you're hurting the people you love while doing it."

"It's not that easy," I say.

"It's not easy to lower your guard, see this incredible opportunity at your feet, and be grateful?" she asks. "Because if I were in your position, that's exactly what I would be."

"You say that, but you don't know until you're in my shoes."

She nods. "You're right, I have no idea what you're experiencing, but what I do know is that we had a big meeting today, and instead of pushing your ego to the side, it spiked, and you let it take an opportunity from us. When I say this could've been big, I meant it, Lottie. Not only is Cane Enterprises worth billions, but they own businesses and real estate all over

Los Angeles, and in other states. Meaning if I were to land an opportunity and they liked what we did, they could have used us not just for their office, but for every property they own. But you didn't think about that when you were trying to put on some show in the conference room, did you?"

"I had no idea how to act," I shoot back. "He's in my head. I don't know how to approach him, how to…treat him."

"Try with a little respect," Kelsey says while opening her door.

"He was the one who provoked me in that room," I say, still on the defensive.

"Because you let him. He seemed perfectly fine from where I stood. You were the one who looked like the fool." And with that, she slams the car door and walks toward her apartment building.

I roll down the window and say, "You forgot your laptop."

"Keep it. The least you can do is fix the website."

Then she walks into her apartment building.

Anger, frustration, and embarrassment clash within me at the same time, hitting me square in my chest, only to travel up my neck, heat up my cheeks, and ultimately bring a wave of tears to my eyes.

"Fuck," I quietly say as a tear cascades down my cheek. What Huxley and Kelsey both said was one hundred percent correct. *Be prepared for every meeting. Know who you're meeting with. Know your own presentation inside and out. Go in with confidence, ready to answer every possible question.* These are basic meeting requirements, and I didn't follow any one of them. *I made a mockery of years of studies.* Why? And of all people to show such lack of professionalism and preparation to, it had to be the owners of Cane Enterprises. *Fuck.*

And Kelsey's business.

Kelsey and I have had our fair share of fights, but for some reason, this one doesn't feel as though it can be fixed with a Double-Double and chocolate milkshake from In-N-Out. This feels deeper.

This feels damaging.

And that frightens me more than anything.

CHAPTER 11
HUXLEY

"I HAVE A QUESTION," BREAKER says as he takes a seat in my office, JP following close behind him.

"What?" I ask, exhausted from the day I've had.

"Are you trying to make sure Lottie absolutely abhors you?"

"She already does. I don't have to do anything to achieve that," I say while exiting out of my inbox and turning off my computer for the night.

"Ever thought about getting her to, I don't know...like you?" Breaker asks.

"Why would I want her to like me? This is a business arrangement. There's nothing more there."

"He doesn't mean it like...sexually," JP says. "But don't you think it would be easier to work with each other if you weren't at each other's throats?"

"Probably," I answer.

"So then why are you pissing her off every chance you get?" Breaker asks. "What you did this afternoon?" He shakes his head. "Brutal, man."

"Yeah, I actually felt bad for the sister. She looked defeated," JP adds.

"I didn't have a choice," I say. "Bower called. That's who I've been working with since I left the conference room."

Breaker perks up. "Everything okay in New York?"

I shake my head. Bower is our site manager; he only calls off schedule if something is wrong. "No. He was calling to tell me there was an electrical fire at the Ninety-Fifth Street location. Fire department was called, building evacuated, a few guys had to be evacuated by the FDNY." I press my hand to my forehead. "It was a goddamn nightmare. I spent the entire afternoon reaching out to all staff affected to ensure they were okay."

"Shit." Breaker drags his hand over his mouth. "Any serious injuries?"

"Two men have third-degree burns on their arms, but they seem to be in good spirits. Everyone else is fine, thankfully."

"Christ," JP says. "Did we send something?"

I nod. "Yes, sent something to the hospital. One of the guys loves a certain type of pizza on Ninth Street, and the other guy is obsessed with Gray's Papaya. I made sure to send them both dinner, along with some cupcakes from Magnolia Bakery. I sent their families something as well. Karla will be taking care of dinners for the crew for the week. I've contacted insurance to let them know what's going on." I lean back in my chair. "I'll have Karla set up another appointment with Kelsey, because I'm quite interested to see what she can do for the company and possibly future offices."

"Seems as though she has an interesting business," JP says.

Breaker chuckles. "I think you were more interested in her…"

My brow raises as I swivel toward JP. "Is that so?"

He shrugs. "She was hot."

"He was thinking more than just *She was hot*. I caught him writing *J and K Forever* on a Post-it in his office."

"Fuck off, I was not," JP says. "I mentioned to Breaker that she was hot and left it at that, and now he's dreaming up some bullshit in his head."

"Could you imagine?" Breaker asks. "Brothers getting married to sisters? That's a fun story."

"You've lost your goddamn mind," I say as I stand from my desk. "Marriage is not for me, let alone to someone like Lottie."

"What's that supposed to mean?" Breaker asks, standing as well.

I put my phone in an inner pocket of my suit jacket and slip my wallet into my pants pocket. "She's a mess. Disorderly, a loose cannon, and too erratic for my liking. She's a total wild card, and I don't need that in my life."

Breaker smiles. "I think you do. You're such an uptight asshole, and she might be able to loosen you up."

"There will be no loosening." We leave my office and head toward the elevators. The floor is quiet; we're the last to leave. We might have a billion-dollar enterprise, but we understand what it takes to make sure employees are happy, and that means making sure they all go home to their families at five.

JP presses the *down* button on the elevator. "I think if anyone needs a Lottie in their life, it's you."

I pierce him with my gaze. "Don't even start with that shit, okay?"

"He's right," Breaker says. "Just from the small glimpse I caught, she looks like a spitfire, and I'd very much enjoy watching her drive you nuts."

"She already drives me nuts."

The elevator doors open, and we step inside. "I don't know. I think there's something there," JP says. "Did you see it, Breaker?"

Breaker nods his head. "I did."

"You both are so full of shit."

We ride the elevator to our private parking garage, and when the doors part, I don't bother to wait for my brothers as I head to my car.

"It was the way you looked at her when she got off the elevator, when she approached you in the conference room, *and* when she sat on your lap," JP calls out. "There was heat in your eyes."

Ignoring him, I unlock my car and get in. The last thing I need is my two idiot brothers putting ideas in my head. There's nothing but a platonic partnership happening between me and Lottie.

Do I find her attractive? I'd be blind not to. She's fucking beautiful, but I can look past that.

And did she look fine as hell in her form-fitting dress today? Yeah, she really fucking did, but once again, I can look past that, because I'm a professional and know how to separate attraction and business.

A knock on my window startles me. Breaker is standing right outside my car. I roll down the window and say, "I don't fucking like her, okay?"

Breaker smiles and leans down so his arms rest on my door. "I wasn't going to say anything about that, but your defensive tone isn't making a solid case." I'm about to roll up the window when he stops me and adds, "Make sure Karla makes that appointment. I feel really fucking bad about skipping out on their presentation. We don't do shit like that."

"I know."

"And make sure Lottie knows it. Explain to her what happened."

"She doesn't need to know."

Breaker nods. "She does. She needs to be able to trust you, Hux. If this is going to work, both of you are going to have to drop the hate and learn to work with each other more harmoniously. If you can't, sooner or later Dave is going to see right through it, and you're going to lose everything you worked toward. And I know that's the last thing you want."

I think back to the conference room and say, "She did give off the wrong energy, even when she was attempting to be the doting fiancée."

Breaker nods again. "You've got to let up, man. I know you like to keep personal and business separate, but I think this is a time when you can't do that. You have to show her you're human, or else it's never going to work."

And that's what I'm afraid of—showing her who I really am—because even though I'll deny my interest in her, I know a part of me, deep down inside, knows if I got to know her, if she got to know me, there might be something there.

Mixing personal with business is a huge risk. Lines get blurred, promises get lost, and it never works out, ever. It's why I need to keep my distance, why we both need to keep our distance.

"I'll give it some thought," I say, even though I know I won't.

All it took was one meal with Lottie, one meal at Chipotle, and I knew she was different. I knew she could be trouble. She's unlike any woman I've ever met. Filter free, she says what's on her mind, she shows no remorse toward her messiness, she's outgoing and up for anything, and there's no holding back with her. It's why I need to remain stoic, why I need to continue to keep space between us; if I don't, I know I'll be wrecked in the end.

Lottie *could* wreck me. But there's no way in hell I'm telling my brother that. *He's far too insightful. Damn him.*

"Will Miss Lottie be joining you?" Reign asks.

I nod. "Yes, she's just finishing up on something." I glance down at the homemade pizza and say, "This looks amazing."

"Thank you. I also made some dark chocolate raspberry mousse for dessert. I'll bring it out when you tell me you're ready. Until then, it's chilling in the fridge."

"Thank you, Reign." He takes off, and I reach for my phone. I texted Lottie five minutes ago, letting her know dinner was ready. I haven't seen her since I got home. From what I could tell, she came home and went straight to her room, where she's been hiding out ever since. There's no doubt the last thing she wants to do is eat dinner with me, especially after everything that happened today, but she needs to eat.

I'm about to stand from my chair and get her myself when she descends the stairs. She's wearing one of the silk robes I had purchased for her. This one matches her eyes, a seafoam green. As she takes the last few steps down, I watch the slit of the robe ride up her tanned bare leg. My eyes travel to her waist, where the tie is cinched tightly, accentuating her petite frame, and then my eyes land on her breasts, which gently sway as she makes it to the main level.

There's no mistake—she's not wearing anything under that robe.

When her eyes meet mine, she says, "I was taking a bath when you texted." Her voice is monotone, devoid of any life. Her eyes are sullen, and even though she looks tempting in that robe, she isn't strutting with confidence like she normally does.

Breaker's words come back to hit me hard in the chest.

You have to show her you're human, or else it's never going to work.

Lottie pulls out her chair and takes a seat. She doesn't acknowledge the place setting, me, or even the food. Instead, she unfolds her napkin, sets it on her lap, and then picks up her fork and knife and cuts a small piece of pizza. I watch as her lips form an O shape and she blows on the steaming pizza.

There's no humor, no anger, just…nothing…to her personality. It's almost as if the bath she just took washed away any remnants of the Lottie I've come to know over the past few days.

The spice is gone.

The hatred is gone.

The arguing is nowhere to be seen.

She's hollow.

Did I do that to her?

And even though she's grated on my nerves for what's felt like every goddamn second she's been around, I'd take that over this Lottie any day.

I think today broke her, and that doesn't settle well with me. I may be a ruthless bastard at times, but this…this doesn't feel right.

The rules I've set firmly in place when it comes to business waver as I feel an inherent need to tell her what happened today, to bring back some of the life that's vanished from her eyes. "It was an important phone call I needed to take." My eyes fall to her, looking for any sort of reaction.

"I'm sure," she says quietly, but her tone has an edge to it, as if she doesn't believe me.

I don't need to explain myself. I don't owe her any sort of explanation regarding my work and how I conduct business, but I still find my gut churning. I want to see that fire in her eyes again.

"Aren't you going to ask what could possibly be more important than your sister?"

She glances in my direction, those cut-down eyes moving over my face for a brief second before they return to her food. "Why would I ask that? I already know the answer."

"And what would that be?" I ask.

"That it's none of my business." She sets her fork and knife down and says, "I know where I stand in your scale of importance, Huxley. Explanation is not needed."

She pushes from the table, stands, and heads toward the stairs.

"You're not done with your dinner."

"I'm not hungry," she says as she walks up the stairs, her robe billowing away from her legs.

She's just going to leave like that?

With nothing else to say?

No fire?

No snarky comment?

No furious glance in my direction?

That won't do.

Eyes still fixed on the stairs, my mind whirls with what to do. I've never dealt with emotion when it comes to business, so I'm in uncharted territory here. But I hate to admit Breaker might be right. I need Lottie to be a solid participant in this scheme, and if she's upset, I'm not sure she'll be willing to work with me the way I need her to.

But how the fuck do I make her happy without getting too involved?

I blow out a heavy breath of frustration, and then push away from the table and charge up the stairs behind her. Not sure what I'm going to do, but I can't let her walk away like that.

She's almost to her room when I catch up to her. "You can't go to bed hungry," I say, unsure of what else to say.

"I can do whatever the hell I want," she says, a touch of that edge coming back to her voice.

That's what I wanted to hear. A snappy response. *Keep pressing, Hux.*

Reaching out, I take her hand and pull her back before she can go any farther. She whips around to face me, her expression registering shock. "What the hell do you think you're doing?" she asks, that spark in full force now.

Better.

"Reminding you who's in charge."

She attempts to yank her hand away, but instead of letting go, I lift her hand up and press it against the wall behind her.

Her eyes widen as I keep her hand held tightly above her.

"No need to remind me who's in charge. Your obscene inability to care about others is quite clear. What you say, goes."

"Is that so?" I ask, wanting to push her further, wanting to drag that personality back out. So I grip her hip with my free hand and steady her against the wall. "Then how come you're always testing me?"

"How do I test you?" she asks. Her chest heaves as it rises and falls at a more rapid rate.

"Do you consider this proper dinner attire?" I ask her, playing with the tie of her robe, gauging her reaction as something comes over me. Something...primal.

But this primal side seems to draw out her personality. It seems to breathe life back into her snarky self.

And that's what I want.

I want Lottie back.

I understand this is crossing the line—touching her, pinning her against the wall like this—but seeing her so sullen, so defeated awoke something inside of me. I don't handle situations like this well, I don't know how to cheer someone up—that's obvious from the way I'm pressing her buttons rather than showing empathy—but my brain doesn't seem to work the way it needs to.

"Wasn't aware there was a dress code for dinner." She glances at my suit pants and rolled-up dress shirt. "Was it business casual? Would you prefer it if I wore my dress instead?"

"I would prefer it if you came back downstairs and finished dinner."

"I told you I wasn't hungry," she shoots back.

Talking sternly, I say, "And I see that as an excuse to not be around me. It was business, Lottie. Nothing you need to take personally."

"Not take personally?" she retorts. "Jesus, I'm so sick of you saying that bullshit." She goes to move, but I hold her in place. "It's hard not to take everything you do personally when there's emotion attached to it for me. I can't be so black and white like you. I have feelings, Huxley."

"Then tell me what you're feeling."

Her chin lifts. "You can't handle what I'm feeling."

"Try me."

She pauses.

Studies me.

Then…

She wets her lips. "Fine. I'm mad at myself for getting involved in this mess. I'm mad that I fucked up my sister's meeting today, one that she worked hard preparing for, given the short notice. I'm furious that I don't have enough courage to tell my mom that she was right, that I never should've taken that job with Angela. I hate that my pride is more important than the truth. And most of all"—her eyes scan me up and down—"I've never despised someone as much as I despise you. I think you're cold, baseless, and have no regard for anyone but yourself. I hate that I have to rely on you, that you need to rely on me, and most importantly"—she catches her breath and her fingers curl around my hand that's pinning her arm to the wall—"I hate that I think you're even remotely attractive."

A light sheen of sweat breaks out at the nape of my neck as I feel this urge to pull her forcibly toward me.

I've seen the way she looks at me. I've noticed her wandering eyes, but she's never voiced her appreciation before.

And, fuck, it makes me feel weak. Weak enough to succumb...

"You don't need to be angry. Your sister will get another chance. I told you, the phone call was important." My tone is clipped as I watch her lips part ever so slightly, just enough to entice me.

Enough to drive me wild. Just enough to make my will slip.

"I don't believe you." Her voice is firm yet soft, and the sound of it pounds another crack into my wall.

My hand presses harder against her hip.

My thumb strokes the soft fabric of the robe.

And to my satisfaction, a low, almost inaudible moan falls past her lips.

"Karla should've already contacted your sister about setting up another meeting." The push and pull between us intensifies as my fingers itch to touch her more, to slip under her robe. "It's done. As for your guilt about not telling your mom the truth, that's on you and none of my goddamn business."

I grip her hand tighter, the one that's pinned against the wall, and when her fingers curl around mine, another part of me becomes unhinged. The need for this woman pummels me, and I can feel myself holding on by a thread.

Continuing, I say, "And your hatred for me...you should know that hatred isn't mutual."

Her piercing eyes match mine. Her voice wavers as she says, "You've only ever expressed distaste for me." But that waver in her voice doesn't match the boldness in her actions as she takes hold of my hand resting on her hip and slowly shifts it inward...

Until my fingers tangle with the tie of her robe.

Don't fucking tempt me.

I may be able to separate business and pleasure, but when the line starts to blur, when my mind feels foggy and confused, there may not be any stopping me.

And I feel confused.

I feel so goddamn foggy.

My body hums with indecision, the wrong decision pulling me closer and closer to her.

"I've expressed annoyance, frustration, irritation, but not hate. You're the one who has expressed hate." My finger toys with the silk ribbon. "I have no problem with you."

"Liar," she says.

"Why don't you trust me?"

"You haven't given me reason to," she says. Her hand glides up my chest, stopping at my shoulder, leaving a trail of heat in its wake.

My teeth roll over my bottom lip as I gently tug on the tie of her robe.

She doesn't protest.

Instead, her body moves closer to mine.

Fuck. My control is barely hanging on; it's teetering, ready to snap.

Ready to combust.

"Have I gone back on anything I've said?"

"No," she says breathlessly, her chest arching away from the wall. The movement pulls at the fabric of the robe. My eyes slide down to her chest, where the lapels of the robe dance dangerously open. Hell, what do those gorgeous tits look like bare? Are they sensitive? If I brought them into my mouth, would she moan in satisfaction?

Unable to hold back, I tug on the tie one more time, loosening one end. The small opening teases me, tempts me even further. It ignites the fire pulsing through my veins.

Fuck, what are you doing, Huxley?

Something you shouldn't be doing.

But, fuck, she's so tempting. I know there's nothing under this robe, nothing but her smooth body. I glance down at her breasts, and I'm rewarded to see her pebbled nipples rubbing against the silk of the fabric. They're so small, so goddamn sexy.

Attempting to focus on our conversation, I say, "So if I've never gone back on anything I've promised so far, why no trust?"

Her hand floats to the back of my neck, where she slowly plays with the short strands of my hair. "Because you're deceitful."

"Normally, I'm not." My fingers itch to tug on the tie one more time so the robe opens. But I hold still.

"Excuse me if I can't take your word for it."

Rolling my teeth over my lips, I ask, "Okay, so how can I prove it to you that you can trust me?"

Her eyes become heady as she removes her hand from my neck and runs it up her body, to the gape of fabric barely covering her chest. Tantalizing me, her fingers caress her cleavage. My goddamn mouth waters. "Don't go back on your promises."

"But I haven't."

Her eyes connect with mine, and she says, "Even your silent ones." Then, to my surprise, she undoes her robe, the sides fall open, exposing the centerline of her body.

Fuck.

Fuck me.

In seconds, I grow hard. But instead of walking away or mauling her, I decide to torture myself and slowly take her in, starting at her chest, where the robe hangs on to her breasts, barely covering them, tormenting me. Then my hungry eyes move down her taut stomach to her completely smooth pussy. My mouth waters from the sight of her. She's only offering a brief preview, but it's enough to drive me crazy. To push me over the goddamn edge.

She's testing me. She's seeing how far I'll go.

Little does she know...

I started this.

I was the one who pinned her against the wall.

I was the one who pulled on the tie.

And I'm the one who should finish this.

"Just what I thought," she says. "You can't follow through on what you start. Like the business meeting."

"I told you, I couldn't prevent what happened today."

"You could've. You chose not to."

My teeth grind.

"And right now, I'm standing here, almost completely naked in front of you. Isn't that what you wanted? To control me? To control my body? And instead of following through, you go still."

Is she fucking kidding me right now?

She thinks I'm all talk?

How little she knows me.

"Not still, Lottie." I step closer. "Stiff. I go fucking stiff." With that, I slide my hand onto her bare hip, continuing to keep her hand pinned above her head.

She gasps from my abrupt touch, and when I slide my hand to her backside and down that sweet ass of hers, she nibbles on her bottom lip.

"And I didn't start this," I say, even though I did. "You showed up to dinner wearing nothing but this robe."

"I showed up yesterday in a negligee. How is this different?"

I float a finger near her crack as I move my hand north, to her lower back, where I grip her tightly, pulling her close to me. "This was intentional."

"As much as you'd like to believe it, Huxley, it is not my intention to try to turn you on. It's to spend as little time with you as possible."

"Then why aren't you leaving now?" I ask, bringing my hand to the front of her body, and I smoothly drag my fingers to just above her pelvic bone. A wave of lust hits her—it's in her eyes, in the way she gently shifts, spreading her legs slightly.

"Calling your bluff," she answers. "You'd never touch me—"

"Touch you like what?" I ask as my finger slides over her aroused slit.

She sucks in a sharp breath as her head falls back to the wall and her pelvis sticks out.

"Touch you like this?" I sweep another finger, but this time I slide deeper, connecting against her clit. *Fuck. She's so soft.* "Because never underestimate what I won't do." Watching how responsive her body is to my touch, I say, "Tell me you want more."

She shakes her head. "No. I'd never give you that satisfaction."

"I see." Two can play this game. Keeping her pinned, I stare down at her smooth pussy as I bring two fingers together and slide them up and down her slit, allowing her clit to catch between them. I gently squeeze and pulse.

"Oh God," she whispers. Her head whips to the side, and her grip on my hand grows tighter.

I pulse my fingers, teasing her entrance. She spreads just a little wider for me, and I take that as an invitation. I slip one finger inside her.

Fuck yes, she's tight.

And wet.

Really fucking wet.

Moving in closer, my lips are tempted to press against her heated skin, but I refrain. This is about proving a point. This is about showing her exactly what I can do to her body with just my hand.

I drag my finger out and then smooth my thumb over her clit. She sucks in a hiss of breath as I apply more pressure and make small circular motions.

"Yes," she whispers, her hips begging for more. But I keep my touch light, allowing the gentle pressure I have on her to drive her nuts.

Slow circles.

Round and around.

Building her.

Climbing her.

Driving her crazy.

Her teeth drag over her bottom lip. Her chest heaves, her robe barely covering her tits now. Any sharp movement and I'll see all of her. And the grip she has on me, on my hand, is so tight that there might be bruises in the morning.

But it'll be worth it.

Because watching her like this—submitting to me, letting me touch her, bring her to her peak—it's all fucking worth it.

"More," she whispers. "Give me more."

Just what I wanted to fucking hear. I release her hand, and before she can protest, I turn her around so she's facing the wall, both hands splayed out as her cheek lands lightly against the white surface. From behind, I cup her pussy and pull her ass against my crotch so she can feel how hard I am.

Her raspy gasp brings me pleasure as I slide my finger across her clit again and again.

"Do you hate me right now?" I ask her, toying with the little nub, making her entire body tremble against mine.

"More now than ever."

"Because I know how to bring you pleasure?" I ask, my lips pressing against her ear.

"Yes." I slide two fingers inside her now. She lets out a low moan.

"You wish that I wasn't fucking you with my fingers right now?"

I start to pull them out but she lets out a protest. "No, I do."

"You do, what?" I ask, my cock so goddamn hard that it's pressing painfully against the zipper of my pants.

"Fuck me. I want you to fuck me."

With my other hand, I smooth up the column of her neck and tilt her head back so I'm talking directly into her ear. "So, you hate me, but you want to fuck me." My thumb presses down on her clit, and she lets out a strangled gasp. "How close are you?"

"Close," she whispers, her body shaking under my hold. "So close."

"Good," I say, just before removing my hand from her pussy.

"Wh-what are you doing?" Her confused gasp gives me great pleasure.

"Why should I give you an orgasm, Lottie? Why should I finish you off?"

"Because you're a bastard if you don't." Her palms flatten against the wall as her head bends forward. Every muscle, every fiber of her being is tense.

I work my finger over her clit again, watching carefully as she tenses more, her back arching. I want to bring her to the edge, to the point where she's about to fall over. "You already think I'm a bastard, so what does it matter? You think the worst of me, Lottie. If I let you come, you will still think the worst about me."

"But at least I'll know you can command my body. And isn't that what you want? Control?"

She knows how to talk to me, she knows what I like to hear, and that's scary. Because, yes, I do want control. I want her to lay her eyes on me and heat up. I want her to crave me when I walk into the room. And I know I shouldn't, I know this is strictly business, but she unleashed something inside me tonight. And now I feel...desperate.

"Tell me." I pinch her clit, evoking a loud moan from her. "When I walk into the room, does your body heat up?"

She doesn't answer right away but takes a second to catch her breath. "No," she finally says.

Pressing my entire body against hers, I ask, "Why the hell not?"

"Because," she gasps as I rub her clit between my fingers. "Fuck," she mutters, her breath heavy. "Because I don't know how...how hard you can make me come."

"Is that a challenge?" I ask her, releasing her clit and causing her to nearly collapse against my chest. Her entire body shakes, and I know she's right where I want her to be. She's right where I need her.

"It's a request," she says, her voice so full of vulnerability that my idea of edging her to her orgasm and leaving her there to finish herself off slips from my mind. Although I'd love to see her beg, plead, and then storm off in anger—knowing she'll use one of those vibrators to make herself come—I want her to know that she's right, that I do command her body.

I move my hand back to her pussy, but I just cup her, making sure to keep my hand still despite the way she shakes beneath me.

"Listen to me, Lottie." When she doesn't acknowledge me, I grip her tighter. "Are you listening?"

"Yes," she answers breathlessly.

"I wasn't going to let you come, I was going to edge you out until you were crying, begging for more, but your lack of trust or even regard for me is disconcerting." I press my lips right against her ear as I start to pulse my finger over her clit. "I'm a good man. You might not see it now, but you will."

"This won't change anything," she says.

"That's a bold-faced lie," I say as her legs tighten around my hand and her body stiffens even more. "This will change everything. You might still hate me, you might still not want to look at me, but you'll damn well know you fucking crave me."

I apply more pressure and move faster and faster until she clamps around me and moans against the wall as her pelvis rocks across my finger. She comes.

And she comes hard. My hand is soaked by her arousal, and she grinds against me, her moans muffled by the wall. She rides out her orgasm and every spasm until there's nothing left inside of her to give.

I pull my hand away and spin her back around, planting her back against the wall. I tilt her chin up so her eyes meet mine, and that's when I drag my finger that was just teasing her pussy across my tongue. Her eyes turn heady as she watches me taste every last inch of my fingers.

"You're fucking delicious." I reach for the sash of her robe and tie the two ends together, closing off the view of her delectable body. "If Karla doesn't set up another appointment with your sister, let me know. I'll make sure her pitch is heard." I cup her cheek, studying those mesmerizing eyes of hers. "Have a good night, Lottie."

Still hungry—*now for the fucking incredible taste of her*—I release her and return to the dining room. I can smell her on my fingers. On my hand. I can taste her on my tongue. As if she's still millimeters from my lips. And I want to taste her some more. I want to fuck her against that wall.

She's. Not. For. You.

My mind races with what she might be thinking. *Does she want me? Does she still hate me?*

Do I still want her to hate me?

CHAPTER 12
LOTTIE

TAKING A DEEP BREATH, I knock on Kelsey's door.

Coffee and donuts are in hand as I wait nervously outside.

I didn't text her last night, I didn't even bother contacting her, because I know how my sister works. When she gets mad, she needs time, and she needs space. I'm hoping a night away was all she needed, because, Jesus Christ, I need someone to talk to.

I need someone bad.

After what happened in the hallway with Huxley, I need to get it off my chest, and Kelsey is the only one who knows what's actually going on in my life.

Last night, I felt...defeated. I felt as though I let down my entire family, and the last thing I wanted to do was have dinner with Huxley. I knew if I didn't show up, he'd make a big deal about it, so I did the absolute minimum. And then I left. I didn't think he'd chase after me, and I certainly didn't think he'd attempt to take off my robe, let alone make me come all over his fingers. I'm not really sure if wearing the robe had been to tease him, if I'm honest.

I nibble on my bottom lip, still thinking about the way his strong, commanding voice felt right up against my ear, how his hand felt so large on my body, how desperately I wanted his lips to trail up my neck and across my jaw.

I truly do hate the man, there's no question about that, but, oh my

God, is he hot. He knows exactly how to use his voice, his body, in a way that will make anyone fall at his feet—me included.

And that orgasm...Christ. It was with just his fingers, and yet, it felt as though he attacked me in a way I can't even describe. I felt as if I were under a spell and the only way to snap out of it was with an orgasm. And that orgasm delivered. It was so good, so satisfying that I was still turned on when I went back into my room, and I had to ride it out on Thor one more time with the memory of Huxley's dominant voice playing over and over in my head.

But what's really rocking my world is not only what he said after, but the way he said it to me. Gently, holding my chin so I was forced to look him in the eyes, he made sure I understood that he'd take care of my sister. That he'd make sure she was heard.

When he left, I stood there, stunned.

There was no harsh tone, there was no sarcastic jab; it was as if I was back in Chipotle, talking to the man I first met. It was confusing. It's why I need Kelsey to forgive me and open this door.

Impatiently I shift my feet until the door unlocks, and I hold my breath. Kelsey appears on the other side, but instead of wearing her usual boss-lady attire, she's in a pair of cotton shorts and a tank top.

Oh God, what happened?

I swallow hard, smile, and hold up the coffee and donuts. "I'm sorry."

She eyes the items in my hand and then opens the door more to let me in.

Step one complete: I'm inside the apartment. I go to the kitchen, grab plates, and set everything out on her dining table. She takes a seat across from me, pulling one of her legs against her chest, and watches as I carefully take out each donut, put it on a platter between us, set the bag on the ground, and then hand her the coffee I know she loves—a house blend with frothed milk and a splash of caramel. She takes a sip, and I hold up the plate, which bears a giant bear claw, an apple fritter, a maple Long

John, and of course, the classic Boston cream. As predicted, she picks up the apple fritter, and I go for the Boston cream.

"I'm really sorry, Kels. Yesterday wasn't my best showing, but I promise, it won't happen again. I worked all day on the website, and I have some things to show you, some things I think you'll—"

"Karla called."

I pause. Why do I know that name? Karla…Karla…

"Huxley's assistant," she offers.

"Oh…OH! She did? Huxley said she would. Did she set up another meeting time?"

Kelsey nods. "She did. This Friday at three. We have more time to prepare, which is nice. We can come up with a great presentation now, fine-tune everything."

"That's great," I say, feeling excited. But I'm sensing Kelsey isn't as excited as me. "What's wrong? That's great, right?"

"It's wonderful."

"Then why is your tone of voice not matching your excitement?"

She sets her coffee down and asks, "Do you know why Huxley left that meeting?"

I shake my head. "He didn't say why, just that it was important. Oh God, was it not important?" I lean forward. "Figures he'd go and lie about something like that."

"He wasn't lying," Kelsey says. "It was important. One of their properties in New York City had an electrical fire. Two men had third-degree burns, others some smoke inhalation."

"Oh…God, really?" I ask, feeling myself shrink into an incredibly small version of myself. He wasn't lying. He'd been needed for something critical. Essential.

"Yes. Karla apologized for taking so long to get back to me with rescheduling, because she and Huxley spent the rest of the day on the phone making arrangements for not only the victims themselves but also the families of the victims." Kelsey leans forward and says, "Apparently he personally called every one of them. Then he sent their favorite meals to the hospital and to the families."

I blink a few times, attempting to comprehend what Kelsey's telling me. "He...he did?"

She nods. "Yes, he did." She picks up her donut. "Do you know why I'm telling you this?"

"To make me feel like an asshole?"

She shakes her head. "No, I'm telling you this so you can lighten up around him. He's a good guy. There might have been some headbutting between the two of you, but at some point, you need to let that go. He's helping you, he's helping us, and that's something you need to be grateful for. Yesterday should've never happened. You know I love you, but it was completely unprofessional. There's no way you'd have done something like that if you were still working for Angela."

I stare down at my untouched donut and swipe at the frosting with my finger. "You're right. I never would've acted that way in front of Angela or in front of prospective clients." I've had a lot of time to think about my reactions throughout the night...*well, before the orgasm, of course.* And when I considered *objectively* how insanely ridiculous and unprofessional my behavior was, I was more than mortified. My wish had been to put my studies to use, to help Kelsey grow her business to the next level. All I could attribute my behavior to was shock. Misplaced anger. *Immaturity.*

"I think I've built this whole situation up in my head, and instead of breathing in a deep breath and taking everything thrown my way one step at a time, I'm reacting without thought." I sigh and lean back into the chair. "I hate to throw out excuses, but this whole thing with getting fired...I think it's fucking with my head. Instead of giving myself time to mourn, I'm taking out my anger on everyone around me, Huxley included."

Kelsey nods. "That makes sense. You've been rather...edgy lately."

I smirk. "I'm always edgy. How about more irritable?"

"Okay, I'll give you that."

I reach across the table and take her hand in mine. "I'm really sorry, Kels. I promise, from here on out, it'll be nothing but professionalism from me. Okay?"

"Okay." She takes a bite of her donut. "Now show me what you've done with the website."

"After I take down this donut. I didn't eat dinner last night and I'm famished."

"Wait, so we can sell the sustainable products straight from our website?" Kelsey asks as we both hunker down at her computer, staring at the screen.

"Yes. I just have to install this app, and we can convert all sales through the website. Mind you, we won't make a huge profit, but it'll be nice supplemental income while clients get the chance to browse the products we work with. And we can sort it by how you'd use each product, so bathroom storage, pantry, etcetera."

"This is great." Kelsey sits back. "Would we purchase the product wholesale?"

I shake my head. "No, I sent an email to your supplier yesterday asking if we could set up a contract where we not only use their product for every project we do, but we also become an official supplier. I explained that we have some major projects in the works and want to make sure we have a solid product base to turn to."

"Seriously?"

I nod. "And I know it's a small percentage, but I said if we land this big client we've been talking to, we would like to start talks about our own product line."

"Stop," Kelsey says, grabbing my hand. "Our own line?"

I grin from ear to ear. "Yup. Mind you, it's a pipe dream, but I wanted them to know that we were going places, and they're our first option when it comes to partnering up."

Kelsey waves her hand in front of her face. "I'm sweating. I'm legit sweating." She faces me. "Lottie, this is huge. Holy crap, where did this all come from?"

"Well, when you feel like a failure, it's a nice swift kick in the ass to get moving, and that's what I did. I got moving."

"Wow, Lottie. I'm really impressed." Whispering, she asks, "Have they written back?"

I chuckle. "Not yet, but I did send it late last night, and it's only ten in the morning."

"True." She sighs. "Wow, wow, wow, I'm really impressed. Impressed and grateful. Thank you for working hard on all of this."

"I'm invested just as much as you are in this business. I've seen you bring it to where it is today, but I know there's so much more potential, and when I take my head out of my ass, I know I can really help build it."

With a chuckle, she asks, "How were things when you got back to his place?"

I shut the laptop and lean back in my chair. "I'm not sure you're ready for this story."

She crosses her legs and rubs her hands together. "Oh, I don't think I've ever been more ready."

And this is what I love about Kelsey. We can have a fight, resolve it, and then just like that, we're back to our normal selves. We don't harp on disagreements; we don't drag them out. We apologize, and we move on. Another reason why I think, in the long run, we'll be great business partners, because we'll be able to read each other well. *But that doesn't mean I'm not incredibly thankful for the second chance.*

"So, when I got home, I was obviously in a really sour mood. I got straight to work and buried myself in the computer. Before I knew it, it was getting late, and I needed to take a second to relax, so I drew a bath."

"Oh, I'm sure he has a really nice bathtub."

"Really nice. Jets and everything. And bath bombs. I dropped a lavender one in the water to calm me. It was really nice."

"But…"

I smirk. "But he texted that dinner was ready just as I was starting to release tension."

"And let me guess, he expects you at dinner."

"The show must go on," I say. "Because I was lazy, I dried off quickly and then just threw on a robe, making sure it was properly cinched at the waist."

Her brow raises in suspicion. "Just a robe, nothing under it?"

I shake my head.

"Girl, were you asking for trouble?"

"I was just trying not to have a moment in front of him after everything that happened. I didn't put much thought into what I was dressed in, and believe me, I was more covered up than the night before. The robe was a step up."

"Okay, so you show up to dinner in a robe. Was he aware nothing was on underneath?"

"It's as if he has X-ray vision. I swear he sees everything. Anyway, we started getting into it again, because that's what we seem to do."

"Naturally, both of you like to be correct, both of you like to be in control. Sparks will fly when personalities clash."

"Boy did they clash." I think back to last night, and it feels like a black hole in my head. "I can't really tell you what we were fighting about. I know I was quiet, and he didn't seem to like that. So he provoked me. I told him I didn't trust him, I think." I tap my chin and then shake my head. "All I know is that I couldn't sit at the table with him any longer, so I got up and went back to my room."

"Oooo, I bet he didn't like that."

"He didn't, and he made it known."

184 | MEGHAN QUINN

"Did he send you a nasty text?"

I shake my head. "Worse. He came after me."

Kelsey sits taller. "Oh, tell me more."

Getting into the storytelling, I say, "I was inches from reaching my room when he snagged my hand from behind. And before I knew it, I was pinned against the wall."

Kelsey gasps, hand to her chest. "Like...in a sexual way?"

I slowly nod.

"Lottie, what the hell did you do?"

"I did absolutely nothing. He was the one doing all the things."

Kelsey nibbles on her thumb. "What kind of things?"

"He tugged my robe open."

"He did not." Her eyes widen and then she whispers, "Did he?"

"He did. But it never fell open, just was undone...undone enough for him to, uh, you know...lower his hand."

Kelsey slaps the table. "Stop, he did not. He...he...fingered you?"

I nod. "Yup. He did."

Hands by her head, Kelsey pretends her head is exploding. "You went from fighting, at each other's throats, to him touching you in the hallway. How the hell does that even work?"

"I don't know, and for the life of me, I couldn't stop it. I didn't want to stop it. I wanted him to keep doing what he was doing, and I wanted it to last all night." I cover my forehead with my hand. "God, Kelsey, am I a whore?"

She laughs. "No. You aren't a whore, but you are confusing, that's for sure. I never would've thought you were interested in doing something like that with him. Not with the way you two seem to hate each other."

"He said I hate him, but he doesn't hate me. But I guess even if I think he's an asshole, I still want his fingers inside me." I shrug. "I'm pretty sure that means I'm fucked in the head."

"They always say there's a thin line between love and hate."

"Oh no, don't start with that. There's no love involved. Lust…yes. The man is a dream, I'm not going to deny that. From the way he talks with such a filthy mouth, to his strong hold, to the domineering stance of his body and how he uses it to his advantage…yeah, everything about him screams 'amazing, drop-everything-you're-doing, ear-piercing sex.'"

"One look at him, and I'd believe that. And his brothers."

"Makes you wonder what their parents are like."

"Ooo, imagine an older man that looks just like them. A man in his sixties, salt-and-pepper hair, slaps you on the ass when you're naughty."

I cock an eyebrow. "Excuse me? Is this some sort of fantasy you've never told me about?"

"Old guys can be hot, too."

"Sixties…that could be our dad."

"I never judge. Love is love. Lust is lust. As long as everyone gives consent, let people live."

"Okay." I chuckle. "That's fair."

"So…did he finish you off?"

I bite my bottom lip and nod. "He did, and it was explosive. Kelsey, I've never had an O like that before. I was shaking after, and I know this is TMI, but when I went back in my room, I had to get off again because I was so geared up from having him that close, touching me, talking to me. It was too much."

"I can imagine. I can't remember the last time I even kissed a man, let alone have someone do that."

Feeling slightly awkward, I say, "He sucked his fingers after."

"Stahp!" Kelsey yells and clutches her chest. "Oh my fuck."

"I know." I cover my eyes. "It was easily the hottest thing I've ever seen. And then he grabbed me by the chin, forced me to look at him, and told me that he promised you'd get your chance to pitch the business. In that moment, when he was speaking to me, it felt as if he was the same guy I went to Chipotle with. He wasn't an asshole; he wasn't provoking me;

he was just being normal, sincere." *Likable.* I look Kelsey in the eyes. "It confused me."

"Confused you how…? Like you might be feeling differently about him?"

I look away. "I mean…maybe. But just differently in the way that maybe I don't hate him as much. I still think he's an asshole, and I think one wrong thing he says to me will set me off, but that gesture…smoothed out some of the rough edges, if that makes sense."

"It does." My phone beeps and I snag it from the table as Kelsey continues. "See? Maybe there's a chance for you two. Maybe you'll have a proper working relationship."

"Maybe," I say as I see a text from Huxley. "Speak of the devil. He just texted me."

I open the message and read it.

Huxley: Are you at your sister's?

"He wants to know if I'm here with you." I text back.

Lottie: Yes.

He's quick on the trigger, and the dots appear right before his text message.

Huxley: I'm sending a car to get you. What are you wearing?

Lottie: Leggings and a crop top that was provided in my approved wardrobe. Do I need to borrow something from Kelsey?

Huxley: No. See you in fifteen.

"What's going on?" Kelsey asks.

"I have no idea. He said he'll see me in fifteen minutes. Something with Dave and Ellie probably. I feel like if he's going to spring these things on me, I need more context so I can prepare."

"Agreed. Ask him what's going on."

I shoot him another text.

Lottie: Can I have some idea about what we'll be doing?
Huxley: Lamaze class. Hope you're good at breathing.

"Oh shit."

"What?" Kelsey asks.

I look up at her. "Lamaze class."

She snorts and covers her nose. "To be a fly on the wall."

I take a seat in Huxley's car and turn toward him as I buckle my seat belt.

"What on earth—"

"Hey, baby," Huxley says, leaning over to kiss me on the cheek. "How's your sister doing?"

Oh yeah…there's someone driving us. Act like the fiancée. When in doubt, from now on, always act like the fiancée.

"She's good," I say in a cheery voice. "Excited about Friday." Wanting to get some information about what the hell we're doing, I say, "This is an unexpected surprise."

"I know how much you like surprises," Huxley says and then turns to his phone.

Okay, so I guess that's that.

I'm about to say something else to him, just to keep the conversation flowing so we don't look like a lame couple, when my phone buzzes in my hand with a text. I glance down and see Huxley's name on the screen.

Ooo, secret communications.

Huxley: This will be your first pregnancy class. You're going just to try it out, and then we'll get ice cream with Ellie and Dave after.

I'm glad he's handing out information. The more I can prepare, the better.

Lottie: Can I ask how you got us wrangled into a pregnancy class?
Huxley: Ran into Dave at the coffee shop this morning. He told me he and Ellie were going to a class. I asked him which one and said we were thinking about taking that one. He told us to join and get ice cream after.
Lottie: What class was it?
Huxley: No fucking idea.

I chuckle and text him back.

Lottie: How do you know it's good?
Huxley: I don't. But I know since we have no clue what the fuck we're doing, it'll be good enough.
Lottie: Isn't it a little early for a pregnancy class for me?
Huxley: Hell if I know. If anyone asks, just say we love education.
Lottie: How eloquent.
Huxley: Ask me a question, we've been too quiet on this ride.
Lottie: Uh…what did you have for breakfast?
Huxley: Jesus Christ. Out loud. Ask me a question out loud.

"Oh," I say quietly and then chuckle. Facing Huxley, I ask, "How's your rash doing?"

His eyes narrow and I have to hold back the straight-up outburst of laughter that threatens to slip past my lips.

"Rash is fine," he answers through clenched teeth. "But now that you bring it up, is your yeast infection improving?"

Ohhh, he plays dirty.

"Faring well," I answer. "Doctor said no sex for a week, though, but don't worry, I won't back out on my promise. I know how much you want to try out my vibrators." A smirk crosses my lips. I find this far too entertaining. I pat him on the cheek. "I can grind your gears tonight, when we get home. You can light that lovemaking candle you enjoy so much."

His nostrils flare, and I cover my mouth, protecting myself from an outburst.

"Sounds good to me. I know watching me come turns you on, but if you could refrain from sounding like a barnyard animal while I come, that would be great. The mooing is a weird habit you've picked up."

"That was one time," I say in defense. "And it's because I watched that documentary on animals reproducing."

"One time is enough," he says, turning back to his phone. His fingers fly across the screen.

My phone buzzes.

Huxley: You realize I'm going to have to find a new driver now.

A hiccup of laughter pops out of me. This is the Huxley from Chipotle, from the sidewalk. This is the side of him I appreciate. The side of him I wish he would show way more often, because if he did, I'm certain we'd be friends.

Lottie: I'm pretty sure this conversation made my year. Also, I can run by the pharmacy tomorrow if you need more cream for your rash.

Huxley: If that's how you want to play this, it's on, Lottie. And remember, I'm relentless.

Lottie: I think you've met your match, Huxley Cane.

CHAPTER 13
HUXLEY

"HUXLEY, LOTTIE, OVER HERE," ELLIE says, waving her hand while she balances on an exercise ball.

I squeeze Lottie's hand and guide her over to the jubilant pregnant woman.

I was worried I'd be encroaching on Lottie's day with this request. I wasn't sure what she was doing, but she didn't seem to mind. She actually seems to be in good spirits today, which is throwing me off. Still has an edge to her, but it seems as though that edge has been smoothed out—slightly.

Lottie turns distinctively into my shoulder and whispers, "She looks as if she just busted out of the insane asylum."

I chuckle and assess Ellie. Bouncing far too high on the ball, wearing leggings and a sports bra, her hair swishing back and forth, while a giant unfaltering grin is plastered to her face. Lottie isn't wrong.

Just then, Dave comes up behind Ellie and settles her down with his hands to her shoulders. He spots me and waves. "So glad you guys could make it."

We walk up to them, and Ellie immediately takes Lottie into a hug while Dave gives me a firm handshake.

"You will absolutely love Heaven," Ellie says. "She's the best in the business."

"Heaven?" Lottie asks, confused.

I place my hand on Lottie's lower back and say, "The prenatal teacher. Remember I was telling you about her in the car?"

I told her nothing. Because her text, *I think you've met your match,* inspired me. Rather than discussing today's outing, I went into great detail about how if she'd actually attend the pedicures I'd set up for her, her crusty feet wouldn't scrape across our beautiful hardwood floors. And the murderous look on Lottie's face when I said we had to get a contractor to come in and check out a spot on the floor where she'd left a gash was priceless.

"Oh yes, sorry." She taps her head. "Pregnancy brain." Turning to Ellie, she asks, "You're sure it's not too early for us to do something like this?"

Ellie waves off Lottie's concerns. "I think the more you can learn and practice the better."

"That's what I told her in the car," I say.

Lottie adds, "We do love education, don't we, Hux?"

I look down at her. "We do. We really love education."

"Then you're in the right spot," Dave says. "Pull up a yoga mat, a ball, and one of those pillows. We should be getting started soon."

"Great."

I head toward the wall when Lottie takes my hand in hers, reminding me to be affectionate in the moment. Together we work our way to the wall where all of the "supplies" are. Out of earshot, she whispers, "What the hell are we supposed to do with an exercise ball, yoga mat, and pillows? I'm not very bendy, Huxley. I'm very stiff, and when I squat, my knees crack. I might be twenty-eight, but my body acts like a seventy-five-year-old arthritic woman's."

"I don't think there's a lot of bending in this class."

"Have you been to one of these before?"

I give her a look. "Do you think I've been to one of these before?"

She shrugs. "I don't know what you do in your spare time."

"Not this," I almost hiss. I really need to start thinking before I react to situations, aka, don't say yes to everything Dave asks. "I don't think we're going to be required to be professionals. This is our first time."

"What if we have to imitate sexual positions?" She glances behind her back.

"Why the fuck would we have to do that?"

"I don't know," she whispers. "We're in LA, and we're in a birthing class. They like granola things here. Hip and trendy things. What if this class isn't about breathing but more about the journey, the process? You know, we did this whole story on Angeloop where they talked about unique birthing classes and how you had to share your entire journey with the class. What if this is one of those?"

"We barely have a journey. You're what, six weeks pregnant?"

Her eyes widen. "I don't know, am I? I don't remember what I said."

"Jesus Christ." I drag my hand over my face.

"Everything okay over there?" Dave asks. "Need help?"

"We're good," I say with a smile, while waving to him. I turn back to Lottie and say, "I think you said you were eight weeks pregnant."

"Are you sure?"

"No," I answer. "But it feels familiar."

"You're the brains of this operation; you're supposed to catalogue these things," she hisses at me. "What kind of mom am I going to look like if I can't even remember how many weeks this little cashew in my belly is?" She pats her flat stomach.

"Then you should've remembered what you said."

Her eyes narrow. "Excuse me for being put on the spot and not remembering. I'll have you know, I often black out in stressful situations, so...good luck with that."

"Great," I mutter and then reach for a pillow. The easy camaraderie from the car is quickly evaporating between us. "Maybe avoid the question if asked."

"You know the teacher is going to ask, everyone asks. Even when they're not supposed to ask, they ask. It's a common pregnancy small-talk specialty. 'Oh, hey, Judy, you're pregnant, look at that. How many weeks are you?' 'Thanks, Carolyn, yeah, this little banana in my belly is thirty-two weeks.'"

"Thirty-two weeks is a banana?"

"I have no freaking clue, Huxley, that was me babbling."

"Well, for the love of God, don't babble."

With a smile on her face, because Ellie is starting to move toward us, Lottie says, "Babbling is what you get for plucking an amateur off the streets."

"Are you two nervous?" Ellie asks when she reaches us. She places her hand on Lottie's arm in a comforting way. "I get it. I was nervous our first time, too. It can be embarrassing, having to do all of these things in front of people, but I promise, you're in a safe zone. And starting when you're only eight weeks pregnant gives you more and more time to be comfortable." She takes a ball from the ball rack and says, "I'll bring this over for you two."

When Ellie is out of earshot, Lottie turns toward me and says, "Thanks to the modern-day Stepford wife, we now know I'm eight weeks pregnant." She lets out a deep breath. "And what the hell kind of *things* are we going to have to do in front of people?"

"I don't know," I say, eyeing the people in the circle. "Can't be that bad, right?"

"Deep breath in and…deep breath out. That's it, and when you're ready, start to lightly pulse into your partner." Lottie is beneath me, legs spread wide as can be, eyes a dangerous shade of bloodshed as she holds on to her knees and I press my jean-clad crotch against her pussy. "Connecting to that moment of conception will bring you closer and closer to the little seedling growing inside of you. Remember that night, the way you felt. Was it passionate? Was it seductive? What was involved? If you're currently in the phases of trying to get pregnant, think about connecting with your partner. Eye contact. Always keep eye contact."

Mouthing to me, Lottie says, "I want to die."

I mouth back, "Right there with you."

As we found out quickly, this is a class for everyone, not just people who are pregnant, but those who are trying as well. It's not Lamaze, per se, it's about learning to connect with your body and your partner, hence the sexual position I'm currently in.

"Dave, such a beautiful rhythm, and your eye contact with Ellie...I can feel your passion building up, your loins stirring as you prepare to give her your seed."

Lottie bites down on her bottom lip as she attempts to keep it together.

"Such a beautiful image, Dave. Now, Ellie, please, with your head thrown back in passion, there has to be something you're doing with your hands. Are you caressing your breasts? Reaching for Dave? The more you evolve this moment into the real thing, the more you will open your flower and receive all the love Dave has to give."

Lottie whispers, "I'm going to throw up."

Strained, I reply, "Shut the fuck up and look as if you're enjoying my pulsing."

"But I'm not. Your pulsing is anything but enjoyable."

"Not what you said last night."

Her eyes narrow. "You finger-fucked me, not *pulsed* with your pelvis. It's different."

I swallow wrong and start coughing, which of course brings the instructor's attention to us. The jangling bracelets on her wrists announce her approach and I wince as I see her clogs come into view. Fuck.

"Our newest couple, Hanley and Lonnie. Now, you look uncomfortable."

First of all, it's Huxley and Lottie.

Second of all, we weren't prepared for a goddamn orgy when coming to this class.

Third of all, yeah, we're uncomfortable, because we've never conceived or attempted to, for fuck's sake.

But I don't say that. Instead, I smile and say, "I think we were drunk the night we conceived."

"It's why it took him so long to get it up," Lottie says, and when I shoot her a scowl, she grins up at me.

"It didn't take long—never takes long with her," I say as I squeeze her sides, reminding her who we're pulsing next to.

"Oh, a drunken night of debauchery. One of my favorite couplings, because nothing is off the table, right? Even going bareback, which I'm assuming is what happened?"

Kill.

Me.

Now.

"Yup," Lottie says. "Totally. We'd been fornicating for quite some time before that, but all it took was one drunken night of Catch Phrase in the backyard with friends, and we were toast. Bumbling up the stairs, we made it all the way to our room completely clothed, and then, *bam*, I turned around and there was Huxley, standing naked, in all his glory. One look at his erection, and I knew what I wanted. I remember saying, 'Screw condoms,' and I threw them out the window before jumping this man. The lovely pool boy found them in the pool the next day. Said he had never fished out condoms before. He's a nice lad."

She's babbling. Jesus Christ, she's babbling.

"Oh, so you jumped him, then?" Heaven asks.

"Yes."

There's no point in stopping her.

"Therefore, would this have been the position you were in?"

"Actually, no," Lottie says. "This isn't the position we were in. I love being on top."

Heaven laughs. "Well, that's why this is awkward, because we aren't thinking back to the actual day of conception. If you're not recreating it properly, then we aren't connecting with our baby." She motions at us with her hands. "Please, please, get up and try again. Really jump back to that night."

"Should I get drunk?" I ask.

Heaven laughs again. "Wouldn't that be a gas?"

Yes, it fucking would.

I roll to my back and rest my head on the pillow, while Lottie climbs on top of me, connecting her center to mine.

"I can already tell this is more comfortable for the both of you." Heaven gets down on her knees and settles right next to us. The other couples are still pulsing, talking to each other—*connecting*—and I can't help wonder, *How the fuck is Dave okay with this?* Not just okay, but a very active participant. Some might say the teacher's pet. "Hanley, walk me through what you remember. Was she topless?"

So we're doing this... step-by-step with the instructor?

Christ.

"Uh, yeah. She was completely naked."

"Good. Good. And when you look up at her like this, her breasts bouncing in front of you, her nipples hard with arousal, would you say it's in that moment where your loins knew you'd be impregnating her?"

Uh...what?

"I, uh, I really wasn't thinking about getting her pregnant. It wasn't planned."

"Oh, I see." Heaven nods. "So, purely a night of passion. That is something for the ages." Moving in closer, she takes Lottie's hands and puts one in her hair and the other on her breast. Then she assists Lottie by gripping

her hips and moving her over my cock. *Whoa, slow down there.* "Would you say this feels familiar?"

"Yes," Lottie says. "Very familiar." Her hips grind down on mine, and she nibbles her bottom lip as I watch her fingers glide over her hard nipple.

Fuck.

FUCK!

There's no way in hell I'm about to get hard at a stupid pregnancy class with Dave right next to me.

But Lottie is making that a difficult task, especially since she's wearing that crop top and I can see peeks of her bare skin, the same bare skin I touched and caressed last night.

"Hanley, I need you to be in the moment. You're thinking too much. Pretend no one is here besides you and Lonnie." Hard to do that with a mother hen yapping in my ear. "Watch the way Lonnie's body undulates against yours. The passion in her expression, the way her fingers glide over her breasts, tug on her hair."

Jesus, this isn't helping at all.

My body tenses, my shoulders practically kissing my ears, and my hands fall to her thighs, trying to get her to slow down so I can catch my breath.

"That's it," Heaven says. "Just like that, Lonnie, keep pace." Slowly, Heaven backs away and moves toward the center of the group. "Don't falter, Lonnie; keep moving as you are."

Lottie nods and then glances down at me. "Trying not to get hard?"

"You're full of yourself," I whisper.

"After last night, I'd have a hard time believing this right here isn't getting you hard." She continues her pace.

"I'm not a teenager. I know how to control myself."

"Okay," she says, then takes her hand that was in her hair and places it on my lower stomach. The shift in position angles her just enough to allow for better friction. She picks up the pace and grinds down on me after lifting, hitting my cock in just the right spot. A wave of heat spikes through me as my cock starts to stir.

My jaw clenches down, I try to attempt to blur her out, to not make eye contact, but every time she angles up, I catch a glimpse of the lacy, dark green bralette she's wearing, and that's not helping the cause.

"I don't remember our conception," Lottie says and makes eye contact with me. "But I sure as hell remember last night and how hard you made me come."

Fuck.

I'm gone and she knows it, because she grins as she drives against me.

"Mmm, having your fingers deep inside me like that." She wets her lips. "I wanted more." She leans forward and, looking me dead in the eyes, she says, "I got off again with my vibrator, because that's how much you turned me on."

Fucking hell. My cock swells beneath her, and a satisfied smile crosses her face.

"There you are. Payback is a bitch, *Hanley.*"

I grind my teeth together, my cock begging for more from her.

"Remember that, because this isn't over," I say while she continues to pulse over me, making me harder and harder until…

"Okay, let's get into another position." Heaven claps her hands.

The tension in the room is palpable, and as everyone disengages from their partners, I realize very quickly from the shift in the room, I'm not the only one turned on.

But it's the sight to my left that really has me rethinking all of my decisions. Standing tall and proud, hands on his hips, is Dave, with a massive erection poking against his pants.

Jesus. Christ.

An image I know I'll never get out of my head.

Nope, Dave is apparently claiming his territory, letting everyone in the room know…he's the boner champ.

I don't know if I should clap, act horrified, or go wash my eyes out with bleach when I get home.

Most likely...the latter.

Huxley: I saw Dave's boner.

Breaker: Uhh...what?

JP: Please tell me you aren't the one who gave him a boner. I'm all about doing whatever it takes, but, man...come on.

Huxley: All I have to say is pregnancy class gone wrong. We had to simulate procreating. There was pulsing.

Breaker: You and Dave had to pretend to procreate? Dear fuck, who was pulsing?

JP: My guess is Dave was pulsing into Hux.

Huxley: No, JESUS. We were practicing with our respective pregnant women.

Breaker: Ohhh...does that mean you pulsed into Lottie?

JP: Things just got interesting.

Breaker: Uh, Dave having a boner is what made things interesting.

JP: Wait...did you have a boner, Hux?

Breaker: ^^^ This. Please answer this.

Huxley: I was fine until she climbed on top of me, gripped her tits, and dry humped me.

Breaker: Holy fuck.

JP: This was a class? Sounds more like a good time. Where can I sign up?

Huxley: You have serious issues.

JP: Says the guy who was boning out during a pregnancy class next to a colleague.

Huxley: You weren't there. You don't know.

Breaker: Did you at least congratulate Dave on his boner?

Huxley: When does a guy ever congratulate another guy on his boner?

Breaker: Might be something nice to do. A solid pat on the back and then a compliment. "Nice bone, man."

Huxley: Fuck knows why I talk to you two.

———

"What a wonderful class, don't you think?" Ellie asks as she licks her mint chocolate chip ice cream in a large waffle cone.

"Oh, quite lovely," Lottie responds, even though I know her voice is full of sarcasm.

That was not a lovely fucking class. That was a nightmare, for many reasons.

"Isn't Heaven a wonderful instructor?" Dave asks me. "She really helps me connect on another level. Ellie and I are so much stronger in our relationship because of Heaven."

"Yeah." I scoot in closer to Lottie, my hand on the back of her chair as we share an ice cream cone. And when I say *share*, I mean she's eating the entire thing by herself. "Heaven was great. She made me think of things I've never considered before." Truth. Heaven definitely brought me to a new level.

"Do you think you'll continue with the class?" Ellie asks, so hopeful.

"Depends on Lottie's schedule," I answer. "She has a start-up business with her sister, so her time is limited."

"Really?" Dave asks, looking interested. "What's the—" He looks down at his phone, which buzzes on the table. "Crap." With a sorrowful look, he says, "That's Gregory. He's been wanting to do a walk-through of one of our properties, and I told him to text me when he's ready. Unfortunately, I have to cut this ice cream date short."

"Totally understand," I say, offering him a wave. "We should probably get going soon as well. After we finish this ice cream, of course."

Dave stands and helps Ellie out of her chair. "Yes, enjoy the sunny day. Hopefully we'll run into you again soon."

"I'd love that," Ellie coos. "Just love you two."

Together, hand in hand, they say their goodbyes, and then they take off toward their parked car.

Instead of releasing myself from Lottie right away, I keep my arm firmly planted where it is and ask, "Are you going to share that?"

"Nope," she says before taking a huge lick of the rocky road ice cream we decided to get together. "This is all mine. It's the least you can do."

"You know, you weren't the only one who suffered through that black hole back there," I hiss into her ear while keeping my posture and face neutral. Dave and Ellie could still see us.

"Are you talking about your blue balls?" Lottie asks, a devious smile on her lips.

Yeah, maybe a little.

Blue balls are in full force right now.

Doesn't help that I keep picturing her above me, grinding down on my cock while she grabs her breast...

"Lottie...Lottie Bug, is that you?"

Instantly, Lottie goes stiff next to me as a leggy blond approaches us. Decked out in a bubblegum pink skirt and white top, the woman looks as if she was plucked from *Legally Blonde*.

Lottie sits up and casually places her hand on my thigh. That move right there, her hand claiming me, tells me one important thing: whoever this person is, she needs *me* to be in character.

"Angela," Lottie says after swallowing her ice cream. "What, uh, what are you doing here?"

Angela? As in...the ex-friend who fired Lottie?

Angela glances my way, and I know the minute she recognizes me, because she tilts her sunglasses down on the edge of her nose and her mouth falls open.

Ignoring Lottie entirely, she asks, "Huxley Cane, is that you?"

Am I supposed to know her? Because she's making it seem as if we know each other.

I shift in my seat, moving closer to Lottie as my arm slips up to her shoulder rather than resting on her chair. "I'm sorry, have we met?" I ask.

Lottie leans in toward me. Her body language is screaming for help. I reassure her with a stroke of my hand over her shoulder.

Angela waves her hand and says, "You're too funny. We met at the Stardom Gala last year. I was the gorgeous goddess in the purple floor-length dress." She tosses her hair over her shoulder.

"Huh," I say, tilting my head. "Can't quite place you."

The softest of snorts escapes Lottie's nose, and I'm sure I'm the only one who heard it.

"Well, there were a lot of people there that night." Angela sets her hand on her hip. "How crazy that we run into each other now." She then looks at Lottie. I watch as her eyes fall on my arm around Lottie, the closeness of our bodies, and then…it clicks. "Oh my, Lottie, are you two…together?"

Lottie glances in my direction, so I take that moment to lift her hand that's holding the ice cream, bring it to my mouth, and take a bite from it before winking at her. "Hiding me from your friends again, babe? What did I tell you? Stop keeping me a secret."

"Wait," Angela says, her mind whirling. "Are you serious? You two are dating?" She motions her manicured finger between us.

Lottie nods. Keeping her eyes on me, she says, "Yes, we're dating."

"Babe, we're more than dating." I take the ice cream from her and then lift her hand, showing off her massive engagement ring. I give it a kiss and say, "We're getting married."

"What?" Angela nearly shrieks. "Since when? You never said anything to me, Lottie."

I turn toward Angela and, with a smile on my face, I say, "We've been busy. Isn't that right, babe?" I lean over and kiss the side of her neck.

Lottie's grip on my leg tightens as she says, "Yeah, very busy. But, yeah, we're engaged."

"I see, well…can't say that I'm not hurt you didn't tell me."

Wow, she has some fucking nerve.

"That's what happens when you sever ties with your best friend, Angela. They take that as a sign to move on." Lottie smiles at me and offers me the ice cream again so I can take another mouthful. "I've moved on."

Angela steps back, hand to her chest. "Lottie, you're being so cruel. And here I was, coming over to see if you wanted to have lunch with me sometime."

Oh, what a load of bullshit.

"We really miss you at the company. Maybe we can figure something out. Especially now that you're dating Huxley Cane, we could partner up."

From the corner of my eye, I see Lottie's jaw clench. Her anger's spiking, and I'm seeing another side of her. Sure, I've made her angry, but those conversations we've had almost seem superficial now, compared to this. This is true anger. This is from the pit of her stomach.

And I can see her wanting to jump down Angela's throat, which will do nothing for Lottie, so I stop it before it can happen. "We're actually late for a meeting, babe." I slip my arm off her shoulder and instead take her hand. "I'm sure Angela doesn't mind catching up with you some other time." I give Angela a look.

"Oh, of course not," she says easily. "Don't let me keep you. But I'd love to chat at some point, Lottie. I miss you. And you know how busy I am. Give the reunion some thought. It needs a nice Lottie touch to it." She twiddles her fingers at Lottie and then heads into the ice cream shop.

Lottie stays silent as she sits there, holding the ice cream but not saying a thing. Not even moving.

Unsure of what to do, I say, "So that's Angela?"

Lottie stands and hands me the ice cream. "Can we leave now?"

"Yeah, if that's what you want."

"It is," she says, and for the first time since I've known her, I take her hand in mine not because I'm putting on a show, but because I think she needs it.

———

The clanging of spoons in our soup bowls is the only sound in the dining room. The silence is so deafening that if someone walked in, they'd think they were walking in on a funeral.

A funeral for my self-respect.

Lottie hasn't really said anything to me since we left the ice cream shop. She doesn't seem mad, more…contemplative. Probably regretting her decision-making, like I am.

I still don't know what kind of class that was. I know Los Angeles is slightly different than other cities, but dry humping in front of strangers while envisioning burying your seed…that's a little much.

And because it was so weird, so off base, I have no idea what to say to Lottie. Should I apologize? Should I ask her if she liked it? Should I sign us up for another class? Should I bring up Angela again?

"How is the soup?" Reign asks, coming in with a basket of biscuits.

"Delicious," I say.

"Really good," Lottie adds. "Are those homemade biscuits?"

"Yes," Reign says. "Chive and cheddar."

"Don't mind if I do," Lottie says as she plucks one from the basket, smiling. *Okay.* She's in better spirits than when we left the ice cream store.

So I decide to test my luck with her.

"Do you want to talk about what happened with Angela?"

Her eyes flash to mine. "No."

"Because it seemed like—"

"I said *no,* Huxley," she snaps at me.

Okay, noted. Doesn't like talking about Angela. Got it. I try a different approach.

"Dave told me Ellie was hoping you'd go shopping with her sometime. For baby items."

She doesn't look at me, not even a small glance. "She said she wanted to get fitted for breast pumps."

"Oh." Shit, that doesn't sound like fun. I have no idea what that entails, but I can already sense it wouldn't be something Lottie's interested in. "Did she say when?"

"Sometime next week." She breaks off a piece of her biscuit and plops it in her mouth.

"Are you going to go?"

"Do I really have a choice? After what happened this afternoon, I'm pretty sure we're bonded to Ellie and Dave for life." She adds another piece of biscuit to her mouth. "When we were putting away the yoga mats, Ellie told me she had an orgasm while Dave was pulsing into her." Casually she dabs her mouth. "Do you understand the kind of damage that does to a person? Knowing someone only a few feet away had an O while their fiancé dry humped them in a pregnancy class?" Her eyes finally meet mine. "I'm not doing well, Huxley."

"Well, you're in good company, because I'll never be able to look at Dave the same, after he proudly stood with his boner for everyone to see."

"I'm surprised you didn't join him." She scoops up more of her soup and sips on it. "You know, since you seem to like to be the best at everything. It would've been fun seeing who packed more heat."

"What happened today was completely unprofessional, and I have no intentions of repeating it."

"I knew it." She shakes her head.

"Knew what?" I ask.

"That a pole was being shoved farther and farther up your ass while we were there."

"Are you telling me you'd enjoy going to another one of those classes?"

"Absolutely not, but chalk it up to a life experience. You don't have to be so stiff all the time, no pun intended."

"I'm not stiff all the time," I say. "I just don't enjoy getting dry humped in front of a business associate, only to see said business associate's erection after."

"He didn't get excited over you dry humping."

I pinch the brow of my nose. "I know that. I was just adding it on to the 'experience' of the day," I say, using air quotes. "You yourself said you weren't doing well. So why are you chastising me?"

"I'm not chastising you," she shoots back and then takes a deep breath while leaning back in her chair. "You know, I don't think this is working out."

"Excuse me?" I say, panic in my voice.

"This." She motions between us. "We can't seem to get on the same wavelength, and frankly, I'm tired of fighting with you all the time."

"You think I enjoy fighting with you?"

"I think you take pleasure in making me angry. That much is true from last night."

"I take pleasure in other things," I say, raising a brow, because I really fucking enjoyed having my fingers inside of her.

She rolls her eyes and sets her hands on the table. "I think this eating dinner together thing is too much. We're forcing something we shouldn't be forcing."

I lean in and speak quietly when I say, "We're not forcing anything. We're putting on a goddamn show." Keeping my voice at a whisper, I continue, "Dinners aren't about spending time with you, they're about keeping the illusion alive."

"You really think Reign might say something? Like that we're not eating dinner together? He seems like a nice, trustworthy guy. He hasn't poisoned you yet, unfortunately."

Cute.

"It's not that he'd deliberately say something. He might casually comment on how we didn't have dinner together; it might get out to someone else, who then spins it for an article to sell to all those bullshit gossip sites. When you're in a position such as myself, you have to be aware of information getting out in any way, even if it is innocent."

"Ugh," she groans and crosses her arms over her chest. "I just don't know how much longer I can do this, Huxley."

Her eyes look drained when they connect with mine, and I realize that maybe she's right. This is really draining, putting on a show, making sure you're saying the right thing all the time. I'm used to acting like someone else—it's how I've acted around all my business associates. Professional, put together, thoughtful, focused. But in reality, I'm like every other guy who just wants to relax, who jokes around, teases, has a good time. For someone who might not be used to putting on a show, it is draining, especially when it isn't just your livelihood at stake, but someone else's.

"How much longer can you do this?" I ask her, growing serious.

Her eyes snap to mine. "What do you mean?"

"Give me a time frame. I can call Dave tomorrow, see if he wants to meet up. Talk about the deal. I wanted to massage the friendship some more before I brought up the deal, but I understand your need to be done with this."

"Well, I don't know." Her eyes are confused.

I nod. "I'll speak with my brothers tomorrow." I scoop up some soup and take a sip, retreating back into myself.

She doesn't move, she just sits there and stares at her soup, leaving it untouched.

After a few minutes of silence, she says, "Do you know what would help?"

"What?" I ask, turning my attention back to her.

"One of the reasons I said yes to this was because when we were having dinner at Chipotle, you seemed like someone I could get along with, but somewhere along the way, that all changed."

"I can't help who I am."

"That's the problem. I don't know who you are. And you don't know who I am."

"I didn't think you were interested in getting to know me on a personal level, given our relationship is strictly business."

She groans. "God, you and your goddamn business. How about setting that *business* mindset to the side for a hot minute and getting to know me instead? Maybe it'll make it easier to do these outings with you. To pretend. Because it won't feel as though I'm dry humping a stranger in a pregnancy class."

I consider what she's asking of me, and it's not much at all. But I do know I've put a wall up around her. If I get to know her more, I'm going to like her more. I can feel it. She's the kind of girl who would easily capture my attention and keep me strung along. I'm not looking for that, to be captured, to start any sort of relationship. I don't have the patience to focus on something like that, nor am I ready to give someone my time. I'm too selfish at the moment. Too focused on my career, on my goals.

But I need her.

Fuck, do I need her.

I need her to help me secure this deal, and if that means switching gears and letting her get to know me better, then fuck, that's what I'll have to do.

"Fine," I say. "Two questions during the day. Two questions at dinner. That should be sufficient."

"Sufficient? You sound like Mary Poppins, all proper and shit."

"Are you taking the deal?" I raise my brow.

"Are you saying these questions can happen every day?"

"Yes. Does that work?"

She shakes her head in amusement. "I wasn't expecting it to be so formal, but I guess that will have to work. Who starts?"

I pat my mouth with my napkin. "You."

"Right now?"

"Isn't that what you want?" I ask as I try to hide my irritation.

"I mean, sure. I guess I wasn't prepared for you to be so open."

"I'm not a complete asshole, Lottie."

Her lips quirk to the side, telling me she believes otherwise. "Okay, fine, I guess I'll start with the questions." Her eyes pin me. "Why is this deal with Dave so important to you that you'd go to such an extent to secure it?"

I should've known her questions weren't going to be easy.

Shifting in my seat, I casually turn toward her and drape my arm over the back of my chair. "It's pretty simple, actually. When I set my mind on something I want, I go after it, no matter the circumstances. Dave has three properties that would be extremely beneficial for our business. He's not going to just sell them to make money; he wants to make sure they go to the right person. I want to be that person."

"Just seems so…aggressive."

"When you're in commercial property development, you have to be aggressive. You can't sleep on anything. You have to know what's selling, where it's selling, and the potential for the spot. Breaker, JP, and I always keep our eyes and ears open, while developing our existing properties to continue to make money for us. Dave's properties would be a huge opportunity that I can't just let slip by because he doesn't know me as a person. That doesn't sit well with me."

She nods. "I can see how that might make sense. I wouldn't go to the extent that you do, but I get it."

The hostility in her voice has subsided and the pinch in her brow has loosened. I hate to admit it, but maybe this questions thing wasn't a bad idea after all.

"Do you want me to ask a question now?"

She nods again. "Yeah, take a whack at it."

Okay, if she's going to come in hot with a hard question, so am I. "Why are you so ashamed of telling your mom and Jeff about being fired?"

"Should've expected that question, given what I asked you." She sighs. "I grew up with Angela, the owner of Angeloop, the lifestyle blog. She's giving Gwyneth Paltrow over at Goop a run for her money. We were on-again, off-again friends."

"What's that?" I ask. "As far as I'm concerned, you're either friends or you're not."

Lottie shakes her head. "Not with Angela. She'd have a friend of the week, kind of like a flavor-of-the-week situation. She had no problem bouncing from friend to friend, and when she got tired of one, she'd move on to the next, and then they were her new best friend. Growing up in a rich city on a blue-collar income, Angela was exciting to me. I know it sounds ridiculous, but when you're a kid, flashy things are fun. Angela had all the flashy things, and we had so much fun together. We'd roll into school in her BMW, spend weekends at her house having pool parties, and then one random day, I'd be dropped as the person she went to. It was torturous, toxic, and yet, I kept accepting her back because of the fun times we had together."

"I see," I say. "That's the definition of toxic."

"I know, and that's what my mom said to me. My mom really hates Angela, actually. So when I graduated from school with a master's in business and Angela offered me a job at her growing start-up, my mom was extremely skeptical about me joining forces with someone who's so hot and cold."

"A natural feeling."

"Yes, perhaps. Mom was so right. She once said something that hits me more now than it did at the time. *'She's treated you with disdain and relentless cruelty as a friend throughout your whole friendship, Lottie, so how do you think she believes she can treat you in business?'*"

"The same way, right?"

"Yeah. But my options were slim. I could go work somewhere that had a hint of the field I wanted to be in, or I could work for Angela, grow a business, and take charge. She offered me a low starting salary and said after a year, if I helped grow the business, she'd give me the raise I deserved. I thought it was a solid situation. My mom, Jeff, and my sister all said not to do it, that Angela couldn't be trusted. But I did it anyway and I excelled. I grew that business to where it is now. I had a huge part in bringing Angela to the forefront of everyone's eyes. And when the time came for my raise…"

"She fired you." I shake my head. "I'm pretty ruthless when it comes to business, but there's no way in hell I'd ever do something like that. I know a good employee when I see them, and instead of cutting them out, I make sure to develop them. They would do so much better under my wing than with a competitor. My guess is Angela felt threatened by you and she wanted to get rid of you before everyone else in the company realized how valuable you were."

"Probably." She glances down at her linked hands. "Either way, I was too embarrassed to tell my mom and Jeff. I didn't want to hear the *I told you so*s, and that's how I came to be sitting here, with you. Desperation to save face."

"I understand the need to protect a reputation. I think it's one of the reasons I'm being so aggressive in my approach with Dave. Everyone in the business knows I'm going after the properties, and everyone knows I get what I want. But Dave is giving me a run for my money, and that puts a blemish on my reputation."

"You can't win them all."

"I do," I tell her. "I always win."

"Glad your perspective is forgiving."

I let out a light chuckle. "What's your second question?"

Tilting her head to the side, studying me, she asks, "You seem so stiff all the time, it's hard for me to imagine you actually having fun, so I guess my question is, what do you like to do for fun?"

I rub my hand over my jaw. "When I get to take a second to breathe, I enjoy going to baseball games."

"Let me guess—you sit in the cushioned seats."

"I wouldn't settle for anything less."

"I know this is another question, but we'll call it question 2a."

"I'll let it slide," I answer.

"Do you have a favorite team?"

I shake my head. "Not really, actually, which seems odd. I like a few of the California teams here, I enjoy going to the different ballparks and seeing how they differ from others, and I follow my good friend from college. He's retiring this year, on his farewell tour."

"Ooo, question 2b, who's your friend?"

I chuckle. "Penn Cutler. He pitches for the Chicago Bobbies, but we went to college together. He's had a bumpy road in the majors, but he's looking solid this season."

"I'm going to have to look him up. But…baseball, that's it? That's the only fun thing you like to do?"

"Nah, I like hanging with my brothers. Pool days. Simple games like ring toss, cornhole, going to the beach. I'm not a surfer, but the boys and I play football on the beach pretty often." I shrug. "Just chilling when we get a chance."

She blinks a few times and then chuckles as she shakes her head. "I never would've pegged you as someone who'd play football on the beach. I figured you're a man who likes to hang out in old smoke rooms, wearing a logoed smoking jacket, cigar in hand, talking about the stock market and how the Dow is fucking you over. You're the kind of guy who goes to the opera and likes it. The kind of man who takes piano lessons in his spare time because he needs to be good at everything."

"I learned to play when I was young."

"Of course you did. But football on the beach, that's a normal person's activity. Next you're going to tell me you enjoy going to concerts."

"I do," I say. "Has to be the right music, though. I'm not about to go to a Bruno Mars concert, but if, let's say, Foreigner is in town, I'll be sure to grab tickets."

"Nope, no way, I don't see that for you. I don't see you at concerts. And if you do go to concerts, you're probably the stiff guy, beer in hand, who doesn't move, doesn't sing, doesn't crack a smile."

"You'd be surprised." She's loosened me up with these questions, and I'm not really comfortable with that. I'm…cautious by nature, ruthless when necessary. But having two brothers as best friends, I've become reticent with others. And here's Lottie, determined to know me more than I'm willing to give.

"Very interesting." She has a smile on her face, an expression so genuine that I'm surprised this is all she needed. A conversation, something so simple. "Okay, your turn, ask your final question."

Giving it some thought, I finally ask, "Dream concert to attend?"

"Dead or alive?"

"Both," I answer.

"If I could resurrect Freddie Mercury, I'd pretty much give my soul to do so. To see him live, to watch him perform…God, it would be the ultimate dream. But to watch alive…hmm, right now…probably Fleetwood Mac."

Surprised, I say, "I was not expecting that answer. From everything you've said, I would've thought you were going to say Foreigner."

"I mean, they are on top of the list, but I'm obsessed with Stevie Nicks—and the new collab she did with Miley Cyrus…ooo, so good. And they're just chill music, you know? You can listen to them on a rainy day or when you're at the beach. And 'Dreams'…" A smile crosses her face. "I think it would be the perfect make-out song. The tempo, the feel of it. It's so good. Are you a fan of Fleetwood Mac?"

I nod. "I am. I'll play them while working sometimes."

She holds up her hand in surprise. "You listen to music while you're working?"

"Every day."

"Wow." She pushes my shoulder. "See? This is what I needed. To see you act like a human." She lets out a deep breath. "I feel better." She picks up her spoon and digs back into her soup.

"You feel better? Just like that?"

"Yup. You should know, Huxley, I'm pretty easy."

"Yeah...found that out last night."

"And would you look at that—he jokes, too. Amazing."

CHAPTER 14
LOTTIE

I CHECK MY WATCH TO see what time it is. A little past one. We ate lunch early today because Kelsey had a meeting with a potential client at one thirty. I've been working on the website for the past hour and a half, and I need to take a breather.

Leaning back in the uncomfortable dining chair—we're going to need an office space at some point, rather than Kelsey's small studio apartment—I pick up my phone and open my text thread with Huxley.

Yesterday was a roller coaster. One minute I'm impressed with the man and how he kept his promise and set up another meeting for Kelsey, not to mention finding out how he cared for his employees, defying the negative image of him I had in my head. Next, he has me going to some creepy pregnancy class that put me far outside of my comfort zone. It didn't help that he couldn't just be fun in the moment. That was the worst part of it—if he'd been laughing with me through the awkward encounter, it would've been a moment to remember, but he was like a robot, and it made it that much worse. And then we ran into Angela.

God, could she be any worse of a human?

I despise her.

The nerve she had to say, *Maybe we can work something out,* when she saw I was dating Huxley Cane—fake dating, I know, but still. She's been showing her true colors lately. But what was even worse than running into her was the way Huxley reacted.

He was protective.

He defended me.

He took hold of the situation.

This man that I'd despised for the past week or so suddenly came through for me, without me even asking. I don't think I'd ever been more confused.

He was just...there. Holding my hand, making sure I was all right.

But while we were in the car, he turned back into a robot.

Stiff set to his shoulders, tight grip on the steering wheel. He shut me out in the blink of an eye.

And I have no idea why.

Now, that robot persona carried over into dinner. I couldn't take it anymore; I was fed up and almost walked out.

Like the mercurial man he is, he dipped and showed that generous personality again, the one I saw while we were at Chipotle.

And he offered me two questions a day and night, something I wasn't expecting either. I'm not sure he thought I was serious about asking them, but I am. It'll make things so much easier if I actually get to know this man. I'll feel more comfortable, and like Kelsey said, maybe I can make things more believable between us.

I send him a text.

Lottie: What are you listening to right now?

When I see the dots appear next to his name, I'm surprised.

Huxley: "The Chain"—Fleetwood Mac. You put me in the mood yesterday. Been listening to them all day.

I smile to myself and text him back.

Lottie: Me, too. Just got done singing my heart out to "Rhiannon." My computer mouse was my microphone, and I used the flashlight on my phone for mood lighting. Did you do the same?

Huxley: No.

Lottie: Baby steps, I guess. Go ahead, ask me one of your daytime questions.

Huxley: Is that what's happening right now?

Lottie: Yes, you said I get two questions during the day, two at night. So…go ahead.

Huxley: Craziest thing you ever did in college?

Lottie: Throwback question. Okay, uh…well, I wasn't really crazy in college. I know it seems as though I might have stories to tell, but I really don't have many, just one claim to party fame.

Huxley: What is it?

Lottie: There was this bar we went to a lot, the Chicken Leg. It was a hole-in-the-wall. They accepted any form of ID, and they had some of the best music ever played, and when I say best music, I think you know what I'm talking about. Old school rock. They had a lipsync wet T-shirt contest one night. Prize was one thousand dollars.

Huxley: I think I see where this is going.

Lottie: I don't have much to work with upstairs, but I wore the thinnest T-shirt I had, no bra, and when it was my turn to lipsync "Don't Stop Believin'," I drenched my boobs in water and went for it. I was one thousand dollars richer that night.

Huxley: What did you do with the money?

Lottie: Paid for parking tickets I accumulated from being lazy and parking in the wrong parking spots at school.

Huxley: That's an unfortunate way to spend it.

Lottie: It was going to bills either way.

Huxley: Did you work in college?

Lottie: Is that your second question?

Huxley: Yes.

Lottie: Then, yes. I was a waitress at a steak joint. I made good money, but the hours were long, the customers were brutal, and I took back at least one steak a week to the kitchen for being cooked too rare. But I served dinner to rich people, and they paid well. It's why I'm not drowning in debt. Well, that and you...

Huxley: Having only thirty thousand dollars in student debt after graduating just a year ago? That's really good, actually.

Lottie: But when you have nothing, thirty thousand is a lot.

Huxley: I get it. What's your second question?

Lottie: What's your favorite board game to play?

Huxley: Don't have one.

Lottie: That's a boring answer. You have to have some sort of board game you enjoy.

Huxley: I don't play board games.

Lottie: Card game?

Huxley: Uno?

Lottie: Is that a question or an answer?

Huxley: Answer. It's the only thing I could think of. Breaker makes us play Uno Attack every once in a while. It's fun.

Lottie: Ooooo, I love Uno Attack. When those cards spit out at you, it's the devil's work. Good answer, Huxley. I accept.

Huxley: Glad to hear it. Now, getting back to work.

Lottie: See you at dinner.

———————

"Did you ask for this on purpose?" I ask when Reign leaves the room.

Huxley, who's looking particularly handsome in a black button-up shirt, places his napkin on his lap before reaching for the homemade horseradish sauce. "You put me in the mood for steak. Hope you don't have to send yours back."

"Cheeky," I say. He dumps some sauce on his steak and then hands me the dish. Our fingers glide over one another, and for some reason, the warm touch of his finger sends a bolt of lust up my arm and straight to my heart. *Where the hell did that come from?*

Clearing my throat, I say, "This looks good though. Fingerling potatoes and...what's this green thing, again?" I ask.

"Broccolini."

He's answering in clipped, short responses, which only leads me to believe one thing—he needs to be warmed up again if I'm going to get him to engage like earlier. He seemed pretty open through texts, but in person, his guard is up. The good thing is I know it can be torn down with some coaxing.

"Broccolini looks like something from a Dr. Seuss book."

"It's good."

"What's this stuff on it?" I ask, seeing if he'll expand on his comments.

"Mustard vinaigrette." Huxley cuts into his steak.

Oh-kay...

I'm wracking my brain for what else I can ask, when he says, "I reached out to Dave today like I promised. I asked to set up a meeting with him to go over business."

Oh crap, I forgot he said he was going to do that, even after admitting he'd like more time to work the friendship angle. I feel guilty. I had a moment of weakness last night when I told him I was done. I was frustrated, and deservingly so, given the closed-off individual I've been interacting with. But that frustration morphed into something else last night—appreciation.

Appreciation for him loosening up and giving my idea a chance without a disgruntled look or thought.

"You didn't have to call Dave," I say. "I was just in a bad state of mind last night. I shouldn't have told you that I was ready to be done." I glance up at him. "I'm sorry."

"It's fine. Business needs to be taken care of," Huxley says rather coldly. "He's going to try to make some time for me this week. When he does, I'll be sure to tell him you're busy and can't meet up with Ellie."

"Huxley, you don't have to do that. I signed a contract. I can go out with Ellie."

His eyes land on me and sternly he says, "It's fine."

It doesn't feel *fine*.

But just like that, the conversation is over. Just when I thought he was starting to warm up to me, he turns into this taciturn man again. Not sure I'll ever understand these mood swings or why he has them, probably because he won't let me get close enough to figure out why he acts the way he does.

But I guess that's "business" for you…right?

I'm so sick of that. Of that term. When did business become this impersonal? When my mom first owned her cleaning business, before being hired as a senior manager in her current position, she was never cold. She was warm, friendly. It was one of the reasons why her customers loved her so much, because she took great care of them, because she was, in fact…not indifferent. Although, to be fair, Mom's business involved *giving* to her clients, whereas Huxley is in the business of acquisitions.

But that doesn't explain why Huxley has the need to act like this.

Let's see if I can loosen him up like I did last night.

"Question time—are you ready?"

His brow raises as he glances up at me. For a nanosecond, I think he's going to deny me the satisfaction of cracking his exterior once again, but then his eyes return to his steak as he cuts into it. "Ready."

Man, it is going to be hard to pull him out of his shell tonight. It has to be a good question, something that will get him talking.

Hmm…

Something to really get him talking.

Something that will appeal to him.

I got it.

"If you had a boat, where would you go?" A simple question with room to elaborate.

"I do have a boat. A yacht, if you care to be correct about the terminology."

Oh, huh.

"You do?" I ask, feeling surprised. I mean, of course he'd have a yacht, he's a billionaire who lives near the ocean. Why wouldn't he have a *yacht*? That would be like…uh…like a knight without a horse. Sure, that works. *Well and a sword, of course.*

"Yes, my brothers and I actually share it because we thought it would be stupid to all have yachts, especially since we don't go out on it all that much."

Common sense.

"Okay…so, if you could go anywhere on your yacht, where would you go?"

"Alaska."

"Alaska?" I ask, feeling even more shocked with that answer. "Why Alaska? I thought you were going to say something like the Mediterranean, you know, because in my head that's where all the rich people go."

"Alaska, because it's breathtaking up there. The cascading mountains capped in snow, the blue waters, the tall pines, and wildlife." He nods. "I'd spend my time there exploring."

"Hold up, are you telling me you're the kind of man who sheds the suit and puts on a pair of hiking boots?"

"Is that your second question?" he asks.

"Consider it 1a," I say with a grin.

The smallest of smirks pulls at the left corner of his mouth before he says, "I do enjoy hiking."

"That wasn't on the list of things you like to do for fun."

He shrugs. "Well, it's one of the things I like to do. There are some decent trails around here, especially up in the hills. The boys and I try to get a few hikes in on the weekends during the month. We haven't been in a bit because of life. But, yeah, I'd take the yacht to Alaska and go hiking, whale watching, camping."

"Why don't you?"

"Time," he says. "Time is always the factor."

"But you could retire right now; you have enough money for more than a lifetime, so why keep going?"

He cuts a piece of his steak and pierces it with his fork. When his dark eyes meet mine, I feel my breath catch in my chest. The intensity throws me for a loop. "We can't just stop what we're doing. A lot of people depend on us for a living. For *their* livelihood. Until I feel comfortable enough to find someone who could take care of the business while we were gone, I'll work for the people who work for me."

An outsider looking in, listening to Huxley and his clipped tones and short-worded answers, would think the man has no heart, but then he gives you an answer like that. He has all the money one person could ever need, he could jet off somewhere and be done with ever working again, but he sees that he owes people his time, because they've given him theirs.

That hits me harder than expected.

"That's a very kind answer, Huxley. You're making me think there's a heart under that pressed shirt after all."

"It's there when it needs to be." He takes a drink of his water and asks, "Best place you've ever gone on vacation?"

"Ooo, you're going to be sadly disappointed. We didn't really go on vacation growing up. My mom didn't have the money, but when she did save enough on occasion, we used to have a fantastic day at Disneyland. Mom would spoil us. We'd get there early before the park opened, have all the food we ever wanted, ride the rides twice, sometimes three times, and then stay until the park closed. Some of my best memories are of going to Disneyland. The only vacation we ever went on was when we went to the Redwood National Park. We went camping. We aren't wilderness ladies, but it was fun. We attempted to cook food over a fire, lived off s'mores, and played cards the entire weekend, when we weren't marveling at the trees. It was a lot of fun."

"Sounds like it. I've always enjoyed camping."

"Let me guess—with your brothers."

He nods. "Yeah, we do everything together."

"I'm sensing that. You know, I've never been formally introduced to them, but I'm guessing they know all about me."

"They do."

"Well, maybe Friday I can get a proper introduction."

"I can arrange that." He bites into his steak, and I watch as his firm jaw moves up and down. Okay, for some reason, that seems sexy to me. Yup, I think I might be losing it. "Your turn to ask a question."

"Right," I say, turning back to my plate. "Uh…who's your favorite brother?"

He chuckles. "Going there, huh?"

"Might as well. I need to be prepared when I do meet them."

"If I had to pick, I would say I'm closer to JP. We're closer in age, we got into more trouble together, and we worked more on building the business together. He's also the one I'd probably go to if I needed someone to help bail me out of jail."

"Jail? Why are you going to jail?"

"We did stupid shit growing up."

"Like what?" I ask.

He shakes his head. "A question for another day. Your quota is up. And don't try that 2a, 2b bullshit on me; you already used it."

"Well, aren't you a killjoy?"

"Just playing the game as it was laid out. My turn." He lifts his glass of water and takes a sip. When he sets the glass down, he looks uncertain. "I'm not sure how to ask this without it sounding harsh, but what happened to your dad?"

"That's not being harsh. He left my mom early on. He was a truck driver. Didn't want to stay in one place. I never had a relationship with the man, but he always sent my mom child support. It's why she was able to afford the house we live in. I remember hearing my mom talk to my grandma late one night when Dad first left. Mom was saying she didn't feel right taking the money from him, but my grandma shot down those feelings very quickly. It was the first time I heard my grandma talk in such a strict tone. She said my mom didn't have her babies on her own. That the money he sent wasn't charity; it was his duty. And from then on, Mom accepted his checks every month. We sent him homemade cards on holidays and his birthdays, but that was the extent of it. Now, I honestly have no idea what he's doing or where he is. And we're okay with that because we have Jeff, and Jeff is all we need."

Huxley is silent for a moment before he says, "I couldn't imagine abandoning my family like that, but at least he had it in his heart to be there in some capacity."

"He helped give us a home Mom wouldn't otherwise have been able to afford. And it's such a great home, full of memories."

"I felt that when I was there. Very homey." He plops another piece of steak in his mouth and then goes quiet.

He remains that way for the rest of the night. And, of course, being the person that I am, I recount our conversation in my head, trying to pinpoint the moment or the thing I said that shut him down so quickly.

If only I could ask…

———

"What are you doing?" Kelsey asks as I bring my feet up into my chair and prop my phone on my knees.

"Getting ready to ask Huxley some questions."

"About what?"

"About him," I answer. "It's part of the deal so I don't freak out about having to live and act with a robot. I get to ask him questions. Two during the day and two at night. He gets to do the same."

"Wow, that seems very...calculated."

"That's Huxley for you. The man needs order."

Kelsey studies me and then scoots her chair closer so she can reach out and poke me in the arm. "You like him, don't you?"

"What?" I ask with a pinch in my brow. "Are you nuts? No, I don't like him. He's...he's a sociopath. Not the type of guy I'd ever go for. But it's nice getting to know him a little bit better, because having dinner with someone who either spends his time irritating me or being completely silent isn't what I'd call fun. This makes the deal easier."

"Uh-huh," she says with a smile as she gets out of her chair. "I'm going to walk to the salad shop around the corner. Want me to grab you something?"

"Please." I smile at her, not giving in to her disbelief. "Chopped salad, no tomatoes. Thanks, sis."

With that grin of hers, she grabs her purse and heads out the door. When it clicks shut, I open up my text thread with Huxley and ask him the question I wanted to ask him last night. Maybe he'd be more receptive to answering over text, where he doesn't have to look me in the face.

Lottie: What stupid shit did you do as a kid?

I smile to myself as the dots appear on the thread.

Huxley: I knew that was coming.

Lottie: So, then you might have a good answer for me, right?

Huxley: Depends on what good is.

He's so much more playful through text. Makes me wonder—does he feel as though he doesn't have to maintain his façade when texting, like he does when we're in person? Most likely he feels as though he can be more himself. Hide behind the comfort of his phone like a protective shield.

Lottie: Stop avoiding. Tell me all the naughty things you've done.

Huxley: You want naughty?

Lottie: Not that kind of naughty…well…huh, now I'm curious. Are you a naughty man?

Huxley: Are those your two questions for the day?

Lottie: You drive a hard bargain, but I kind of want them answered, so, yes, those are my two questions. I'd like the jail-time question answered first.

Huxley: For the record, we never went to jail, because we were never caught. But we were bored assholes and would fuck with our neighbors, stealing stupid shit from lawns and putting it in other people's yards. So, Mr. Galstone on the corner would end up with Mrs. Dreerie's potted plants, but we would alter them somehow, like spray-painting the planters. Stupid shit, but it got the neighbors talking, arguing. It was entertaining.

Lottie: You little assholes. Man, that would drive Jeff nuts if something like that happened to him. He's very protective of his yard. He wishes he'd be acknowledged by The Flats yard committee, but we're one street off from being considered. Jeff believes he deserves recognition. We all do.

Huxley: I noticed the yard was very well manicured. He does a great job.

Lottie: He'd appreciate the compliment. Now…ask me a question.

Huxley: You don't want my answer to your other question right now?

Lottie: I'll wait. Hit me with a hard one.

Huxley: Okay...have you ever been in love?

I stare down at my phone, reading his question over and over again. For such a robotic man, I never thought he'd ask a question like that. When I said hard, I meant something like "Who would you die on a sword for? Team Jacob or Team Edward?"

Side note...glitter dick, all day, every day.

But have I ever been in love? Now that's a heavy question.

Huxley: I'm waiting...

And he's relentless. I guess it's only fair I answer.

Lottie: Have I ever been in love? Umm, that would be a no. A solid no. I've been with a few guys, dated, but no one has ever captured me. I'm pretty sure my heart will wait to fall for someone when I least expect it.

Huxley: How many guys have you been with?

Lottie: Is that your second question?

Huxley: Yes.

Lottie: Throwing away a second question on such a menial subject. I've been with five guys, and I'll throw you a bone, only one of them has made me come. That one guy...was you.

My face heats up as I press *Send*. *Dear Jesus, why did I say that?* That wasn't flirting, was it? No, I'm not flirting with him. That was just telling the truth, and knowing the kind of man Huxley is, he'll be proud he's the only one, because he's an alpha and he thrives on information like that. It'll help him open up to me more...hopefully.

Huxley: Clearly, you've been with some assholes. Glad I could make you come all over my fingers.

Oof...okay, things are getting acutely sweaty over here.
The back of my neck feels dewy; my upper lip also seems to have a sheen to it. What an "attractive" reaction to a decently dirty text.

Lottie: You're the only one, other than myself.

Huxley: If I give you one more question, will you give me one more?

Lottie: I'm intrigued. So...yes.

Huxley: Ask another question first. The naughty one?

Lottie: No. I'm saving that for last. I want to know if you've ever been in love.

Huxley: Never. No one has even come close to making me feel as though I could spend the rest of my life with them, as if I can't go another day without laying eyes on them, as if I need them in my arms just to get a solid night's sleep. I've only ever had surface-level relationships with the women I've been with.

Lottie: I wouldn't have guessed that would be your answer. From the way you act, your clipped tone, your standoffish behavior, I would've sworn someone broke your heart.

Huxley: There was someone who fucked me in the head, but I wasn't in love. I was more...attached for the wrong reasons. For business.

Lottie: Oh, I see. Well, that explains your need to keep everything business-related between us.

Huxley: There's a reason for everything.

Lottie: What's your third question for me?

Huxley: You said I'm the only one who got you off, besides

yourself. Tell me the best way you've ever made yourself orgasm.

Cue more upper lip sweat. Because I know precisely, without a doubt, no question in my mind, which moment. But my answer is only going to puff up his chest more.

Lottie: It was the night you got me off. When I went back to my room, I fucked myself with my purple vibrator and came so hard just thinking about how you commanded my body only moments before. And I realize how inappropriate that answer is, but it's the truth. You worked me up that night. There was no turning back.

Huxley: Your body was easy to command.

I set my phone down for a second and take a deep breath. Okay, yes, the man is attractive, he has a way with words. And when he shows it, his personality is actually one I like, but I need to tread carefully here. Even though this is strictly business, a part of me believes if I let him, he wouldn't think twice about it.

Lottie: It's a thoughtful body, always wanting to include everyone.

Good God, what does that even mean?
Before he can respond to that, I quickly send him another text.

Lottie: Okay, so what's the naughtiest thing you've ever done?

Huxley: Naughty in my eyes probably isn't naughty in someone else's. I've fucked women in some pretty weird places, but that's just fucking. Naughty to me means crossing a line, a line that probably shouldn't be crossed. Something forbidden.

Lottie: I'd agree with that.

Huxley: So then, the naughtiest thing I've ever done was undoing your robe and slipping my fingers inside your sweet cunt.

Blinks.

Swallows.

Nearly chokes on own saliva.

Okay, what's happening? What is actually happening? Is he flirting? Is he just being blunt? What's going on in that head of his? Inquiring minds want to know, because his answer is blowing my mind right now.

Lottie: There has to be something naughtier than that. Like, you know, taking someone on your office desk, or maybe whips and chains? I don't know, I can't be it.

Huxley: I crossed a line that night. You're forbidden, off limits, part of a business deal, and I lost control. I allowed myself to give in to temptation. Be happy I only touched your pussy, because if I would've had it my way, that robe wouldn't have stayed on. I have a meeting. I'll see you for dinner.

I set my phone down and slowly look up. *How the hell am I supposed to have dinner with him now?*

"Steak and arugula salad with candied pecans, fingerling potatoes, peppers, Gorgonzola cheese, and a balsamic glaze. Enjoy," Reign says before leaving us to our plentiful salads. We had steak last night, but this looks different. Thinly sliced steak and potatoes in a salad…I've never heard of such a thing, but I'll be honest, I'm here for it.

When I got back to Huxley's house, I went straight to the tub, where I took a nice long bath and used one of my vibrators to take the edge off from the text messages. There was no way I'd be coming to dinner all worked up. Nope, I edged myself off and then let the warm water soak into my tense muscles until I was utterly relaxed.

By the time I got out, Huxley was rushing me with a text saying dinner was ready.

I threw on a robe—and a thong, for obvious reasons—and charged down the stairs to where Huxley was sitting at the table wearing a navy-blue button-up shirt, the sleeves rolled to his elbows and the top two buttons undone. Talk about someone who wears business clothes well.

"This looks so good," I say while moving the food around on my plate, mixing everything together.

When I glance at Huxley, he looks tense once again, stiff as a board.

"Uh, everything okay over there?" I ask. What could he possibly be angry about now? It never ends with this man. I thought we'd made peace, that we were getting along. But with every dinner, it feels like two steps back.

"Why are you wearing that?" Huxley asks, his eyes falling to the robe.

"Uh, I was in the bathtub again when you texted. I got dressed quickly in the nearest thing. Don't worry, I put on underwear this time." I wink, as if that's supposed to help.

Reign comes back into the dining room and says, "The kitchen is cleaned and set. If you just leave your plates in the sink, the morning staff will tend to them. I'm going to catch my daughter's recital."

"There are flowers in the pantry fridge for her," Huxley says. "Enjoy your evening with your family."

"Thank you," Reign says with a smile and then takes off.

"He has a daughter? I didn't know he had a family."

"He does. It's why I eat early, so he can get back to them."

See…there he goes again, being thoughtful. Are you annoyed? Because I am.

After a few moments of silence, Huxley asks, "Are you going to ask your questions?"

"Oh yeah…sure," I say. "Umm, let me see. A question, a question." I tap my chin as nothing comes to mind. Not a single freaking thing. All I can think about is the way his steely eyes shot to my robe as he asked why I was wearing it. Dark, sinister, as if he was about to rip the damn thing off my body with his teeth.

"We can skip the questions for tonight," he says with a firm tone.

"No, no, just give me a second. Uh, what…uh, what can you cook?"

"Cook?" he asks, brows raised.

"Yeah, are you a cook in any way? Any dishes you lay claim to? Anything you're super proud of? Like, let's say JP is having a backyard barbecue and everyone has to bring something homemade—what would you bring?"

"JP would have it catered," he answers.

"Play along," I say.

"I don't really cook, but if I had to make something, I'd grill, because that's the only thing I'm decent at. So, if I were to bring something, probably burgers Reign prepared for me, and I'd grill them."

"Wow," I say with a laugh. "That was a very wealthy response."

He barely smiles as he says, "I've lost touch with some things after being in the business for so long. Cooking is one of them."

"What's another thing you've lost touch with?" I ask.

"Is that your second question?"

I nod. "Yeah, that's a good second question."

He lifts his water glass to his lips and says, "What have I lost touch with? Probably everything a thirty-five-year-old man does. Dating, cooking, hobbies."

"So, you're all about work, then?"

"That's what happens when you're in a position like mine. It consumes you." He looks over at me, eyes intrigued. "Have you ever had something consume you?"

I'm assuming that's one of his questions, so I give it some thought.

"Are we talking consume my time, or consume me as a whole, like work has consumed you?"

"Consumed you as a whole."

"Hmm…I hate that I know what my answer is because I wish something else would consume me."

"What is it?" he asks.

"Angela," I answer. "She's consumed me, but not in a healthy way. The relationship I've had with her has been toxic. At times, she's made me feel important, special, only to throw me away as if I didn't matter." I shake my head. "I've allowed her to have too much of my headspace, and I wish I could find something else that would consume me, something that would make me forget everything that happened between me and her."

"You still think about how she let you go?" he asks.

"Yes all the time, because that's the reason I'm here right now. And I don't mean that to be offensive to you, but this is very unconventional. So yeah, I just wish I could let it go, not give her any more of my time. Any more thought. I just need to find something that will take over that headspace, you know?"

He slowly nods.

"And even though I love working with Kelsey, I don't want my headspace to be taken over by work. I want it to be something healthy. Something that brings me joy. I guess I'm still trying to figure that all out."

Huxley's tongue drags over his teeth, and he pushes his salad to the side. *What's he doing?* He pushes his chair out, putting space between him and the table. In a commanding tone, he says, "Come here."

"Uh…what?" I ask.

His laser-sharp eyes meet mine. "I said *come here.*"

"Why?"

"I'm going to teach you something, something to help with that consuming feeling you're trying to fulfill."

"Oh," I say. Simple enough. I stand from my chair, but before I can even set my napkin down, he grabs hold of my hand and pulls me over to between his legs and up against the thick wood of the dining room table. "What the hell?" I say as he sits me on the table in front of him. I squeeze my legs shut and adjust my robe so as to not reveal anything. "What are you doing?"

"You want something to consume you? You want those thoughts out of your head? This is how you do it." His hands go to my thighs, and realization finally kicks in. His eyes stay on mine as he says, "Say it right now that you don't want this, and I'll go back to eating my salad. If not, I'm going to eat you."

Oh.

Dear.

God.

Mixing business with pleasure, always a bad idea. Huxley has said it so many times, but how on earth can I deny the satisfaction of having him make me come again? After the texts, the tense conversations, the revealing questions…how can I say no?

There's no chance.

I want to be consumed.

I want to forget.

I want to move on to something that isn't going to make me feel bad, but rather make me feel completely satisfied.

"Why do you want to do this?" I ask him, wanting to figure out where his head is at.

"I'm a giving man, Lottie, but my offer doesn't last forever. There's a time limit. It's either a yes or a no."

I bite my bottom lip while staring down at this man. I can practically feel him between my legs already, that coarse five o'clock shadow rubbing on my inner thighs, while his delicious mouth presses against my arousal.

I want it.

I need it.

I don't want him anywhere else.

I nod, giving him the go-ahead, but he doesn't move. Instead, he says, "From your mouth. I want to hear you say you want me between your legs."

I wet my lips, my heart racing a mile a minute.

"I want you, Huxley, between my legs. Your tongue on my clit. I want to come on your mouth."

His eyes darken, and his hands slide up inside my robe and to the waistband of my thong. He drags it down, and I lift up to help him pull it all the way off me. He drops it to the side, almost seeming insulted that I'd wear such a thing to dinner.

Exposed, I press my hands behind me, my robe still cinched tight at my waist, and I watch as his hands slowly crawl up my inner thighs. He doesn't say anything, doesn't even look at me; instead, he's fixated on my center, slowly pushing my legs farther and farther apart until I'm completely open to him.

I don't have to smooth my hand over my pussy to know I'm already wet. Just the thought of him being near me, in this position, turns me on.

His hands glide inward until his thumb gently connects with my clit. He passes over the nub a few times, a satisfied grin tugging at his lips. "Wet, just as I expect you to be when around me," he says as his thumb makes circles. "Were you wet at the pregnancy class when you were pulsing over my thick cock?"

Jesus Christ, no man has ever talked to me like this.

"Yes," I answer honestly. "I was."

"Did you play with yourself when you got home?"

I suck in a sharp breath as he places a kiss on my inner thigh. "I've played with myself every night since I've arrived at your house."

His eyes meet mine. "I don't hear you at night."

"I make sure of it," I say.

"Don't." He stops his fingers. "If you play with yourself at night, I want to fucking hear it. I want to hear your moans. I want to know that you're satisfied."

"Would you want to watch?"

His mouth presses another kiss, and another. "Yes. I'd watch."

"Would you masturbate while you watched me?"

"It would be difficult not to, but no."

"Why not?" I ask. His mouth is so close, I want to scream, but he goes to the other leg, his tongue lightly dragging over my pussy for a brief second before tending to my other thigh. I groan in frustration. He's worked me up in a matter of seconds. It usually takes me a few minutes, but not with Huxley, not with the way he commands my body. Well, and the text messages from earlier. Just thinking about how I'd caused him to tug on the ties of my robe...makes me hot.

"I wouldn't touch myself because the only way I'd want to come is inside of you." And then his mouth descends on my clit, and my back arches, the tie of my robe dangerously close to coming undone from my abrupt movement.

"Oh God, Huxley...yes."

His tongue moves over my clit, circling it, applying just enough pressure to drive me mad.

"You taste like goddamn honey." He sucks my clit into his mouth, pulling, teasing, making every bone in my body feel like mush.

"Jesus." Before I can catch my breath, he slips two fingers inside of me. "Fuck," I yell, hoping Reign was the last person to leave tonight. Knowing Huxley, he wouldn't be doing this if someone else was in the house.

Simultaneously, he curls his fingers up inside of me, hitting a spot that makes my vision go black as his tongue rotates over and over my sensitive nub.

There's rhythm to his movements, a precise synchronization that's building my orgasm fast and hard.

My legs go numb, and my shaky arms can barely support my weight. Huxley notices and gently pushes me back with his hand until I'm lying down, my pussy at the edge of the table, right in front of his face. And he takes advantage of the position, because he spreads my legs even farther, holds them both in place, and then his mouth laps me up.

Over and over and over.

He takes no breath in between.

He doesn't attempt to kiss me anywhere else.

Instead, he's focused on my clit and my clit alone.

It's my undoing.

The pressure builds at the base of my spine, delicious, swirling pleasure. My vision fades to black, forcing me to shut my eyes and feel what this conceited yet commanding man does to my body. I'm swept away, brought into another world where I can't feel anything but the distinct pleasure of Huxley between my legs.

"God, yes, Hux. Please don't stop. Please."

He doesn't.

He doesn't even falter.

Instead, he adds more pressure to my clit before moving his hands to my inner thighs, where he spreads my lips with his thumbs, granting him undisturbed access.

And in this position, he takes advantage.

His tongue swirls.

"Fuck, yes," I yell, my arm going over my eyes.

His tongue pulses.

"Oh my God." I grip my hair.

His lips suck.

"Holy fuck, yes, Huxley, yes."

The pressure builds and builds and builds until…

"I'm coming. Oh, fuck, Huxley, I'm coming."

My body spasms, my clit pulses in his mouth, and my scream of ecstasy bounces off the pristine white dining room walls as I ride out my orgasm on his tongue.

Delicious. Addicting. Life-altering pleasure.

Feeling out the rest of my orgasm, my hips pulse under him, and I slowly come back down to earth as I catch my breath.

"Jesus," I say, my voice hoarse.

Huxley places one last kiss on my pussy and then sits up in his chair. He takes my hand in his and gently helps me up so I'm sitting in front of him. He adjusts my robe over my legs and says, "Let that consume you tonight, and nothing else."

With that, he stands from the table and attempts to step to the side, as if he's leaving. I grab his hand quickly and ask, "Where are you going?"

"I had my dinner." His alluring eyes pin me. "Now it's time for bed."

Eyes trained on mine, he brings my hand to his mouth, places a soft kiss on my knuckles, and then breaks our connection as he backs away. Before he turns and retreats from the dining room, I spy his hard erection, pressing and aching against the zipper of his dress pants.

God, he's so hot, so tempting.

I want his dick in my mouth.

That's my initial thought, and then the desire to have him in my mouth grows immensely larger with every breath I take. Should I chase after him? What would I do if I did? Hell, I think we all know what I would do. Pull his pants down and suck him off. I'd revel in the act of having his heavy cock in my mouth.

But if I know one thing about Huxley, it's if he wanted his cock in my mouth, he would've asked for it. That's the type of man he is.

And based on his quick retreat, he doesn't want it from me.

Yet.

CHAPTER 15
HUXLEY

I CAN STILL TASTE HER on my tongue.

I can still feel the beat of her clit pulsing with pleasure.

I can still hear her cries of ecstasy as she came all over my face.

And, fuck, I can't think of anything else.

This is exactly why I didn't want to get involved. Why I knew crossing that line with her would be a bad idea, because she's too consuming. Because she's the type of woman you don't have one taste of and say *take care.*

No, she leaves a lasting impression. An imprint. She doesn't fade away.

I find myself checking the clock, seeing what time it is, counting down the goddamn minutes until she texts me a question, waiting desperately to see her today for the meeting with her sister.

And all it took was one goddamn taste. Now I'm a fucking mess.

I want her.

I didn't see her this morning. I snuck out early with my gym bag, came to the office, got a workout in, and showered here, too worried that if I did see her, I'd bury myself between her legs again, searching out her sweet taste, wanting to hear her cry out my name again.

Fuck.

What is wrong with me?

I never should have crossed that line. I never should have even considered her an option, and the big reason why is because I think I'm developing feelings for the girl, and I know those feelings most likely are not returned.

Yeah, she's getting to know me, though not because she likes me—fuck, I sound like a teenager—but she's getting to know me so she's not doing business with some jerk-off who doesn't know how to act around women.

And if she was really into me, she'd have followed me upstairs last night. I didn't expect her to, and I'd never expect a woman to return the favor, but if she had any draw toward me, she'd have been at my bedroom door, at least listening as I came all over my stomach, my hand pumping like a goddamn workhorse while my mind focused on the sounds and taste of her orgasm.

But she didn't, and I need to be conscious of that. I need to remember exactly what I'm doing. Trying to secure a deal.

I turn my attention to my computer just as my phone beeps with a text message. I squeeze my eyes shut, attempting to have some self-control, but I fail miserably as I reach for my phone and open up the text from Lottie.

Lottie: What's for lunch today?

I lean back in my office chair and text her back.

Huxley: Is that one of your questions?
Lottie: Consider it a freebie. Inquiring minds are curious.
Huxley: Not sure. Probably nothing. Getting a lot of work done.

She doesn't need to know that what I really want for lunch is her goddamn pussy, and if she were here right now, I'd be feasting on her before she could even take her next breath.

Lottie: How can you not eat lunch? I had a donut an hour ago, a
     huge breakfast burrito for breakfast, and I'm starving, ready
     to gnaw my arm off. And you skipped out on dinner.

Huxley: I recall it differently. I had my fill of dinner.

Fuck, I can't help myself. I can't stop myself from reminding her of how I make her feel, hell, how she makes me feel.

Satisfied.

Lottie: Question—have you always been this dirty?

Huxley: When you know what you want, you go after it. There's nothing dirty involved, just the truth.

Lottie: Well, that was a scapegoat answer that worked really well for you. Now ask me a question. Distract me while Kelsey fetches us lunch.

Huxley: Do you feel as though you know me a little better?

Lottie: I do, but I'm not sure I would've without these questions. I'm glad you've been open to them.

Huxley: Your turn.

Lottie: That's all you're going to say on the matter?

Huxley: Yes.

Lottie: Okay, I see that I'm getting the closed-off Huxley today, that's fine. Hmm, question—when was the last time you had sex, and with who?

Huxley: That's two questions.

Lottie: It's a two-parter, linked together. It passes.

Huxley: Why do you want to know?

Lottie: Is that your question?

Huxley: Consider it linked as well.

Lottie: Just interested in what your life was like before I rolled in.

Huxley: Last time I had sex, probably three months ago, with a girl I've known for a few years. Occasionally we get together just for the hell of it, no strings attached. Don't have time for anything else.

Lottie: A booty call. I wouldn't have expected anything less. But three months seems like a long time. I would've thought once a week for you.

Huxley: No time. Plus, I told you, when we're in contract, I don't seek out anyone else but you.

Lottie: I don't know how to respond to that.

Huxley: No need. My last question before I go—are you nervous about the pitch today?

Lottie: Honestly?

Huxley: Always.

Lottie: I am. I'm nervous because we've been working hard on this. I know we offer a great service, I know a lot is riding on this, and I know you're not going to just give us something for the hell of it. You're going to make us earn it.

Huxley: That's correct.

Lottie: This means a lot to us. Even the opportunity to pitch means a lot. We've been practicing, making sure everything is perfect, and when the time comes, I really hope we can show you how beneficial we'd be for Cane Enterprises.

I already know they're perfect for the job. I've done my research on Kelsey, but I'm going to make them pitch anyway, because I'm not the only one who makes the decisions. Breaker and JP have to be a *yes* as well. More so, this is good practice for Kelsey and an excellent boost in confidence for Lottie. She needs to find her niche in business, given it's what she's studied. I see the potential in her. She needs to prove it to herself more than to me.

Huxley: We look forward to your presentation. We'll see you then.

I set down my phone and turn back to my computer. I look through my emails, but the letters become all jumbled and mashed together. Nothing makes sense.

My mind is unfocused.

Because even though I don't want to admit it, the only thing I can think about is this: Will I be able to go down on Lottie again and...when?

———

"They should be here any minute, right?" JP asks, adjusting his suit.

"Yes," I say. I can see one of the elevators climbing toward our floor. That has to be them.

"Do we know if the sister is single?" JP asks. "She's really hot."

"No idea, but if we sign a contract with her, it wouldn't be a good idea to pursue her," I say.

"Uh, says the guy who ate out Lottie on the dining room table last night."

"What?" Breaker leans in. "Why the hell did I not know about that?"

"I conned him into telling me," JP says. "I could tell he was in a good mood when he came in this morning, so I needled him until he told me."

"Dude, what the hell are you doing?" Breaker asks.

"Not the place or time," I say to Breaker as the elevator dings with their arrival. I set my shoulders back and prepare to lay my eyes on Lottie and whatever dress she chose to wear today.

But when the elevator doors open, it isn't Lottie and Kelsey I see, but rather Dave.

"Wow, what a greeting," Dave says as he steps off the elevator, taking us all in. "I wasn't expecting to see all three of the Cane brothers waiting on the other side of the elevator."

What's he doing here?

Better yet, where are Lottie and Kelsey—

The elevator on the far left dings, and the doors slide open, revealing Kelsey and Lottie, both with a more feminine-looking briefcase in hand.

Kelsey is wearing a deep purple dress that shapes to her torso and flares ever so slightly at the hips, while Lottie—hell, is she trying to distract me? She's wearing a navy-blue dress that hits her midthigh, fits like a glove, and cuts just low enough on her chest to make me want to rip the dress right off her with my bare hands. And then those heels.

My teeth wander over my bottom lip as my eyes stay fixed on her. On her…confused face.

"Would you look at that? Lottie, how nice to see you," Dave says, pulling me out of my daze. "You look fantastic."

Shit, should she be showing?

Hopefully not.

I had no idea Dave was going to come to the office. I thought he couldn't work anything into his schedule and that's why we never heard from him. I guess I was wrong.

"Thank you," Lottie says. "Nice tie, Dave." Smoothly, she walks toward me, and I watch her every step in those heels as she marches right up to me, places her hand on the back of my neck, and says, "Hey, handsome." Then, before I can catch my breath, she's bringing my mouth toward her. It feels like hours as she closes the space between us, but when her lips meet mine, something possessive runs deep through my veins.

Life.

Her lips on mine are giving me life.

My hand snags around her back, and I pull her in close to anchor her against me. Her other hand holding her modern briefcase falls to my chest as she steadies herself. My lips get lost in hers.

The fact that we're in the office fades to black.

The peering eyes are nonexistent.

And the meeting we have planned goes on the back burner as I taste Lottie's lips for the first time.

Smooth.

Interested.

Passionate.

I knew, just from the way she gets lost in my touch, that she'd be a good kisser, but this reaction, this press of her body against mine, fuck…it's so much better than I ever expected.

When she finally pulls away and looks up at me with searching eyes, she slowly swallows and says, "Hey, you."

I pinch her chin with my forefinger and thumb. "Hey." When I finally look away from her, I catch Kelsey's look of total disbelief, followed by Dave's excited response.

"I love you two together," Dave says, as if he's known us for years and finally got us to hook up. The man is kind of weird, I've grown to find out as we've spent more time with him. He claps his hands together. "I'm sorry to interrupt, though. Huxley, are you ready for our meeting?"

"Meeting?" Lottie asks quietly. I glance at her. There's a confused look in her eyes, and I know how this might seem.

Like once again I'm skipping out on her and her sister.

"I wasn't aware you set up a meeting with Dave as well," Lottie says, and there's defeat in her shoulders. She knows how hard I've been trying to get Dave to talk to me about the properties.

"We didn't," Dave says. "I was hoping to sneak in before the weekend. You know how I don't like to talk business after hours."

Didn't know that, but now I do.

"Oh." Lottie pats me on the chest. "Then I won't keep you waiting, Dave." Lottie steps away. I see the protest on Kelsey's lips as Lottie slowly shakes her head and moves her sister toward the elevator. "It was great seeing you, Dave." She gives him a gentle wave and presses the *down* button on the elevator. The doors open right away.

But, before they can step on, I say, "Lottie, Kelsey, meet us in the boardroom. We'll be right with you."

The look of surprise on Lottie's face gives me all the confirmation I need. *I just did the right fucking thing.*

"Huxley?"

"We'll be right there. Go set up." I let her know with my eyes that I mean business.

Without arguing, she leads Kelsey into the conference room, but I can feel her eyes on me the entire time.

I turn to Dave and say, "Man, you know I'd love to have this conversation with you more than anything, but I promised Kelsey and Lottie I'd listen to their pitch."

"Pitch?" Dave asks. "You make your fiancée pitch to you?"

I smirk. "She wouldn't have it any other way."

"Pardon my intrusion, but can I ask what they're pitching?"

I stick my hands in my suit pockets and say, "They own an organizational business that focuses on using sustainable and earth-friendly organizing products. We're thinking of having them go through our properties, especially this office, to make our spaces more efficient."

"Wow." Dave blinks a few times and glances toward the conference room. "I had no idea Lottie was a hustler." He slowly nods. "With all the money you have, she doesn't want to just sit around and enjoy it; she wants to make something of herself. I respect that, a lot." He keeps his eyes on her and a spike of jealousy…possession…pulses through me.

"I'm a lucky man. It's really sexy seeing her work as hard as she does."

"I can imagine." Dave rocks on his heels and says, "Well, how about I set up a time with Karla to speak so we don't have a run-in like this again?"

"Great, and I'm sorry about today."

Dave waves me off. "It actually makes me respect you even more, sticking to your prior commitments, realizing when something is important." Dave nods. "You're a good man, Huxley Cane."

Hell, if he only knew.

I turn to Breaker and ask, "Can you help Dave find Karla to set up that meeting?"

"It would be my pleasure," Breaker says as he guides Dave to the back of the office. When they're out of earshot, JP turns toward me, mimicking my stance.

"You're fucked."

"What do you mean?" I ask. "Dave said he respected me more."

JP shakes his head. "Nah, man, not with Dave. You're just fucked, because that girl in there, the one in the blue dress—yeah, she has you by the balls. The Huxley I know never would've passed up on the opportunity to meet with the guy he's trying to strike a deal with. As a matter of fact, he'd drop pretty much anything to make it happen." He glances behind him. "Who knew a girl in a blue dress would be your kryptonite?"

"I made a promise to her," I say, my jaw clenched tight. "I'm not about to walk out on that promise."

JP pats me on the shoulder. "Keep telling yourself that, man."

He heads toward the conference room, and when he opens the door, both girls look up, but Lottie doesn't say anything to JP. Her eyes stray to mine through the glass windows. There it is, plain as day—she's grateful.

The surge of pride that pummels me in the chest from that one simple look is scary.

Terrifying.

———

Exhausted, I flop onto my large bed and let out a deep sigh. From the lack of sleep this week to the tension-filled moments I've shared with Lottie, I've never felt more tired in my entire life.

When I got home, I sat at the kitchen island and scarfed down the sandwich Reign made for me, and then I spent a good ten minutes in the shower, washing the week away, then slipped into a pair of boxer briefs and lay on top of my bed.

Lottie and Kelsey delivered today. There didn't seem to be an ounce of nerves when they were presenting. They were confident, knowledgeable, and when we drilled them with questions, they had an answer for every single one of them. But not just answers, answers that were well thought-out and informative.

There was no question. After they finished, I looked at the boys, they gave me the nod, and we told them they were hired. We'd start with the main office and then work our way out from there. It's a huge contract for them. A contract that's going to put them at the next level.

They held their composure as they packed up their things and thanked us, but after we left, Lottie sent me a text message full of emojis and said she and Kelsey were going to celebrate. She asked if it was okay if she missed dinner.

As if she needs to ask my permission. I told her to have fun.

Which leaves me here, alone, in my bedroom, contemplating my decisions.

Knock. Knock.

My eyes glance over at the door.

I sit up on my bed, hands gripping the edge as I say, "It's open."

The door cracks and Lottie pokes her head inside. "Can I come in?"

"Yes," I answer as my eyes drag over her body in that dress. What I wouldn't give to peel it off her body right now and celebrate her victory with her, the only way I know how—by worshipping her body.

"Hey." She waves shyly.

"Hey," I say as I wet my lips. Lottie looks like a juicy piece of meat, standing there in front of me, waiting to be devoured.

"I just thought I'd stop by before I went to take a bath. I wanted to personally thank you again."

"No need to thank me, Lottie. You and Kelsey put on one hell of a presentation. It was an easy yes for all of us."

She shakes her head. "No, I mean, thank you for the sacrifice you made. You didn't have to do that."

"Do what?" I ask, confused.

Her head tilts to the side. "Huxley, I know you've been waiting to talk to Dave about business for a while now, but when the opportunity presented itself, you didn't back down on your promise to us."

"I told you, I can be an honest man. Dave could wait."

"Well, I know what a sacrifice it was, and I'm really grateful."

"You're welcome," I say simply. And when she doesn't leave, I ask, "Did you have fun with your sister? You're home sooner than I thought."

"We went for celebratory drinks. Some guys bought us a few drinks." My jealousies rise, my anger taking root. "Kelsey was vibing with one of them, and the other guy was trying to get my number."

My jaw tenses, my fingers grip the side of the mattress tightly.

"But I told him I was engaged." Lottie smirks and holds up her hand, showing off her ring. "When he saw the size of the diamond, he knew there was no competition."

Damn fucking right.

"He doesn't need to see the size of the ring to realize there's no competition. Especially when I'm the man who gave you the ring."

She folds her arms over her chest. "Am I sensing a hint of jealousy, Huxley?"

"Not jealousy, just protecting what's mine."

"I'm yours now?"

"Until we've fulfilled our duties spelled out in the contract," I say, my fingers itching to let go of this mattress and bury themselves in Lottie's long dark locks.

"Well, you have nothing to worry about, my loyalty lies with you." She walks toward me, those mile-high heels of hers clicking across the floor. My eyes fix on her toned legs, and when she stops in front of me, her chest rests just at eye level. And then she squats to her knees, right between my legs.

"What are you doing?" I ask, my body erupting in excitement from her position.

Her hands fall to my thighs. "Thanking you."

Her hands slide up to my already stiff cock, but I stop her before she can touch anything. "I don't need your thanks. I told you, you earned everything you got today. It has nothing to do with our situation and everything to do with your ideas and merit."

Her eyes match up to mine. "Do you not want me to suck you off?"

"Not like this," I say, offended. "Not with the thought in your mind that you're thanking me for hiring you. I don't want your mouth like that."

I move my hand to her cheek and caress her lips with my thumb. She opens her mouth, capturing my thumb, and she sucks on it, hard. Her cheeks hollow out, and fuck, what I wouldn't give to have my dick replace my thumb.

But not like this.

Not when there's the possibility that she thinks she's repaying me.

No fucking way.

When she releases my thumb, she smooths her hands up my thighs and stands. She pushes at my chest until I'm lying down and then crawls on top of me, her legs spread, her heated warmth connecting right with my aching cock.

I'd love to fuck this woman, to peel her out of this dress and show her the kind of lover I am.

And I don't want to fuck her just because she's beautiful, or because her smart mouth turns me on, but because I saw a side of her I haven't seen before. A professional side, a spark of excitement for her goals, for her achievements. It was really fucking sexy. It's making me see her in a completely different light, which is so goddamn dangerous, because I'm already sticking my toes over the line here. I'm already crossing into damaging territory.

"Lottie, what are you doing?"

Her hips rub against my cock, and she smiles. "You're hard."

"What's your point?"

Her face falls, and her hand braces on my chest. "Why are you angry?"

"I'm not angry."

"You're pulling away. I know when you're shutting down, and that's what you're doing right now. You're shutting down. Why, Huxley?"

"You've already asked your questions for today."

She shakes her head. "Not my dinner questions."

"You didn't have dinner with me tonight, so you forfeited that right."

Growing angry, she lifts off me, and I sit up as she rights her dress. "Just when I think you might not be an asshole anymore, you prove me wrong. You're the most infuriating man I've ever met."

Yeah, I'm pretty fucking annoyed with myself as well. But when I remain silent, she huffs and turns toward the door.

Before exiting my room, she says, "I'm meeting up with Ellie on Tuesday at ten to look at breast pumps. Thought I'd let you know. I'm still keeping up my end."

"I told you, you don't have to do that."

"Apparently it's the least I can do," she says with such venom that I grow irritated.

"You owe me nothing, I told you that," I say as she reaches for the handle of my door.

"Consider it part of the contract." She goes to leave but then pauses. She looks over her shoulder, her petite frame tense, causing her movements to be jagged. Exhaling deeply, she lowers her head and barely above a whisper, she asks, "Could you at least do me a favor and unzip my dress for me?"

"You can't reach it?"

She shakes her head. "No, Kelsey helped me earlier."

I stand from my bed and close the distance between us, my cock hard in my briefs as I approach. When only a few inches separate us, I swipe my hand across her long hair and swoop it over her shoulder, exposing her back. I reach up to the small zipper and slowly pull it down her back, painfully revealing that she's not wearing a bra. When I reach the end of the zipper, I keep my eyes fixed on her back as she pushes the dress down until it pools at her feet, revealing her bright white lace thong and her round perky ass.

Fuck.

Me.

Arm clasped over her breasts, she turns toward me and drops to a squat to pick up her dress. As she stands back up, her shoulder grazes my cock and I nearly jump right out of my briefs from the touch. Her eyes meet mine, and she blinks those long lashes before she says seductively, "Thank you."

I wet my lips.

My hands itch to reach out and grab her.

My cock begs for relief.

But I don't move. I don't even flinch.

With a disappointed look in her eyes, she heads out of my bedroom but doesn't shut the door. She crosses into her bedroom and leaves her door open as well as she drops the dress on her bed and sashays to the bathroom.

Fuck. An open door. That's an invitation.

She's tempting me, not giving up in her pursuit. For the life of me, I don't think I can hold back.

Not after seeing her perfect ass.

Not after undressing her.

Not after that kiss we shared earlier.

Not after seeing her on her knees, cheeks hollowed.

Not after knowing she wanted my cock in her mouth.

My will has cracked, my strength is wavering, and all my rules are jumbled in my head, not a single one making sense.

I hear the shower turn on in her bathroom. Hell. My cock grows even harder as I stand still, staring into the other room, pleading with myself to make a move, but to also keep it the fuck together.

But then…she walks across the bedroom…completely naked.

Tits, the perfect handful.

Hips, just enough to grab on to.

Pussy, waxed and so goddamn tempting. One taste was not enough.

Mother.

Fucker.

She looks over at me, flips her hair over her shoulder, and then goes to her nightstand. She opens a drawer and pulls out her dildo with the suction cup at the end. Turning toward me, she offers a full-frontal view, and my mouth goes dry as my eyes take in her tight nipples, hard and craving my mouth. Aware of my staring, Lottie takes the end of the dildo and rubs it across her chest, allowing her head to fall back as she brings it up to her mouth.

Her tongue peeks out…

And she licks the goddamn top.

I'm fucking gone.

My cock jolts in my briefs.

Sweat breaks out on my lower back.

And just like that, my willpower snaps.

Satisfied with herself, she moves toward her bathroom, dildo in hand, with me crossing the barrier between our rooms and following her inside.

The moment I step into her bathroom, she shuts the door to the shower, and I catch her watering down the dildo before she suctions it to the wall. I built this house to include two-person showers in every bathroom, so there's plenty of room in there. *Especially if I wanted to join her.* She steps away and wets herself down in the shower as well, but instead of just letting the water soak her, she puts on a show.

Seductively, with purpose, her hands cascade down her breasts, where she pauses and pinches her nipples. A low moan falls past her lips as her hands continue to move south. Water runs down her chest, off the tips of her nipples, and all the way down her flat stomach to her smooth pussy.

My mouth waters.

My hands itch to touch her. Feel her.

My body aches to be in that shower with her.

Once she's doused in water, she turns her back toward the dildo and then bends at the waist, angling herself just enough to...oh...fuck.

My teeth bite into my bottom lip as she slowly backs up onto the dildo, inserting it into her tight hole.

"Yesss," she moans softly as she pulls her wet hair to one side.

Intently fixated on what she's doing, I watch her pelvis move around in soft circles.

Fuck, my cock grows so tight that it's painful. I swore I wouldn't masturbate in front of her, that if I were to come, I'd come inside of her.

But seeing her like this, wanting so badly to touch her goddamn nipples and suck them into my mouth...it drives me crazy.

It makes me snap.

It causes me to want to go against everything I've said.

"God, Huxley," she says in such a satisfied tone that my ears perk up from the use of my name. "Yes, Hux," she says, pumping a little harder. "So good. Feels...so...good."

My cock jumps.

My body tenses.

My arms tremble at my sides as one of her hands snakes between her legs, and she begins to massage her clit.

"Yes, right there. Right there, Hux. God, I love your hands. I love how they make me feel."

Fuck.

Her eyes slide open, and her head tilts to the side as her gaze connects with mine.

Heady.

Lustful.

Passionate.

"Mmmm, yes," she moans, her eyes never leaving mine.

I take a step forward, my need possessing me.

"Your tongue. I love coming on your mouth." She sticks her finger past her lips and sucks. "I love it when you taste me. Lick me. Suck me." Her other hand goes to her breast, where she pinches her nipple hard. "You're so good at making me come, unlike any man I've ever been with," she groans.

Her hips pulse in and out.

The finger once in her mouth drags down her chest.

Fucking hell…

Another two steps forward.

"Ahh, ahhh, yes. Oh God, you're so huge. I knew you would be; I knew your cock would be just what I needed."

Her head falls forward.

Her hips pulse faster.

Her fingers pinch her nipples, pulling a hiss past her lips.

Motherfucker.

I want that to be me.

I *need* that to be me.

The last thread of resistance snaps, and before I can stop myself, I strip out of my briefs and throw the door to the shower open. The water pelts me in the back as Lottie smiles up at me right before her hand reaches out and grabs my cock, which is standing at attention.

"Just what I wanted for dessert," she says before taking my cock into her mouth.

Fuck.

I reach for her hair and gather it to one side so I can watch as her mouth descends over my thick cock. Her plump lips suck me in, and her hand strokes me at the base of my cock. But it's her mouth that's making me drive my hips forward, begging for more.

Hot.

Wet.

Perfection.

She takes me deep in her throat. My eyes roll to the back of my head, and I move closer so she can keep pleasuring herself as well.

Just as I thought—allowing her to touch me, suck me—it's everything I dreamed of. So fucking good. I move my hand over her cheek and stroke her soft skin with my thumb. "Take my cock, deep into that dirty mouth." She sucks me harder. "Just like that. Fuck, yes, Lottie." My hand goes to the back of her head, and I help her keep pace, moving her over my erection again and again, building the pleasure deep within me.

"Oh God," she mumbles against my cock as she swivels her hips against the dildo.

Can't say I particularly like her getting off with something other than my hand or mouth, but it is hot having her fuck herself while she fucks me with her mouth. I'll allow it this time. *But it's my name she's been saying. My hands she's imagining on her body. My tongue on her clit and pussy.*

Her mouth drags to the tip of my cock, and her hands reach for my balls, which she gently rolls between her fingers. I spread my legs so she has better access, because I want to be played with. I want her to be able to do whatever the fuck she wants to me. And she does. She smooths her palm over my balls and plays with my tip, sucking just the end, licking, flicking.

Fucking teasing.

And I love it.

I love the buildup.

The way she focuses on one particular area and then takes a part of me in her mouth again, pressing me to the back of her throat...

"Fuck," I mutter when my cock jolts against her luscious lips.

"I love your cock," she says when she removes me from her mouth and licks my length. "It's so big, Huxley. So thick." Her tongue flicks the underside of the head, teasing that sensitive part, and I swear I grow another inch from how she's holding my balls, gently, and I mean gently, tugging on them. It's just enough to drive me crazy, to send a chill of pleasure up my spine.

"I want to come in your mouth," I say as I grip the base of my cock, but she swats my hand away.

"This is mine, you don't touch it."

My brow raises from her demand, and if I weren't so desperate for her to finish me off, I'd tell her exactly what is hers, but I need her perfect mouth all over my cock. And I need it now.

"Then fuck me with your mouth," I say through clenched teeth.

She stops pulsing on her dildo and, instead, focuses on my cock, taking me deep in her throat.

She sucks.

She gags.

She repeats the process until I can't feel anything but her sweet mouth.

I grip the side of the shower wall as pleasure rips up my legs and pools at the base of my cock.

"Fuck, I'm going to come." I brush my hand over her cheek. "Take every last drop."

Her eyes turn hazy, and, in that moment, she finishes me off, pumping, sucking, giving me the best head of my entire life. My balls tighten, my cock swells, and I explode with a roar that erupts from my chest as I come in her mouth.

And she takes it all.

Every last drop, like I said, until I'm completely spent and trying to catch my breath.

She releases me and smirks up at me.

It takes me three seconds to grab hold of her, flip the shower off, and then lay her across the built-in bench. I spread her legs, get down on my knees, and press my mouth to her pussy.

"Yesss," she draws out as her hand falls to my hair. She grips the strands tightly and moans as I lap up her already aroused pussy.

She's so close. Her legs squeeze at my shoulders, the tremble in her hands, which loosely grip my hair.

"I won't ever get over how you taste," I say while taking long lapping strokes and inserting two fingers inside of her. "I could eat you all goddamn day." Stroke after stroke, the tension in her core grows tighter and tighter until her fingers dig deep into my scalp and her hips shift.

"Huxley, I'm going…oh fuck, I'm coming," she shouts as I hold her pelvis down, making it impossible for her to move as I eat her out, pleasure her how I want her to be pleasured.

She moans, her voice echoing off the tile.

She yells my name when I don't let up, taking every last ounce of her orgasm from her.

And when she slowly relaxes, I give her a few more strokes before pulling away slightly, only to give her a kiss on her pussy.

When I stand, she looks up at me, her eyes showing disbelief. Her hand shakily moves up her body, to her neck. She searches me as she catches her breath, and I'm not sure what's on her mind, what she might say, so I decide to beat her to it.

"Have a good night," I say, before stepping out of the shower. I have to cut it off here. I have to get the fuck away, or else I can see myself taking her back to her bed and fucking her through the night until she can't take my cock anymore.

Regret for leaving her pulses through me, but I push past it and grab one of her spare towels, wrap it around my waist, and head toward my bedroom, shutting the door behind me.

Dazed, confused, and unsure of what came over me, I enter my bathroom, where I flip on the shower and rest under the hot water, trying to gather myself.

What the actual fuck am I doing?

I'm blurring lines all over the goddamn place, and now that I've had her mouth on me, I don't think I'll ever be the same. Not after seeing her take me so deep, after the way she drank every last drop of my come.

I won't be able to get that image out of my head. Not for a very long time.

And as I step out of the shower to dry off, all I can think about is how I want to go back across the hallway and explore Lottie's body. How I want to thank her for putting up with my shit. For opening me up when I don't really want to be opened up.

I stare at myself in the mirror and slowly drag my hand over my scruff, the same scruff that marked Lottie on her inner thighs as mine. *What the actual hell are you doing, man?*

And why do you look…happy?

Happy in a moment when I shouldn't be happy, because chaos is swallowing me whole. The deal, the lies, the blurred lines…it's all up in the air—something I don't normally put up with—but here I am…dealing with it.

Christ.

My phone beeps on my nightstand, and I glance over at it, wondering what the hell time it is.

I take a seat in my towel on my bed and read it.

Lottie: Your mouth is absolutely decadent. I love coming on your tongue.

Fuck.

Is she trying to get me hard again?

Huxley: I can't get enough of your pussy or your trembling clit.

I drag my hand over my mouth, willing my body to not get excited again. Once tonight is enough. Crossing the line more than that is asking for trouble.

Lottie: I've only come like that for you. No one else. Only. You.

Yup, she's trying to get me hard again, she's trying to entice me. She wants more. I can feel it deep in my bones.

Huxley: Are you naked on your bed right now?
Lottie: How did you know?
Huxley: You're trying to get me to come back to your bedroom.
Lottie: I want your dick inside of me, Huxley. My legs are spread, my nipples are hard, my body is heated just thinking about it.

My cock jolts and I grind my molars, trying to keep it together.

Huxley: I'm not coming back over there.

Even though I want to. Fuck, do I want to sink myself between her legs. But I'm growing addicted, and that needs to stop. I have no idea where her head is at, if this is just fun for her while we pass the time, but I can see that it would be more for me, and I'm not about to risk it. I place my phone down, thinking that Lottie won't respond after that last text. Is she angry? Frustrated? Confused? *Everything I feel too?*

Lottie: If you won't come back over here, then will you reconsider answering my two questions?

I let out a deep sigh and push my hand through my hair. *She still wants to know me...*
But I still need to keep boundaries.

Huxley: Those are dinner questions only.
Lottie: Please, Huxley?

And just like that, the conversation switches from sexually charged to innocent. I can hear her voice saying those two words, asking me, begging me to participate.

I apparently have no willpower, because I nod even though she can't see me and text her back.

> **Huxley:** What are your questions?
>
> **Lottie:** Thank you. How about I ask the two questions and we both have to answer?
>
> **Huxley:** Fine.
>
> **Lottie:** Your enthusiasm is infectious.
>
> **Huxley:** You're on borrowed time...
>
> **Lottie:** Okay, question number one—what would you say is your favorite quality about yourself?
>
> **Huxley:** Not sure where you're going with this, but I guess I'd answer my drive.
>
> **Lottie:** I could see that.
>
> **Huxley:** What's your favorite thing about yourself?
>
> **Lottie:** My loyalty, even though it got me into trouble with Angela. I think having loyalty is very important. Another reason why I'm sticking to my word and going breast pump shopping with Ellie.
>
> **Huxley:** Being loyal is a very admirable quality.
>
> **Lottie:** Okay, second question—what do you like most about me? And I'll answer what I like most about you.
>
> **Huxley:** Fishing for compliments?
>
> **Lottie:** Since we're working together and you tend to pull away a lot, I thought it would be beneficial if we say what we like about each other. As a reminder.
>
> **Huxley:** Okay. I like that you're loyal.
>
> **Lottie:** No way, you can't use the thing I said. Come on, Huxley,

I know it might be painful for you to offer me a compliment, but you can at least try.

My lips press against my teeth in frustration as I flop back on my bed. Okay, she wants to know what I like about her. Might as well tell her.

Huxley: You're fearless. You might not make the right decision all the time, but no matter what, you go into the situation without fear and you don't hold back. It's a characteristic you don't find with many people. Pair that with loyalty, and it makes you someone I'd spend time with.

She doesn't reply right away, and I worry if I overstepped, if I said too much, but then there's a knock on the doorframe of my door. I sit up and find Lottie standing there in one of the many lingerie sets I had purchased for her.

This one is red. The shorts are loose-fitting, made entirely of lace and see-through. The top is cropped at the belly button and offers no support. Therefore, her breasts just float freely.

Yup, she's easily the sexiest woman I've ever seen in my entire life.

"What's up?" I ask, feeling uncomfortable from my honest text and also, once again turned on.

"Wanted to see if what you said was the truth."

"Why would I lie to you? Have I lied to you yet?"

"No," she says. "But...I don't know, just felt as if I needed to see your face."

"It's the truth. You can count on that from me."

She toes the ground as she stares down at the carpet. "Thank you."

"Is that all?" I ask her.

"No. I need to tell you what I like about you."

I shake my head and stand from my bed. "Not necessary."

"Your helping heart," she says, her eyes meeting mine. "You don't let people see it; you hide it away from the public eye. But as a spectator, having paid close enough attention, I've seen it, and it's beautiful."

I don't take compliments well.

I don't really care for them, actually.

So, listening to her, to her praise doesn't settle well, and I don't understand how to handle it.

"You don't need to say anything," she says, sensing how uncomfortable I am. "But I thought I'd let you know." She offers me a soft smile. "Good night, Huxley."

Quietly, I say, "Good night," as she walks away.

My mind feels as though it's been eclipsed by a heavy foggy night. I can't think straight. I can't seem to put two thoughts together as to what the hell I should do. How the hell do I reconcile Lottie's observation of me...her favorite thing about me? *"Your helping heart. You don't let people see it; you hide it away from the public eye. But as a spectator, having paid close enough attention, I've seen it, and it's beautiful."* No one has ever talked to me—argued with me—the way Lottie does. No one has seen me the way she sees me. Sure, my brothers know me for the person I am, but anyone who's walked into my life sees Huxley Cane, the billionaire, the mogul. They've never seen me as Huxley, the man with a heart. Because I know it's fucking there. I pride myself on being compassionate when the moment presents itself. But no one has picked up on it.

Until Lottie.

Knowing I'm in trouble mentally, I go back to my nightstand, grab my phone, and text my brothers.

Huxley: I'm fucked.

They're immediate with their responses.

JP: Let me guess—you realized you like your fake fiancée?

Huxley: I like her. I shouldn't, but I do.

JP: Called it.

Breaker: Every person watching this could've called that.

Huxley: I don't know what to fucking do.

JP: What any other person would do if they liked someone. Ask them out.

Huxley: Ask her out? But we have a business agreement. And I don't think she likes me like that.

Breaker: Look at our big brother being all insecure. It's cute on him.

JP: Dare I say, I'm enjoying this humbling moment?

Huxley: Don't be assholes. I need fucking help.

JP: You don't need help. You know exactly what to do, you're just too scared to pull the trigger.

Breaker: ^^^ Facts.

Huxley: It's complicated. What about the deal with Dave?

JP: I don't think that's anything you need to worry about right now. I'd focus on what you want, something you want that's not business related. Breaker and I can both attest to this and say, you need something in your life other than this company.

Breaker: You need to learn to live, man. You're not living. You have all this money, and you do nothing with it. Now you have a reason to do something. Take her out. Date her. If you like her, go for it.

Huxley: You don't think it'll fuck things up between us?

JP: It'll only make it better.

Breaker: He's right. What could go wrong? Seriously.

Huxley: Famous last words.

CHAPTER 16
LOTTIE

I STARE UP AT THE ceiling of my bedroom, my mind drifting to last night.

What I wouldn't have given to have Huxley come to my room again, to taste his lips one more time, to feel him driving between my legs with his magnificent cock.

I groan in frustration and sit up, not bothering to adjust my swimming cover-up that I put on before I flopped on my bed. If Huxley hadn't already seen me naked, I'd consider skipping the cover-up, because the swimsuit he provided me barely covers my nipples.

This morning, he was out on a run when I went down to the kitchen for breakfast; at least, that's what the note on the kitchen island said. It was a plain note, nothing special about it. It just said, "on a run." His staff doesn't work on the weekends anymore, so I had his house to myself. I grabbed a yogurt parfait Reign had made the day before, devoured it, and then worked on our website for a bit before spending a decent amount of time putting my hair into French braids and then pulling on one of the provided swimsuits. I went with a simple black one.

I need to get some sun. Clear my head. Get the hell out of this room where I'm reminded of how amazing it felt to have Huxley's five o'clock shadow roughly rub against my inner thighs.

The sides of the cover-up flap open as I snag my sunglasses from the dresser and head for the stairs. I leave my phone behind because I don't want any distractions. I want it to be me and the sun.

I take the stairs down to the main floor and glance around, noticing that the space looks untouched, and then head to the back of the house, where I open one of the overly large sliding glass doors. Of course there are towels folded neatly and stacked in an outdoor linen closet, along with anything else you might need while swimming—goggles, sunscreen, and even those little plugs for your nose.

From the closet, I snag a towel and take it to one of the black-and-white striped lounge chairs bordering the pool. Undoing the ties of my cover-up, I let the fabric fall to the ground, then set my sunglasses over my eyes. The California sun is relentless, making it great tanning weather, which makes me think… I glance around, knowing damn well I'm alone in this incredibly large house, so I reach behind and undo my bikini top. Oops, would you look at that, completely topless. That's more like it. I revel in the way the heat of the sun immediately warms my nipples.

Should I strip down completely?

I glance around one more time and then think, *Why the fuck not?*

Once my bottoms are pushed down to my feet, I step out of the fabric and place the bottoms with my top.

Nude.

And it feels so good.

There's a white lounge float in the pool calling my name, so I walk over to the edge, reach for the float, and pull it toward the stairs to carefully get on. The cool water against my heated skin is a wonderful contrast that my body appreciates. Once I'm situated on the float, I adjust my glasses and then sink into the comfort of floating on the water as the sun heats my naked skin.

Wouldn't be the first time I've gone skinny-dipping.

I close my eyes and listen to the subtle breeze swishing through the palm tree leaves, offering a relaxing soundtrack to my midmorning swim. Yes, this is just what I needed.

Eyes shut, I'm just about to doze off—

"What the hell are you doing?"

Huxley.

And from the tone of his voice, he's not happy.

I open my eyes and lift my sunglasses to see him at the edge of the pool, wearing nothing but a pair of running shorts and running shoes. His thick bare chest is covered in sweat, and his hair is soaked, wet strands clumping together.

God, he looks yummy.

I shift on the raft—I'm not shy at all; the man has seen it all already—and say, "Floating."

"You're naked."

"Am I?" I ask, glancing down. "Well, would you look at that, I am." And just for the hell of it, I spread my legs wider than the raft and let my feet dip into the water.

"Why?"

I fix my sunglasses over my eyes. "Because I wanted to. Because you've already seen me naked. And because your staff doesn't work on weekends anymore." I tilt my head toward the sun. "God, I love skinny-dipping. Have you tried it?"

"No."

"Really? You have a pool. You should at least try it once." I wave toward him. "Come in, join me."

He doesn't say anything, so I crack my eyes open to see what he's doing. I find him standing on the edge, but now his hands are balled into tight fists at his side.

Someone needs to relax.

The man is a pent-up ball of stress, ready to explode any minute. He's had small moments here and there where he's allowed himself to relax, but he hasn't fully unclenched yet. Maybe slowly but surely, I can help him do that.

"I won't bite. Promise." I dip my fingers into the water and splash them around before bringing them up to my chest, where water drips from my fingers and onto my breasts. I'm tempted to circle my nipple but I'm not looking for him to come in here sexually charged. I'm just looking for him to relax.

When he still doesn't move, I sigh in frustration and shift my body off the raft and into the cool water. My nipples harden immediately from the shock of the temperature change to my skin, but I power through and make it to the stairs.

Huxley's eyes stay fixed on me, pulsing through me with such intensity that my stomach bottoms out momentarily as I grow close to him.

With a shaky hand, I take his in mine, guide him to a lounge chair, and forcibly make him sit. When he doesn't protest, I kneel in front of him and remove his socks and shoes. I can feel his gaze on me the entire time, watching my every move. When I'm done, I stand and take his hand in mine again. I leave him in his shorts, because those are easy to swim in, and after I've checked for his phone and wallet, I guide him to the steps of the pool.

Oddly, even though I'm completely naked, I don't feel self-conscious in front of him. I don't even feel as though I'm naked. *He makes me feel comfortable in my skin.* He hasn't quite voiced his appreciation for my body as much as one would think, given the confidence I have around him, but it isn't about what he says; it's about how he acts when I'm exposed to him. The way his eyes rake over me with desperate gratitude. The firm grip whenever he places his hands on me. The domineering commands when we're in the moment.

Not to mention, how he gets so incredibly hard any time we're intimate.

I step into the water and bring him in with me. He doesn't protest, so I keep moving forward until I reach the raft, which is definitely big enough for the both of us. I pull it closer and say, "Get on."

He scans the raft and then looks at me. "Are you going to join me?"

"Yes," I answer.

With that, he gets on the raft and then helps me on. With the added weight, we sink lower into the water, but we're still floating, just the occasional splash of water lapping up over the edge. I situate myself so I'm facing him while he lies on his back and places his hand behind his head.

"See? No need to get your panties in a twist. Isn't this nice?"

In a gruff voice, he says, "My panties weren't in a twist."

I press my finger to his brow and say, "This was all scrunched up."

"You're naked."

"You didn't seem to have a problem with that last night."

His eyes shoot to mine. "You weren't outside."

I can't hide the smirk that pulls at my lips. "Afraid someone else might see me?"

"Yes," he says.

"You act as if you care."

His eyes flash to mine again, and he stares at me for a few breaths before he turns and faces me on the raft. His hand falls to my hip, and from that little possessive touch, my entire body heats up from the inside out.

"I do fucking care." His thumb rubs over my skin. "This is for my eyes only."

I twist my lips to the side, trying to tread the line carefully as I ask, "Was my body contracted to you as well? I can't quite remember that part."

He wets his lips and drags his hand up my side, down my arm, and then straight to my breast. His fingers connect with my nipple, and casually, as if this is what he does on Saturdays, he rolls my nipple between his fingers.

But the feeling pumping through me from his touch is anything but casual.

"Did I or did I not have my mouth all over your cunt last night?" He twists my nipple, and I squeeze my eyes shut, my breath stolen from me momentarily.

"You...did," I answer.

"Then that means I laid claim on this body." He pinches me. "Understood?"

A hiss escapes past my lips. "Yes," I answer.

"Good." He releases my nipple, and I can't help but utter a sound of protest. The smallest of smirks passes over his lips, and I glare at him.

"You think that's funny? Teasing me like that?"

"Not funny...more enticing. Makes me want to do more. Seeing you like this, naked in my pool, makes me want to do so much more."

"Like what?" I ask, intrigued. After the last couple of encounters with him and the mind-blowing orgasms he's pulled from me, I'd pretty much let him do anything to me. And I mean anything.

"Bend you over the side of this pool, spread your ass, and eat you out."

Oh.

Jesus.

My legs grow tight as a dull throb pulses between them. I can't imagine what that would feel like, but now I'm wondering just how good it would be.

"Have you ever done that before? Ever done anything with anyone in your pool before?"

He glances to the side, avoiding eye contact with me. "Yeah."

For some reason, that disappoints me. I know I shouldn't care, and I have no right to care at all, but a small part of me wishes that I were the first woman he had in this pool.

But playing it cool, I ask, "Oh really? Was she any good?"

This time his eyes flash to mine. "No."

Well…that, uh, that makes me want to smile.

"Interesting," I say, keeping my smile to myself. "Why wasn't she any good?"

He runs his fingers over my breast again and then passes his thumb across my nipple. "She was aggressive. Over-the-top. It was as if she was trying to impress me."

"When she did the exact opposite."

He nods as he rolls my nipple between his thumb and index finger. A small moan falls past my lips. I'm unable to control it, control how he makes me feel. This is the first time in my entire life that I can say that when I look at a man, all I want is his mouth on mine, his hand between my legs, his body commanding mine.

Every.

Single.

Time.

"I don't appreciate theatrics," he says softly, his eyes fixed on my breasts. "I want real when I take a woman to bed."

"Do you think I'm being real?" I ask.

His thumb releases my nipple, and he moves his hand back to my hip, stroking me gently. I'm turned on and want so much more. And yet, I also want him to relax, and that's what he seems to be doing. "Yes, I do think you're being real. You hate me too much to pretend I'm giving you pleasure. If I wasn't turning you on, you'd let me know."

He's very much right about that, but there is one thing he's not entirely correct in stating.

"I don't hate you, Huxley."

"Could've fooled me," he says softly. The tone of his voice is more teasing than accusatory.

"I mean, there are moments when I hate you; I'm not going to lie about that. But I don't have an overall hatred for you. I actually appreciate what you've done for me."

"It's a mutual appreciation," he says before he closes his eyes.

His breath evens out as his grip on me relaxes. *Is he…taking a nap? With me naked like this?*

When he doesn't move, but continues to lie there, eyes closed, hand on me, I realize that's exactly what he's doing.

And maybe, in other circumstances, I'd take offense to this. I'm a naked woman lying right next to him. I'd expect him to want to take advantage of the situation, but Huxley doesn't need to. He can lie here in comfort, knowing that I'll probably lie right here with him.

Which I will, because this moment feels comfortable. It feels normal.

I close my eyes as well and let out a deep sigh as I allow the raft to float us around the pool. The incoming clouds slowly block the sun from crisping up our skin, giving us the opportunity to just enjoy the warm heat.

I'm not sure how long we stay like this.

I can't be sure how long we nap, but it isn't until I'm being carried up the stairs of Huxley's house that I realize I'm no longer on the raft.

In a haze, I open my eyes and blink a few times. "What's happening?" I ask, confused.

"I didn't want you to get burnt. The sun came out again," he whispers softly.

Carrying me down the hallway that leads to our bedrooms, I half expect him to kick open the door to his bedroom, but he doesn't. He opens my bedroom door and then softly places me on my bed, rolling down the blankets and then slipping them up over my naked body. When he straightens, he grips the back of his neck and asks, "Can I get you anything?"

Caught off guard from his one-eighty in attitude, I shake my head. "No, I'm…uh, I'm good."

He nods and takes a step back. "Sorry about that back there."

"Sorry about what?" I ask.

"Touching you. I shouldn't have. I'm just having a hard time keeping this professional, especially when I walk in on you naked. You're damn hard to resist, Lottie."

I tilt my head, trying to understand him. "When has touching me ever stopped you before?"

"I'm trying to respect what we have, not fuck it up."

"Do you know how you can fuck it up?" I ask.

"How?"

"By closing yourself off."

He grips his neck even harder. "I'm trying, Lottie."

"I've noticed," I say. "And I appreciate you opening up and talking to me. Answering my questions. It means a lot to me. It makes this situation easier, and honestly, I like getting to know you, Huxley. You're a...neat guy."

His brow quirks up while a slight smile pulls at his lips. "Neat?"

I smirk. "Yup. Neat."

"Pretty sure no one has ever called me a *neat guy* before."

"Such a shame." I remove the covers he placed over me and stand from my bed. As I walk toward my bathroom, I feel his eyes tracing my every move. I walk into the walk-in closet and grab a fresh pair of underwear—if that's what you want to call them. The fabric barely covers my ass. I look for an oversized shirt but remember all of my clothes are in storage. Groaning, I walk back out. His eyes immediately rake over me, from head to toe. It's a heated gaze, reminding me that he might not have done anything with me this morning, but there's no doubt in my mind that he wants to. "Can I borrow a shirt?" I ask. "I really just want to wear something oversized and comfortable."

"You want to borrow one of my shirts?" he asks.

"Yeah, do you mind?"

His eyes grow darker, and he pauses before answering. *What's the big deal? It's a shirt.*

I'm about to tease him, when he says, "Sure." He turns away from me and heads into his room. I follow behind him, not caring at all that I'm topless. What's the point in covering up now?

He goes to his dresser drawers and pulls out a faded black T-shirt. "Don't lose it. It's one of my favorites," he says before handing it to me.

I take the threadbare shirt from him and unfold it, revealing a picture of Creedence Clearwater Revival. I quickly look up at him. "CCR? You have a CCR shirt?"

He nods. "They were one of my dad's favorite bands. I only have a few memories of my dad, because he divorced my mom when we were young, but the memories I do have of him always involved CCR playing in the background."

I slip the shirt on, loving how it smells like him.

He takes a step forward and tugs on the sleeve. "You're swimming in this."

"The way I like it."

He nods again. "Yeah, you look pretty damn good in it."

I hug myself. "It's really comfortable. I might steal it from you."

That playful brow of his quirks up again. "You better not."

Teasing him, I say, "You shouldn't have offered up this shirt if you didn't want me stealing it." I move past him, only for him to grip my wrist and pull me against his chest.

He tilts up my chin and says, "Don't make me peel that shirt off you right now."

"Is that supposed to be a threat? Feels more like a reward to me."

His lips thin as they press together. His eyes search mine, bouncing back and forth, and I wait for his next move. His comeback. But he doesn't say anything. He just…shakes his head and then laces his fingers with mine to bring me back downstairs to the kitchen, where he spins me toward the counter and lifts me up onto the island. The cold surface makes me squeal for just a second until my skin becomes acclimated.

"What do you want for lunch?" he asks.

"I thought you can't cook."

"I can't," he says. "But a sandwich is in my wheelhouse."

"Is it now?" I cross one leg over the other and lean my hands back on the counter. "What kind of sandwich? Grilled cheese? Or is that asking too much?"

He looks over his shoulder at me. "That's asking too much."

I snort and cover my nose at the same time. "You poor wealthy man. Can't even make a grilled cheese. Let me show you how it's done."

I hop off the counter and go to the fridge to find the cheese. Butter is on the counter in a crock, and I turn to find Huxley handing me the bread.

I know the pots and pans are in the island cabinets, so I open one of the doors and find exactly what I'm looking for.

When I turn toward the stove, I feel Huxley crowding me. "Don't worry, I'm not going to break anything."

"I'm not worried about you breaking anything," he says. "I'm hoping you teach me."

I pause. "You really don't know how to make a grilled cheese?"

"Never made one before."

"Oh God, why do I find that so endearing?" I ask.

His hand falls to my lower back as he moves to my other side. "Maybe because it's a weakness of mine and you enjoy watching me struggle."

I chuckle. "I do like seeing the almighty Huxley Cane having to come back down to earth." I elbow him, showing him I'm teasing. And when he glances in my direction with a smile, I can feel all of my anxiety wash right out of me.

With one simple look.

That's all it takes.

"So how do we make these things?" He holds up two pieces of bread.

"You really are helpless." I turn on the stovetop, warm up the pan, and then grab a plate and a knife, which I hand to him. "Do you know how to butter bread?"

He gives me a mocking look. "I'm not completely inept."

"Just checking." I smile widely. "Butter one side on each slice of bread."

He lifts the top to the butter crock and swipes butter over the bread. He's not smooth about it by any means. He's actually quite clumsy, which I find adorable, and at one point, he pierces the knife through the bread, making it seem as though I'm sitting in the front row to an awful infomercial where they don't know how to do simple things like cut a slice of cheese.

When he's done with the butter, I hand him the cheese. "Put that on the sandwich and then, with the butter facing out, set the sandwich on the pan."

"Easy enough," he says, though he gets butter all over his fingers in his attempt to put the sandwich on the pan. I hand him a towel, which he uses to wipe his hands. "Now we wait?"

"Yes. I have the heat on medium, and we're going to cover the pan with this lid so the cheese melts, and then we'll check on it in a minute or so."

He stares at the pan and then runs his hand through his hair. "This seems far too easy. I'm looking like an asshat right now."

I let out a loud laugh. "No, just…interesting, is all. If no one showed you, how would you know?"

"I could ask."

"Which you did." I pat his bare chest. "You asked me. Aren't you lucky to have me as your teacher?"

"Very," he says, his eyes serious.

Well…okay then.

Uh, let me just go, uh, get something so I don't have to feel like a wilting flower under this man's strong gaze.

I smile awkwardly and then head into the pantry to get some chips I saw in there the other day, as well as two bananas.

I don't know what's with the change of attitude on his end, but I'm going with it, because this is a Huxley Cane I could very much get along with. And given the man fell asleep with me on a pool float and then carried me upstairs to rest, I think I'm the Lottie Gardner he could get along with, too.

"It doesn't taste that bad after you scrape off the burnt parts," I say, examining the sandwich.

"You realize this is your fault, right?" He takes a bite of his partially burnt grilled cheese.

"How is this my fault?" I ask.

We're sitting at the outdoor dining set, a small bowl of chips between us, as well as precut veggies from Reign. I must say, the personal chef thing is pretty nice, a luxury I'll miss when this is all over.

"You left me in charge while you went to the bathroom."

"I told you to check it in a few seconds to see if it was done and then to take it off the heat. You turned up the heat."

"Something the supervisor should've been there to watch."

I roll my eyes and lean back in my chair. "Keep telling yourself that, Hux."

He sets his sandwich down and picks up his water. Casually, he leans back in his chair as well and looks out toward the pool. "Do you have any questions for me today?"

"I always have questions."

"Fire away," he says, looking way more relaxed than I've ever seen him. Which means he very well might be open to answering some hard-hitting questions.

Don't mind if I do.

I rub my hands together and ask, "What was your first impression of me?"

He takes a sip of his water and keeps his gaze forward as he speaks. "First impression. Well, you were wearing leggings and a sports bra that made your tits look amazing. It was hard not to think right off the bat how hot you were." He stuns me with his stare. "But then I quickly realized you were a lunatic."

My mouth falls open in amusement. I poke at his arm and say, "And yet, you still asked me to be your fake fiancée."

He scratches the side of his cheek. "Desperation does crazy things to a person."

"Aren't you a charmer today?" I bring my feet up on my seat and hug my knees to my chest, getting more comfortable. "Go ahead, ask me a question."

Studying me, he tilts his head to the side and asks, "Your dream man, who is he?"

Color me shocked. Didn't expect that kind of question to fall past his lips.

"You seem surprised," Huxley says.

"Yeah, wasn't expecting that. Almost thought you were going to ask me what my first impression of you was."

"I already know that. You've been quite vocal about how I was a different man on the sidewalk and in Chipotle."

Yeah, I have.

"Okay, then. My dream guy? Hmm...I've never really thought about it before. I know I want someone who cares for me, like Jeff cares for my mom. He thinks she's an absolute queen and treats her like it. I'd also like him to have fun with me. We don't have to have everything in common, but I'd love to be able to just let loose, have fun with him. But also, a man with a good head on his shoulders. I'm barely keeping my head above water; I don't want someone I have to babysit, if that makes sense."

He nods.

"And then, of course, the obvious—he has to be a killer in bed. I've had my fair share of bad lovers. I've paid my dues. Whoever I end up with needs to be able to get me off with barely trying."

"Is that it?" he asks.

"I think so. You caught me off guard. I'm sure there are other things, you know…like celebrating my wins just as much as we celebrate his. Respect. The usual items."

"Think you'll ever find him?"

"Is that your second question?"

"Yeah, it is." He props his chin on his fingers as he leans further into his chair.

"Will I ever find him?" I shrug. "I don't know. Maybe, if I'm lucky. I've never been a super-romantic person, so I don't really give any of this much thought at all, but would I like to have a dream guy by my side one day? Yeah. I've seen my mom alone, and I've seen her with someone who truly adores her. She's so much happier, stress free. I want that for me one day. Not saying I need it now, but someday." When our eyes connect, I ask, "What about you? Think you'll find your dream girl one day, settle down?"

He doesn't waver when he says, "Yeah, I think I will."

"Care to elaborate on that answer?"

He shakes his head. "Nah, I'm good."

I roll my eyes. "God, you're infuriating."

He chuckles. "I don't know what you want me to elaborate on. Do I think I'll find her? Yeah, I fucking do. Do I think I'm ready for her? No. But life doesn't really work like that. It doesn't wait for when you're ready. So, whenever she comes along, I know I'm going to scramble to figure out how to make her happy, to try to keep her."

"Here's a hint—don't be a dick to her." I wink at him. "That will give you a fighting chance."

"I'll take that into consideration."

Tired, I close Kelsey's laptop and flop back on my bed. Since I spent a good portion of my day yesterday doing absolutely nothing, I figured

I'd try to get some things done today before I go to Kelsey's tomorrow morning.

But I've been working on the website for a good three hours now, and I'm over it. I need a break.

Wow, it's gotten dark in here. What time is it?

I wake up my phone to see it's only four in the afternoon, so I glance out the window and take in the dark clouds and the early signs of rain.

A rare day in California when it rains.

My phone buzzes and I glance at the screen.

Angela.

My nostrils flare as I angrily pick up my phone and unlock it so I can see what she has to say. Honestly, she's so delusional that she thinks she can just text me as if she didn't fuck me over. Why I haven't already blocked her number is beyond me.

Angela: Hey, girl. Didn't get your RSVP for the reunion. Should I count on you coming solo?

Why would she just assume that when I had Huxley's enormous rock on my finger?

Probably because she believes Huxley is way too good for me.

Which, yeah, she might be right about that. I'm not necessarily the dream girl he's searching for, even though he didn't describe her. I know I don't quite fit into his high-profile life. I'm not an idiot, but for Angela to just assume...

What a wretched bitch.

Should I even bother with texting her back?

If I don't, she's going to assume she got the best of me and I don't want that, so, out of pure anger, I text her back.

Lottie: Sorry, been totally busy with Huxley. Count us in for two.

There, that should set her fake-blond roots on fire.

Smiling to myself, I lift off the bed—still in my robe from my shower earlier—and go to my closet. I throw on a pair of lace pajama shorts and matching bralette. It's actually one of the more comfortable sets, and I've worn every color besides this white one so far.

My phone buzzes and I quickly read it, wanting to see the kind of snarky response Angela has for me.

> **Angela:** Oh, you're together still? Huh, I thought I saw him with someone else the other night.

What a fucking liar!

I'm not stupid enough to fall for that shit, nor am I insecure enough to even question Huxley's intentions. He's told me, point blank, I'm it while we're in contract. And if anything, I know when Huxley talks business, he means it.

I walk into my bedroom and start pacing as I furiously text her back.

> **Lottie:** Funny…he's been with me every night. Are you trying to start drama, Angela?

There, call her out on her bullshit. It's not as if I have anything to lose.

> **Angela:** Why on earth would I want to do that?

I laugh out loud. She must think I'm a complete dumbass.

And maybe I am in her eyes, since I'm the idiot who's followed her around and been at her beck and call only for her to turn her back on me. Not anymore.

> **Lottie:** Because you're jealous.

Angela: Jealous? Of you? Oh, honey, that's cute.

I don't think I've ever despised someone as much as I despise her.

I'm about to text her back when there's a knock at my door, and then Huxley cracks it open. When he catches sight of me, his eyes heat up, and he gives me a strong perusal before he pushes the door all the way open.

"What are you doing?" he asks. I'm not sure I've ever seen him so casually dressed. Shorts and a T-shirt, his hair a rumpled mess, and he didn't bother shaving today. He looks...yummy.

"Texting with Angela. Did you know I hate her?"

"Yeah, I did." He walks up to me, removes my phone from my steel grip, and tosses it on the bed. He then laces his fingers with mine and guides me toward the hallway.

"What are you doing?" I ask.

"It's raining."

"I noticed."

He pauses and says, "When I asked you what you'd want if it was a perfect world, you said to work with your sister, move out of your mom's house, stick it to Angela, erase your student loans, and to have a place where you can lie in the rain without judgment."

He remembered that?

He tugs on my hand. "I told you I'd take care of all of it. I've come through on everything else. This is the last thing."

He pulls me down the hallway, to the opposite side of the house, and to a door I've never explored before. When he opens it, we're greeted by another set of stairs.

"Where are you taking me?" I ask as we ascend the stairs.

He doesn't answer. Instead, when we reach the top, he opens the door to a surprise rooftop deck.

What on earth?

It's not very big at all, and he's done nothing with the space. Just four short walls to prevent you from rolling off the side.

"Here you go," he says, "the perfect spot to lie in the rain without judgment, without being disturbed." He nods toward the teak-covered floor. "Does this work?"

"This more than works." I glance up at him. "Thank you. This means a lot to me."

"You're welcome," he says softly and steps aside so I can make my way out into the rain, just as it starts to pick up.

When I get outside, I spread my arms wide, tilt my head back, and let the rain soak through my clothes and into my skin. When I open my eyes, I smile at Huxley, who's watching me intently. I motion for him to join me.

He doesn't skip a beat and steps out into the rain with me. I take his hands in mine and spin him around. He chuckles lightly, letting me be goofy with him.

"Don't you love it? The rain?" I ask.

"Not as much as you do."

"You clearly don't know how to appreciate it." I guide him to the ground and lay him out next to me, keeping my hand in his as the rain pelts down upon us. Eyes closed, I say, "The sound, the smell, the feeling of not caring if you get wet—isn't it the best feeling?"

He doesn't answer right away, but I feel him take a few deep breaths. "I've never stopped to feel the rain."

I turn my head, open my eyes, and see him staring back at me.

"Thank you."

He's so genuine in this moment.

So real.

There's no domineering asshole trying to control me.

There's no sign of the man who's been playing Dr. Jekyll and Mr. Hyde.

This is Huxley.

The true man.

And it feels like a bullet to the chest. I like this side of him. I like him like this more than I probably should.

Together, we lie in the rain, letting it soak us to the bone and gather on the rooftop surface. The plops from the water hitting the hard surface fill the silence between us, while the smell of wet blacktop wafts around us.

Pure perfection.

"When did you start doing this?" he asks, turning toward me.

I turn toward him as well. The rain has let up so it's more of a sprinkle now. "When I was in high school. I've always loved the rain, especially since it rarely rains here in California. I loved the feeling of being caught up in something other than everyday life. Especially when I was hanging out with Angela. I felt out of control at times. The rain would help me slow down." Being with Angela often felt like being in a dark, unwelcome storm. *But the rain, by contrast, was soft. Safe. Clean.*

He reaches out and places his hand on my cheek before wiping away a few droplets of water with his thumb. It's a sweet, intimate gesture, and instead of shying away, I lean into it.

"How often do you come up here?"

"Not often enough," he says. "I've probably come up here once or twice. But when you said you wanted a place to lie in the rain, I knew exactly where I'd take you." Seeming insecure, he asks, "Do you like it?"

I nod. "I like it a lot. It could use a piece of furniture." I chuckle. "But I think it's perfect. Thank you."

When he doesn't say anything, but instead continues to stare at me, I take that moment to scoot closer to him. The heat of the day doesn't quite break through all the rain, so my body is slightly chilled, but not chilled enough to force me to leave. I just need a little warmth.

Noticing my intention, he lifts his arm, and I scoot in even closer until he wraps his arm around my waist and pulls me against his side. *And, oh God, does he smell good. Like fresh, masculine laundry—if that makes sense.*

"Should've put on something warmer," he says.

"I didn't know I'd be out in the rain, and these are the clothes you provided me." I look up at him. "I've come to realize you're a pervert."

He lightly chuckles. "I'm not a pervert."

"Everything in that closet of mine is scandalous. I'm going to start working my way into your dresser drawers and taking all your shirts."

"Have whatever you want. You look sexy in both."

I lift up, my hand on his chest as I stare at him. "Was that a compliment, Huxley?"

"Want me to take it back?"

"No." I shake my head and press my hand to my heart. "I need to cherish this moment. Huxley Cane complimented me. Not sure this moment could get any better."

"It can," he says and pulls me on top of him. Compared to his tall and muscular stature, I feel so miniature, so petite. Both of his hands fall to my lower back and then slip an inch under the waistband of my shorts.

"Is this comfortable for you?" I ask him.

"Very," he says.

"And I thought you wouldn't appreciate having a shrew of a woman draped across you."

He laughs, and it's such a beautiful sound. "I might enjoy the shrew more than I thought."

This causes me to sit all the way up until I'm situated on top of his lap. "Are you saying you enjoy my company rather than despise it?"

His hands fall to my thighs, and he moves them farther north until they connect with the insides of my hips. It's a small touch, but it carries a large impact as a bolt of lust shoots right up my spine.

"I never despised you. You have to stop thinking that. Did I find you mildly irritating at times? Of course."

I laugh. "Such a charmer."

"Wasn't aware I needed to charm you." His eyes speak of pure playfulness. "Do you need charming?"

I pretend to fluff my wet hair. "Wouldn't hurt you to throw a little charm this way."

He wets his lips even though they probably don't need it because of the rain. "What do you consider *charm*? Words or actions?"

"Both can qualify."

He glances at my chest and then back up at me. "So, if I were to say your tits look hot in that see-through lace top, would that charm you?"

It's see-through?

I glance down and see the clear definition of my nipples. Well, I guess it is see-through when it's wet.

"I guess that would charm me marginally, but I believe you could probably do better."

"Yeah?" His hands snake up my sides until they loop under my bralette and pull it up and over my head. He tosses the drenched fabric to the side and then brings his hands to my thighs. "What about now? Charming?"

I sit there, on his lap, topless, in the rain, and to any other person, this action could be defined as "horny man."

But, God, with one blink of his eye, he could charm these shorts right off me.

"From your silence and heavy breathing, I'm going to take that as a *yes*."

He's so cocky, so sure of himself. It's sexy and also vaguely annoying. The annoying part causes my next action.

I rest my hand on his stomach and shift my pelvis over his lap. His playful eyes immediately turn dark, seductive.

"What are you doing?"

"Showing you what charm really is." I rotate my hips again, and this time, I'm rewarded by him growing harder underneath me.

I'd be lying if I said I didn't want his cock. After giving him head in the shower, there's nothing I want more than to experience him driving into me over and over again. But he's also a bit of a flight risk, and while we've made some progress this weekend—progress toward what, I'm not sure, but at least he's engaging with me—I don't want to push him too far, just enough.

Water drips down my face as I smile at him. "You see, Huxley"—I rub my center over his erection in a continuous motion, finding just the right spot for both of us—"charm can easily come in the form of dry humping."

He lets out a roar of laughter right before the most gorgeous smile I've ever seen lights up his face. *God, he's beautiful.* Sexy and hot, yes, but right now, I see a boyish cuteness to him as well.

"I had no idea charm could be translated through dry humping. I always thought the universal translation for dry humping was...'Hey, I'm horny.'"

I steady my hands on his stomach, which causes my breasts to press together. "It can mean both."

Still smiling, he reaches up to my breasts and rolls my nipples with his fingers. "Good to know." He then envelops my right breast in his hand, squeezing, massaging. "Have I ever told you how fucking hot your tits are?"

"Mmm," I moan, picking up my pace just a notch. "I can't remember. Maybe. But tell me more."

"They're sexy as fuck, Lottie. Not too big, not too small, tight little nipples that beg me to touch them. I could spend hours just playing with your tits."

"Hours seems excessive." My head falls back as he sits up and brings his mouth to my breast. He sucks tightly on my nipple and...that's it. The scruff of his jaw rubbing against my sensitive skin combined with the intimate feeling of his lips on my nipple sends a crazy rip of pleasure down my spine and all the way to my curled toes.

"Hours are necessary." He moves his mouth to my other breast and pays as much attention to that nipple as he did the other.

My hand floats to the back of his head, and I hold him in place, not wanting him to stop doing what he's doing, because it lights me up, makes me feel alive.

The patter of rain around us heightens the mood, as well as the way the water runs over our two bodies, soaking our clothes, our hair, our skin. It's erotic. The only thing that could make this better would be if we were both completely naked.

"God, Huxley," I groan when he tugs on my nipple with his teeth. "I want more."

He takes that as a sign to flip me to my back, laying me across the cold wet surface of the teakwood flooring. His gorgeous body hovers above mine, blocking the rainfall from hitting me in the face. His chest ripples above me, his hair's wet with droplets, and his eyes are so intense with need that I find myself spreading my legs.

He positions himself between them, his large frame causing me to make even more room. He lowers his pelvis to mine, and when they touch, immediate gratification strikes me in the chest.

Yes.

He feels so much better like this.

Heavy against me.

Hard as stone.

But he's the one in control, something I've come to love when he touches me. I want him to own me, own my body, and make me forget everything around us.

"I want your shorts off," he says in a tortured tone.

He pushes his hand through his hair, sopping the water away, and lifts off me only enough to pull down on my shorts. I help him remove them with a lift of my hips, and once they're off, he drops them to the side and positions himself against me again.

I've never been naked in the rain.

And I'm going to be honest, it might be my new favorite thing.

It's exciting.

Daring.

Erotic.

Huxley hovers over me, the only thing between us his shorts, and they do nothing to hide his massive erection.

"I love seeing you like this," he says, "submitting to me. I've never seen anything sexier in my life. This is it, right here, you naked, wet, legs spread, waiting for me." He wets his lips. "How much do you want me?"

"More than I care to admit," I say, looping my hand behind his neck.

"Still hate me?"

"No."

"Still want to help me?"

"Do I even have a choice?" I ask, wondering where this questioning is coming from.

He flashes his eyes to me. "Even if I don't want to admit it, you always have a choice." He rubs his length along my aroused clit. Oh God, that feels too freaking good. My hand trembles against his neck as he reaches up to my breast and teases it with his fingers. Looking me in the eyes, he says, "If you told me, tomorrow, you want out, I'd destroy the contract."

He thrusts against me.

"What?" I gasp as he pushes again, and again, and again. "Oh God," I moan, his pace stirring pleasure deep within me. "Wh-why?"

"Because," he says, thrusting again. I catch the tension in his shoulders. He's holding back. From the thick veins in his neck and the tight clench of his jaw, he could give more, wants to give more. "Even though you might not believe it, I want you to be happy." He thrusts again, and my back arches as my body pulses. Begs. "I don't want to trap you." Another thrust. Two more, that's all it's going to take. "I don't want you to feel trapped." Thrust.

"Yes, God, yes, Huxley." I grip him and meet his thrusts with my own. I'm right there, on the edge. Pleasure pools at the base of my spine, this euphoric feeling amplifying with every push of his erection against my clit.

So close.

God, I'm so close.

"I just want you happy," he says, and I hear him.

I'm listening to everything he's saying to me, but it's not quite registering in my head.

His words aren't making sense, because all I can focus on is teetering on the edge of my orgasm and wanting to fall over. I want to fall over with him.

"How close are you?" I ask him.

"Right...there," he groans.

"Then take it, take me. Harder, Huxley."

He smooths his hand down to my ass, where he grips me tightly and pulls me all the way against him, intensifying the connection. That's all it takes.

One thrust and I'm done.

Every last ounce of pleasure gathers, coils, into the center of my body, only to be ripped into millions of joyous pieces as my body combusts underneath him.

"Oh, fuck," I yell. "Yes, Huxley."

"Jesus," he mutters as he drives harder and harder until he stills, groans loudly, and then collapses on top of me.

He props his weight up with one arm on the ground, but his head tilts down, our foreheads connecting. It's as close as our mouths have been this entire time, making me realize that the man might have just dry humped me to completion, but he never once laid his lips on mine.

Why?

My eyes search out his, and I catch him taking a few large breaths before making eye contact with me. Rain continues to fall on us, and in the distance, I hear the rumble of thunder for the first time since we've been out here.

Huxley wipes the water off his face before blinking a few times. "We should, uh...get back inside."

"Yeah," I say, breathless, still staring up at him. The pull between us is so damn strong that I want nothing more than to cling to him and be carried to his bed.

But when he stands and offers me his hand to help me up, I notice a change in him. Hesitation. Uneasiness.

And I'm not sure if that's a good thing or a bad thing.

Huxley tugs me quickly toward the door, opens it, and hurries me inside. Then he snags my garments and guides me down the stairs carefully, making sure we don't slip. When we reach the hallway, he takes my hand and maneuvers me toward our bedrooms. I'm curious which way he'll take me—maybe to his shower so we can warm up?

But then he stops in front of my bedroom door and lets go of my hand. Our time is up. With a step back, he grips his neck and scans my naked body. "You should take a shower, get warmed up."

"Yeah," I answer awkwardly.

"Do you need anything?"

You.

A conversation.

Some understanding of what the hell we're doing.

Maybe a brief recap of the things you said up on the roof.

"Um, I don't think so," I answer.

He nods. "Okay. If you want, I can order something for dinner."

I shake my head. "It's okay. I'm not very hungry."

"Sure." He takes another step back, and my hope plummets as I see him retreat once again.

Why?

Why does he do this?

Why does he take one giant leap forward only to take two steps back?

And why do I even care?

Yeah, I know…I know.

Everyone knows. Because somehow, someway, I've started to care about him.

CHAPTER 17
LOTTIE

"WHERE ARE YOU?" KELSEY ASKS over the phone as I lean against the white brick of the breast pump store.

"You don't want to know."

"If I didn't, I wouldn't have asked."

"Okay, I'm at a breast pump store, waiting for Ellie to show up so we can shop together."

"You were right, I don't want to know."

"Told you."

"Aren't you a little worried you're leading this girl on? She seems to be getting attached to you—I mean, you're going breast pump shopping."

"I know." I nibble on the corner of my mouth. "I actually feel kind of bad, but I don't know what to do. I don't like faking this pregnancy since so many people try so hard to get pregnant, and there's no way in hell I'd ever act as if I'd miscarried to end all of this pregnancy stuff. Remember Aunt Rina? She had five miscarriages, and holding her hand through them with Mom was devastating. The more I think about it, the more uncomfortable I feel."

"So maybe...tell her the truth."

"Are you insane? Huxley would lose the deal for sure."

"What are you going to do when you're supposed to start showing and you don't?"

"I don't know. But you don't start showing until around thirteen weeks

298 | MEGHAN QUINN

or so with your first baby, right?" At least, that's what I read when I looked it up last night. I press my hand to my forehead. "God, I'm in such a mess."

"Has more happened?"

I bite down on my index finger. Yesterday, Kelsey was gone most of the day running errands and interviewing another supplier since the one we contacted hasn't gotten back to us yet. Therefore, I haven't talked to her much.

Actually, I haven't spoken to her at all.

She has no idea what happened this past weekend with Huxley.

Hell, I barely have a grasp on what happened, but this is something I'd normally tell my sister right away. But after the rooftop, I wasn't sure what to do. I felt...weird.

As if something wasn't right.

And I know it wasn't what I did but more so what happened after. I wanted more, so much more with him, but, for the life of me, didn't know how to express it. He's been so hot and cold with me, so inconsistent with how he treats me, that I'm scared. I like him, a lot, and I'm unsure what that means for us, for me. I'm not sure if I can make a move, if I can tell him. If he even wants more with me.

He didn't kiss me on Sunday when he had the perfect opportunity to do so. We were drenched from the rain, and there was nothing around us but nature. If he was going to kiss me at any point in time, it would've been then, but he didn't, which leads me to believe that he has no desire to shift this relationship in any way. He's told me he's not wanting to blur the lines. He's also told me he wants me to be happy. *But why? Why does that matter to him, if I don't really matter to him?*

I joked about our agreement replicating that of *Pretty Woman*, me being the less whore-y version of Vivian, but instead of Vivian being the one who doesn't kiss on the lips...it's Huxley.

And if I learned anything from that movie, it's that kissing means so much more. It carries weight. Kissing connects you on an intimate level, and Huxley doesn't want that. It's evident. He might want my body, but he doesn't want me.

Which, in return, makes me feel weird. But does that mean I want him?

"Lottie, you there?"

"Yeah, sorry." I clear my throat. God, why am I getting emotional? I shouldn't be getting emotional.

"What's going on? Did something happen that you're not telling me about?"

Wincing, I look up to the sky as I say, "I, uh, I might have done some things."

"What kind of things?"

"Um, you know, like...I might have given him head in the shower, and then possibly dry humped him on a roof."

"What?" Kelsey screams into the phone. "Lottie, are you serious right now?"

"I wish I wasn't." I let out a deep breath. "God, Kelsey, I don't know what's happening to me. It all started with our pitch. He chose us, Kelsey. He chose us over Dave, and that, God, that crippled me. When I saw Dave show up, I thought we'd have to reschedule—that our chance was gone again—but he took our meeting instead, like he promised. It put a dent in the negative thoughts I had of the man. And then, this weekend..." I let out a deep sigh and rest my head against the brick. "He was different. Softer, didn't have the edge he usually does. He joked, laughed, teased. And, yeah...he did more things than I care to admit."

"Holy shit, Lottie. What does this mean?"

I squeeze my eyes shut, completely shocked I'm about to say this out loud. "It means I like him."

"Wait...like...you *like him*, like him?"

"Yeah. And I shouldn't. God, he's been so mercurial. So up and down and straight-up assholish at times, but he also has this giving heart I can't seem to ignore."

"Oh, the same heart I kept telling you about?"

"This is your fault. You made me look at him differently."

"This is not my fault. You're the one who set out to find a rich husband."

"I didn't think it was actually going to happen," I hiss into the phone. "Stuff like that doesn't just work out for me."

"Okay, so you like him, you put his penis in your mouth—what now?"

"I have no clue. I don't know how to act around him. Not after what happened over the weekend, and there's one thing I didn't tell you about."

"Uh, what else could there be? You dry-humped him on the roof." She's silent for a second and then says, "Let me guess—he has a big penis?"

"As if God couldn't stop with the good looks, he had to bless him with the penis of all penises."

"Figured as much. A man with such a stern gaze doesn't have a floppy noodle between his legs."

"More like a steel rod made to build skyscrapers."

Kelsey lets out a laugh. "The imagery on that…too much."

"But that wasn't what I was going to say."

"Obviously," Kelsey says. "So, what is it?"

Feeling slightly embarrassed, I turn so my side is pressed up against the brick. For some reason, the position makes me feel less exposed. "He, uh…he didn't kiss me."

"What do you mean?"

"I mean, during all of our escapades, he never once kissed me."

"Oh…"

"*Oh?*" I repeat. "That doesn't sound like a good *oh*, that sounds like a sympathetic *oh*."

"Not once?"

My stomach twists, and once again, my emotions roar with shame. "No," I say solemnly. "What do you think that means?" When Kelsey doesn't answer right away, I add, "That he's Vivian-ing me, right?"

"Vivi-what?"

"You know, how in *Pretty Woman*, Vivian doesn't want to kiss Edward, or any of her clients, because it's too intimate? I feel as though that's what Huxley is doing."

"Oh, I get it." Kelsey pauses, and I swear it feels as though I'm waiting on pins and needles for her response. "I don't know, Lottie."

"That's not what you were supposed to say," I nearly screech into the phone. "You were supposed to say, '*No, that's not it at all*'."

"I'm not going to lie to you."

"God." I press my hand to my forehead. "Look at me. I like a guy who's Vivian-ing me. How did this happen?"

"Stupid luck?"

"You are not helpful today. I'm really freaked out, Kels. My stomach is twisted in knots. I—ugh…"

"What?" Kelsey asks.

A car pulls up on the street and I recognize it immediately. "Ellie is here. I should go."

"Okay, I'm sorry that I'm not being a helpful sister. Honestly, all I can think to say is maybe just see where it goes."

"But that complicates things."

"Hate to tell you, sis, but things are already complicated. Might as well see if he's worth your time."

"You're confusing me."

"Then I'm doing my job. Love you, Lottie."

Groaning, I say, "Love you, Kelsey."

I hang up the phone just as Ellie pops out of the car and waves at me frantically.

She's a little…much…for me, but she is incredibly nice. I do feel bad about deceiving her. Why couldn't I just have been the fake fiancée? Why do I have to be fake pregnant, too?

"Oh, I'm so glad you're here," Ellie says as she comes up to me and gives me a huge hug. "Are you excited?"

"Uh, you know, this might be a little much for me," I say honestly. "But I'm more than happy to help you."

"Oh, are you uncomfortable?" she asks.

"Overwhelmed with everything." There, not a lie. I really am overwhelmed, especially with Huxley.

"I can understand that completely." She takes my hand. "But don't worry, I've got you." She charges us into the store and all the way to the back, where there's a designated area of breast pumps. Fake breasts of all shapes and sizes and colors line the wall—good for them—and below them are these weird suction-cup things with bottles at the end.

Is that what's supposed to go on the breast?

"I love this place so much," Ellie says. "When my sister was pregnant, we went to the same store, but in Georgia—oh, you might know where it is, actually. Off Clive Street?"

Uhhh…

Oh yeah, I'm supposed to be from Georgia.

I tap my chin. "Sounds familiar."

"It's right next to Peaches Bakery."

"Ohh, Peaches." I nod as if I've been there a million times.

"Wouldn't you just kill for one of their cupcakes right now? Which one was your favorite?"

Oh God.

My favorite.

Err…

Think of something unoriginal that every bakery would have.

"Chocolate," I say with a nod.

Her face contorts in confusion. "Chocolate?"

Oh fuck, do they not have a chocolate option? What bakery doesn't have chocolate as an option? That would be absolutely ludicrous.

"Well, you know—"

She nudges my shoulder with a laugh. "I was sure you were going to say their crumble-cake cupcake, as you just give me those vibes."

Never in a million years would I have said crumble-cake cupcake.

I shrug playfully. "A chocolate girl here."

"I'm a chocolate girl myself. Have you tried their pink velvet cupcake? I honestly don't understand how it differs from vanilla."

"I was just about to say that," I say as I pick up a fake breast and examine it. God, it's so lifelike. "What do they do, just splash some food coloring in it and call it a day?" I ask.

"Totally. But their peach pie…"

I wave my hand at her. "To die for."

"Hello, ladies. Welcome," a saleswoman says. "Do you need help with anything?"

Ellie spins around with a smile and says, "Looking at breast pumps. I'm Ellie, and this is my friend Lottie. She's not ready to find a perfect fit, but I'm here to squeeze breasts and figure out what works for me."

"Wonderful. I'm Ann, and I'm an expert when it comes to breast pumps. Now let me see your breasts."

Uhh…

Ellie goes to lift her top—wow, just like that, no shame—but Ann says, "No, no. Just puff your chest so I can have a better look."

Ellie laughs. "Oh, okay. I was ready to strip down for you."

That was obvious.

And entirely unnecessary.

Ann reaches out and asks, "Do you mind if I touch?"

"Please do. It's why I came here." Talking to me, Ellie says, "They can fit you perfectly to your needs, and you can test them out on the wall of breasts to see how they would work."

I glance at the wall of breasts. "Seems as if you have every size there," I say awkwardly.

"We do," Ann says as she fondles Ellie. This is weird, really freaking weird. "And you can adjust the flow, too."

"The...uh, the what now?"

"The flow," Ellie says. "They produce actual liquid, so you can get the full experience."

Who on earth comes up with a place like this? Floating breasts glued to walls with an actual "milk" flow. I'm confused...and uncomfortably intrigued.

"Like almost every woman I come across, there's a sizeable difference between your right breast and left." Ann lifts both of Ellie's boobs.

"Yeah, guilty. The left just can't seem to catch up."

"No breasts are symmetrical, but some women have a large difference, and you're one of the lucky ones."

Ellie looks at me. "What boob is bigger on your body?"

"Umm..." I grip my boobs. "I think my right?"

"If you're right-handed, it probably is bigger," Ann says. She then asks Ellie, "Can I ask nipple size?"

"Why don't I just show you? It'll be so much easier." Before I can even excuse myself to give her some privacy, Ellie lifts her shirt and bra at the same time, flashing both me and Ann.

And there are her boobs, just like that.

Now what the hell am I supposed to do with this? Do I look, do I not look? Do I pretend to find something fascinating on the ground? Do I stare at the wall of breasts? Do I pray the floor swallows me whole?

I was not mentally prepared for this.

"Oh, wow, you have wonderful nipples," Ann says, and from the corner of my eye, I see her get in close and pinch Ellie's nipple between her fingers. "Very firm nipple. That will serve you well."

"Oh, really? I'm so happy to hear that. Do you have firm nipples, Lottie?"

"Huh? What?" I ask, glancing over at Ellie, but keeping my eyes north.
"Sorry—these…books," I pick up a book from a table. "Fascinating.
What did you say?"

"Firm nipples. Do you have them?"

Awkwardly, I smooth my hand over my breasts, attempting to feel
them through my layers of clothing—because this, the topless party happening in front of me, is not something I'll be joining. "Well, you know,
I have small nipples."

"Nipples or areolas?" Ann asks.

"Both."

She nods. "I think I have the perfect breast pump for you, then. There's
only one that works great with small nipples. But for you, Ellie, we have
some choices to make, because these nipples are just spectacular. Lottie,
come here, feel this."

I wave my hand at Ann. "Oh, you know, that's really okay." I laugh. "I
can see from here." I look at Ellie's boobs. And yup—bare, everything
bare. "Those for sure look firm." I give her a thumbs-up. "Good job
growing."

Ellie laughs. "Isn't she fun? Come on, Lottie, just feel. You can feel
what the baby will be sucking on. You know I don't care at all."

She might not care, but I do.

"It's very educational," Ann says. "You can mimic the sucking
sensation."

I laugh and shake my head. "I'm all about education, but I think I'm
good with not sucking my friend's nipple."

Ann and Ellie both look at each other and then throw back their heads
and laugh.

"Not with your mouth," Ann says, grabbing my hand. "With your
fingers."

In a flash, my hand smacks right into Ellie's left breast, and her
extremely hard nipple rubs against my fingers.

Thick, tight, just…a solid nip.

And I'm touching it.

I'm touching another woman's nipple.

Fondling is more like it, as Ann makes me move my fingers all over it.

"Ooo, that tickles," Ellie says, and that's it for me.

I yank my hand away and fold my arms across my chest. "You've got some baby suckers there," I say, trying to mentally block this day already from memory.

Huxley is going to owe me big time.

"I'm so excited you think so." Ellie lowers her shirt and bra. "So, what do you think, Ann? Can we milk some breasts?"

"You didn't come here not to." Ann pats me on the shoulder. "This is where the fun begins."

"Lottie?" Huxley calls out. "Where are you?"

I don't say anything.

I don't even move.

Instead, I sit in the living room, on the most comfortable couch I've ever sat on, stiffly perched at the edge, hands in my lap, as I stare at the elaborate fireplace right in front of me.

There are no words for what my morning was like. No words at all.

After being squirted in the eye by a fake breast glued to a wall, I've done my fair share of adulting for today.

"There you are," Huxley says, stopping in the living room doorway. "I just got a text from Dave. He told me Ellie won't stop raving about this morning." When I don't look at him, I hear him shuffle across the floor to get in my line of sight. "Uh, everything okay?"

Lips pressed together, I shake my head. "Nope. Not even close."

"What happened?"

"I touched her bare boob, Huxley. I touched Ellie's bare boob."

"What?" he asks as he takes a seat on the coffee table so he's sitting across from me. His handsome face comes into view, but it does nothing to ease the tension in my shoulders. "What do you mean, you touched her boob?"

"And I got squirted in the face."

"By her boob?" Huxley practically yells.

"No, by a boob on the wall."

He sits taller. "You're going to have to run through it for me, because I'm confused."

"As am I." I pat his knee. "As am I." I let out a deep breath and say, "I don't have it in me to recount what happened. Just know, if I ever proved how serious I'm taking this deal, today would be the day."

"Sounds like it." Guilt washes over his face. "I'm sorry you had to do that."

I snap out of my funk and connect with his eyes.

There he is.

The Chipotle guy.

Right there. The stern scowl on his forehead is gone. The boyish charm is brimming in his eyes. And the way he pulls on the back of his neck—unmistakable.

"It's fine," I say. "Traumatizing. I will have to bleach my eyes, but I'll make it."

He smirks and then reaches behind him to his back pocket. That's when I notice he's wearing jeans and sneakers. Well, hello, Mr. Casual.

"I got something for you."

"You did?" I ask.

He nods and brings a rolled-up piece of fabric out in front of him.

"What is it?"

He unravels it and holds it up. "Thought you might like it."

In front of me is a cream-colored, vintage rock band T-shirt with Fleetwood Mac on the front, the image from their *Rumours* album.

"Oh my God." I take it from him. "This is amazing." I hold it out and study it.

"Check out the back," he says.

I turn it around and take in all the city tour dates.

"Wait, is this an original tour shirt?"

"Yeah," he says. When I glance up, I catch the pride in his eyes.

"Holy shit, Huxley. This is...wow, this is amazing." I clutch it to my chest. "Thank you. This means so much to me."

And this is exactly why I'm having such a hard time. Because the thoughtfulness behind this T-shirt only makes me like him that much more. The gesture cracks open my chest and pulls on my heart, forcing me to look at him in a different light.

He rubs his hands on his legs. "Glad you like it." He glances to the side, and it almost looks as though he's...nervous. *Nervous about what?* "I wasn't sure if you had anything else planned for today. Do you?"

He's acting really weird.

Very strange.

Not like the demanding man I've come to know very well.

"Uh, nothing on the docket. Just trying to erase what happened this morning."

He nods and continues to rub his hands on his thighs. "Well, if that's all you have planned, I was thinking I might take you somewhere."

Take me somewhere?

An inch of hope blooms in my belly. It's coupled with excitement.

Is he...is he asking me out?

Is that why he's nervous?

Is that why he's rocking back and forth?

Because he's nervous to ask me out?

Don't get ahead of yourself, Lottie. Remember, he wouldn't kiss you over the weekend. Even when the rain was dripping off his chest and he was thrusting into you, he kept his lips to himself.

I choke down my raw emotions and ask, "Like on a date?"

His eyes land on mine. And for a torturous second, I'm terrified I read him completely wrong, until he says, "Yeah, like on a date."

Oh God. He's serious.

The honesty.

The shadow of hope in his eyes.

The nervous tick in his hands.

How could I possibly say no? There's no way I could say no, not when my body gravitates toward him, when I can sense my heart opening up to him, even when I try to hide it or hold back. He's got me hooked. It's undeniable. I'm positively hooked on this man.

I try to keep my emotions casual, though. "What were you thinking?"

His nervous ticks morph into a confident smile as he reaches to pull out something else from his back pocket. He holds a piece of paper in front of me and then flicks his fingers so the one piece of paper in his hand turns into two. "Care to go to a Fleetwood Mac concert with me?"

"What?" I shout, standing from the couch and grabbing the tickets to look at them closely. "No way. There's no way…" My eyes scan the tickets. "Holy shit, these are tickets, these are real fucking tickets. Huxley, did you know these are real tickets?"

He chuckles as he stands as well. "Do you think I'd buy fake ones?"

"No, I mean—I just thought, you know, it would be like a fake ticket, and then we go on the patio and play the music, pretending it's a concert, but these are real. They have a barcode on them."

"The barcode makes all the difference."

In disbelief, I stare down at the tickets. "I can't believe this. I didn't know they were going to be in Los Angeles. I—Huxley…" I glance up at him. "Wait. This concert is in Portland."

Hope falls as I realize the mistake.

He tilts up my chin and says, "I know. The jet is ready to take us once you get dressed."

"Jet?" I ask.

A cocky smirk appears on his face. "Yeah, you do realize I have a private jet, right? We can go wherever we want, when we want." He winks, the confidence in full swing now. "That's what happens when you have a rich fake fiancé."

"Wait...so we're flying to Portland tonight, and we're really going to go see Fleetwood Mac...in concert?"

He nods. "Yup. There's also this burger place in Portland called Killer Burger. We should go there for dinner. Maybe Voodoo Doughnut for dessert. That's if you're up for it."

"Are you kidding me?" I nearly shout. "Of course I'm up for it." I look him in the eyes. "Thank you, Huxley. This is..." I catch my breath. "This is really thoughtful."

This is why I'm falling for this man. This right here.

That smile.

That kind heart.

That attentive, sexy mind of his.

"I wanted to do something nice for you." He pinches my chin with his forefinger and thumb. "I'm really grateful for everything you've done for me." And for some reason, that comment diminishes my hope that this is something more. He's grateful for the work I've done for him. *Deep sigh.* I can't let that ruin my night, though. He might not be in the same headspace as me, but at least I can enjoy tonight. He looks at his watch. "Think you can get ready in half an hour?"

"On it," I say while squeezing the shirt to my chest. "I have the perfect shorts to wear—ugh, you took my clothes away. I don't have jean shorts."

"I had your clothes brought over this morning. Figured you'd want something casual to wear tonight. Everything is in your room."

"God bless you." I stand on my toes, lift up, and, because I have a death sentence, I place a kiss on his jaw. "Thank you, Huxley."

And then with my T-shirt in hand, I run up the stairs to my room so I can get dressed. I can't believe I'm about to see Fleetwood Mac in concert.

But more importantly, I can't believe I'm going on a date with Huxley Cane.

Kelsey: He's flying you to Portland? What? For a date? Where can I find myself a Huxley?

Lottie: He has two brothers.

Kelsey: Unlike you, I don't mix business with pleasure. But enough about that. HOLY SHIT, Lottie, you're going to see Fleetwood Mac. Did you tell Mom?

Lottie: Not yet. I figured I'd send her a picture.

Kelsey: Where are the seats? Front row?

Lottie: I didn't even look. Probably not.

Kelsey: He's flying you to Portland in his private jet. I'm pretty sure he didn't mind spending money on expensive tickets.

Lottie: He has the tickets. I'm getting dressed. I'll let you know where the seats are when I look at them again.

Kelsey: What are you wearing?

Lottie: He gave me a vintage tour T-shirt with the Rumours cover on the front, so I'm wearing that and my ripped jean shorts. Hair down and curled, and my boho hat. Ankle boots.

Kelsey: It's perfect. Think he's making a move?

Lottie: I honestly can't think about it. I asked him if it was a date and he said yes. But he also thanked me for the work I've done. This was what I was worried about. I really like him, and I don't think he returns the feeling.

Kelsey: Then just enjoy. Maybe this is the olive branch, him trying to connect the two of you on a different level.

Lottie: I'm nervous. All the teasing, the sexual tension, that felt easy, but a date? That just feels all too real.

Kelsey: Because it is real. Don't waste your time worrying about it. Just enjoy it, because when do you ever get whisked away on a private jet?

Lottie: Never.

Kelsey: Exactly. Enjoy the moment, sis. Take lots of pictures and enjoy yourself. I love you.

Lottie: Love you, too.

CHAPTER 18
HUXLEY

"YOU'RE GRIPPING THE ARMREST PRETTY tightly. Are you nervous?"

Lottie looks away from the window and says, "Just never been on a plane this small. It's different."

She's sitting across from me, looking sexy as hell in short denim shorts, her vintage T-shirt, which she tied in the back so it shows two inches of her midriff, and that goddamn hat, which is doing things to my libido I never expected. When she came down the stairs in her outfit, I knew I was in for a long night of staring and appreciating, with the secret hope that when we're at the concert, she'll let me hold her.

"Want to do something to distract you?"

She raises a brow, and I roll my eyes.

"Nothing like that." I reach to the side panel of my seat and pull out a pad of paper and a pen. There's a table between us so we have the perfect playing space. "Want to play some Hangman?"

"Is that Huxley Cane–branded stationery?"

"Just Cane Enterprises."

"God, you *are* rich."

I chuckle. "I am. So how about it? Want to play?"

Cutely, she cracks her fingers and says, "I'll have you know, I'm an expert."

"Yeah, guess we'll have to see about that."

I draw out the game board and then put spaces on the paper for my chosen word.

Lottie takes her time, studying the paper. Her eyes shoot to mine, then to the paper and then back to mine. She leans back in her chair, crosses her arms, and says, "Pussy."

My eyes nearly bulge out of my sockets. "What?"

She taps the paper. "That's your word. *Pussy.* I'm right, aren't I?"

How the actual fuck?

She smiles and chuckles. "I'm right. God, I told you I was good." She takes the paper from me and fills in my blank spaces. "Are you impressed?"

"Terrified."

The laugh that falls past her lips is so goddamn sexy that I'm tempted to pull her across this table and put her on my lap, where I can kiss her senseless.

Fuck, do I want to taste those lips again, desperately. But for the first time in my life when it comes to a woman I like…I feel unsure. I wouldn't say we've had the best track record when it comes to getting along, nor has our relationship so far been one filled with ease. It's been tense, uncomfortable at times, a lie. That's no way to start a relationship, which makes me question, does she even want to start anything with me? Although, I'm sure I saw happiness in her expression when she asked if this was a date. *I think.*

She marks down some spaces on the paper and says, "Okay, your turn."

I study the six-letter word. Glance up at her. Then back at the paper. I grip my chin and say, "*O.*"

Her eyes flash to mine; they're lit up with humor as she marks *O* as the first letter.

Smiling widely now, I say, "*M.*"

"You know." She tosses the pen at me.

"Orgasm." When she rolls her eyes, I say, "You're not the only one good at this game."

"It seems as though we're both perverts." She presses her hand to her chest. "I'm uncultured. What's your excuse?"

"Uncultured?" I laugh. "What makes you uncultured?"

She rubs her fingers together. "I didn't grow up with money."

"Money has nothing to do with it. Some of the richest people are uncultured swine. Complete assholes. Money has nothing to do with it."

"Oh, then tell me, what makes a cultured person?"

"Your heart. Your mind. Your soul. It has nothing to do with status and everything to do with who you are as a person."

Thoughtfully, she tilts her head to the side. "So, based off those criteria, would you say I'm cultured?"

Giving her a hard time, I say, "Well, your heart is beautiful. Your soul is spotted with black, but overall, a kind one, and well, your mind...that's all kinds of fucked up."

Her mouth drops open in amusement as she stands from her seat and charges toward me. I don't flinch. When she reaches out to poke me with her rose-colored nail, I take her hand and pull her forward, so she's forced to sit on my lap.

She playfully fights me, poking me all over my chest. "I'll show you a spotted-black soul."

I chuckle and gain hold of her hands, only to pin them at her side.

"Let go of me at once. I'm attempting to prove a point to you."

"What are you going to do? Poke me to death?"

"To death seems a bit extreme, don't you think, Huxley?" She arches a brow. "A bit dramatic."

"You're the one who came over here with your fingers. How am I supposed to know what you're doing?"

"So, your first inclination is that I'm going to poke you to death...to death, Huxley."

I shrug. "You did harbor some strong hate for me at the beginning."

"Yeah, at the beginning, but not anymore."

My lips turn up in a grin. "Not anymore, huh?"

She rolls her eyes and attempts to get off my lap. "I'm not here to boost your ego."

I keep her firmly in place. "I'd never expect you to. Now cutting it down, that's another thing."

"Someone has to keep you grounded."

"You do a damn good job at it."

"Would you say I'm the best at it?"

I release her hands and rest my palm on her thigh. She doesn't flee but stays in place, which I fucking like. "Between you and my brothers, it's a tough competition, but I think you edge them out."

"I shall wear my medal with honor."

"Mr. Cane," the pilot says over the speaker. "We'll be landing shortly. Please take your seats and buckle up."

I pat Lottie's leg. "Are you ready for this?"

She shakes her head. "I don't think so, but it doesn't look like I have time to prepare myself." Before she gets off my lap, she reaches out and cups my cheek. Her facial features turn soft, endearing, as she says, "If I forget to say it tonight, thank you, Huxley. Thank you so much for this. You're really making a dream of mine come true."

I place my hand on hers and move it to my mouth to kiss her palm. "You're welcome, Lottie."

"I'm sweating."

"What?" I laugh. "What do you mean you're sweating?"

We're standing in line, waiting to enter the concert hall, and this is the first thing she's said to me since we left the car after finishing off our donuts. We shared a burger and fries at Killer Burger, opting for the peanut butter burger, before we headed over to Voodoo Doughnut and each got a donut, but split them, so we could have a taste of each. Lottie's idea. But she's been silent ever since the donuts were consumed. I asked

her a question at one point, but she didn't answer, instead, continued to stare out the window. I wasn't sure what was going through her head, so I chose to just let her have her peace.

Holding on tightly to my hand, she leans in close to me and says, "I'm so excited, Hux. I'm sweaty. I'm nervous. My body doesn't know what to do with itself."

I like it when she calls me *Hux*. It sounds good coming from her lips.

"Are you going to fangirl out?"

"Uh, yeah," she says with confidence. "If you didn't expect that, you clearly don't know me at all. And I expect you to fangirl out as well."

"I'll get my girly scream ready."

She chuckles. "What I wouldn't give to hear it." The doors open and the crowd grows closer as people begin to filter into the vintage art deco building.

"Before we head in, want to take a picture with the marquee?" I ask. She's nervous, so she might say no.

"Oh, great idea," she answers.

Thank fuck.

I take my phone from my pocket and switch it to camera mode. Lottie curls against my side and places her hand on my chest, and I angle the phone just right to capture my height, her height, and the marquee above us.

Once I take a few, I say, "I'll text you the best one."

"Please do. I want to send one to my mom. She's going to freak out."

"Is she a Fleetwood Mac fan, too?" I pocket my phone as we move closer to the building.

"Yes. She was the one who introduced me to their music—basically to all the music I love."

"If I knew, I would've invited her as well."

"Stop. It's better like this, making her jealous." Lottie smiles, and... fuck...I like that smile. I'm obsessed with that smile.

I'm obsessed with her.

"Daughter of the year."

"I think so." She bumps my shoulder with hers. "What about your brothers? Are they jealous?"

"They don't know I'm here."

"Really?" she asks, surprised. "You didn't tell them?"

I shake my head. "No."

She pauses and asks, "Didn't want them to know about me?"

I clutch her hand tighter to ease any doubts that might be popping up in her head. "Didn't want to hear their *I told you sos.*"

"What do you mean?" she asks, confused.

This is not the place I want to have this conversation, in a throng of people, but thankfully, we're at the front of the line so I can press pause on my answer as I hand the ticket attendant our tickets. Once they're scanned, we walk into the concert hall. From the outside, it stands above the rest, with its gothic-style columns surrounding the marquee, but on the inside, it's decked out in gold wallpaper from floor to ceiling. Pops of a dusty sky blue are carved into the pillars surrounding the lobby, while the floors are a colorfully glazed tile that must be original to its era of build. Breathtaking. Art deco at its finest.

"Do you want a drink?" I ask her as we move toward a concession stand.

"Uh, sure," she answers quietly, and I know the shift in her mood is from the question she asked that went unanswered.

I work her through the crowd and find a concession stand that just opened. I order us each a beer, and then, with the drinks in hand, I guide her to our seats, which are on the first row of the mezzanine level, dead center. The perfect view, in my opinion. Just close enough, but not so close that we're craning our necks.

"Wow, these are great seats," she says.

"Yeah, I'm pleased with them."

She takes a seat, and once she's settled, I hand her a beer and then take a seat as well, being sure to turn toward her. Everyone is still filtering into their seats so I take this opportunity to elaborate on my answer.

I just hope she's on the same page as me, because I'm about to put myself out there—put my personal life over business—and that's fucking terrifying. *What if she doesn't feel the same way about me? What if I've been reading her wrong this entire time?* I can't keep living in this unknown, so there's only one way to find out.

I set my drink in the cup holder and reach for her hand, which she lets me take. I bring her knuckles to my lips and place a gentle kiss there. Her cheeks stain with a hint of pink as she smiles at me.

"My brothers were skeptical about our situation." I look her in the eyes. "They told me there was no way I would be able to keep this strictly professional—our agreement." I rub the side of my cheek, a bout of nerves hitting me all at once. *Christ, man, just say it.* "They were right. After our first night hanging out with Ellie and Dave, I knew you were different. And then I had a taste of you, in the hallway, I got to watch you come apart on my fingers, and I was fucking done. I tried to deny it, to ignore it, but my need for you has grown too strong, Lottie." With a deep breath, I say, "I want more from you. And I know this crosses the line of our agreement, but I can't pretend I don't have feelings for you, because I do. I like you, Lottie. I like you a lot."

"I was not expecting you to say that." She takes a deep breath. *Fuck, she doesn't feel the same way.*

She stands from her chair, and I panic that she's about to leave, but instead, she sets her beer in her cup holder and takes a seat on my lap. She places her hand on the back of my neck and plays with the short strands of my hair.

"I like you a lot, too, Huxley. And I want you to know how painful that is for me to admit."

I chuckle as I'm filled with relief.

Her hand cups my cheek. "You've slowly won me over with your heart, something I never thought I would say. Given how things first started, I wasn't sure there was a heart in that barrel of a chest of yours, but I know now that you were hiding it."

"Because I didn't want to show you. I wanted you to think I was cold, soulless, just a man to work with, nothing else."

She chuckles. "Well, you did a good job at that, but too bad for you, I have people in my life who like to point out the good in you. Which they pointed out to me. I wanted to deny it; I wanted to think it wasn't true, that your soul wasn't just spotted black, but encompassed by it. I was wrong." She shakes her head and lets out a curt laugh. "God, I thought you didn't like me at all, that maybe I was just a toy to you."

"Why the hell would you think that?" I ask.

Shyly, she moves her hand over my shirt as she says, "Because this weekend, when we were intimate, you never kissed me."

For a goddamn reason.

I tilt her chin up so she's forced to look me in the eyes. "Because I knew if I did, I wouldn't be able to stop." I wet my lips, moving closer. "And honestly, I wasn't sure you even wanted me to kiss you."

"I do," she says, her voice sounding breathless. "I don't think I've ever wanted something as much as I want you to kiss me." Her hand falls to my cheek. "You've commanded my body, Huxley, now I want you to command my mouth."

There's no way in hell I can deny myself now, not with that confession, not with the way she's pulling me closer.

No, I want this. I want her.

This might go against every goddamn thing I've said from the very beginning, but it seems as though it's inevitable. There's no more denying our attraction, our need, our yearning.

It's out in the open, and I'm going to take advantage of it.

I gently place my hand at the side of her neck, and with my thumb, tilt her chin up just before I lower my mouth to hers.

It's a simple kiss but with a powerful punch behind it, packed with pent-up restraint and desperation.

And now that I'm not in front of my brothers or Dave, I don't have to make a show of our kiss. I can really let myself enjoy.

Enjoy how beautifully soft her lips are.

Enjoy the firm grip she has on my cheek, keeping me still, showing me how much more she wants from me.

Enjoy the soft noises that fall past her lips when she needs to catch her breath.

My mouth moves across hers, slowly exploring. Her tongue swipes against my lips and I open my mouth to allow her to explore. Timid at first, her tongue gingerly strokes mine, but as I grip her more tightly, her timid kiss turns more desperate, and before I know it, we're making out, in our chairs, waiting for the concert to start.

Her hand snakes behind my head and up into my hair, while I move my other hand to her rib cage, just below her breast. I'm tempted to cop a feel, to increase this burn between us, but right as I start to move my hand, a guitar chord strums through speakers.

We pull apart just in time for Fleetwood Mac to come onto the stage.

What?

No opening band?

No announcement?

Just...here they are?

The entire place erupts in cheers, and my comfortable make-out session turns into Lottie hopping off my lap and throwing her hands in the air as she starts jumping up and down and cheering.

Still seated in my seat, I give myself a few seconds to collect myself before I join her.

Lottie, she's...hell, she's fucking special. And I knew that from the first time she turned me down. She was someone in need, yet she only thought about her sister. She didn't want her parents to be disappointed in her, so she looked out for them, too. She fought me on things that deserved fighting me on, and even though I attempted to deny it from the beginning, I don't think there's a chance in hell I'll be able to let her go.

And that means one thing: I have to make this work. I want to date Lottie, make her feel special, because that's what she is—special. *And I suspect she has no clue.* No thanks to her "friend" Angela.

Standing from my chair, I wrap my arm around her and settle my hand on her stomach, keeping her close to me just as the chords for "Dreams" start to play. Lottie glances up at me, tears in her eyes. She reaches for the back of my head, brings me down to her, and places a passionate kiss across my lips, turning me into a goddamn desperate man, wanting so much more.

When she pulls away, she says, "Thank you, Huxley. Thank you so much."

I press a light kiss to the end of her nose. "You're welcome, Lottie."

Smile still on her face, she spins in my arms and leans into my embrace.

And while Fleetwood Mac performs, Lottie never leaves my side, never shifts away. She sways to the music with me while we sing together, letting the night take ahold of us. And while I've been to many concerts before—a private jet makes it so easy—this is one of my best concert experiences. *And it's all about the girl in my arms.*

"Mr. Cane, you're free to remove your seat belts and move about if you'd like," the pilot says over the speaker.

Lottie is curled up in her seat, staring at me, the biggest smile on her face that I've ever seen.

"What?" I ask, unable to take it anymore. "Why do you keep staring at me?"

"Because I can now."

"Didn't know there was a rule that you couldn't before."

She cutely tilts her head to the side. She ditched her hat when we got back on the plane, and she tied her hair up into a ponytail so her hair was out of her face. "There is, when all you keep saying to me over and over again is 'contract, contract, contract.'"

I chuckle. "I had a protective shield up. Can't blame me for that."

"You weren't like that when we first went out at Chipotle."

"Because I didn't know the effect you'd have on me," I admit. "Once I realized you were a temptation I couldn't have, I shut down."

"I see," she says while standing from her chair. She walks over to me and says, "And what am I now? Still a temptation?"

"Undeniably," I answer.

Her finger moves over my shoulder. "But you can have me now?"

"You tell me," I say.

Smirking, she takes my hand in hers and pulls me out of my chair and toward the back of the plane. I pause her at the door of the bedroom situated in the back.

"What are you doing?" I ask her.

"What do you think I'm doing?" she asks, pushing the door open and walking backward into the space while holding my hand and smiling up at me.

"Lottie, you don't have to do this."

"You say that as if it's a chore." She pulls me into the bedroom with her and shuts the door behind me. Her hands fall to the hem of my T-shirt, and she pulls it up and over my head before dropping it on the floor. "I know I don't have to do anything." Her hands fall to my chest. "But, God, Huxley, do I want to feel you inside of me."

Just like that, I grow hard.

"Ever since that night when you made me come on your fingers, I've wanted to know what it would be like to come all over your cock."

"Fu-ck," I mumble.

Her fingers drag down my chest to the waistband of my jeans. She undoes my pants, but instead of pushing them down, she leaves them hanging on my waist and lifts her hands above her head.

"Undress me, Hux."

Skin burning with lust for this woman, I reach for the hem of her shirt and pull it over her head. I drop the shirt with mine and take in the see-through black bra she's wearing. Her nipples are puckered, pushing against the threadbare lace, and her breath appears erratic as her chest rises and falls rapidly.

Eyes connected with mine, she takes my hands and puts them on the front clasp of her bra. I don't bother to look at the clasp as I undo it. Her breasts push the unhooked bra away, and she lets it slide down her arms to the ground.

I reach out and pass my thumb over one of her nipples. "You have the sexiest fucking tits I've ever seen. I could spend hours worshipping them." I smooth my hand down her stomach to her jean shorts. I undo them and push them down to the ground, leaving her in just her black lace thong. "But I'll wait to worship them another day. Now...I need to be inside of you." I turn her around and lay her upper half down on the bed, keeping her lower half arched up for me. I take the sides of her thong and drag them down her legs until she can step out of it for me.

I glide my hand over her naked ass and relish in her naked body.

"So goddamn hot." I squeeze her ass and then give it a light slap, pulling a moan straight from the depths of her throat. "If I were to reach between your legs right now, would I find you wet, ready for me?"

"Yes," she groans, pushing her ass into my hand.

"Then spread wider for me."

She does just that, spreading her legs and then sticking her ass higher in the air.

I glide my thumb down her crack to her arousal, where I'm rewarded with her slick pussy. "Such a good girl," I say, smoothing two fingers over her clit. Her hands curl into fists as she gathers the comforter beneath her.

"Don't tease me, Huxley."

"Do you really think I would tease you at this point? My cock is as hard as stone seeing you like this. There's no way I'd fucking tease you."

"Show me how hard."

Easy. I push my jeans and briefs down and take them off, along with my socks. My cock jolts upward, hard...ready. I grip the base and take a step forward to rub the tip along her slick arousal.

"Oh my God," she says as she grips the comforter tighter. "Huxley, I want you inside me. Now."

I want her, too. So fucking bad. But I want to see her.

I grip her hips and twist her on the bed, so she's flipped to her back. She scoots upward, offering me room, so I climb onto the mattress as well and move toward the headboard with her. She's waiting for me, legs spread and arms open wide, so I ease down onto her and prop my body up with my forearms, which cradle her head.

"You're beautiful, Lottie. I'm not sure I've ever told you that, but you are. Fucking breathtaking."

Her eyes go soft as she reaches up and presses her palm to my cheek. "Thank you," she whispers before pulling my mouth down to hers.

With a featherlight touch, she moves her lips against mine in a tantalizing, teasing performance, giving me a little, but not giving me nearly enough of her delicious mouth. I growl in frustration, which causes her to smile and pull her lips away even more.

"Kiss me, Lottie. Let me taste those lips."

"You sound as though you've been wanting these lips for a long time."

I move my hand closer to her face so I can float my finger over her cheek. "I have been. Now let me fucking enjoy."

Her smile grows even brighter, and she tugs on my neck so my mouth swoops down on hers. I capture her lips, claiming her with my kisses.

My mouth moves over hers with savage intensity, begging her for more but savoring every moment.

Her hand moves to the back of my head. With my thrusting tongue, I part her lips so that our tongues clash in heated passion.

Our once calm, leisurely kiss has now turned into something frantic, something completely carnal. Her grip on the back of my head grows tighter. My hand falls to her jaw, and I hold her mouth in place, gaining control over this kiss.

Because I'm falling.

In this moment, with her legs spread and my erection resting against her center, our hands holding on tightly, our mouths claiming each other…I'm fucking falling. I can feel it in my bones.

She's not what I was expecting.

But she's everything I fucking want.

Pulling my mouth away, I kiss her chin, then her jaw, then the column of her neck to her collarbone. Her body shifts under mine, and I move down to her breasts, dragging my tongue along her skin, until I meet her pert nipple. I massage her right breast as I pull her left into my mouth, sucking hard.

"Yes," she whispers. "Yes, Huxley."

She pulls on the strands of my hair as my teeth massage her nipple. When I nibble, a hiss escapes her lips, followed by a drawn-out moan.

"I'm so wet," she whispers, and then takes my hand and brings it between her lips. "Feel me. Feel how drenched I am for you."

I slide my finger across her pussy, and fuck, she's right. She's dripping.

I lift off her breasts, and her eyes connect with mine. "I want you," she says softly. "Please, Huxley."

"I'm all yours, baby," I say as I press a sweet, gentle kiss to her mouth.

Her legs spread even wider, so I take the opportunity to smooth my hand down her leg and then carefully lift it until it's draped over my shoulder.

"That okay?" I ask, wanting to make sure she's comfortable.

"Yes, so good."

"Perfect," I say as I grip my cock and tease her entrance with it. She thrusts her hips toward me, and I smile at how impatient she is.

Hell, I'm just as impatient.

I move my hips forward and shift my cock inside her just an inch.

But that inch is all it takes.

Her warmth sucks me in, and I push farther, not giving her much time to adjust.

"Fuck," I mutter. "You're so goddamn perfect for me." I take a deep breath and ask, "Are you okay?"

"More," is all she says. "I want more, Huxley."

Given the green light, I thrust all the way in until I bottom out, unable to push any farther. She groans as her eyes fly shut and her chest arches toward me. I take that moment to bring her breast to my mouth again, wanting to make sure she's as relaxed as possible, because I'm not going to be able to hold back very long. Not when she feels this good.

Needing to feel her, I slowly thrust into her, while my mouth plays over her taut nipples.

"You're so big," she says, letting out a deep breath. This relaxes her more, and I'm able to thrust farther.

"Baby, you need to relax some more; you're tense."

"Then bring those lips back to my mouth," she says, pulling at my chin with her finger.

I don't automatically move up to her lips. I drag my tongue along her skin and pepper kisses up her neck and along her jaw, leaving a path of pleasure in my wake. I own every last inch of her. When I reach her mouth, I waste no time in tangling our tongues together.

And I feel her relax even more.

Fuck. I thrust again, and I go deeper, so deep that my vision narrows.

"Yes," she whispers against my lips.

Mouths connected, I pick up my pace and thrust harder, quicker.

"Never been this good," I admit as my tempo becomes frenzied. "Never in my goddamn life."

"Same," she cries, her back arching more, her leg clamping around my shoulder. "Oh God, I'm getting close. More, Hux." *I'm so close. So fucking close. So good.*

I lower her leg from my shoulder, press her thighs wide open, and say, "Hold your legs."

She does, and I brace myself on the mattress as I pound into her harder. My hips are relentless. Pushing and pushing and pushing.

The pleasure between us heightens.

My body begins to float as the first ripple of pleasure shoots up my spine.

"Fuck, Lottie. I'm going to—"

"Yes," she moans as her pussy clenches around my cock. "You're making me come. Oh God, Huxley."

With a cry of absolute pleasure, so goddamn loud I'm almost positive the pilots can hear us, she comes all over my cock, and I use her spasms to push me over the edge while she gasps in sweet agony.

My balls tighten, and with one final pulse of my hips, my orgasm rips through me like a goddamn wrecking ball through my rib cage.

It takes my breath away.

It rocks me to my very core as I come over and over inside her.

The lasting ripples of pleasure casually throb up and down my spine as I collapse on top of her.

Her arms wrap around my back, and her hands gently caress my shoulders as we both catch our breath. After a few seconds, I lift up just enough so not all of my weight is on top of her, and I reach up to brush my thumb over her cheek.

"Are you okay?" I ask, worried that I was too rough.

"I'm perfect," she answers with a sated smile. She lifts up and presses another kiss to my lips. "I'm really so perfect, Huxley."

And she looks like she is. Heady eyes. Satisfied smile. Relaxed body.

"Are we able to just lie here for a second?" she asks.

"As long as you want. Let me just get something to clean us up." I press one more kiss to her lips and then lift off her. There's a bathroom attached to the bedroom, thankfully, so I walk in there, clean up quickly, and then wet a washcloth for her. When I turn to go back to the bedroom, I discover her standing in the bathroom doorway, wearing my shirt.

Fuck.

She looks so damn good with her hair rumpled, coming loose from her ponytail, and a satisfied expression on her face.

I hold out the washcloth. "Here," I say.

She presses her hand to my chest, kisses my jaw, and then takes the washcloth and goes into the bathroom. Giving her some privacy, I step into my boxer briefs, then hop into bed and under the covers. We have an hour before we have to be back in our seats.

After a few minutes, she comes out of the bathroom, looking sexy as hell in my shirt, and crawls into bed next to me. I open my arm, and she curls against me, her head resting on my shoulder and her hand on my bare chest. I curl my arm around her, clutching her tight.

And just like that, I'm a taken man.

Fucking besotted.

This is what I want.

Her, in my arms.

Exactly like this.

It's as if the last few weeks have been the most intense foreplay of my life, because the end result, Lottie in my arms...yeah, the best fucking thing that could happen.

"I'm on the pill," she says softly.

"I figured," I say, moving my hand over her hair.

"I don't want you thinking I'm trying to trap you."

"I'd never assume such a thing. You have too much pride to consider doing anything like that."

"That's true." She chuckles. "But I thought I'd let you know anyway."

"Thank you." I kiss her forehead and close my eyes.

After a few beats of silence, she says, "Can I ask you something?"

"Anything," I answer. I don't think I've ever been this comfortable, this carefree, as I am in this moment.

"When you said, It's *never been like this*, did you mean that?"

"Fuck yes," I say without skipping a beat. "I wouldn't lie about shit like that."

She lifts up, and I open my eyes to find her staring at me. "Are you saying I'm the best you've ever had?"

I chuckle. "Looking for a trophy?"

I mean it's not a lie, she is the best, hands down. And I know a lot of that has to do with this connection I feel toward her.

"I wouldn't mind one."

I tickle her side and she squirms against me, laughing.

"After all you've put me through, I'd say a trophy wouldn't kill you."

"Call it character building."

She rolls her eyes. "Such a businessman-like thing to say."

"Get used to it. That's who you're dating now. A businessman."

Her brow arches in question. "Oh, are we dating now?"

"Yeah," I answer. "What the hell do you think tonight was?"

"A lucky night out with my fake fiancé?" She smirks.

"Is that how you want to see it?" *Fuck. I hope not.*

She shakes her head. "No, I don't want to go back to whatever it was that we were. That was stressful." She's right. It was stressful. Not only did I have my normal job to do, but I felt enormous pressure to be someone I'm not around her. I'm not a hard-hearted asshole. I'm reticent. Slow to show my inner self. *Protective.* And yet, somehow, she's managed to pull deeper parts of me to the surface. But thank fuck, she's not tossing that back in my face. *She wants more of me…and I want her to have it. Willingly. Gratefully.*

"So then, we're dating."

She pauses, thinking about it for a second, and then she chuckles. "Never thought I'd date my fake fiancé, but then again, I never thought I'd do half the things I've done since I met you."

"And we haven't even gotten started yet."

CHAPTER 19
LOTTIE

"I'M NERVOUS. WHY AM I nervous? Should I be nervous?" I twist my hands in front of me as I pace the entryway of Huxley's house.

He's sitting on the stairs, a grin spread across his face.

"And I don't like that you're finding joy in my pacing."

He chuckles and stands, then steps in front of me to keep me from wearing a path into his beautiful floors. He stills me with his hands to my shoulders and then lifts my chin. Only to bend down and place a soft kiss to my lips. Not sure I'll ever get tired of receiving his affection.

Ever.

"You have nothing to worry about."

"Easy for you to say. My mom already loves you, but I've never really spoken to your brothers before. Besides a few pleasantries, they're strangers to me. And they must know I'm some kind of lunatic for agreeing to be your fake fiancée." I grip my forehead. "God, what they must think of me." Eyes wide, I ask, "Do they think I'm a gold digger? Because I'm not. I'll break up with you right now to prove them wrong."

"They don't think you're a gold digger. If they're judging anybody, they're judging me. Trust me, I've taken enough shit from them over the past week about us getting together. They're going to be ecstatic to get to know you better."

"They've given you shit?" I ask.

"They said from the very beginning that I liked you, but I was in denial. So basically, them just rubbing it in my face." He shrugs his shoulders as if it's nothing.

"And they know my mom thinks we're engaged?"

He nods. "They're well aware. Everyone is going to act as though we're engaged."

I blow out a deep breath and step into his embrace.

His hand rubs up and down my back. "It's going to be okay, Lottie."

"Why did we think it would be a good idea to have our families over for a barbecue? This seems like a recipe for disaster."

"I thought it was because you wanted to tell everyone how amazing my cock is."

My head shoots up, and I catch the blatant humor in his expression. "What is wrong with you?"

He chuckles. "Trying to lighten the mood, babe. It's really going to be okay."

"And what if your brothers don't like me?"

"They will, trust me. Anyone who can give me as much shit as you do and bring me to my knees, they're going to love. I wouldn't be surprised if they showed up wearing Team Lottie T-shirts. Trust me, they're fans."

"Team Lottie. I like the sound of that." I press a kiss to his jaw. "And you still don't have any regrets?"

He shakes his head. "None."

It's been a little over a week since the concert, since we confessed our feelings, since Huxley Cane took me by storm. When we got back home, he brought me back to his bedroom and fucked me until we passed out. The next day, he called in sick—I told Kelsey I'd be working from Huxley's place—and we spent the entire day getting to know each other all over again. He told me about how when he was an Eagle Scout, he used to boast about it to get girls to notice him. Sadly, none of them cared, which made me laugh so hard I snorted. And I told him about the time I caught my mom making out with Jeff in the pantry when they first started dating, and how Mom said she lost her Tic Tac in his mouth. She was trying to find it. Which then inspired Huxley to proceed to push me on my back and say he lost a Tic Tac as well…

I'll be honest, I've never had this much sex in my life. I've never been contorted the way Huxley contorts me. And I never knew there were so many surfaces you can have sex on.

Bathroom counter.

Stairway landing.

Lounge chairs.

Patio table.

Fence.

Hood of a car…

Basically if I can sit or lean on it, Huxley can fuck me on it, and he has.

And it's been amazing. So amazing that I admitted to Kelsey yesterday that I'm embarrassingly addicted to his cock. So bad that any time I see him, I can practically feel him already between my legs. Yup, I've lost it completely.

And yet…it's not just that. In fact, it's making me see how superficial my previous boyfriends were. Especially Ken. *God, I dated an idiot.* I knew Huxley had a deeper soul than it seemed when I first met him. And I've gotten to know *him.* Yes, he has pretentious business goals and aspirations, but he's also generous with his time. He looks for opportunities to grow his employees by offering his expertise when that benefits *them.* He encourages growth in employee skills. He shared some of his drive with me, and it got me even more excited about opportunities for Kelsey's company. *And for what I'm actually capable of.* He complimented *me* for my business acumen, and that felt extraordinary. *He is* extraordinary.

Grabbing me by the hips, Huxley asks, "Do you have any regrets?"

"Are you serious?" I ask. "The only regret I have is not stripping down for you on day one."

He laughs. "Pretty sure you hated me too much to strip down."

"Angry sex is better than no sex." I reach up to kiss him just as the doorbell rings. I stiffen in his arms and whisper, "Oh God, they're here."

"They're going to love you. I promise." He kisses me one last time, then takes my hand in his and brings me to the front door. When he opens it, he reveals Breaker and JP, both holding Tupperware and flowers in their hands.

"There she is," Breaker says, pushing through the door. "The girl who turned our brother into a walking pile of lusty mush."

"Jesus," Huxley mutters.

"These are for you." Breaker hands me flowers and then pulls me into a hug.

JP follows behind him, handing me flowers as well. "You're a goddess," he says, giving me a hug as well. "We want you to tell us everything."

Huxley inserts himself between me and his brothers and separates us. "That won't be necessary. You know enough."

"You can't protect her all night. We *will* get her alone, and we'll ask her embarrassing questions. We need as much ammo as we can get," JP says.

There's a knock at the door.

With a warning glare, Huxley says, "Be on your best behavior."

His brothers roll their eyes—which I think is hilarious—and they walk toward the kitchen as Huxley answers the door. "Maura, Jeff, Kelsey, welcome."

Huxley swings the door all the way open, revealing my family on the other side. Mom made homemade churros, and Jeff brought a fruit salad I know he spent at least an hour making. He takes his fruit salads seriously. It shows. They're positively beautiful and really freaking delicious.

"Thank you so much for having us. I've been itching to see where our Lottie has been staying," Mom says as she steps in and gives Huxley a hug. Jeff offers him a handshake, and Kelsey gives him a fist bump, which I think is kind of funny. We've had two meetings with Cane Enterprises, and even though Huxley is extremely professional, Breaker and JP have made the business relationship more easygoing. I can see that in the easy manner Kelsey has around Huxley now.

I give them a quick hello before we all head back to the kitchen. Reign prepared a spread of food, which he arranged on the kitchen island while Huxley and I were busy doing...other things.

The sliding glass doors to the backyard are open, and there's music playing softly in the background.

"Wow," Mom says in awe. "Your place is spectacular."

"Thank you," Huxley says while taking the food Mom and Jeff brought. "Can I get you anything to drink?"

Over the past week, I've come to know the real Huxley. The Huxley I thought I met when we ran into each other on the sidewalk. Easygoing, fun. The once stiff and unapproachable man I knew is no longer in sight. Actually, the only thing stiff about him is his cock.

After we're all settled, pleasantries and introductions behind us, we head out to the patio with our food and take a seat at the large table on which Huxley and I have had sex three times. But no one needs to know that.

Huxley leans into my ear and whispers, "Your mom is sitting in the exact same spot where you came so hard, you squirted."

"Can you not?" I whisper back, feeling my face go red.

He chuckles and kisses my cheek.

"What are you whispering about over there?" Kelsey, who's sitting across from me, asks. The glint in her eye tells me she knows exactly what we're talking about, because I told her about our patio table escapades.

"Nothing," I say, glaring at her.

"So, Jeff, are you going to tell them the news?" Mom asks, thankfully changing the subject.

"What news?" I ask, glancing down the table at Jeff, who's partaking in some of his fruit salad and Reign's homemade macaroni casserole.

The table grows quiet as Jeff sets down his fork and lifts his head. "I received a letter in the mail yesterday. Apparently, someone contacted the beautification committee and suggested they take a look at our house. They came by last week while visiting the other properties and congratulated me on a well-preserved yard with exquisite definition and color selection in our planters." Mom squeezes Jeff's arm.

"Seriously?" I ask, in complete shock.

Jeff nods, his smile so large that it's contagious. "Unfortunately, the house isn't within the boundaries of the contest, but they did give me an honorary award and said they'd be working with the city on expanding the boundary line so I can possibly be included in the future."

"Holy shit," I say. "That's amazing, Jeff. Oh my God, you've worked so hard."

He nods again and his eyes well up. He looks at Huxley and says, "Thank you, Huxley. I'm not sure you know how much this means to me."

Huxley?

I turn around to look at him, and he offers Jeff a simple nod. "I just made a phone call. You did all of the work."

"Wait, you called the beautification committee?"

"Nothing to make a big deal about," he says under his breath. "Congrats, Jeff. It's a well-deserved honor."

In the most sincere voice, Jeff says, "It means the world to me to be recognized, Huxley. Thank you."

And then the table falls silent as my mind swirls with this new information.

Jeff heard from them yesterday.

But they did their rounds a week to two weeks ago.

Which means...Huxley must have called them before we were together, when we were at each other's necks with anger and frustration.

And he did that. He called.

He put that smile on Jeff's face.

"Huxley," I whisper.

He picks up my hand, places a kiss across my knuckles, and says, "We'll talk about it later."

———

"Please tell us you have some embarrassing stories," JP says as he takes a seat across from me on a lounger. Breaker joins him.

I glance over at the patio, where Huxley is in deep conversation with Jeff and my mom. Kelsey left a while ago because she claimed she had another engagement, but I saw right through her. She was avoiding JP and his flirtation. Frankly, I was enjoying the show, but Kelsey could only take so much.

Hunkering down with the boys, I say, "I'm not sure the man is capable of doing anything embarrassing."

"Obviously he's been able to hold it together so far in front of you. Trust me when I say, the man can embarrass himself."

"Oh yeah? Why don't you delight me with a story?"

Breaker and JP exchange glances. "Did he mention the time he did a presentation at NYU about entrepreneurship, and the entire time, his fly was undone?"

"What?" I laugh out loud. "No, he didn't."

Breaker nods. "He did. At the end of his presentation, one of the dick-head college kids asked him if he was hot."

"Oh God." I clamp my hand over my mouth, giggling.

"Of course, Huxley was confused and answered no and asked why. Then the kid said because he didn't know why else his fly would be undone unless it was for a cross breeze."

I burst out in laughter and draw Huxley's attention away from his conversation. He eyes his brothers suspiciously, and there's no doubt he knows what his brothers are doing.

"What did he do?" I ask.

Breaker rubs his hand over his jaw, something I've noticed Huxley does as well. "He of course was humiliated. Zipped up his pants, cleared his throat, and then thanked everyone for their time before bolting. Bro was an epic dick for days after, blamed us for sending him out there unzipped."

"What?" I ask.

JP presses his hand to his chest. "Exactly. Explain to us how that's our fault. Are we supposed to hover over him like a helicopter mom?" JP shakes his head. "No, not our job. Be an adult man and zip up your pants."

"Now, before we go into any meeting, we always whisper to Huxley to check his fly."

"Stop. Do you really?" I chuckle.

Breaker nods. "Yeah, he hates us so much for it, but to hell if we're going to be blamed again for his mistake."

"You're protecting yourself," I say.

"Exactly," Breaker says to JP. "She gets it."

"She gets what?" Huxley asks, joining us, my mom and Jeff at his side.

"Nothing," JP says. "This is between us. Nothing you need to concern yourself about."

"If you're talking to my girl, I'm concerned," Huxley responds, which of course makes me all weak in the knees because of the possessive tone he uses.

"Ooo, I like this side of him," JP says. He stands and slaps his brother on the shoulder. "As much as I love talking to your fiancée about your embarrassing moments, I need to head out."

"Me, too," Breaker says.

"We're headed out as well," Jeff says. "We came over to say bye."

I stand and give Jeff and my mom a hug, making sure to squeeze them extra tight. It was good seeing them again. I've been so wrapped up in my hectic life that I've missed spending time with them. Hopefully things are slowing down now, though, so we can plan more things like this.

Together, as a group, we head to the front door, where we all exchange hugs, thank-yous, and goodbyes. Once the door is shut, Huxley turns toward me and asks, "What did they say to you?"

I chuckle and head into the kitchen to start cleaning up. "Afraid they said something that would deter me away from you?"

"Yes."

"It's going to take a lot more than a story about your fly being down to tear me away."

He groans and leans against the counter. "They didn't."

I pin him with a look. "Was it for the cross breeze?"

The look in his eyes is absolutely murderous, and it just makes me laugh even more.

"You're no longer allowed to talk to them."

"Such a shame," I say. "We got along very well." Since we already took care of the food earlier, I just stick the dishes in the dishwasher and then turn toward Huxley. "I'd love to talk to them more. They seem really grounded."

"Yeah, I'm sure you would." When I close the dishwasher, he comes up to me and tugs on my hand, pulling me in close. "Did you have fun today?"

"I did." I smooth my hand up his chest. "But I do have to ask you something."

"What's that?"

"That phone call you made—"

"It's not a big deal, Lottie." He starts to move away, but I stop him.

"It's a big deal to me. I'm not sure you realize this, but you made Jeff's year. He works so hard on our front yard, and to be recognized like that, it means everything to him." I force Huxley to look at me. "When did you make the phone call?"

"Why does it matter?"

"Because it does. When did you make it?"

He lets out a deep sigh. "I don't know, like four weeks ago."

"Four weeks ago?" I ask, astonished. "As in, right after we met?"

He pulls on his neck. "Yeah, probably around then. But like I said, it doesn't matter."

"That's where you're wrong," I say, reaching up to him and gripping his cheek. "Huxley, you did this out of the kindness of your heart, because you knew it meant a lot to someone else. Not many people would stop to do something like that."

"We don't have to make a big deal out of this."

I pause and observe him. The fidgetiness of his body. The inability to look me in the eyes. "You don't accept compliments very well, do you?"

"I don't think it's necessary to make a big deal out of something that, in the grand scheme of things, was small on my end."

"But it wasn't small," I counter. "It wasn't small at all. You made Jeff, a man so special to me, happy. You truly made his year, Huxley. I can't tell you how grateful I am for that."

He grips my hips and leans forward, pressing a kiss to my forehead. "If you're happy, then I'm happy."

He takes my hand and guides me up the stairs to his bedroom. The entire way, I keep thinking about how things have changed, and so quickly. We went from being at each other's throats with insults to not wanting to let each other go. Kelsey was right—there really is a fine line between love and hate, and we crossed over it.

"I don't feel comfortable with this," I say as we wait for Dave and Ellie to show up. "We need to tell them."

Huxley looks just as uncomfortable as I feel. "I know, but I don't know how to fucking do it. I still haven't secured the deal, because he keeps cancelling on me."

We're waiting outside a tall brick building for a newborn class. Dave asked if we wanted to join them, and of course, Huxley—still on his quest to secure Dave's properties—said yes. But now that we're here, it doesn't feel right at all, especially since we're actually together now.

"What do you think he'd do if he actually knew the pregnancy thing wasn't true?"

"I don't know," Huxley says, looking out toward the street. "I'm pretty sure he'd never do business with me, because I lied. And my worst fear would be the news getting out to everyone around us, all the people I work with. It could be absolutely disastrous."

"Yeah, I can't imagine people wanting to do business with you after you've claimed a fake fiancée and child all in one day."

"Doesn't bode well for me."

I nudge him with my shoulder. "I know I've said it before, but it was a pretty idiotic move."

He chuckles, pulls me closer against his chest, and kisses me on the top of the head. "Yes, you've made that statement before."

"Hey, you guys, over here," we hear Dave say from behind us. Together, we turn around to find Dave and Ellie wearing jeans and matching white button-up tops, walking toward us with their arms wrapped around each other's waists. They are something else.

Huxley lifts his hand in a wave and then quietly says to me, "I'll figure out a way to make this better, I promise. Let's just get through today."

"Okay." I give him a squeeze, and then we join Dave and Ellie.

"Oh, wow, you look amazing," Ellie says, pulling me into a hug. "You're positively glowing in this dress." I chose to wear a flowy dress just in case I'm supposed to be showing, which I'm not. "Isn't she glowing, Dave?"

"She is," Dave says with a sly smile. "She looks like a woman in love." I nearly choke on my own saliva.

I cough a few times and Huxley rubs my back. "You okay?"

"Yeah, sorry." I cough again. "Just swallowed wrong for a second." I gather myself and smile at everyone. "Uh, so, are we going in?" I thumb toward the door awkwardly.

"Yes, I'm so excited. I heard the dolls are so lifelike in this class that they actually pee on you. Doesn't that sound thrilling?"

Keeping my composure, I answer, "Oh yes. Very excited for that surprise." About as excited as I was for the fake breast milk to fly across my face.

Dave and Ellie walk in before us, and Huxley hangs back for a second, tugging on my hand. "Everything okay?" he asks.

"Yeah, everything is fine. Why?" I ask, pasting on a smile.

"Because you're acting weird."

"Am I?" I ask in a high-pitched tone. "I feel as though I'm normal."

He studies me for a few beats before reaching for the door and opening it for me. Hand on my lower back, he guides me in to where Dave and Ellie are waiting for us. Ellie holds up a baby doll and says, "We got our baby. His name is Enoch. Isn't he dreamy?"

Dreamy?

It's a doll.

I really want to know what species Ellie is, because there's no way she's human. Not even close to it. She's an odd one.

"What a lovely baby," I say. "Very...plasticky."

Huxley tugs on my arm toward the registration desk. He lowers his mouth to my ear and in an amused tone, he asks, "Plasticky?"

I chuckle softly. "I don't know how to compliment a fake baby."

"Hello, who is the reservation under?" the receptionist asks.

"Mr. and Mrs. Cane," Huxley says, shocking me.

"Ah, I have you right here. Let me go grab your baby and supplies."

When she takes off, I turn to Huxley with an arched brow. "Mr. and Mrs. Cane?"

He smirks. "Has a nice ring to it, don't you think?"

"Uh...what?" I ask, about to choke on my saliva again.

He laughs and tugs me closer to him to place a kiss on the top of my head. "Your fear of being attached to me is making me feel like a god today."

The receptionist comes back out and hands us a girl doll. "Her name is Judith. She's a cranky one."

Judith?

Are we taking care of a seventy-year-old?

I take the baby and glance down at it...

"Good Jesus," I whisper. "She's missing an eye."

The receptionist nods. "Not all babies are perfect."

"But this baby doesn't look as though it was born like this, it looks as though it was mauled by a pack of coyotes."

"More like a brothel of chihuahuas," the receptionist says. "Judith has been through a lot, but I know you two will take great care of her." The receptionist motions toward the room. "Hurry on in, the class will be starting soon."

I tuck Judith in my arm and turn toward Ellie and Dave, who are cuddling Enoch as if he's their own. *Sorry, Judith, we probably won't be having the same bond.*

"She's what nightmares are made of," Huxley whispers in my ear.

"I wouldn't be surprised if somehow she finds a way to hitch it back home with us and stare at us in the middle of the night while we're sleeping."

With his hand on my lower back, Huxley says, "If I look over my shoulder as I'm pounding into you and see her, I'm telling you right now, I'm going to leave you."

I whisper back, "I don't blame you."

"Are you ready?" Dave asks, looking up from cooing at Enoch.

"We are," I say, even though I have no idea what to expect or what Huxley got us into.

As a group, we walk into the room, which is filled with couples holding babies. At least ten other couples all hover over their baby stations. The only tables left are one in the back and one in the front.

"If you don't get that back table, I'll never suck your cock again," I whisper to Huxley, who chuckles and moves forward in front of Dave.

Hands out, he says, "Ah, damn, looks as if we can't sit next to each other. We'll take this back table."

"Oh, what a shame," Ellie says, scanning the tables. "Well, might be for the best, I think our little Enoch is crushing on your one-eyed Judith." Ellie winks and then takes off toward the front with Dave.

I glance up at Huxley and ask, "Do you think that was sarcastic? Do you think she was hating on Judith?"

"Does it matter? I thought you were terrified of Judith."

"I am," I say as we make our way to the back table. "But she's ours to be terrified of, no one else's."

"I think you're taking this baby thing too seriously."

"Are you saying you're not actually here to learn the ins and outs of taking care of an infant?" I ask him.

"I'm just hoping there's some kind of snack break." He glances around the room. "But I don't see a snack table, so I'm guessing I'm out of luck."

"Why do I like you?"

Leaning in toward me and talking closely to my ear, he says, "Because you can't get enough of my cock."

"If only that were the case," I reply as the instructor walks into the room. Wait..."Is that Heaven?"

"Who's Heaven?" Huxley asks.

"Uh, the lady who made me dry hump you in front of a bunch of strangers."

"Oh Jesus," Huxley says, trying to get a better look at the instructor. "Fuck, I think it's her. Thank God we're in the back."

"Welcome," Heaven says, her voice booming through the speakers. "I'm so glad everyone could join us on this wonderful journey of getting to know your newborn. I see some familiar faces, and I'm sure I'll see more as I make my way around the classroom to work with each of you individually."

"Oh, great," I mutter. "I'm sure she's going to be focusing on us again." I glance up at Huxley. "You owe me, *Hanley*."

"I'm starting to realize that."

"Now, please go ahead and turn on your babies. The switch is on their back. They'll wake up, and we'll get started."

I flip Judith over and find her *on* switch. I move it to the right, turn her back over, and then with one eye, she blinks at me.

Blinks again.

And then...wails.

"Dear Christ," I say, tossing her on the table, which only makes her wail even louder.

"What are you doing?" Huxley asks. "You're drawing attention to us."

"Not on purpose."

"Why is she so loud?" he asks, picking her up by the leg.

"Because she has one eye and isn't happy about life," I answer while looking around. "I don't think you should hold her like that."

"Like what?"

"Like she's a snake you found on the trail." I nudge him. "She's not going to bite. Coddle her."

"Easy for you to say, she's not staring at you with her one eye." She wails even louder and Huxley grimaces. "Good fuck, what has possessed this thing?"

"It doesn't like being held upside down like that," I say.

"It doesn't know. It's not alive."

"Says the man who's scared of the blinking doll. No, I think it has a sensor. Hold it close to you."

"Maybe we shouldn't call Judith *it*, maybe that's hurting *her* feelings."

"Then hold *Judith* close to you," I say as she screams even louder.

"Like to my chest?"

"Yes," I say in exasperation. "Like an actual baby, Huxley." Judith wails again, and I catch sight of Heaven walking toward us. "Oh shit, Heaven is coming in this direction. Quick, coddle her. Coddle her, damn it."

"Ugh, okay." Huxley brings Judith to his chest and holds her, but that doesn't stop her wailing. "She's still acting like a wretched crotch."

"Then pat her."

"Pat her?" he asks.

"Yes, you know. A light tap to the back. Soothe her, Huxley."

Awkwardly, he pats Judith, which only makes her scream more. "It's possessed. It's because she's missing an eye; there's no other explanation." He hands me the doll, which I hold out in front of me. The plastic doll wails, blinks, and wails some more.

"I don't like this thing."

"You're not coddling it," Huxley says as Heaven draws closer.

"Because I'm afraid Judith is going to suck my soul right from my body if I bring her in closer."

"Here, I'll pat her while you hold her." Huxley reaches out and pats Judith on the back a few times.

After the fourth pat, Judith stops crying.

"Oh my God, we did it."

"Did we?" Huxley asks, unsure. "Would she just stop like that?"

"I think so. I think we soothed—"

Before I can finish my sentence, I'm sprayed in the face with some sort of milky liquid.

"Oh fuck," Huxley says, jumping back to avoid whatever hellish liquid the doll is spewing.

"Get it off me, get it off me," I yell as I run in place, holding Judith as far away from me as possible. "Oh my God, why does it smell?"

"I have a wash—" Huxley makes a gagging sound. "Jesus fuck, it smells so bad. What is that?"

"I don't know, just get it off my face."

"Everything okay over here?" Heaven's voice cuts through the chaos.

I pause my theatrics and try not to vomit from the putrid smell on my face. "Judith is experiencing an exorcism," I say.

"I can see that. It seems as though she's not feeling well. Is that how you'd hold a baby who's not feeling well?"

"This is how I'd hold a baby that just sprayed sour milk all over my face. She's lucky she's not rolling on the ground by herself."

Huxley wipes my face with a washcloth, and I allow myself to take a deep breath once most of the liquid is gone.

"Why does it smell?" I ask Heaven, who's standing in front of us with a judgy look on her face.

"We try to make the experience as authentic as possible, which is why I'd ask that you treat the baby like a real one."

"I am. I was just caught off guard, I wasn't expecting for—"

Judith gurgles.

Judith makes an odd sound.

And then, to my horror, Judith starts leaking something brown.

Without even thinking, I screech, drop Judith on the table, and step away as a fresh round of putrid stench comes from Judith's plastic bottom.

And of course, because she's Satan's baby, she wails so loud that everyone is looking at us now, even Dave and Ellie, who are coddling Enoch.

This is not going well.

———

"I'm sorry," I whisper as we sit outside of the building, cleaned up, thankfully all remnants of Judith wiped away.

"Don't be; that doll was possessed."

"Yeah, but I got us kicked out of the class."

After Judith had another "upset belly," as Heaven liked to call it, I swore at the doll, which caused our eviction from the classroom.

I'm sorry, but if that was a real child, I probably would've reacted the same exact way, except the whole dropping-the-baby thing. But I doubt there's one parent out there who would've been able to keep their cool as they were being blasted by their baby from every hole. Please show me one parent who would've been able to handle that situation with dignity and grace.

None.

"Kicking us out of class was aggressive," Huxley says. "Just because of your litany of swear words? Frankly, I thought it was a colorful combination."

I lean against him and press a kiss to his cheek. "I appreciate you appreciating my ability to combine swear words."

The door to the building opens, and Dave and Ellie step out, holding hands. When they spot us, they smile with apologetic looks.

"We weren't sure if you two left or not," Ellie says. "That was a bit of a rough situation in there."

Huxley helps me stand and places his arm over my shoulder, keeping me close to him. "I'm not sure we were expecting things to be so volatile," Huxley says with humor in his voice.

Dave chuckles. "I don't think I've ever seen such a string of unfortunate events before." He smirks. "And congrats on the swear words. Quite impressive, Lottie."

I feel my face heat up with embarrassment. I was so thrown off by Judith that I completely forgot about all decorum and the purpose of being in the damn class to begin with—to impress Dave. I really hope I didn't just screw things up for Huxley. This deal that seems to have been dragged on forever.

"Sorry about that." I wince. "I think I was so overcome by the smell that I lost all ability to act like a normal human."

"No need to apologize," Dave says. "I'm not sure I would've been able to hold it together if the same thing happened to me."

"I wouldn't have been able to," Ellie says, resting her hand on her belly. "I'm starving. Would you guys care to join us for some dinner?"

"That would be great," I answer for the both of us before Huxley can come up with an excuse. I think I owe it to him to give this outing one more shot.

"Wonderful," Ellie says. "Right around the block, there's a quaint sandwich shop I'm obsessed with. Does that sound good?"

I nod. "Lead the way."

Dave and Ellie take off, but Huxley holds me back a few steps. Whispering into my ear, he says, "You don't have to do this. I know you probably want to get home." *And shower. Yes, God, yes.* But...

"I owe it to you," I answer.

His lips run over my ear, sending chills down my arm. "You owe me nothing. I want to make sure you're okay."

I link my fingers with his, twining them together. "I promise, I'm okay. Let's see if we can make a dent in this deal." I wink and let him draw me in closer as we trail behind Ellie and Dave. He leans away suddenly and clears his throat.

"Is something wrong?"

"Yeah, um...I don't think you got all the baby vomit out of your hair."

Oh fuck.

"Don't you just love a meaty sandwich?" Ellie asks, taking a ravenous bite of her Philly cheesesteak. Cheese drips off her chin as she smiles and chews.

Dear God.

"I love all the meat in my mouth," I answer, causing Huxley to snort next to me. Huh, I guess that didn't sound quite right.

"So sad that you opted for the soup. You could've really chowed down on this cheesesteak."

I got the chicken noodle soup because, frankly, I had no idea what a pregnant lady could eat, and since Ellie and Dave insisted on us ordering first, I went with something neutral. Trust me, that cheesesteak looks phenomenal.

"Not sad at all," I answer, scooping up a spoonful of the boring broth.

"Love me a good soup." I shovel the spoon into my mouth and pretend to enjoy the lackluster meal.

"Is that so?" Dave asks. "Are you a big souper?"

"She's obsessed with soup," Huxley steps in to say. He's been done with his sandwich for a bit now, having opted for something small with a side salad. His arm is draped over my chair, and he's been casually twirling my hair with his finger. "Remember that barley soup you made for us that one night?"

Uhhh…no.

And frankly, soup is ehhh. I'm not much of a heated-liquid person. I prefer a hearty sandwich, so where is he going with this?

"Oh yeah, the barley soup," I answer.

"You used a whole jar of dried barley." Huxley laughs and turns to Dave and Ellie. "I tried to be the doting fiancé and eat it, but it wasn't swallowable."

"Oh, I've had my fair share of unswallowable things," Ellie says, looking at Dave with a certain glint in her eye. *Good…God!*

Dave raises his hand apologetically. "Not the best cook…in any aspect."

Is it just me or are these two throwing down sexual innuendos?

If they are…gross!

"And then there was the beef and potato stew you made," Huxley continues, being Mr. Chatty today. "Now, that was good."

Since we're throwing out sexual innuendos…

"Because I'm great at handling meat."

Huxley's eyes fix on mine. "You're very good at it."

We stare at each other, smiles playing on our lips. Is he thinking about last night? Because I am. I'm thinking about how I spent a good ten minutes handling his meat while he writhed beneath me, begging for release.

"Oh, Dave, do you see that?" Ellie asks.

Huxley and I both snap out of our ogling and turn toward the couple opposite us.

"Yep." Dave has a huge smile on his face. "I think that's our cue, sweetheart. We need to leave these two alone."

Ellie nods. "Those pregnancy hormones are kicking in, and they're about to tear each other's clothes off."

I mean, I wouldn't mind seeing Huxley's well-built chest right now. At the sandwich shop, not so much, but you know, when we get back home.

"You don't have to leave," Huxley says, clearing his throat, but his grip on me grows tighter, more possessive.

Dave laughs. "I think we do." He offers his hand to Huxley and asks, "Next week, think we can discuss this acquisition?"

Huxley straightens and takes Dave's hand, giving it a good shake. "Yes, I'll have Karla call you to see when we're both available."

"Perfect." Dave lifts my hand and places a kiss on the back of it. "Lottie, always a pleasure getting to see you. Good luck...handling your meat."

My cheeks flame. "Th-thank you," I say awkwardly.

Ellie gives us a quick goodbye, and once they're out of the restaurant, Huxley turns toward me, a huge smile on his face. "Babe, did you hear that?"

I love it when he calls me babe. It means he's relaxed, in a good mood, and the stick he likes to wear up his ass most of the time has been temporarily removed.

"That he wants to meet up with you?" I ask.

He nods, that lopsided grin so damn endearing that I find myself drawing closer to him.

"I think he's ready to make a decision. Fuck, could you imagine if this is all over next week?"

My smile fades as realization hits me square in the chest. What if this is all over next week? I never really gave much thought to what would happen after Huxley secured the deal. I know we're sort of dating, but do I leave his house? I'm making some money now that Kelsey and I were paid an advance by Cane Enterprises for our work. Does that mean I could afford my own place now?

"That, uh, that would be great," I answer with a smile, but my mind is wandering. My head is swarming with *What if it really is all over?*

No longer hungry, I pack up my soup and let Huxley know I'm ready to leave. He texts his driver, who meets us outside. Together, we head out of the restaurant and straight to the waiting car, where we take a seat in the back. I buckle up and look out the window, willing my emotions to stay as calm as possible.

The unknown is scary.

Being unprepared is even scarier.

I need to have a plan for when Huxley does secure the deal.

I have a job—thankfully.

I still have my old car, and to my knowledge, it still works, so I have a way to get around.

School loans are paid off—that's still a miracle.

Huxley has already said he'll go to the reunion with me, so I don't have to worry about that. Sticking it to Angela will still be a possibility.

But a place to live...

That's the one thing I don't have under control.

Needing to calm down the worry, I pull my phone out of my purse and go to Zillow, because where else should I look for an apartment? And I do a search for places in West Hollywood. I won't be able to afford anything near Huxley, but near Kelsey would be good.

A studio, that's all I need.

Not a basement apartment, though. That's just asking to be murdered.

God, rent is so high. That's okay, I don't have much in the way of bills. Spend more on rent, save by forgoing luxuries.

"What are you doing?" Huxley asks, the angry tone of his voice catching me off guard.

I glance up at him and catch the confusion in his face. "Uh..." Keeping my voice down, I whisper, "Looking for a place."

"Why the hell would you be doing that?"

I turn toward him now and say, "Well, if you secure the deal, there's no need for me anymore."

His brows narrow. "Are you saying you're going to leave once I secure the deal?"

"Isn't that—isn't that what you want?" I ask, completely confused.

"What I want is you. So why the hell would I want you to leave?"

"Uh...I don't know," I answer. "I mean, I assumed we'd still date, right? Is that a bad assumption?"

"That's a correct assumption. But what I don't understand is why you're trying to leave."

"Because I didn't think you'd still want me around," I whisper to him, not wanting the driver to hear us, even though there's a privacy shield.

Huxley grips my chin and holds me in place as he says, "You're not going anywhere. You hear me? What we have goes beyond the contract. To me, the contract doesn't exist anymore. What's between us now is real. Is it not real to you?"

"No, it is," I say quickly. "I just didn't want to, you know, impose."

He chuckles and leans in, placing a soft, open-mouthed kiss to my lips. When he pulls away, he quietly says, "Lottie, trust me when I say you're not imposing. I want you in my house, in my room, in my bed. I want you on my couch, holding my hand while watching a show you've forced me to reluctantly binge. I want you in my pool, skinny-dipping like you enjoy so much. I want you on my roof, feeling the rain bounce off you during a storm. I want you at my dining room table, eating dinner next to me, giving me a hard time for whatever reason you come up with that day." He lifts my knuckles to his lips and places a soft kiss to them. "I want you, okay?"

The smile that crosses my lips stretches from ear to ear. "Okay. So no apartment searching?"

"No, Jesus." He chuckles while shaking his head. "No more giving me a heart attack."

I press my palm to his cheek. "Aw, you act as if you're attached."

"I am. I'm very much attached to you, Lottie. I don't know how you did it, but I'm addicted. You're not going anywhere."

"Good to know." I nod casually. "Very good to know."

I glance at him, holding back my smile.

He smirks.

I attempt to play it cool.

He calls my bluff and reaches out to tickle me, causing me to laugh, right before he captures my mouth, placing a muffling kiss across my lips. I melt into his embrace and enjoy him laying his claim.

He's not the only one who's addicted, because I need this man just as much as he needs me. I need his teasing, his annoying habits, and his ability to rile me up. I need his caring heart, his blessed soul, and his ability to make me feel safe and protected within the comfort of his arms.

My feelings changed for him so quickly, like the snap of a finger, which makes me wonder, did I always feel like this with him? Were my true feelings just masked by annoyance?

From how much I've fallen for this man, my answer is probably going to be a *yes*.

Yes, I do believe I've always had feelings for him. I've always felt drawn to him. A connection that's unmistakable. But now I've lifted the veil, and I'm able to acknowledge the truth.

I not only like Huxley Cane, but I'm falling in love with him.

CHAPTER 20
HUXLEY

I PRESS MY LIPS TO the curve of her neck as her hand glides into my hair.

"Yes," she whispers, being quiet for once.

My hand slides up her stomach and cups her breast as I continue to pump in and out of her.

I woke up this morning needing my girl. Not because I missed her—she hasn't left my goddamn sight unless I'm at work—but because I craved her. I wake up every morning craving her, and thankfully, she craves me just as much.

Hard as stone when I woke up, I moved in close behind her, and I can still remember the sound of her moan as she lifted one leg and let me in.

This has to be one of my favorite positions—lying down, fucking her from behind as she rests on her pillow.

"So good, so close," I say.

"Me, too," she breathes out heavily.

There's nothing feral about what we're doing right now, more like comfort. It's lazy, but it feels so fucking good.

I give her a few more pumps as I feel her tightening around me, and when I know she's about to fall over, I pinch her nipple, and that's all it takes with my girl. She screams my name, tightens, and then sends me over the edge as well.

Together, we ride out the wave of euphoria until we're both sated and breathing heavily.

I don't move, and neither does she as we catch our breath. I casually play with her breast and pull her in closer.

"The perfect way to wake up," she says, her voice all dreamy.

"Yeah, I'm one lucky son of a bitch."

She chuckles and rests her hand over mine. "I'm lucky that you can keep up with my libido."

"Are you saying you're more…needy…than me?"

"Do you not remember what happened in the middle of the night?"

How could I forget?

I woke up to her riding me. I had no idea I was hard, but apparently I was, because in a dreamy haze, I opened my eyes to find Lottie hovering above me, her tits bouncing beautifully as she used my dick to make herself come.

Hottest thing I've ever experienced.

"I do recall." I place a kiss along her neck. "Not sure I'll ever forget that."

Pulling away from me, she turns in my embrace and asks, "Should I be embarrassed?"

I laugh out loud. "Babe, you should be rewarded. That was really hot."

"Yeah?"

I nod. "Yeah. Please, feel free to do that again, whenever you want."

Her fingers play over my chest. "You were so hard last night, you woke me up, and even though you were still sleeping, all I could think about was how it would feel to slide over you."

"And how did it feel?"

"Amazing." She glides her leg over mine and her hand falls to my pec, her thumb passing over my nipple.

"If you keep that up, I'm never getting out of this bed."

"Would that be a bad thing?"

I grip her ass and give it a squeeze. "You and I both have work to do. Calling in sick won't work anymore. Everyone would know we weren't actually sick."

"Ugh, I hate real-world responsibilities."

"You and me both," I say, pressing a kiss to her nose.

Sighing, she rolls away from me and gets out of bed, much to my dismay. I was hoping for more cuddle time.

The shower turns on, indicating the start of the day.

Groaning, I get out of bed as well and trudge across the hardwood floor to the bathroom, where I find Lottie standing next to the shower, holding up one of her vibrators and sporting a mischievous grin.

"Care to have some fun in the shower?"

She doesn't have to ask twice.

"Dude, are you listening?"

"Huh?" I ask, looking at JP, who looks more than irritated with me.

"I'm trying to talk about our business here, and you can't give me two seconds before you're daydreaming."

"I'm not daydreaming," I say, even though that's exactly what I'm doing. I keep thinking about Lottie and the wicked smile she gave me before rubbing her vibrator up and down my cock, making me come in thirty seconds—she counted in her head.

"Bullshit," Breaker says. "You haven't paid attention to a goddamn thing we've had to say this entire meeting."

"That's not true at all."

"Oh?" Breaker asks. "Then who did we say is arriving in five minutes?"

Someone is arriving in five minutes?

"Uhh…Karla?" I ask, sounding more pathetic than I'd like.

Breaker rolls his eyes, while JP throws his arms up in annoyance.

There's a knock on my office door, and Karla stands there with her tablet in hand. "Mr. Cane, Mr. Dwayne Hernandez is here to see you."

"Thank you," I say to Karla. "Send him in." When she takes off, I quickly say to my brothers, "Dwayne is arriving."

JP offers me a slow clap. "Wow, man. Impressive."

I don't have time for a snarky retort, because Dwayne makes his way into my office.

I've done plenty of business with Dwayne in the past. He's a good man, someone I trust, someone I wouldn't mind doing more business with, especially since he's leading the area in clean, sustainable, and on-time construction. He's our go-to man. And if I were paying attention earlier rather than daydreaming about Lottie, I'd know exactly why he's here.

But I've winged it before.

I stand from my desk and round it, welcoming the man.

"Dwayne, it's good to see you." I give him a handshake.

"How are you, man?" Dwayne asks before shaking my brothers' hands as well.

"Good. Good. Please, take a seat." I join them in the sitting area of my office.

Dwayne unbuttons his suit jacket and takes a seat, his large frame eating up most of his chair.

"How are the girls?" I ask him. Pretty sure he has eight-, six-, and two-year-old daughters.

"They have me wrapped around their little fingers. We just installed a slide to our pool yesterday, and I spent so much time in the water with them that I think my balls have become raisins."

We let out a hearty laugh.

"But seeing those smiling faces as they flew into the water—worth it."

"I bet," I say. "And Maxine? She's good?"

He nods and shifts in his seat. "She is. She, uh, she's pregnant again."

"Wow, that's great," Breaker says. "How do you feel about it?"

"Excited." Dwayne rubs his hands together. "Hoping for another girl. Maxine wants a boy, but not me. I know if we have a boy, he's going to end up being a punk just like me. I want to have another girl, another angel like my wife."

And this is exactly why we hire Dwayne for every job. Because he's just an all-around good man. A family man. An honest man. A man with integrity.

"You know, having another Dwayne Hernandez in the world might not be a bad thing," I say.

"Your flattery never goes unnoticed." He then motions his hand to me and says, "And I guess congratulations are in order to you, or…fake congratulations." He laughs.

Eh…what?

"Fake congratulations?" I ask, confused, even though I feel a sense of dread falling over me.

"Yeah." He chuckles and then shifts in his seat. "Had dinner with Dave Toney the other night, and he told me all about your fake engagement and pregnancy." Dwayne shakes his head. "I'm not sure I'd be able to pull off something like that, but Dave said you were killing it."

What.

The.

Actual.

Fuck?

Breaker and JP both stare at me with horrified expressions, most likely mirror replicas of mine.

"He, uh, he told you that?" I ask, unsure of what else to say.

"Yeah. He said he had no clue until his fiancée, Ellie, told him all about it."

My mind races. My pulse hammers in my head as I try to wrap my mind around what Dwayne is divulging.

Ellie told Dave it was fake?

How could she have known?

Unless…

No.

Lottie wouldn't have said anything. Right?

Her loyalty is with me. That's what she said.

But…

"But, yeah, the plans he has for the empty lots down on the south side—great idea," Dwayne continues.

Plans?

The south side?

Is he talking about the lots I'm trying to acquire?

A burning rage of confusion erupts in the pit of my stomach.

No, there's no fucking way.

"Wasn't sure I could fit him into my schedule, but I put together a quote anyway. Dude is kind of a strange one. Have you spent much time with him?"

Too much goddamn time. *And now I know why he's been blowing off meetings with me. The bastard.*

"Uh, yeah," I say, trying to keep my composure, but I'm not doing a good job of it as sweat breaks out over my upper lip.

"Solid guy, though, even if he has his quirks." Dwayne claps his hands together. "Okay, should we go over the Malibu estate?"

"Um…" I hold up my finger and stand from my chair. "Would you be able to give me one second?"

"Of course." He pulls his phone from his suit pocket. "If it's okay with you, I'd like to call Maxine to make sure she's okay. There's a message from her, and as she was having odd back pain this morning, I want to check up on her, make sure all is well."

"Ask Karla for access to the conference room. She'll be more than happy to help you."

"Thank you," Dwayne says, standing from his chair.

He makes his way out of my office, and the moment the door clicks shut, JP asks, "What the actual fuck? Dave knows?"

"First I've heard of it," I say, pushing my hand frantically through my hair.

"How the hell does he know? You didn't say anything, did you?"

"Are you insane? Do you think I'd tell him the truth while trying to secure this deal with him? A deal it seems as though he has no intention of taking, seeing he has plans to capitalize on our goddamn idea." Angrily, I stand from my chair and start pacing the room.

He knows.

Dave fucking knows.

And he's telling people, people I work with, ruining my reputation.

My worst fears come to the surface, pinning me in the chest with mortification.

"Who else do you think he told?" I ask. "Fuck, this could be bad."

"This could be really bad," JP adds. "If he told Dwayne, then he's told others. Dwayne is cool enough to laugh it off, but I couldn't say that about everyone we work with."

"Especially people we might want to work with in the future." I grip my hair with both hands now. "Fuck, he's probably turning us into a laughingstock with everyone. What the hell do we do now? I have a meeting with him tomorrow."

"What the hell for? Clearly, he's not going to sell us the properties," Breaker says, his face contorted in a worried expression. My stomach plummets from that one look.

This is what my brothers feared would happen, that my mistake and ignorance would come back to bite us in the ass. I'm not only fucking over myself, but I'm fucking them over as well, and that hurts more than anything.

Through thick and thin, they've been there for me. We've created this business together, from the ground up. We've grown, we've been through the aches and pains together, the ups and downs, and the successes with minimal failure. If this lie took me out individually, that would be something I'd have to live with, but taking out my brothers...fuck, I can't imagine carrying that burden on my shoulders.

"I...I don't know."

"I think you need to figure out how he found out," JP says.

"And how do I go about doing that?" I pin my brothers with a look, and I can see it on their faces. The same thought is going through their minds that passed through mine.

"Dwayne said Ellie knew," Breaker says gently. "I think—"

I shake my head. "Don't say it."

"You need to ask her," JP says. "You need to confront Lottie."

And there it is, the elephant in the room, the one thing I didn't want to consider.

"I don't think she said anything," I say, defending her.

"Didn't she hang out with Ellie in the beginning? Before you two were a real couple?" Breaker asks.

"Yes, but she wouldn't have said anything."

"You don't think she might have said something out of spite? You two fought a lot in the beginning. I'm pretty sure you said there were times when you thought she actually hated you."

There were times when I think she could barely look at me. Didn't even want to be around me.

But…

"She was under contract."

"Sometimes that doesn't matter to some people," Breaker says. He glances over his shoulder to see if Dwayne is coming. "Either way, you need to ask her, because if it was Lottie, we need to know exactly what she told Ellie."

"Fuck," I say as a nervous tension fills my muscles.

"I hate to say it," JP adds, "especially since I like Lottie so much, but he has a point. We need to get to the bottom of this. She's the only one I can think of that would have that close a connection to the truth and tell Ellie."

I drag my hands over my face. "And what if she did say something? Then what?"

Breaker leans back in his chair. "Then I think we call it like it is—we were fucked over. And not sure if we're going to recover."

And that right there sends a cold chill of resentment through my veins.

Fuck with me—fine.

Fuck with my brothers—that's a different story.

CHAPTER 21
LOTTIE

"WHAT DO YOU THINK ABOUT this dress?" I ask Kelsey, holding it up to my body while looking at it in the mirror.

"That color does nothing for you, which surprises me, since Huxley seems to be perfect at picking out clothes that showcase your best features."

"This is one of my dresses."

"Then that makes sense."

Rolling my eyes, I toss the dress at her, which makes her laugh.

"Remind me why you're getting dressed up for dinner, again? Isn't it just another normal night in this crazy, dreamlike life you've been living?"

I pick up a purple dress that has a deep V-cut in the middle and hold it up to my body. This one makes my eyes stand out, and it's sexy—just what I want.

"No particular reason." I smirk and take the dress off the hanger.

"Uh, I don't believe that for a second."

Not caring if my sister sees me in my bra and underwear, I remove the shirt I borrowed from Huxley and toss it on the bed, then slip the dress over my hips and up my torso. I situate the straps on my shoulder, adjust my boobs, and then look in the mirror.

Yup. This is it.

"Can you zip me up?" I move my hair to the side so Kelsey has easy access to the zipper.

She stands from the bed and grips the zipper of my dress but doesn't pull it up right away. "What are you planning tonight?"

Then she zips up the dress, and I watch as the fabric clings to my silhouette. God, it's perfect. Huxley will tear it off in seconds, no doubt in my mind.

"Nothing," I say, even though that's not the truth.

Kelsey, being the intuitive sister that she is, turns me to face her and grips my shoulders. "Talk to me, now."

Sighing, I lie back on my bed and stare up at the ceiling. "I love him, Kels."

"What?" she asks, her voice coming out high-pitched. "What did you say?"

I lift up to look her in the eyes. "I love him."

Her jaw drops as she blinks a few times. "You love him. As in, you love Huxley Cane, your fake fiancé?"

"Yes, exactly. I love him."

"What? When? How? I mean, I know you're dating and things have progressed, but love?"

I nod, totally sure of it. "Yeah, I love him. It feels as though it came out of nowhere, but there's no doubt in my mind. You were right—there's a thin line between love and hate. I crossed that line."

"Wow, just…" She pauses, and when my eyes connect with hers, she smiles, and then reaches out and pulls me into a hug. "I'm happy for you, Lottie."

"Thank you." I return her embrace.

"Are you planning on telling him? Is that why you're getting all dressed up?"

"Yeah." I bite down on my lip, nerves shooting up my arms. "Do you think that's too forward?"

"No." Kelsey shakes her head. "Because I think he has the same feelings for you."

I perk up. "You think so?"

"I've seen him before you two were together and since, and I'm telling you right now, I've never seen a man so into a woman as Huxley is into you. He worships you, Lottie."

"I think *worship* is a strong word." But I still smirk, thinking about how he was reluctant to leave me this morning after I played with him in the shower. I can still hear his deep groans as he came on my chest while I ran my vibrator along his balls.

It was one of the hottest things I've ever seen, his godlike body contracting, straining. Every muscle vibrating as he lost control of all his senses. I've been replaying the visual in my head all day, to the point that I sent him a dirty text letting him know exactly what I wanted to do to him when he got home. He hasn't replied yet, but then again, he's a very busy man.

"When is he supposed to get home?"

I glance at the clock on my nightstand. "Any time now."

"Really?" Kelsey jumps off the bed. "Then I should get going. I don't want to be the one who interrupts a special homecoming." She snags her purse and then snatches me into a hug. "I'm happy for you. Huxley is a good guy; I've said it from the beginning. You both are lucky to have stumbled upon each other." She chuckles. "Still can't believe you went looking for a rich husband and actually found one." With that, she gives me one last hug and then takes off.

I take another look at myself in the mirror. There's no doubt this is the dress I should be wearing. Huxley is going to love it. The only question is—do I pair it with shoes, or do I go barefoot?

Knowing Huxley, he'd want heels.

I walk into the expansive closet and try on a few pairs before settling on a pair of strappy black heels I know he'll love. I walk over to my dresser where I keep my perfume and spritz myself a few times. I hear the front door open and close.

He's home.

Butterflies erupt in my stomach, knowing this is a huge step for me. I've never told a guy I loved him before, let alone been the first to acknowledge feelings. But there's something about the way Huxley talks to me with such honesty. He instills confidence…comfort, a safe place to be able to express myself. And I don't think there's a chance in hell I'll be able to go another day without telling him how I feel. Lord knows I told the man I hated him several times.

It's about time I told him I love him.

I head down the stairs, being careful not to slip in these heels, and work my way to the entryway, where I catch Huxley staring down at his phone.

"Hey, you," I say, walking up to him. I place my hand on his chest and curl against him as I press a kiss to his jaw.

Instead of wrapping his arm around my waist like he normally would, or forcing me to kiss him on the lips, he stands there stiff, almost unwelcoming.

Nervous, I pull away and ask, "Is everything okay?"

Slowly, he lifts his head until his eyes connect with mine, and that's when I see it: the disconnect in his gaze. The same disconnect I saw early on, when he barely talked to me, when he wanted nothing to do with me.

This is not the man I left this morning.

This is not the man who texted me this morning saying how he wished he didn't have to go into work.

And this is not the man I planned on telling I love him.

"Huxley," I whisper. "What's…what's going on?"

He stuffs his phone in his pants pocket, and I watch as the muscle in his jaw tenses as his eyes narrow on me.

"What did you say to her?"

"Say to who?" I ask, completely confused. "Say to Kelsey?"

Oh God, she didn't tell him anything we talked about, did she?

No, she'd never say anything.

"No, to Ellie."

"To Ellie?" I feel my face contort with complete confusion. *What on earth is he talking about?*

Growling, he says, "Yes, Lottie. What the fuck did you say to Ellie?" His voice sounds like venom, lashing out at me, spitting in my direction. This was not what I was expecting when Huxley came home. Honestly, if he hadn't been looking down at his phone when I saw him, I would've leapt into his arms, so excited to see him. But the anger vibrating off him, the hostility...I have no idea what's happening.

"I...I don't know," I answer, my voice stumbling with nerves.

"You must have said something," he yells, pushing past me while gripping the back of his head. "Because Dave knows."

Dave knows...

"As in, he knows about us?" I ask.

"Yeah, he fucking knows, and guess who told him? Ellie. So, tell me what the fuck you said to her, because whatever it was, I need to know so I can assess damage control."

"I don't know what you're talking about, Huxley. I didn't say anything to her about us."

"Don't fucking bullshit me, Lottie," he yells. His eyes are devoid of any loving tenderness toward me. They're empty, as if...as if he's already written me off. "You're the only one who's been alone with Ellie. You're the one who hated me so much at the beginning of all of this, so I wouldn't put it past you to say something to her in confidence."

Wait...

Wait a goddamn second.

Is he actually accusing me of telling Ellie our entire engagement is a hoax? He can't possibly be doing that.

But when I look him in the eyes, take in his heavy breaths, the steeliness of his jaw, the emptiness of his eyes...I see that's exactly what he's doing.

"You think I said something to Ellie?" I ask, just needing to confirm his assumption.

"Yes," he says in an exasperated tone. "Dave is telling people about our fake engagement, ruining my reputation, and I want to know what you told Ellie so I can see how fucked I really am."

Yup, he's blaming me.

He thinks I'd go behind his back. He thinks I'd so easily betray him like that.

After all of those conversations about the contract, after all those threats, he really believes I wouldn't care, that I'd say something anyway.

Not only does that make me incredibly angry, but...a wave of emotion clogs my throat, because that breaks my heart. That he'd think so lowly of me.

Unable to muster up the courage to have this conversation with him, I turn on my heels and walk away. The early signs of a panic attack start to surface as my breath shortens and my chest tightens.

I can't believe that he thinks I'd say something. That he doesn't trust me. I stalk up the stairs.

I hear him call out, "Where the hell do you think you're going?"

I don't stop; I don't even stumble as my feet move faster than my body. Instead, I propel myself forward, and when I reach my room, I slam my door and reach behind my back for the zipper of my dress. I struggle to reach it for a few seconds, and just as I grab it and pull down, unzipping my dress, the door to my bedroom flings open.

"Are you going to answer me?" Huxley asks as I step out of the dress and heels, leaving them on the floor.

I turn to the closet and throw on a pair of jean shorts and the only simple T-shirt in there, which is the Fleetwood Mac shirt he got me. It'll have to do. I slip on a pair of my sandals and grab my phone from my nightstand. I'm about to storm past him when he blocks the door.

"Lottie, I need to fucking know."

"Why do you need to know?" I ask him. "It seems to me as though you've already made up your mind."

374 | MEGHAN QUINN

"Are you saying you didn't say anything?"

"The fact that you even have to ask that is so incredibly insulting."

"That's not an answer," he says.

"You want an answer?" I reply, trying to hold on to my composure as best as I can. "Fine, here's your answer. No, I didn't say anything to Ellie, because despite what you might think of me, despite how horribly you treated me in the beginning of all of this, I still found it within myself to be loyal and keep our secret just that...our secret."

I go to move past him, but he stops me. His facial features have softened now, and so has his voice. "You...you really didn't say anything, Lottie?"

"No. I didn't."

His eyes search mine and his expression slowly turns to one of regret.

"Shit, Lottie. I'm—"

"Don't," I say, holding up my hand. "Don't even bother." Able to catch him off guard, I slip past him and head down the stairs, him trailing behind me.

I barely register his pleading for me to stop over the pounding of my own heart, over the sound of it cracking, shattering.

I thought we trusted each other. I thought we'd established a connection, a bond so strong that nothing could penetrate it. I thought we were moving toward more, but apparently, I was wrong, because, with the flip of a switch, he turned on me.

How could he possibly ever accuse me of such a thing? Have I not proven myself? Have I not done everything he's asked, and done it exceptionally well? Have I not shown how he can trust me?

I charge toward the front door, where Huxley catches up to me.

"Lottie, wait." He steps in front of the door, his breathing labored. "I'm sorry. Okay? That was stupid of me to ask."

"You didn't just ask, Huxley; you accused."

"I know." He pulls on his hair. "I was thrown off, okay? I wasn't expecting to hear that Dave knows about the fake engagement."

"So, the first thing you do is blame me?"

"No, I mean—hell, I was told Ellie told him. What was I supposed to think?"

"What were you supposed to think?" I ask incredulously. "You were supposed to trust me. You were supposed to approach me with the problem so I could help you find the solution. But you *shouldn't* have come charging in here, blaming me. Not when I was—" I catch myself before I admit to what I was going to tell him tonight.

"Not when what?" he asks.

I shake my head. "Nothing." Raising my chin, trying to be calm, I say, "I should've known this was all too good to be true, that you were going to end up hurting me somehow."

He takes a step back. "Talk about fucking assumptions."

"Uh…did you not just do that? Did you not just hurt me?"

"Not on purpose. I'm kind of fucked right now, Lottie. In case you haven't noticed. This could ruin my entire business."

"Maybe you should've thought about that before you started lying to everyone about having a fiancée and baby on the way. This is no one's fault but your own."

"I'd do anything to secure that deal," Huxley says, snapping back at me.

"Including blaming me for something you should've known I never would've done."

He scrubs his hand over his face. "You hated me early on, Lottie. It was a question I had to ask."

"No, it wasn't." I close the space between us and poke his chest. "You should know I'd never screw someone over, especially when it comes to business, not after I was fucked over by someone I thought I could trust. I lost everything, Huxley. Angela took away the one thing I thought I was good at, made me feel small and not worth a goddamn penny. She denigrated me. After being treated so poorly, having everything ripped out from under me, do you really think I'd turn around and do that to someone else?" When he glances down at his feet in shame, I say, "No, I wouldn't. I might have disliked you in the beginning, but that dislike would never have enraged me to do something as low as tell Ellie the truth about us."

I move past him and open the door.

"Lottie, stop. Where are you going?"

I type out a text to Kelsey telling her to come get me. I know she won't ask any questions; she'll just show up and ask questions later. I just need to get out of here. I can't possibly be around him.

"Kelsey is coming to get me."

"I'm sorry, okay? I lost my cool. Let's talk through this."

"There's nothing to talk about, Huxley." I continue to walk toward the gate.

"So, you're leaving? Just like that?"

I turn to face him. "Do you think I can stay here?"

"It was a miscommunication."

My eyes nearly bug out of my head. "How can you be so apathetic about this?"

"I'm not being apathetic. I'm just trying to wrap my head around this."

"Well, wrap your head around this, Huxley. I was planning on expressing my feelings for you tonight, and instead of me being able to do that, you placed blame where it shouldn't have been placed, tore down the trust we built between each other, and you broke my heart."

"Wait...what?" he asks, his eyes going soft with regret. "Your...feelings? What feelings?"

"Doesn't matter anymore," I say as a tear falls down my cheek. I didn't even know my eyes were leaking. I quickly wipe it away, but not before Huxley catches sight of it.

"Fuck, Lottie. I'm sorry. I'm really fucking sorry. I shouldn't have said what I said tonight."

I move toward the gate, unable to listen to him over the roaring of my heart.

"Please, stay. We can work this out."

"I can't." I shake my head. I feel so fragile in this moment. "I need some space."

"Space?" He catches up to me as I walk through the gate and onto the sidewalk, where I wait for Kelsey. "What do you mean, you need space? Lottie, please, don't do this. Don't leave me."

Kelsey's car comes into view.

"Lottie." Huxley reaches for my hand, but I pull it away.

"Don't."

"Just fucking talk to me, please. We can work through this. We don't need space."

I turn around to face him as the tears gathered in my eyes start to fall again. "I can barely look at you right now, Huxley. What makes you think I want to stay with you?"

Caught off guard by my tears, he rears back, and it's all I need for my escape when Kelsey pulls up. I open the car door and start to get in, but Huxley says, "Please, Lottie. Babe, don't leave."

I don't listen. I get in, shut the door, and buckle up.

Kelsey doesn't say a thing, just drives away. We drive in silence all the way to her apartment.

Even when my phone blows up with texts from Huxley, she doesn't say anything.

It isn't until we're in her apartment that she opens her mouth.

"God, Lottie, I'm so sorry."

My eyes are puffy at this point.

I have no more tears left to cry.

And I'm curled in a ball on Kelsey's floor, wrapped up in one of her blankets.

"I don't understand," I say quietly. "I thought…I thought he trusted me."

"Sounds like he was caught off guard."

I glance at her with a warning stare.

She holds up her hands in defense. "I'm not giving him an out; I'm just trying to understand where he's coming from. I mean, could you imagine hearing that? He's worked so hard, and for it all to just blow up in his face, he must be stressed."

"He most likely is, but that doesn't give him the right to lash out at me. He should've come home and asked me for help rather than accuse me. He basically threw everything we built between each other right out the window, as if…as if his business is more important than me." And then it hits me. "Maybe…maybe his business is more important than me. Maybe I didn't matter as much to him as I thought I did." My lip trembles. "Maybe I liked him more than he liked me."

"No." Kelsey shakes her head. "That's not the case. He likes you, Lottie. He came after you. I saw his face. He was devastated." *I wish that were the case.*

"Maybe outwardly he acted as though he cared, but someone who cares about another person doesn't treat them the way he treated me."

Kelsey sighs and leans back on her bed. "Can I say something and you not hate me?"

"No. I have all the right to hate you for whatever comes out of your mouth."

Kelsey grumbles something under her breath and then says, "I think you need to look at this from his perspective. He just found out his secret wasn't a secret after all, that word is getting around that he's a liar. He most likely blacked out and had a one-track mind. He didn't think; he just reacted."

I sit up from my balled-up position on the floor and look Kelsey in the eyes. "But that's the thing you're not getting, Kelsey. He reacted without thinking, and his reaction was to not trust me. I was about to tell him that I loved him. That he makes me so incredibly happy and every day

I'm grateful to wake up in his arms." Tears flow down my cheeks. "But to him, I'm something he's willing to throw away over an assumption. Do you see the problem?"

Slowly, Kelsey shakes her head. "Yes, I see the problem. I wasn't thinking about it that way." She gets down on the floor and crawls toward me to scoop me into a hug. "I'm sorry, Lottie. I can't imagine how much you're hurting right now."

"Too much," I say with a sniff. "Way too much." I wipe at my tears. "I wish I'd never agreed to any of this. I wish I'd called his bluff. I wish I'd never gotten involved, because now I feel more broken than ever."

Kelsey brushes her hand over my head, which brings back the tears. What I said to Huxley about Angela wasn't wrong. Her betrayal cut me deeply, even though she was simply acting according to her character. She's a spineless, manipulative liar. But I had trusted in Huxley's character. His determined, intense nature. *Unrelenting, yet decent.* Now I should be wondering how I could fall in love with someone who paid people to lie for him. Who wrote contracts to cover up his barefaced fiction because his business meant everything to him. There's something very wrong with me that I could look past that. *That was our foundation.*

And yet, my heart and soul feel destroyed.

Sniffling against her shoulder, I ask, "Why did he have to break me, Kels?"

"I don't know," she says quietly. "But you need to remember just how resilient you are."

"Not this time," I say as I wipe at my cheek. "I don't think bouncing back from this will be easy. Not in the slightest."

The gurgling sound of Kelsey's coffee maker wakes me up from my spot on the ground. Just from an attempt at opening my eyes, I know they're puffy from all the crying I did last night. And the ache in my back is from the lovely mattress of pillows I attempted to sleep on as well.

"Did my coffee wake you?" Kelsey asks from the kitchen.

"Yeah," I answer, my voice sounding as if I smoked an entire carton of cigarettes last night. "But I should get up."

Knock. Knock.

"Was that your door?" I ask her.

"I think so," she replies before going to the door to answer it. When she props it open, I hear her ask, "Huxley, what are you doing here?"

Crap.

"I was hoping to talk to Lottie." I glance behind me and make eye contact with him. When he takes in my appearance, concern quickly washes over his face. "Baby, please, can I talk to you?"

"Uh, you know, I really need to get in the shower," Kelsey says. "And I don't know how to handle awkward situations. I want to be a good sister, but I also can't handle it when guys do that whole puppy-dog-eyes thing, and he looks so pathetic, so basically, I'm just going to bolt."

And she does just that.

She takes off running to the bathroom, shuts the door, and turns on the shower.

When I hear the door click shut, I know Huxley has stepped into the apartment, but I refuse to look up at him, not when my eyes are starting to water all over again.

I don't want to see him, I still feel too raw, but he has other plans.

He kneels down next to me and places his hand on my cheek. When our eyes meet, his are not only bloodshot but also heavy with concern. But is he concerned about his career, his business, or is he concerned about me?

"You slept on the floor last night?"

"There are pillows underneath me." Which happened to shift when

I shifted, leaving me partially on the floor, but he doesn't need to know that.

"Lottie, I'm sorry." His voice is tight. "I know what I did last night was inexcusable. I should never have treated you the way I did, and I'm ashamed." He swallows hard. "I'm just really fucking scared I fucked over my brothers. I took my fears out on you rather than leaning on you." His thumb brushes over my cheek. "And I'm sorry." He picks up a bag from his side and sets it closer to me. "I wasn't sure if you had any clothes or overnight things here, but I thought I'd bring you some of your things." That's annoyingly thoughtful. "I have to get to the office to do some damage control, but I wanted to see you first. Can we have dinner tonight?" When I don't say anything, he says, "Please, Lottie."

I slowly nod as a tear slips down my cheek.

He growls in frustration and wipes it away for me.

"Fuck, I'm sorry." He stands and makes his way to the door. "I'll text you the details."

All I do is nod.

Once he's out of the apartment, I unzip the bag he packed for me, and right on top is a printed picture of me and him at the Fleetwood Mac concert. He has his arm around me possessively, his hand tucked into the front of my pocket, and I'm leaning against his broad chest, with one arm up, my hand gripping the back of his neck.

I remember taking this and the exact feeling I felt while taking it. I was completely overjoyed.

Now, I'd give anything to feel that feeling again. Instead, all I feel is... empty.

CHAPTER 22
HUXLEY

"WHAT ARE YOU GOING TO say to him?" Breaker asks while pacing the length of my office.

"I'm just going to come out with it. Ask him point-blank if he knew. What's the use of beating around the bush?"

JP bounces his legs up and down as he perches in one of the chairs in the sitting area of my office. "I think being direct is key. I believe he'd appreciate that more."

"I think so too," Breaker adds. "Are you going to pass it off as a funny thing you did? Or take it seriously?"

"Seriously," I answer as my mind switches over to Lottie.

Seeing her lying on the goddamn floor, tears streaming from her eyes, is fucking gnawing at my stomach. Eating away at me with every breath I take. Instead of staying with me, she thought it would be better if she stayed at her sister's, where she had to sleep on the floor. That's how much she didn't want to be around me. That's how much I should be ashamed. My girl would rather sleep on the floor than share a bed with me. *Or even in a bed across the hall from me.*

"I think if I go in with a serious tone, explain everything rather than joke around about it, then I'm going to save my ass."

"Smart approach," Breaker says and then lets out a deep breath. "Fuck, I hope he hasn't said much to anyone."

"I still don't get how he knows," JP says. "How did they find out? We haven't said a goddamn word to anyone, and everyone else has an NDA."

JP scratches his head. "Do you think it was Kelsey?"

I shake my head. "No."

"Did Lottie seem happy to see you this morning?" JP winces.

After Lottie took off yesterday, I sent a text to my brothers, telling them it wasn't Lottie, and then went into detail about how I fucked up everything with her. I blamed them; they blamed me. I took responsibility because, let's be honest, this entire mess is my fault. Because I have some sick drive to prove—*to prove what? That I can secure a deal? What's the point of securing a deal if, in the end, I hurt the people who matter the most to me?*

I hurt my brothers.

And I hurt Lottie.

No deal is bigger than that.

"No," I say, remembering the grief-stricken look on her face. "She didn't even say much."

"Did you apologize?" JP asks.

"Of course I fucking apologized. Do you think I just went over there for the hell of it?"

"I'm just checking," JP says in a defensive tone. "You've screwed up a lot lately. Just wanted to make sure you didn't screw that up, too."

"Oh no, I did. I fucked that up big time. The only thing I have going for me is that she said she'd have dinner with me tonight."

"Oh shit, really?" Breaker asks. "What are you going to do?"

"Beg for her forgiveness. What else is there to do?"

"Prove to her how sorry you are."

"And how would I do that?" I ask.

Breaker shrugs. "Hell if I know. It's why I'm not in a relationship. I don't know how to handle women."

"I don't think that's the reason," JP says. "You're just an idiot."

"Says the guy who's not in a relationship either," Breaker says.

"By choice," JP shoots back. "If I wanted to be in a relationship, then I would be."

"Uh-huh." Breaker eyes him up and down. "And how's that flirting going with Kelsey, by the way?"

"Fine. If I turned it up a notch, she'd be all over me."

Breaker scoffs. "Yeah…all over you." He rolls his eyes, and I'm about to snap at my brothers when Karla comes into my office.

She raps her knuckles on the doorframe and says, "The front just informed me Mr. Toney is on his way up."

"Thank you, Karla." She gives me a curt nod and then disappears. "You two need to get the hell out of here." I need to deal with this on my own.

They gather their things and head toward the door. "Good luck, man," Breaker says with a nod. JP gives me a quick nod, too, and then I'm left alone in my office.

Idly, I sit in my chair, staring at my computer screen. I'm a lucky son of a bitch that my brothers are supportive rather than wanting to murder me for possibly fucking up our reputation. *Our livelihood, as well as the company's employees.* They could be dicks, but they're choosing not to be, and I'm really appreciative of it. It's tough enough knowing I damaged my relationship with Lottie; I'm not sure I'd know what to do without my brothers. And, yes, I said *damaged.* It's not over. I'm going to get Lottie back. She's mine. *Forever.*

Karla knows to send Dave back to my office when he arrives, so when there's a knock at my door, I'm not surprised to see him.

"Dave." I stand and walk over to him, offering him a firm handshake. "Thanks for making it over here."

"I thought I was going to be late." He chuckles, completely unaware of how my stomach is turning in on itself. "There was a huge accident on the 405. I was able to get off at an exit before I hit parking lot–type traffic."

"When is there not an accident on the 405?" I ask.

"Very true."

I gesture toward the sitting area in my office while I shut my door behind him. "Take a seat. Can I get you anything to drink?"

"I'm good. I downed a coffee on the way here. Don't worry, I went to the bathroom before I came in, so I won't be requiring the use of your personal toilet."

I chuckle and take a seat across from him. "My personal toilet is always available to you."

He presses his hand to his chest. "The sentiment hits me hard."

My smile fades as I clear my throat. I figure I might as well just jump right to it. "I, uh, I was hoping to have an honest conversation with you today."

The smallest of smirks appear on Dave's face. "I think I know what this is about."

"Do you?" I ask, wanting to see where he's at.

He nods. "You know, when Ellie first told me, I didn't believe her at first, but after the baby class, I knew right away that Ellie was right."

I clear my throat again, tempted to pull on my tie, to loosen it, but I hold strong. "And what was she right about?"

"Excuse me for being forward, but that your relationship with Lottie wasn't real."

Yup, there it is.

Shame and embarrassment flow through my veins, heating up my body. *Damn it, I wish I'd thought to take off my suit jacket for this conversation.* It's too late now.

I go to say something, but Dave continues, "She told me after the dinner at our house. She suspected you two were faking it. I thought maybe it was some crazy pregnancy hormone at first, because I couldn't fathom why you'd lie. Especially about a relationship. Ellie pointed out the stiffness in your shoulders when Lottie touched you, the robotic way you talked to each other. There was something missing, and even though you were quite convincing, there were things here and there that gave you away."

I drag my hand over my face. "Listen, Dave. I can explain."

"I found the whole thing quite comical, to be honest. How far would Huxley Cane go? Just how unethical was the man who wanted my business?" He pauses, and I think I'm going to be sick.

Unethical.

He's not wrong. God, I feel ashamed. Especially that he'd known.

"Ellie kept finding these crazy things to do and thought it would be fun to drag you two along."

I sit a little taller. "You mean, you invited us even after knowing it was a ruse?"

Dave laughs. "Oh yeah. You're probably the most uptight man I know, and granted, it's gotten you very far in business, but there's more than making a deal, Huxley, and I wanted you to see that. I thought that maybe if we carried on with the charade, that maybe something would come of it. There was a connection between you and Lottie, and Ellie and I were hoping to see it grow stronger." He smiles. "And it has." He laughs. "I can assure you, had I not met Ellie, I may have never known what true love was, either."

"Wh-what?" I ask, trying to comprehend and process everything he's saying.

"Correct me if I'm wrong, but you love her, don't you?"

My teeth roll over my bottom lip, and I stare down at my connected hands. I nod. "Yeah, I do."

"I knew it." Dave slaps his leg. "Ellie thinks Lottie was the one to crack first, she seemed to be more into you, but I told Ellie you're a professional at masking your emotions, and if I had to bet on it, I'd say you developed feelings sooner than she developed feelings for you."

Since this is the conversation we're apparently having, I say, "I think it started the minute I ran into her."

"Which wasn't in Georgia..."

I shake my head.

"Ellie was also struck by that. Lottie wasn't very convincing about knowing much about Georgia."

I wince. "She's never been."

"Then how exactly did you meet?"

"On the sidewalk in my neighborhood. She was lost; I was blowing off steam. Just so happened we both needed each other." I grip the back of my head. "A not-so-meet-cute."

"You know, I beg to differ. Meeting on the sidewalk has its charm."

"Not if you add in what we were both after. I needed a fake fiancée, and she needed a rich husband to impress someone. That doesn't really scream romance."

"Sometimes it's not the beginning that screams romance, but rather the journey. And I have to say, your journey has been quite interesting to watch unfold." Dave scratches the side of his face. "I do wonder, though... why did you do it?"

Sighing heavily, I lean back in my chair and say, "Because I'm a dumbass."

"Well, this much is true, but give me the real reason."

The real reason. Wasn't that enough? That I was a dumbass? But Dave had taken every answer in stride so far, so even though this showed how manipulative I could actually be, *how much of a liar,* I was now all in here.

"Breaker and JP said I'd never succeed in making a deal with you because you were a relatable guy. You honored the connection in a business deal, not just the money. They said I wasn't relatable to you. I wanted to prove them wrong. When I saw you outside the deli and you introduced me to Ellie, the lies just poured out of my mouth before I could stop myself. I thought that maybe if we could connect on another level, you'd consider a deal with me."

"And what would have happened if we did make the deal...? What would've happened to Lottie?"

"We would've gone our separate ways. I probably wouldn't have mentioned anything to you."

"I see." His smile fades. "Seems very untrustworthy."

"I know." I drag my hand over my forehead. "Trust me, I fucking know. My brothers, from the very beginning, told me it was a bad idea. And when I was able to look past my determination, I knew what we were doing was wrong, but I was so inflexible that I couldn't look past the deal. I ended up hurting my brothers, and even worse…I ended up losing Lottie."

"What?" Dave asks, looking concerned. "She left you?"

I nod. "Last night. I, uh, I spoke with someone who offhandedly told me you knew we had a fake engagement. I couldn't possibly understand how you'd know, so I blamed Lottie, thinking she was the one who let it slip to Ellie. I said some shitty things, and she left." I shake my head, completely disgusted with myself. "I fucking blew it because I was so caught up in my image, my reputation, that I forgot one thing—none of that matters if I don't have someone to share my life with. She took off for her sister's." I pinch the bridge of my nose. "She chose sleeping on the floor over sleeping with me. If that doesn't tell you how fucked I am, I don't know what does."

"Let me ask you this, and look me in the eyes when you answer. If you could choose one, Lottie or the acquisition with me, what would it be?"

"Lottie." I look him straight in the eye. "Lottie. *She* is everything. I don't know how it came to this, how I fell for a girl so fast, so hard, that I actually feel physical pain from losing her, but here I am, a desperate asshole willing to do anything to get her back."

That brings a smile to his face. Dave leans forward and holds his hand out to me while he says, "This might surprise you, Huxley, and in some ways, it surprises me too, but you have a deal."

"What?" I ask, awkwardly taking his hand, unsure what we're shaking on. Dwayne said he was developing the land with him. *How is this happening?*

Dave stands from his chair and buttons his suit jacket. "Your brothers were right. I wasn't sure I wanted to make a deal with someone I didn't quite know. I wasn't sure you were going to develop the lots into something I could consciously be okay with. I've been incredibly disappointed in deals I've made in the past, promises that weren't kept. It's why I spoke with Dwayne. I knew you'd be working with him. I wanted to see if your plans were feasible. I wanted to see if he knew about you and Lottie. I wanted to see what kind of deal I might be getting myself into. But when Dwayne genuinely looked surprised to hear about you and Lottie, I knew, even though you were lying, you weren't making me into a laughingstock."

"Fuck, I would never. If anyone is going to be laughed at, it's me. I had all my employees sign an NDA—even Lottie was under an NDA. And those who didn't have an NDA believed we were actually engaged. She moved into my home and everything. Trust me, I didn't want this getting out."

"I believe you," Dave says confidently. "It's why the lots are yours. I'll have my lawyers work with your lawyers on the details. I'm trusting that you're not lying to me now, and that you'll follow through on the terms of our agreement."

"I will. It's not in my nature to lie, Dave. I honestly felt wretched every time we *pretended* around you. Lottie and I both did. So I won't let you down in your trust in me."

"I feel confident in you. *Now.* And maybe another man would've told you to fuck off, but I find the whole scenario quite fascinating, and I've enjoyed seeing you change. You were a hard man to understand before, but Lottie has smoothed out your rough edges. You understand your priorities now. And frankly, you're more relatable. I've had some fun times, not only watching you struggle, but also having some honest conversations with you. You've grown, Huxley, and I do consider you a friend, even if under some false pretenses. I only hope you can fix things with Lottie, because we truly did enjoy your company."

"Wow," I say. "I honestly wasn't expecting you to say that. I thought this conversation would go a completely different direction, and I was ready to beg and plead with you."

Dave glances at his watch. "I have about five minutes if you want to get down on your knees and do a little begging." He chuckles, and I nervously laugh because, hell, I would do it. "But in all seriousness, I can't stop thinking about seeing you two interact after the baby class. I knew you'd changed. I knew you'd gentled. Your severity had disappeared, and I appreciated that. I enjoyed the transformation, and I hope it continues. You're a good man, Huxley. Now, figure out a way to fix this with Lottie, because I know Ellie is going to want you two over for a celebratory dinner."

"That would be great, Dave. Thank you. Truly, thank you for everything."

He heads toward my office door. "I'm a pretty understanding guy who can find joy in almost every situation. But know, you probably won't see the same respect from other business associates, so I'd keep the fake fiancée and fake pregnancy thing out of business deals from here on out."

"Trust me, never again."

"Good to hear. We'll be in touch." He offers me a wave and then takes off. When I know he's farther down the hall, I slump in my chair and let out a pent-up breath.

Holy.

Fucking.

Shit.

After a few minutes, Breaker and JP come barreling into my office.

"Oh fuck, he doesn't look good," Breaker says. "Is that sweat on his brow?"

JP takes a step closer. "Fuck, it is sweat. He doesn't ever sweat."

"What happened? Are we ruined?" Breaker asks.

I clasp my hands together and chuckle.

"He's laughing. Is that a *good* laugh or a *he's-lost-his-mind* laugh?" Breaker asks.

"Sounds slightly maniacal. I think he's lost it," JP answers.

"He's signing the deal."

"What?" Breaker and JP say at the same time.

"I don't have time to talk about it. I have to figure out how to fix things with Lottie. That's what I care most about." I stand and push my hand through my hair. "Fuck, I don't even know where to start."

"You can't half-ass it," Breaker says.

"You went all in on this contract with her; might as well go all in on a relationship," JP says, laughing.

But a light bulb goes off in my head.

"I have an idea," I say as I go to my desk to pocket my phone and keys. "Have the lawyers connect with Dave's lawyers. I'll give you a call while I'm in my car to explain everything."

And without a goodbye, I head out of my office and past Karla.

I have some shit to do before tonight.

CHAPTER 23
LOTTIE

"WHAT AM I DOING, KELSEY?" I ask, staring out the window, the rich, elegant homes in The Flats passing me by.

"You're going to hear him out," she says through the phone, her calming voice doing nothing to soothe my raging nerves.

I got a text from Huxley a few hours ago telling me a car would be at Kelsey's to pick me up at six thirty and that he hoped I got in the car. I almost texted him that I'd changed my mind, that I couldn't make it to dinner because the thought of seeing his face tonight made me nauseous.

But Kelsey made me take a few deep breaths, she talked me through the positives and told me that the reason I was so upset was because I loved him, and that upset feeling wasn't going to go away until I listened to what he had to say.

At the time, I thought she was right. Now that I'm nearing his place, I'm starting to think maybe she was wrong.

"I don't feel pretty. He's going to think I look like a mess."

"You look freaking amazing, and who cares if you do look like a mess? If he loves you, he'll think you look beautiful no matter how tear-streaked your cheeks are."

"I should've dressed up. I should've done my makeup."

"You couldn't stop crying long enough to do your makeup. Remember? We tried; it just smeared down your face."

"This was a mistake, Kelsey. I really don't think I should do this. I'm not ready."

"I'm not sure if you will ever be ready, Lottie."

"I feel broken inside," I say softly. "I don't think I've ever felt like this before. When Angela fired me, I thought that was rock bottom, but that feeling is nothing compared to this. I thought we had something, and then he just ripped that away from me." I suck in a deep breath as a lone tear falls down my cheek. "I'm not sure how to wash away that feeling."

"And the emotions you're experiencing, they're all valid," Kelsey says. "But, Lottie, there's a reason he wants you to come over tonight, why he stopped by this morning. He knows he messed up. We all make mistakes—granted, his might have been larger than most—but he's trying to make it right. If you truly love him, you will give him a chance to do that. That's what love is, isn't it? I mean, haven't you and I had to forgive each other for jumping down each other's throats without considering the truth?"

More tears stream down my face as I take in the familiar gate that protects Huxley's house. She isn't wrong. God, I'd hurt Kelsey only weeks ago with my stupid mouth, talking without thinking, and...*and she forgave me.* I take a deep breath as the driver presses a button and the gate slides open. *No turning back.* As we drive through, I see Huxley standing outside his door, on his porch, waiting for me.

"Oh God, I see him. Kelsey, I can't do this. I can't. I'm a mess."

"Then be a mess in front of him. I love you, sis. You have a beautiful heart. Share it with him." And then she hangs up just as the driver puts the car in Park.

I wipe frantically at my tears, but unfortunately, they keep falling, even as Huxley steps up to the car and opens the door. When he catches sight of me, I see the devastation that passes through his eyes before he offers his hand to me.

Not ready to hold his hand, I get out of the car without his help.

He doesn't say anything, but I see the disappointment in his shoulders from my denial.

Clearing his throat, he says, "Thanks for coming over."

I wipe at my face and just nod, my throat tight, so choked up that squeezing out a word right now feels next to impossible.

Raw, tumultuous emotions beat through me, and from the sight of him in a pair of simple jeans and a T-shirt, his hair ruffled from his hand running through it, those emotions skyrocket, sending me into a tailspin of uncertainty.

Should I be here?

Should I give him a second chance?

If I feel this awful from one bout of heartbreak, what could he possibly do to me in the future?

And why exactly am I suffering from such intense emotions?

Probably because Kelsey is right. I love him so much, more than I thought. My heart is drawn toward him. My heart aches for him. But my heart is also wary. He's playing tug-of-war with my heart, ripping and tearing it in every direction, stirring up anxiety and uncertainty.

"Do you mind if we go inside?" he asks. When I shake my head, he gestures toward the door, and when I step in front of him, he places his hand on my lower back. It feels like a bolt of lightning to my spine, forcing it to straighten, go stiff. He notices quickly and removes his hand, probably interpreting it as me not wanting his touch. But my reaction wasn't because I didn't want the touch, it was because I didn't realize how much I'd missed it...

He opens the door for me, and when I walk through, he says, "I have everything set up in the dining room."

Everything set up? What does that mean?

What exactly did he have to set up?

Anxious and nervous, I walk toward the dining room, where I see the table set for two. Two large cloche serving dishes, two glasses filled with water, and a manila folder with two pens have been laid on the table. The lights are dimmed, Fleetwood Mac plays in the background, and there doesn't seem to be a soul in the house other than me and Huxley.

He walks past me to the chair I normally sit in, and he pulls it out, waiting for me to take a seat. Questioning everything in my head, I take the seat and glance toward the folder, my mind racing. *What's inside it?*

Huxley takes a seat as well, but instead of facing his plate, he scoots his chair close to mine and turns toward me.

"Lottie."

Taking a deep breath, I turn toward him as well, a tear slipping down my cheek.

"Baby..." he says quietly while reaching out and wiping away the tear. "Please don't cry."

"Wh-what do you...want, Huxley?" I ask, getting the words out.

With a concerned gaze, he sits straighter and says, "I want you, Lottie."

"You screwed that up."

"I know. Trust me, I know how bad I screwed this up. It's been the biggest mistake of my life, charging into our house and sticking blame on you for something I know, deep down, you would never do." It doesn't slip past me that he said *our house.* "And I've tried to figure out how to make this up to you, how to show you how sorry I am, and I realized, maybe I should bring it back to where we started."

Slightly confused, I ask, "What do you mean?"

From the folder, he pulls out a stack of stapled papers. When my eyes land on it, I realize it's our contract.

He stands from his chair and walks over to the corner of the dining room where a buffet table lines the wall. Sitting on top of it, plugged in, is a paper shredder. Without a pause, he sends the contract into the paper shredder, and the deafening sound of it eating up our contract echoes through the room.

And for some reason, it hurts. That was the thing that bonded us together. It's what freed me of my student loans. *Is that gone, too?* It's what brought me close to Huxley, and he tore it up without a blink of an eye.

"Why did you do that?" I ask, my anguish clear in my voice.

"Because we need to start fresh, Lottie." He walks back to the table and takes a seat. He reaches for my hand, but I don't let him have it. Dipping his head in defeat, he says, "Lottie, please, you're not making this easy on me."

"Do you think I should?" I ask. "Because you sure as hell didn't make it easy on me last night when you were accusing me of telling Ellie the truth."

"I know, but—"

"And do you think it was easy on me, seeing the absolute disdain you had for me?"

"No, but—"

"And do you think it was easy on me, knowing the man that I trusted, that I was falling for, didn't trust me to keep him safe with our secret?"

"No. But, Lottie—"

"I don't know why I came here." I stand from my chair.

Huxley stands as well. "Where are you going?"

"I'm leaving," I say. "This was stupid."

I head toward the entryway, but Huxley tugs on my hand, spinning me back around. With anger in his eyes, he says, "Sit down, Lottie."

"Excuse me?"

"I said sit. Down." He speaks through his teeth, and in that instant, my sorrow turns to anger.

"Who the hell do you think you are—"

He moves toward me and gently pushes me up against the dining room wall, cutting my words short. My breath catches in my throat as his one hand pins me in place and the other strikes the wall, propping him up.

"I'm trying to apologize, damn it," he says, his anger spiking.

"And you think this is the way to do it?"

"Do you have a better idea?" he asks, his eyes never leaving mine. "You're so goddamn stubborn that pissing you off seems to be the only way to make you listen."

"You hurt me, Huxley. I don't want to listen."

"If you didn't, you wouldn't be here." *He sees right through me.* "If you didn't want to be here, then you never would've gotten in that car, and I know you, Lottie. You love me—"

"No." I shake my head. "I don't."

He presses harder against me, trapping my breath in my lungs. "Don't you dare fucking lie to me. You don't lose feelings like that overnight. Now is that how you want to have this conversation, with me possessing you? Because I'd rather be civil with you, not revert to our old ways of communication. But if I need to, I'll hold you here like this, all night, until you listen."

I wet my lips as my body heats with lust.

Goddamn it.

I don't want to lust after him.

I don't want to envision the kind of delicious torture he could put me through in this position, waiting for me to communicate properly.

"Are you going to listen to me?" he asks, repeating himself.

I give it a few breaths before I say, "Fine."

He releases me and then takes my hand, which I let him have, and he walks me back to the table, where we both take a seat.

When we're settled, he asks, "Are you done being stubborn?"

"Are you done being an asshole?"

And just like that, the smallest of smirks pull at his lips. Just like the beginning of our relationship, we're back at ground zero—me irritated, him taking some sort of joy out of it.

Annoyed with the smirk, I fold my arms across my chest and ask, "Do you find humor in this?"

"I do. Reminds me of our early days."

Me, too.

"I was more partial to our later days." I look away.

"Don't get me wrong; so was I, but it's nice to bring things full circle, don't you think?"

"I think we need to get on with whatever presentation you might have so I can move on."

That pisses him off, judging by the narrowing of his eyes and clenching of his jaw. Given the shift in our relationship, I didn't think it was possible to revisit what it was like when we were first together, but I was wrong. We could very much get there.

But what I hate is that it invigorates me.

His jaw twitches as he reaches out and takes one of my hands, and this time I let him. Holding it firmly, he stares me down and simply says, "I love you."

The words stun me.

They take my breath away.

But they also don't feel entirely real.

"I don't believe you," I say. "How do I know you're not just saying that?"

Frustration laces through his eyes as he reaches for the folder and opens it, revealing another contract. But this one is less formal. Instead of legal jargon, it looks as if he typed it up himself, and it only consists of bullet points on a single sheet of paper.

"What's that?" I ask.

"Our new contract."

"You think I'm going to sign a new contract with you?"

His eyes flash to mine. "Cut the goddamn sass for a second and hear me out."

"That's one way to win me back." I roll my eyes.

"Do I need to bend you over this table just so you knock it off?"

My body heats up, and I can feel my eyes widen from the thought.

He catches it.

The intrigue.

The yearning.

The need.

"Don't," I say, holding up my hand as he shifts. "Don't even think about it."

"Then hear me out, and I won't be forced to take extreme measures."

God, it's annoying how commanding he is.

Domineering.

Possessive.

But I also love it. *What is wrong with me?*

Some of the steel leaves his eyes when he says, "I'm sorry, Lottie, for a lot of things. I'm sorry that I blamed you for something I had no right blaming you for. I'm sorry for breaking our trust. I'm sorry for not leaning on you when I should have. And most importantly, I'm sorry that I hurt you. To see you cry, see you so upset, and know I'm the one causing that pain...it kills me."

And just like that, with his soothing voice, the irritation drains from me as the tension lessens in my shoulders and...I listen.

"I quickly realized my mistake when you started to leave. My heart leapt in my throat when you got in your sister's car. And when I saw you drive away, I knew you'd taken a huge piece of me with you. It gutted me seeing you leave, which made me realize I love you. I love you more than I ever thought it was possible to love someone. And it hit me like a ton of bricks. I need you to be a part of my life, Lottie. I need you to be a permanent fixture. Which is why I came up with this contract."

I don't take it, but instead, I say, "Read it to me."

Clearing his throat, he says, "My legal terms aren't up to par, so don't make fun of me." That makes me inwardly smile. "'This contract binds Huxley Cane and Lottie Gardner once terms are agreed to and signatures are present at the bottom.'"

"You're right, your terminology is way off."

"I was drawing a blank when writing this up. Bear with me." He sets his shoulders back and reads some more. "'The following requests must be followed by both parties. Request number one—after some careful thought and consideration, Lottie agrees to forgive Huxley for being a massive ass.'"

"I appreciate you using *massive* as a descriptor, because that's what you were."

"I was," he agrees, and more tension eases.

"'Request number two—after a solid makeup session, which will include whatever Lottie wants'"—I smirk at that—"'Lottie will be required to permanently move in with Huxley, and into his bedroom, where he's already made space in the closet for her clothes.'"

"My clothes or the personal items you picked out for me?" I ask.

"Whatever you want."

"I prefer a mixture of both."

"Done." His facial expression lightens as he continues. "'Request number three—Lottie drops all previous roles of fake fiancée and fake pregnant woman. Huxley realizes what a bad idea this was and has already cleared the air with Dave. He wants Lottie to live her best life now, free of any fake premise.'"

"*Her best life?*" I ask with a raised brow. He nods. "And things are cleared up with Dave? Really?"

"Yes, I spoke with him today. He wasn't happy when I told him I'd fucked things up with you, and told me I'd better get you back."

"Dave is a smart man." I push my hair over my shoulder, needing to busy my antsy hands.

"'Request number four—even though the previous contract has been destroyed, Huxley is still indebted to Lottie and therefore will attend any social event to help her stick it to her old boss, but this time, he prefers to act as her real fiancé.'"

His eyes peer up at me.

Uh, did I hear that right? Real fiancé?

"'Request number five—Lottie realizes that Huxley is a shell of a man without her. That he not only craves her in his life, but he needs her in his life. She's become a permanent fixture, and not having her in his life is nonnegotiable.' Which brings me to 'Request number six—Lottie follows Huxley to the rooftop.'" Huxley stands and holds out his hand.

I don't take it right away.

I'm not even sure I can with how shaky I am.

"Lottie..."

Mustering up some words, I say, "I'm, uh...I'm going to need my lawyer to look at that contract."

His smile nearly knocks me over, it's so brilliantly handsome and full of joy. It propels my hand into his and guides me through the house, up the stairs, and to the rooftop. When Huxley pushes open the door, he allows me to go through first, revealing the beautiful setup.

Two wooden lounge chairs occupy the middle of the space, decorated with rose petals and surrounded by fake candles that offer just enough light to set the scene.

"Wow," I say, taking it all in.

The door shuts behind us, and I turn to find Huxley bent down on one knee, holding a ring box.

This can't be real. This seriously can't be the life I'm living right now, but when he opens his mouth and says my name in a breathless tone, I realize this is very much real.

"Lottie, I love you. You're beautifully frustrating, annoyingly right most of the time, and you bring me more joy than I ever thought I'd be lucky enough to have. You complement my surly attitude. You put me in my place when I need it, and you listen to me when I need a listening ear. Plain and simple, you complete me, and I know for certain I can't live this life without you in it." He pops open the ring box, revealing a beautiful, cushion-shaped diamond ring with diamond accents on the band. It's different than the current ring on my finger. Edgier, just like me. "I love you so goddamn much. Please, would you accept the contract, and will you also do me the honor of being my wife?"

I stare down at him, those deep, mysterious eyes piercing through me, holding me captive.

They always will.

I believe he's had my heart from the very beginning. Even through our ups and downs, there was a connection, an unrelenting bond that drew me toward him. There's no denying I love this man; there's no denying I'll always love him. He's it for me. I realize this. But…

"You hurt me, Huxley."

He stands up and quickly closes the space between us. "I know, Lottie, and I'm really fucking sorry. I can't promise you I won't hurt you again, because we'll always have disagreements, but I'll promise you this— you're my number one; you're the person I trust, the person I know will always be by my side, cheering for me *and* telling me when I'm an asshole. And I'll do everything possible to make you happy. To make sure I never—on purpose—make you cry again." His hand rises to my face and his thumb gently rubs across my cheek. "I love you, baby."

I wet my lips, get lost in those eyes, and on a leap and a prayer, I say, "I love you, too."

"Fuck," he says in an exhale before tilting my jaw up and pressing his lips to mine. My arms instantly wrap around his neck, and I deepen the kiss, letting go of the anger and tension that's drained from me.

Oddly, he's everything I've ever wanted. He challenges me. Teases me. And passionately loves me.

When he pulls away, he grips my cheeks and rests his forehead on mine. "Please tell me it's a *yes*. Please tell me you'll be mine forever."

Locking gazes with him, I say, "I'm yours forever, Huxley."

"Thank fuck," he says, lifting my hand and pressing a kiss to my

404 | MEGHAN QUINN

knuckles. Then, he takes the fake engagement ring off my finger and replaces it with the real thing. He gives it a kiss and asks, "Do you like it?"

I smile. "I love it, just like I love you."

He presses another kiss to my lips and then quietly says, "Looks like you snagged yourself a rich husband after all."

I chuckle. "I think it was the braids."

"It was the braids for sure."

He pulls me into a hug, then lifts me up and spins me around as we both laugh.

Just when you think you've hit rock bottom, when you don't think there's any way you could climb the mountain again to find happiness, you stumble across a trail, one that has its bumps and bruises, but offers a gorgeous outcome. I might not have known the outcome of saying yes to Huxley and his crazy scheme, but I'm so glad I did. I can't imagine what this life would be like without him.

EPILOGUE
HUXLEY

"DOES MY BUTT LOOK GOOD?"

"For the tenth time, your ass looks amazing," I say, though I don't even bother to look at it this time. I'm sure it hasn't changed in the last minute, and the more I stare at it, the more I'm going to get hard. And the last thing I want to do is be hard when we walk into Lottie's high school reunion.

"This dress wasn't too much? It feels like too much."

I stop her and spin her toward me. She's wearing a deep-purple dress that clings to every curve of her body and lifts her tits, giving her impossible cleavage. When she stepped out of our bathroom, my jaw hit the floor and my dick grew in seconds. She paired the dress with four-inch black stilettos, my kryptonite. I immediately reached for her, but she blocked me with a stiff arm, saying I wasn't allowed to touch her sexually until after the reunion because she didn't want me ruining her hair and makeup.

I didn't touch her in the house, but the moment we got to the car, I put up the privacy shield, lifted her legs over my shoulders, and ate her out until she came twice. In return, she gave me one of the quickest blow jobs of my life. I was primed and ready from her taste on my lips, so it didn't take long. *Even if I wasn't allowed to pull on her hair like I normally love to do.* Both satisfied, we made our way into the Beverly Hillshire Hotel, which made Lottie laugh, given the start of our relationship and its *Pretty Woman* vibe.

"The dress is perfect, babe. I promise, you look amazing." I kiss her

406 | MEGHAN QUINN

cheek and then lean toward her ear. "So goddamn amazing that it's taking every last ounce of my control to not fuck you right here in this hallway."

My hand presses to the curve of her hip, and I move her against the wall.

"Huxley," she says breathlessly.

"You can't say my name like that. You're going to make me hard," I whisper, placing a kiss on her neck. She tilts her head to the side. "Babe, you're taunting me."

"You're the one doing the taunting," she says as I kiss the spot beneath her ear. She lightly moans.

"Lottie...do you want me to fuck you right here—"

"Excuse me, we're hosting a high school reunion here," a shrill voice says.

When I pull away, I'm met with a woman in a bubblegum-colored dress. There's a man attached to her arm, but he honestly looks fake. There's no connection in his eyes, no caring. It's as if he's just present. When I finally notice the woman speaking to us, I realize it's Angela.

"Oh, Lottie," Angela says, placing her hand on her chest. I watch as her eyes rake over my fiancée. Her lips turn down, and I know right then and there, she's jealous. When Lottie's hand clutches around mine, I know Lottie saw it, too. "I didn't realize that was you." Angela turns to me. "Huxley, how are you?"

I hate that she thinks we're friends.

"Great," I answer, lifting Lottie's hand and placing a kiss on the back of her knuckles, the same hand that bears her engagement ring. Angela's eyes land on it, and she has a very hard time masking her emotions as jealousy rips through her. "Sorry about that PDA, but my girl is stunning in this dress, and I can't seem to keep my hands off her. She made me swear I wouldn't ruin her hair and makeup. I think I did a good job of that in the car, don't you?"

Her eyes narrow, but then she must realize she has to put on a show, because she straightens up and leans against her man, who is, unfortunately for Angela, checking out another woman.

"Oh yes, Brad and I had a hard time controlling ourselves in the car as well. The man is horny all the time."

He doesn't acknowledge her, but instead bites the corner of his lip as a blond walks by.

"What happened to Ken?" Lottie asks.

Angela dismissively waves her hand. "He got boring."

Aka, he broke up with her.

"But Brad and I are just having the best time. Isn't that right?" She tugs on Brad's arm.

"I'm going to go to the bathroom," he says, taking off without another word, following that blond.

Still putting on a happy face, Angela asks, "So have you two actually set a date?"

"December tenth," Lottie says. "We're going to Tulum and flying our closest friends and family down for a two-week-long wedding celebration."

"Oh, how exciting." Angela perks up, clearly missing the mark that she's not invited. "Should I book my flight now?"

Really, really obtuse.

"No, that's okay. We'll be fine getting married without you."

She frowns. "Lottie, I'm your best friend."

"Nope, that's not accurate." Lottie shakes her head. Her confidence is making me so goddamn horny right now. I hope she doesn't plan on staying at this reunion very long. "But thank you for thinking so kindly of me." Lottie smiles. "Oh, and hey, sorry to hear about your top two sponsors pulling out of advertising. That must have been hard."

Angela's frown deepens.

"I know how hard it was to keep those accounts happy, as it was always me ensuring they had everything they ever needed. Such a shame, but, hey"—Lottie winks—"at least you're saving money when it comes to hiring mediocre employees."

That frown grows even more.

"Did you happen to see Kelsey and I are in business now? We just signed a one-million-dollar contract with Dave Toney. We're in way over our heads and plan on hiring quite a few hands to help us get the job done. Don't worry, though; we'll keep the mediocre employees at your disposal. We only want the best, so we pay them what they deserve. Anyway"—Lottie reaches up and presses a kiss to my cheek—"I'm kind of over this. Want to go grab a burger?"

I smirk. "Care to fly to Portland? I'm craving Killer Burger."

"I couldn't think of anything more perfect." Lottie turns to Angela. "So *not* nice to see you again. Take care, Angela."

And with that, hand in hand, we walk out of the hotel and straight to where my car is waiting. I call up my pilot and tell him to meet us at the airport. My girl wants a burger, she's going to get one.

As we drive through the city, I think about how lucky I am.

I had been so wrong in so many ways. In suggesting a flagrant deception was the way to get a business deal. To think that Dave, who I'd always known to be a stand-up guy, hadn't believed in Cane Enterprises all along. To believe that this gorgeous woman in my arms was capable of the sort of betrayal I'd suggested. *Ridiculous.* I'm fucking lucky. I've had to eat humble pie, and I won't ever take her for granted again. Nor will I fabricate a story to get a deal.

Lottie leans into my embrace and gently lifts her lips to my jaw. "I love you, Huxley."

"I love you, too, babe. I'm proud of you. Really fucking proud."

"I wasn't too bitchy?"

"You were incredibly bitchy, but I loved it."

She chuckles. "That last jab was maybe uncalled for, but I couldn't help myself."

"Do you have closure?"

She nods. "Very much so. Thank you."

"No need to thank me, babe. You did this all on your own."

"You mean snag a rich husband by haphazardly getting lost in The Flats?"

The best damn day of my life. Thank fuck Angela was truly that vacuous to fire Lottie.

"Exactly. You have no idea how glad I am that you lost your way that day, *and* that you said yes to my crazy proposal."

"Well, I have to say, I liked your most recent proposal even more."

"And you said yes."

"And I said yes."

Thank God.

"Angela was very wrong about many things, you know."

"Oh, I know, but what do you mean?"

"You're my best friend, Lottie. And my life is only better for it. I love you, wife-to-be."

"And I love you, husband-to-be, even with all your crazy."

I laugh and then blow her mind with a deep and passionate kiss. *My gorgeous, sexy, incredible girl.* Life will never be boring with this spitfire by my side. Rainy days will never be dismal. Life will be fun, adventurous, crazy, and better than I ever thought life could be. Better than I ever deserved.

ABOUT THE AUTHOR

#1 Amazon and *USA Today* bestselling author, wife, adoptive mother, and peanut butter lover, as well as an author of romantic comedies and contemporary romance, Meghan Quinn brings readers the perfect combination of heart, humor, and heat in every book.

Website: authormeghanquinn.com
Facebook: meghanquinnauthor
Instagram: @meghanquinnbooks